THREADS

By CONNIE TEAL

The story begins in Nottingham, England. Spring 1902

Also in this series.
Volume Two. Yes, Sergeant Victor

Volume Three. The Other Arf

Polladras Publishers
Penrose Farm
Trew, Breage,
Helston. Cornwall.
England.
TR13 9QN
writerconnieteal@mail.com

Published 2011

Connie Teal asserts the moral right to be identified as the author of this
work.

A catalogue record of this book is available from The British Library.

ISBN 978-0-9562599-2-9

Printed and bound by the MPG Books Group Ltd

Cover by Knight Design
www.knightdesign.co.uk

NOT TIL THE LOOM IS SILENT

AND THE SHUTTLES CEASE TO FLY

SHALL GOD UNROLL THE CANVAS

AND EXPLAIN THE REASON WHY

THE DARK THREADS ARE AS NEEDFUL

IN THE WEAVER'S SKILFUL HAND

AS THE THREADS OF GOLD AND SILVER

IN THE PATTERN HE HAS PLANNED.

FROM A POEM 'THE WEAVER'

AUTHOR

BENJAMIN MALACHI FRANKLIN

1882—1965

This book is dedicated to:-

Annie & Byron

Golden threads both.

CHAPTER ONE

"Keep out o' the bloody way, I can't 'old 'is 'ead, when I catch the miserable blighter as spiked 'im I'll flog the last breath from 'is scrawny little body."

The driver bellowed his threat over the rear of the horse as they careered past Annie, she stood at the threshold of the entry, her legs trembled, someone could be killed. The waggon had swayed violently across the cobbles, spilling the last three bags of precious jet black nuggets, sending them randomly side to side the street. A rough looking lad, the likely perpetrator, ran into Sherwood Road, Annie had seen him before, Constable Quigley holding him by the collar, a ne'er-do-well as aunt Bella would say.

Winnie Bacon had been scrubbing her step, every Tuesday without fail, Winnie would take a bucket of washing water from the dolly tub and with admirable purpose, maintain a whiteness of the old stone which Annie, many times had observed from the opposite side of the street as looking like one gleaming tooth in an otherwise full set of decay. None of the other women applied such devotion, aunt Bella certainly wouldn't place herself on public view.

"Make haste Annie dear, fetch a bucket never mind Saul Eddowes, 'e wouldn't walk by a windfall, it'll disappear like snow in the sun, you mark my words."

Indeed within seconds doors opened in unison and pinafore clad women with scuttles and buckets converged upon the scene. Winnie hurled the soapy water over the pavings and began to grab at the coal, all the other women did likewise.

Annie could still hear faintly in the distance the sound of the waggon and driver as he called to the horse to bring it under control.

The women seemed to abandon all decorum in the battle to secure as much coal as they could, the last nub was literally fought over, Nellie Draper, Winnie Bacon and Martha Ingle all determined to add that one last nub to their haul. Then Nellie, with a thrust that would have been the envy of many a wrestler, sent Winnie to the ground, where she landed in a deposit of still steaming horse manure which the terrified animal had shed as it charged. Annie rushed to the aid of her neighbour.

"Are you alright Winnie?" She asked, helping the dishevelled woman to her feet, by now their company had retreated behind closed doors. Winnie stared across the street to Nellie's house, shaking her skirts.

"Do you know young Annie, she wer' allus 'lousy' at school, forever itchin' an' scratchin', 'twas 'er every time as give us all nits."

"If you're sure you are alright then I'll go to the workshop," said Annie anxiously.

Winnie picked up her bucket of coal, minus that one last nub.

"You go dear," she said, patting Annie's arm, "bit of 'oss shit never hurt nobody, an' don't you pay no mind to 'im if 'e fusses at yer bein' late."

Winnie gazed at the step, still only half scrubbed, gathered her brush from where it had come to rest on the paving and with a disgruntled 'huff' said.

"Bugger it," she too retreated behind the closed door.

The walk to Saul's took but a few minutes and varied seldom, today had been unusual, normally her journey was uninterrupted unless Mr.Brooks was in his doorway but it was too cold this morning for Alfred. He had no legs, lost in some terrible accident they said. Evelyn, his wife, on fine days would lift him to the door and place him in a strange wooden seat that in sympathy with Alfred, had no legs either. His face always seemed set, incapable of any other expression than the bleak stare he gave to the world. His door was tightly closed so Annie walked briskly by saving her tentative smile and polite good morning for his next appearance. She reached the double iron gates which Saul insisted be always latched. The aged iron creaked its resistance and its flaking demeanour gripped at Annie's gloved fingers menacingly. Any stain from the iron transferred from Annie's fingers to the white cotton meant disaster, the material, no longer usable, now became a loss on the books which could be balanced only by an adjustment of pay.

Annie had worked for Saul since she was ten years old, over the eleven years that had passed her skills had developed greatly. The mainstay of Saul's business had always been the collarless working man's shirt, produced by Annie, May and Edna in impressive numbers. When Annie opened the workshop door Edna's face showed her concern.

"God almighty, what wer' all that about, shoutin' an' ollorin', we thought as somebody wer' bein' murdered."

Saul called through from his office.

"Are you alright Annie?"

"Yes, I am quite alright, it was a runaway coal waggon, I think someone had scared the horse on purpose, the driver was irate."

Satisfied that all was well, Saul prompted the women to get on with their work. Edna, out of sight of Saul pulled a face and stuck out her tongue roguishly.

Edna was an enigma to Annie. Edna embraced life with such confidence, her tales of exploits with men were quite shameless and embellished with such vivid colour. Annie would listen to these accounts and would pay them as much heed as her delicate senses would allow and yet it was impossible to dislike Edna.

May was older and had two children cared for by their grandmother whilst May worked. May's husband had developed into a sickly man, weakened by repeated bouts of bronchitis, she seemed always to be preoccupied and Annie respected her desire to be still.

The room in which the three women worked held four sewing machines, three were for everyday use and the fourth allowed much more elaborate stitching for the elegant and expensive garments which oft times Saul was commissioned to create for the gentry.

The women sat on plain wooden stools, having no support on which to lean back, served to encourage the relentless action of the machines. A doorway to the room beyond revealed two long trestle tables, worn smooth by the passage of cloth along their surface. These tables occupied half the space, the other side of the room held the racks of cloth, boxes of braids and silks, buttons and hooks, all the numerous items which were transformed into gowns and frocks. The stock was positioned with such precision that Saul, sitting at his desk in the back office was able to survey his holding without leaving his seat. Not one of the women held inclination to remove items for themselves but Saul was a businessman, now more by habit than design.

He was not a young man, his wife Hilda had died three years before, a fine woman from good stock. It was commonly considered that the backing of her family had enabled Saul to progress. Hilda had been taken by a fever which neither doctor nor physician could control. Since his wife's death Saul had bowed under the weight of weariness that wrapped about his shoulders and drew his once fine features to the gaunt, tired expression that daily scrutinised his books.

Charles Eddowes, Saul's son, worked as a clerk at the bank and came to the workshop on occasions to bring packages from the bank to Saul. Charles had failed to display any interest in the working of his father's trade. Hilda had kept the boy at the centre of her life, her love for him had been entire, complete, leaving only slight allowance for Saul. He however, had grown deeply fond of his wife over the years and the void which now starved his soul had been offered no comfort by the arrogant young Charles.

Annie, working at her machine felt unease whenever Charles came. His eyes were demanding yet forbidding, only when she heard the latch fall on the gates as he left did Annie find calm.

Charles had been married to Enid for eight months, an attractive young woman in appearance but with a grasping nature that rendered her less desirable company to other young women.

Annie knew only that her own mother had died giving birth to her and had been told that her father had died of a broken heart. She had been raised by an aunt who, despite the account of Annie's tragic beginnings, gave her not a thread more than was needful, placing her at Saul's on her tenth birthday. Annie was a bright child, with an ability to concentrate and learn far beyond her years, her value, very early on, had been recognised by Saul. Her aunt allowed Annie no reward for her labours until she reached the age of twenty one, at this milestone in life Annie was permitted to keep sixpence each week.

'Now my girl,' aunt Bella had said, 'you will clothe yourself'. Her manner was as cold as the flags on the scullery floor. Annie held no expectations, her days were varied only by the elements of nature, warm sunshine finding her spirit, cold grey days passing it by, one day conceded to the next with little to mark its occupation.

Annie had found herself with a strange new feeling of independence, an allowance of sixpence seemed to herald a fresh chapter in her life and inspired by the confidence it gave she took to strolling through the arboretum on a Sunday afternoon. Sunday mornings had always been spent at the Mission Hall where the Minister would preach his threats of 'Hell and Damnation' to all sinners. Annie had pondered many times why Jesus should want her for a sunbeam when she had caused her mother's death and broken her father's heart.

The gentle surroundings of the arboretum made Annie feel much closer to God than did the echoing chill of the Mission Hall. The grass bank sloped down to the flower beds where the plants ordered their cheerful blooms to dance around the laburnum trees as the ladies promenaded the pathways bedecked in finery. Sometimes Annie would recognise a gown which, back at Saul's she herself had draped across her lap to hand stitch the embroidery and fastenings.

"Want a mint?" Startled, Annie turned toward the voice. Standing just a few feet behind her, at the top of the bank stood a young man. Annie, sitting on the grass, looked up at the generous smile that fell around her like the beam from a lamp. Before she had a chance to reply he was on his haunches beside her, his arm outstretched, his hand in front of her cupping a crumpled paper bag in which nestled a cluster of humbugs.

"I'm alright thank you," replied Annie nervously.

"Go on, do yer good," he said.

There was something compelling about his manner and Annie's slight fingers reached into the paper bag and not without a degree of difficulty, managed to part one reluctant humbug from the rest. He laughed out loud.

"Sticky little buggers aren't they," he said. Then with no further pause, "my name is Harold Boucher, what's yours?" By now he was sitting alongside Annie, his legs anchored into the grass bank by the weight of his hobnailed boots.

"Annie," she said, "Annie Bundy".

The humbugs had been deposited in his jacket pocket and his hand took hers with such speed she had no time to offer it, only to accept his.

"Pleased to meet yer."

Annie felt the strength of his grip and the roughness of the skin on his fingers but he caused her no alarm, she found herself smiling back at him quite readily. He had brown eyes, a head of dark wavy hair and a complexion which could only have come from spending much time outdoors.

"I live down Mitchell Street, work at Toft's," he said. Josiah Toft owned the slaughter yard where the cattle were brought for killing.

"I work for Saul Eddowes," replied Annie.

"Oh you must know Edna," he said.

Slightly unnerved at this remark she ventured, "Yes, is she a friend of yours?"

"She's Billy's girl," he replied. Annie perceived this to mean friend not offspring, the wry grin with which he delivered the statement defined it clearly enough.

"It's time I was going home," said Annie.

"I'll walk with you".

Harold had no intention of allowing Annie to leave his company until he had somehow found out where she lived. There seemed to be a quiet understanding between the two of them as they left the arboretum to walk along Sherwood Road into Winchester Street. Annie stopped just a few yards short of the entry.

"Goodbye Harold," she said, "thank you for the mint".

"Ta-ta," came the reply, his hand raised to wave. The powerful warmth and brightness of his smile clung to her for a few precious seconds until she turned into the dark draughtiness of the entry. There the cool air brought a shiver to her shoulders and the now, closeness of aunt Bella, weighted her steps. Annie opened the privy door to provide just a few more moments of sanctuary before she must face the constant reminder of her past. Aunt Bella never failed to charge her with the duty, 'You just remember what you are my girl!' Annie had for so long asked herself the question, 'What am I?', 'what,' not who, perhaps one day before I die I shall know she told herself.

Aunt Bella sat in the deep leather chair in the corner by the bottom of the stairs, her face fixed on Annie as she entered through the scullery door.

"The bucket needs filling," Bella commanded.

It was seldom that Bella made it a request, Annie gathered up the empty coal bucket and returned to the yard. The door of the coal shed seemed to display its loyalty to Bella by clinging to the cobbles, making the task as hard as it could for Annie. The short wooden handle on the shovel had become loose over the years and in order to scoop up the coal, Annie must hold one side of the shovel to steady it. Her fingers blackened by the coal dust now gripped the edge of the wretched door and with all the strength Annie could muster, she lifted and pushed it back into its frame where now secure, it would doubtless plot its next campaign of resistance. Annie placed the bucket on the hearth of the range, Bella dispensed the coal, just enough to keep the bed of the fire alive in the grate but never enough to allow it to thrive. As a result she sat hindered by several layers of clothing, a bonnet, fingerless gloves and bootees over heavy woollen stockings. Her skin always sallowed by constant chill, never able to achieve the remotest hint of pink. Annie found more warmth outside where at least when the sun shone its rays reached her blood and she felt truly alive. The house was drab and dark and only at the height of summer, for the briefest of periods did the dreary surroundings make any attempt to mellow.

Annie poured a little water from the heavy stoneware jug into the bowl that sat on top of the scrubbed table in the scullery, placing the jug back on the shelf below. She turned the soap about between her palms until her wrists ached from the effort. Bella hardened the soap bars between paper in the bottom drawer of the dresser for months at a time, this caused the soap to last much longer. Annie tried desperately to prise enough lather from the soap's unyielding meanness to remove the sooty black staining from her fingers, she could risk not the faintest shadow to blight the white linen at her work next morning. Looking hard at her upturned hands she satisfied herself, 'that will do' and emptied the soiled water into the pail. By now her fingers had taken the chill of the water and rubbing them dry on the rough cloth was almost a pleasure. Annie glanced at the clock on the living room wall, as was her routine each Sunday she filled the kettle with water and placed it on the now reddened coals, Bella spoke little. Bread with dripping or butter and jam made up Sunday tea and the meal shared by the two women passed mostly in silence.

"Aunt Bella," Annie said, "I saw one of my gowns at the arboretum."

"Your gowns," Bella spat the words mockingly, "your gowns," she said again. "You just remember what you are my girl."

Annie lay in her bed recounting the day's events in her head. Earlier in the day, Mr.Shawcross, the Minister, had enforced the wonders of Zion with the relentless rapping of clenched fist on the pulpit until the old planking of the Mission floor seemed to shake beneath Annie's feet. The afternoon was now a treasured dream, to be brought from the secret chambers of her mind whenever harsh reality threatened. It felt to Annie a good dream, one she wished to imagine over and over, its comforting balm soothed her to sleep.

Annie and Edna had been left with the responsibility of completing an order for Blackmore's school. Oliver Blackmore and his wife ran their establishment for the education of boys. The uniform garments, by their very design, limited the young wearers to an exclusive group, such apparel was never seen on the lads who kicked the bladder, tossed over the wall by Josiah, up and down Bingley Street.

'Give us a bladder mister,' would be the cry. They knew that if they agreed to hold tight the rope which Josiah fed through a hole in the slaughter yard wall, their determined show of strength would be rewarded with this makeshift ball. The lads not seeing the fearful plight of the beast being pole axed on the other side, remained ignorant of this gruesome act and revelled in the street games which followed. Annie voiced this observation to Edna as casually as she could, hoping that to mention the slaughter yard might illicit a response that somehow shed light on Billy and Harold, her shrewdness paid a dividend.

"Billy works at the slaughter yard," Edna said quietly. A telling blush crept up Edna's cheeks and Annie knew instantly that Billy was more than a mere acquaintance.

"I don't think I've heard you talk about him," said Annie, recalling the many tales with which Edna had regaled May and herself.
Edna's mouth spread to a wide grin and with obvious delight at feeling fit to reveal her secret, declared Billy to be,

"Bloody lovely, real copper, different to all the others."
Annie detected a greater depth to Edna's words than she had ever heard her speak before, these were not uttered simply to entertain the women through their monotonous hours spent at the machines as was usually the purpose, no, these words were delivered by Edna as would be a passage from the Bible, truthful, pure and binding. Annie felt a slight guilt at prompting Edna further, surely her pleasure should be enough in sharing this open hearted moment with Edna. She wished so much to hold just a little knowledge of Harold for herself, not to let the opportunity pass without adding to her own precious dream.

"Billy gets on alright with Josiah," Edna said ,"they both do 'im an' Harold."

"Harold," said Annie in an enquiring tone.

"Yes," said Edna, "Harold's a good laugh, 'e tells these stories about 'is dad, 'is old man's a chimney sweep an' last week, well, what a 'to-do'. E's been trying to get 'is money from this woman on Lenton Street for weeks, every time 'e goes there to ask for it she tells 'im that things 'ave been really 'ard this week but she'll 'ave the money for 'im next time, she's no better than she ought to be neither," said Edna.

Annie felt at this point that Billy had surely brought about a conversion in Edna but suppressed her bemusement.

Edna continued, "Anyway, last Thursday 'e knocked on 'er door an' she give 'im the same response so 'e told 'er 'never mind missus, it don't matter any more 'cause I've brought your soot back' and 'e chucked it in through the open door, it went everywhere." Edna erupted into gales of laughter. For an instant Annie bore a measure of compassion for the wretched woman, but Edna's glee was highly infectious and the two were united in merriment.

Aware that Saul would return in due course expecting their work to be completed both women resumed their task with a will. This afternoon they were content and their happiness propelled their fingers apace.

Saul had been bidden to the home of Mrs.Wright. It was an elegant house in The Park, there was to be a wedding in the family. May accompanied Saul on these duties, he of course, would deal with the pecuniary matters and May would measure the good lady for her new ensemble. Mrs.Wright was known to be of ample proportions, a sobering comparison to the slight frame which comprised May.

The latch on the gates rattled, Annie looked up to see Saul and May enter, Saul nodded briefly to the two women before passing into the stock room behind. He stood before the racking, his gaze deliberate, ponderous. Having reassured himself that nothing was amiss he crossed into the back office where he transferred the afternoons instructions to the copy book and ledger. May enquired of Edna what should be her immediate occupation at such a late stage of the day.

"Six more sets o' buttons to sew on these jackets," suggested Edna.

May sat quietly at her table, Edna always curious about the upper class, quizzed May about the household in The Park, this area of the city contained all the large houses which accommodated the wealthy and commercially successful 'gentrified' section of the population.

"Well what was it like?" asked Edna.

May was a timid soul always afraid to be noticed, more than happy to hide behind her machine, seemingly to believe that if her eyes were trained downwards to the needle and cloth this would render her invisible to all. This total discretion doubtless convinced Saul of May's suitability for the clients' appointments.

"It was big," said May, "it smelled of grate polish and beeswax." That was it, that was as much account as May's retiring nature could bear.

The shadows began to invade the workshop and the last button was firmly secured just as the light became too fickle. The women donned their coats and each obtained from Saul the required release. Annie was the last to leave, she thought his face looked tired and felt concern. He had, over the years she had worked for him, always been fair, not ever showing any malice, never wounding her with words too sharp. In the very early days when she had been no more than a child her initial fear and alarm at this unknown man and surroundings had calmed quite soon. His almost constant presence and his desire for her to be helped and guided by a seamstress had granted Annie an anchor, life at home had been ever dominated by Bella's anguished moods. The work at Saul's was often tedious, though not always, as the expensive gowns on which she sometimes worked, transported Annie to imaginary worlds, but the sameness and reliability of Saul and the workshop gave Annie a sense of belonging and for that she was indeed grateful.

Annie set off to walk home, as she progressed up the street her nose reminded her it was Monday, the wind carried the powerful evidence of the 'tub' man's visit. The horse and waggon which came to Winchester Street each Monday driven by the poor man whose duty it was to bid everyone to bring out their tubs for tipping, managed in the few hours of their presence to pervade the air for miles around. Annie hastened her step, it was more desirable to be indoors with aunt Bella than to breathe such potent air. All doors were tightly shut today, no need of polite gestures or courteous conversation, she was just a few yards short of the entry when a head appeared from within its threshold, a silly grin straddling it. Annie recognised the face instantly as Harold. He stepped out in front of her and with his typical spontaneity, produced from behind his back a bunch of large white daisies saying.

"Well Annie Bundy, 'tis a bit ripe round 'ere, 'tis wiltin' me flowers," he laughed with a glorious honesty that made Annie blush vividly, she felt at that moment that she alone was responsible for the obnoxious smell simply because she lived there.

"These are for you," he said and thrust them at her with a determined show of pleasure. Annie took the flowers saying, "Thank you Harold," already wondering inwardly how she would explain her possession of this bouquet to aunt Bella.

"Will I see you at the arboretum on Sunday?" He asked.

Annie felt drawn to him, his eyes shed a kindness over her which caused her feelings to lift toward it like seedlings to a rain shower.

"Yes," she answered, "I'll go to the arboretum on Sunday."

Harold's face revealed his delight, he turned to walk away, his feet were powered by his excitement and quickly reached a skip. Annie stood by the entry just knowing that he would pause before disappearing round the corner. He will look back she told herself. Harold stopped, turned, raised his hand as if to wave but at the last moment his fingers brushed his mouth and he blew back a kiss to Annie, shouting as if he needed everyone behind their doors to hear.

"See you Sunday Annie Bundy," then he was gone.

Annie gazed down at her flowers, their fine white petals framed a centre more embroidered with colour than any gown she had ever sewn, she must face aunt Bella. Whatever else, Annie knew that her life was changing. Bella didn't like change, the days, weeks, months and years had seemed to

Annie to be fettered always by aunt Bella's morose soul.

The scullery smelled of onions and the old pan, encrusted on the outside by years of charring from the fire sat in the hearth. Bella looked across the room at Annie and the daisies.

"A friend gave them to me," said Annie, "I should put them in water."

In the far corner of a shelf on the scullery wall she found an old jar with a chip on the rim, she took water from the jug and placed the flowers in the jar. Her fingers were awkward, made nervous by the threat of Bella's inquisition.

"Shall I put them on the sideboard Aunt Bella?" She asked.

Bella stared at Annie, her expression bore prosecutor and judge yet she uttered not a word except to order the coal bucket be filled.

Still Annie knew not why she was so condemned.

CHAPTER TWO

The workshop had been busy fulfilling orders and Annie had spent many hours sewing the dress for Mrs.Wright. It was now necessary for Saul and May to attend the house in The Park in order to carry out a fitting. Outside, the latch rattled on the gates and a knock came at the door. Saul looked up from his papers, across from the back office he nodded to Annie, the opened door revealed a child, a young boy, his face pale, his breath tight from his hurried mission.

"Mam," he gasped, "grandma says you must come."

May rose from her stool, franticly attempting to gather the length of cloth from her lap and transfer it to the safety of the table. Saul had crossed to the door and now stood in front of the child, he calmly placed his hand on the youngster's shoulder and said.

"Catch your breath boy whilst your mother fetches her coat."

Annie felt truly grateful to Saul, he questioned neither the urgency nor the necessity of the child's plea. Annie knew that life was ever difficult for May and her timid spirit could easily have been overwhelmed but Saul caused her no further anxiety and May and her young son were despatched immediately.

When quiet was restored and the incident passed, Saul turned to Annie and said.

"I shall need you to go with me to the house in The Park, I cannot change the appointment at this hour, Mrs.Wright is expecting us."

Annie reached up to the top shelving, a box had now to be prepared in which to transport the dress. There was still much needlework to do on the gown but before the garment went any further it must be established that the bodice and waist fit neatly, the neckline and hem must be tacked into position, the sleeves checked for length and any alterations agreed with Mrs.Wright, who must at this stage, choose the lace and ribbon trimmings and type of fasteners. Annie removed the lid from the box and lined the bottom with a large piece of unbleached calico. The dress was folded loosely and laid onto the calico then wrapped across neatly with the surplus material, when the lid was replaced, the delicate silks from which the dress was made could find no way of rolling into a bundle and any creasing would be kept to an absolute minimum. She made ready the bag of samples, so many times she had observed May's preparations, always eager to learn more.

Saul turned to Edna, "When you have completed those shirts, move to May's machine and carry on there, we shall not be very long."

A horse and carriage drew up outside, Saul gathered up the box and Annie the bag, he gestured that Annie should step up into the carriage, he passed up the large box then sat beside her, the box resting across their knees. It was a simple carriage driven by Edward Meade, Saul used Meade's services on these occasions, the arrangement was long standing and mutually beneficial.

Annie had never in her life before been inside a carriage, to be travelling by any other means than on foot seemed to her to be of another world, one which she had not previously been permitted to enter, it felt so grand, oh what a story she would have to tell Harold on Sunday. Then Annie was overcome by a feeling of terrible guilt, that she could for even the briefest of moments allow herself to enjoy this interlude when poor May was almost sure to be struggling amidst the darkest despair. The carriage jolted over a pit in the road, Saul firmed his grip on the box but said nothing and Annie looked ahead at the broad shoulders of Mr.Meade. She listened to the regular 'clip-clop' of the horses hooves over the cobbles, her mind pulling her thoughts toward the big house, Mrs.Wright and that gracious world which was still a wonder to her but her emotions dashed her back to Winchester Street, to the reality of her world, of aunt Bella, and the cold of the entry. Meade called to the horse and the carriage halted, they were outside a house which could be barely seen for shrubs and trees, the entire protected by railings.

Saul alighted and took the box, he offered a hand to assist Annie but she, so unused to her new situation, had her feet on the ground before even noticing his courtesy. Saul instructed Meade to return for them in one hour, he handed the box to Annie and opened the gate for her to pass through, they walked to one side of the house and around to a door which was unseen from the road. Eventually the door was opened by a maid, a young woman with a pleasant manner, she recognised Saul and bid them enter and wait whilst she announced their arrival.

Annie's eyes had never beheld such surroundings, the richly grained floor beneath her feet gleamed from the daily polishing, the ceilings were so high that every word spoken echoed as if to emphasise its importance. Heavily gilded pictures adorned the walls, images of stately gentlemen, elegant ladies in expensive attire, dark oil paintings of wild country scenes. A huge mirror dominated the hallway and made the area appear so big, it felt to Annie she might be swallowed up by it. The maid opened a heavy panelled door and led Saul and Annie into a large room which despite its grand dimensions was reduced in actual space by so much furnishing and a host of ornaments. Every colour bedecked the room and reflected its hue in an enormous marcasite brooch worn by the lady herself.

"Ah my fitting," said Mrs.Wright as she looked at the two arrivals. "You have brought me a different seamstress today Mr.Eddowes."

Saul appeared somewhat intimidated by Mrs.Wright and his voice in reply sounded thin and wavering.

"May has family matters to attend, however Annie is very competent and will carry out the fitting, we have brought many samples from which you might choose the finishes to your ensemble."

"Of course Mr.Eddowes, we shall go to my dressing room right away and delight in our project." The words were returned in a volley, her ample person entirely animated, she looked to the maid and said, "Bring a tray of tea for Mr.Eddowes Ivy," then, "come on my dear young Annie, I shall carry the bag if you can manage the box."

Mrs.Wright crossed the floor like a ship in full sail, Annie was drawn up in her wake and found herself following the lady up a wide staircase, intent on the safe passage of the box she gripped it tightly with both hands so the rich rosewood banister served only to guide the corner of Annie's eye up the two flights and on to a landing.

"In here my dear."

Mrs.Wright had entered a room so scented by perfumes that Annie's nose demanded to sneeze. Her predicament was dire, her hand achieved to reach her mouth just in time but the box fell to the floor, it remained intact and Annie quickly apologised and begged pardon. Mrs.Wright smiled in genuine amusement.

"No harm done my dear," she said, "here take one of these and suck it slowly."

She held out a dainty dish of very small sweets, Annie accepted graciously and popped the tiny candy into her mouth. No determined stickiness on these, inwardly she laughed at the thought of Harold's humbugs and for a moment tried to imagine Mrs.Wright and Harold in one another's company.

Annie surveyed the room, its pastel shades were very different from the bold colours of the drawing room below. It was draped in pretty lace and the ornaments were of fine china, small figurines, little posies that looked almost real, cut glass dishes and perfume atomizers with silk cords, the hair brush and mirror on the dresser caught the light on their engraved silver handles. The rug was the colour of well churned cream and just as thick with fleece, Annie felt it could not possibly experience the indignity of being placed over a wall and thoroughly beaten! A full length mirror beckoned to Mrs.Wright, with a gentle command she bid Annie assist her in disrobing. Annie's fingers moved carefully down the back of Mrs.Wright's dress, undoing the hooks and eyes which eventually revealed a fine silk undergarment, she slipped the shoulders aside and went to the front to help the lady's arms from the sleeves.

"So you are Annie," said Mrs.Wright, "tell me what is your full name my dear?"

"Annie Bundy ma'am," she replied, aware that Mrs.Wright's eyes were intent on her own, her gaze couldn't hide her curiosity.

"So, Annie Bundy," Mrs.Wright continued her obvious analysis of the information, "Hmm, well now, Annie Bundy."

Annie could hear aunt Bella's words, 'You just remember what you are my girl', she felt suddenly unnerved. Mrs.Wright sensed Annie's discomfort.

"Come my dear" she said, "we must fit my well made self into that delightful gown."

Her enthusiasm bolstered Annie's confidence and the task was undertaken by both women with good heart. Annie tucked and pinned, her fingers moved over the expensive material with skill, all the time feeling the warmth of Mrs.Wright's plump figure. She could not ever remember feeling the warmth of aunt Bella's body, whilst they lived under the same roof and ate together, the distance between them had always been set by Bella, Annie knew love only as a duty not as a passion.

The samples produced the delighted cry, "Just what I wanted!"

Mrs.Wright was pleased and satisfied by the afternoon's effort. Annie placed the gown carefully back in the box and gathered up the sample bag, she made mental note of the lady's choice and would see that Saul entered the order accordingly on their return to the workshop. Although her learning had been for a short period, Annie could nevertheless read and write very well. Saul was waiting downstairs, the tea tray on a small table by his chair, a piece of parkin remained on the tea plate.

"My dear Mr.Eddowes have you entered a decline?" Asked Mrs.Wright, her eyes focused on the portion of cake.

"Thank you, but tea alone was sufficient," he said politely.

"You will keep me up to date with my account?" Mrs.Wright asked.

"Of course, I shall attend to it directly."

Ivy was summoned to escort Annie and Saul to the side door. Edward Meade was waiting outside the main gate, it had been sixty five minutes since the carriage had brought them to the house. Annie's head was occupied by so many thoughts that she was firmly ensconced in the seat of the carriage with the box over her knees without being aware of how she got there, Saul stepped up and sat beside her, as the horse pulled away on Meade's command Annie heard Saul sigh deeply.

"I have Mrs.Wright's instructions for you to enter when we get back," she said.

He turned his face towards her and spoke softly, "Thank you Annie, you did well."

Then he asked Meade to make haste, the only sound was the hooves of the horse as they quickened over the road, the minutes passed by and the big house in The Park was left behind. The scents of lavender, rosewater and gardenia faded under the increasing smells of leather wax and street odours. Back to the real world and that constancy it provided.

Edna looked pleased to see them, "It's been so bloody quiet, like a morgue in 'ere," she said.

Annie shuddered, fearful of what May's situation might be. Edna had busied herself in their absence and was just completing the work at May's machine. Saul entered the paperwork and turned to the women.

"It is too late to begin more work now, pack away and go home."

Saul seemed preoccupied, apparently seeking his own society, Annie felt perhaps he too was thinking of May. It was not too far to Peverell Street, Annie had not before visited May, the private nature May displayed had always seemed to forbid it. This day was different, the opportunity Saul had provided in dismissing her early propelled her feet away from Winchester Street, she feared what she might find but remembering the boy's anxious face at the workshop door and his urgent bidding, Annie could not turn away from their troubles.

She reached the corner of Peverell Street, it looked to Annie as if God had passed it by, when making the world he must surely have missed this spot and Satan had seen his chance to jump in and seize Peverell Street for his own. Not even the bold dandelion had dared to venture through the chinks and cracks of the rough ground, a single blade of grass far too pure to withstand the oppression. The course stony street and the veiled sky holding between their grip, a layer of noxious fumes from the tannery. As Annie walked slowly along, trying to find the door of No.28, angry shrieking voices rent the air, almost knocking her to the ground, a man poured out of a doorway into the street and within seconds he was doused with urine from a chamber pot emptied from the window above. His curses rang out in a continuous stream of abuse, he paused, spat into the dirt and with the speed of a hunted rat disappeared into the shambling chaos of the street. Annie's heart beat wildly, her legs had for a moment lost their strength, her will tested to its limit. Somewhere amid all this damnation May and her family hid themselves. Just a few more frantic paces revealed No.28. Annie's knuckles rapped the door urgently. The boy's tousled hair and dark eyes peered from the slight opening he had allowed the door. She smiled at him with all her features, forcing her eyes, brow, cheeks and mouth to reassure him with their cheerfulness. He recognised her and turned his head to tell someone in the room behind him that.

"A lady from Mr.Eddowes is here."

Annie heard muffled tones from within the house and the boy opened the door to allow Annie to step inside.

From the kaleidoscope of colours that danced around Mrs.Wright's drawing room she now entered a room so plain, so bare, the former must surely have robbed the latter, how else could one be so bright and adorned and the other so dull and bereft. A man sat in the corner, his frame emaciated, his eyes set so far back they could barely see beyond the ridges of his cheekbones, his voice was faint but kindly.

"May is upstairs, go to her," he said.

Annie pulled aside the curtain at the foot of the stairs and trying to tread so lightly that her shoes made little sound she found the open doorway to a bedroom. May sat on a small wooden chair, leaning towards the bed, holding the hand of an elderly woman. At first Annie didn't see the child nestling into May's side away from the doorway, it was a little girl, a tumble of blonde hair, the thumb of one hand riveted into her pursed mouth, the fingers of the other hand gripping the folds of May's skirt like a vice. The old woman murmured and repeated a name over and over several times.

"Joseph, Joseph."

May looked at Annie, her reddened, swollen eyes evidence of her distress.

"I don't know what to do Annie," she said.

Annie looked at May's mother on the bed, she crossed to the top of the stairs and called to the boy, he was about nine years old, quick in his movements, alert to Annie's words.

"Go to Hucknall Road, the doctor's house, tell them that the doctor must come to your grandma, tell them Annie Bundy sent you and that I will wait for the doctor to come."

"It will be alright May," she put her arm about May's shoulders, unlike the well rounded fleshy arms of Mrs.Wright whom she had attended just a short time ago, May's frame was as spare as a clothes horse and shaking with worry.

"What is your name?" Annie asked the small girl, reluctant to remove the comforting thumb she gave no answer.

May prompted her, "Tell aunty Annie what you are called."
A distorted response due to only partial removal of the thumb, nevertheless informed Annie that her name was Mabel.

"And what is your big brother's name Mabel?" Enquired Annie gently.

The little girl's adoration of her brother was immediately obvious, thumb forgotten she declared, "Alfred, he's my Alfred".

Annie smiled at May and said to Mabel, "I wish I had an Alfred, I don't have a brother, you are very lucky to have an Alfred and I'm sure you are his very special sister."

The child seemed pleased at this notion and locked the moist red thumb back into position.

Some twenty minutes passed before Annie heard the door downstairs, voices made a brief exchange then the purposeful steps of the doctor trod the stairs. He crossed to the bed and spoke softly asking the old woman her name.

"Grace," May answered for her, "Joseph was my father."

Annie encouraged the little fingers of Mabel's hand to release the gathers of her mam's skirt. "Come with me Mabel," she said "we will go downstairs for a few minutes to see Alfred."

May's husband whispered to Annie, "We cannot pay the doctor."

"Don't trouble yourself about that Mr.Watkinson, it will be alright."

Annie saw the doctor to the door and stood just outside as she spoke with him.

"I can pay you sixpence a week until the bill is settled doctor," she said.

The doctor sighed as if resigned to a situation he had met so many times. "There will be a charge for the medication only, it is perhaps fortunate young lady that the gentry also become sick."

Annie was bright enough to recognise the inference. "Thank-you doctor, I will call at your house at the end of the week. You know my name, I am in reliable work sir."

Grace had at last found some sleep, no doubt induced by the medicine.

"I must make my way home May." Annie said.

The two women comforted each other with a brief embrace, May now had to face whatever the future held and Annie must face the more immediate trauma of her journey on foot back to Winchester Street.

CHAPTER THREE

May had worked for Saul for many years, her quiet ways made it easy to overlook the valuable 'constant' she had become. Annie had learned a great deal from May and she determined herself to approach Saul with a plan that would help May and enable the workshop to continue as before. Annie had told Harold the story of the appointment in The Park and the events of the same afternoon, they had sat in the arboretum and debated the situation in earnest. Harold made everything seem so safe and sound. Her confidence rallied to its fullest, she waited for Edna to leave and asked Saul if she might speak with him for a moment.

"What is it Annie?"

"About May, we shall miss her speed and skills at the machine, it isn't that May is ill and can't work, it's just that she can't work here."

Saul looked puzzled but waited for Annie to continue.

"If we took a machine to May's home and some cloth and thread May could stitch the shirts. I could take cloth to her every other day and collect the completed work, that way it would not be more than I could carry."

"Annie," said Saul, "even if I waited until dusk it would be a perilous undertaking to travel along Peverell Street in Meade's carriage."

"We've thought of that," replied Annie, "Harold says Josiah Toft takes his horse and waggon along Peverell Street each week with the hides for the tannery. There are two seats behind the horse, we could put the machine beside Josiah, no one would think anything of him stopping briefly at May's, I doubt they would even notice."

"Harold," said Saul, "who is Harold?"

Annie's character had no inclination to coyness, certainly not at this moment when her mind was set on the success of her plan.

"He is a good friend of mine, he works at the slaughter yard for Josiah."

Annie's sincerity impressed Saul, so often he had seen in Annie all the qualities he would have hoped to find in Charles but the boy had become a man and Saul now knew that Charles' nature was beyond changing.

"It would not be desirable for you to walk alone in Peverell Street, by the time you finish your work here it is too late." Saul was concerned.

"I know," said Annie, "that it why I should leave the workshop at three in the afternoon, I would be back by four and I would work an hour longer in the evening."

"You have it all planned Annie," he said "but you have overlooked the fact that I too would need to stay at the workshop on those evenings."

Annie's face fell , her eyes filled with disappointment, but even as they lowered, Saul caught their dismay.

"I don't really have any need to go home at a particular time, I could give the arrangement a trial," he said.

"It will be alright Mr. Eddowes," declared Annie, "I promise."

And so they agreed Annie's scheme. Her visits to Peverell Street were always eventful but no one had shown her any real malice or interfered with her progress. In walking up and down, she had passed an entry which had a low iron gate, sitting behind it, like a mighty sentinel was a bulldog. Annie had noticed other people cross over the street rather than walk by the entry and its occupant but Annie spoke each time she passed saying.

"Hello Shawcross." The dog's wobbly jowls, large paws and dominance of people, reminded her of the double chins, big hands and overbearing nature of the Minister.

Josiah Toft had proved to be a good man, he had delivered the machine to May's home and seen for himself the family's plight. May's mother was made more frail daily by her failing heart and Alfred Watkinson senior, May's husband, so sickly in his constitution that Josiah had taken to handing May a marrowbone for broth, an ox heart, a little tripe whenever he could.

Annie had taken more cloth for May and collected the finished shirts, she had spoken with Mr. Watkinson, she felt pity for the man, his poor health confined him to the house and his life held so little interest, Annie felt it necessary to chat to him for a minute or two. As they talked Annie could see on the table an enamel dish accommodating a marrowbone that had relinquished every shred of marrow and had been simmered until it shone like marble.

"Oh Mr. Watkinson," said Annie, "do you think I might have that bone?"

"Whatever for Annie?" He asked surprised.

"Well I think I know someone who would enjoy it," she said.

"There's nothing left on it Annie dear, no one could use that."

"It is for a dog," said Annie, "I walk by him each time I come here, he is a big bulldog, he sits behind an old iron gate just a few houses along."

"Be careful Annie," he said.

"Oh I don't believe the dog will cause me any harm."

"It is not the dog I think of," replied Alfred, "you have seen folk around here, you know how it is, if someone is able to provide food for a dog such as you describe, then they almost certainly have a trade which is pursued out of the sight of others."

"I will take care Mr. Watkinson."

Annie gathered up the bone and wrapped it loosely with her handkerchief. The parcel of shirts safely tucked under the other arm she bid Alfred goodbye, and made her way along Peverell Street.

"Hello Shawcross, I have a surprise for you."

She managed to coax the hanky from the bone and lowered her hand, still gripping the edge of the bone over the gate and let it fall to the side of the dog's huge paw. As she slowly withdrew her arm a big, sloppy wet tongue enveloped her wrist. Shawcross seemed to smile, she was convinced of his pleasure and patted him on the head.

"Cheerio Shawcross," she said happily.

A feeling of assurance came over her. If I should ever be alarmed by anyone my new friend would come to my rescue, the old rusting gate which holds him now would act as slight impediment if I called to him urgently, she told herself. The thought amused her and lifted her spirits as she resumed her walk back to Winchester Street.

That evening at the workshop, Annie was busy with Mrs.Wright's gown. Saul was in the back office reading, the two had become quite comfortable with the new routine. Aunt Bella had been surprisingly sympathetic of May's predicament and presented no additional complication to the situation. Annie had found her waiting with their meal on the evenings she arrived home later and had sensed no resentment from Bella, Annie had noticed her earlier bedtime of late, she ate but a small meal and retired soon after. Aunt Bella had always seemed old and Annie had no knowledge of her actual age. Never displaying mirth or merriment, the lines of her face had become pronounced, no laughter to distract them so they had progressed unhindered and now travelled across her skin like the embossed patterns on the workshop brocades. These thoughts caused Annie to look at the clock, it was almost time for her to pack away her task and bid Saul goodnight.

Just then the gate latch rattled outside, the door opened and Charles entered. He cast a short 'Hello' to Annie and crossed quickly to Saul who was surprised by his arrival. Charles' voice became lowered and Annie felt uncomfortable. She secured her thread and placed the gown, which was now well advanced, onto a hanger in the stockroom, this she did with haste then she took her coat from the hook and called to the men.

"I'll be off now." Outside, she set to pondering the purpose of Charles' visit. It was too late to be the business of the bank, he seldom seemed to bring Saul any gladness, she reprimanded herself for being curious, it was none of her concern, her steps quickened as she turned her thoughts to home.

"Why do you need money Charles?" Saul's tone demanded explanation. "You have a good job and steady income!"

"Enid has many wants Father," replied Charles, "she is going to have a child, she is showing now, it is due in three or four months."

Saul knew of Charles' fondness for drink, it was not always taken from a jug in the ale house but at the more elite gatherings in the back room of the bank, where doubtless a few hands of cards accompanied a glass or two of spirit. Charles was still young but his arrogance had gained him entry to this clique.

"I have no cash here now," Saul informed him, "come to me at home on Sunday." Charles left.

Saul sat in the stillness of the workshop, the machines his only company. He had been such a driven young man, his ambition to rise in the world of commerce, to establish a powerful industry in the name of Eddowes had dominated his thinking and being in those days. Fate however, chose not to favour Saul's designs for the future, as the years went by, with no kindred spirit to share his dreams even Saul lost the stomach for it. Neither his wife nor child had shown the slightest regard for his efforts and at some moment in the past it had all lost the taste that once fired his appetite. The sprawling warehouses and factory floors that had filled his imagination lost themselves somewhere beyond his consciousness, the workshop at the bottom of Winchester Street was Saul's reality. He had been fortunate in always securing good women to his employ, a seamstress with unreliable ability could quickly lose the reputation of the business, this had not been the case, the merchandise produced at Saul's had ever been of excellent quality and his reputation for supplying 'the best', was widely acknowledged. He worked the women hard but unlike some bosses, he was not an aggressive man. His circumstances and age seemed to have mellowed him further and a day's end free of trial satisfied Saul.

Charles' shoe caught the side of an abandoned tobacco tin, he kicked it angrily into the road in his frustration. Disturbed from its resting place, the tired tin protested the violation by clattering noisily over every cobble in its path until it found sanctuary once more in a hollow made by the heavy waggon wheels on the other side of the street.

He and Enid lived in a small house not far from his work at the bank. Enid carried a look which could turn a man's head as she passed, fully aware of this she had an enlarged sense of her own importance and played Charles against any situation she felt might win her the latest prize at which she had set her sights. Charles' weakness for the cards had on a number of occasions eaten into his finances. Enid's seemingly endless wants only achieved to drive him more frequently to the back rooms of the bank, the inevitable shortfall of both funds and favours had now led him to crisis point. Enid heard his footsteps as they approached the back door, she stood in front of the hearth, her back to the grate, the fingers of one hand tapping the wooden shoulder of the mantel clock, her swollen figure was indeed evidence of her impending motherhood. Her naturally impatient manner was now even more volatile due to her condition, she was aware of Charles' extended activities at the bank, made so by some of the older women with whom she associated. Enid seemed unable to find companionship in the young women about her.

"Couldn't you return home to your pregnant wife and leave your cronies to their dealings just for once," she shrieked in a tone that stung the already wounded Charles. It was a strange irony that not until this evening had she challenged him on the subject, the very evening his time had been spent away from his usual undertaking.

"I have been to see father," he said.

She scoffed, her obvious disbelief taunted him further.

"Pray God this child doesn't have your avarice." He raised his voice to her harshly, "your wants could drive a man to his end."

He threw his jacket onto the back of the chair and stormed into the scullery where he cupped his hands in a bowl of cold water and sank his head down into the biting chill.

He had missed his mother greatly after she died. She had been sweet and naïve as a young woman and kept her pleasant demeanour as she aged. Her attentions had possibly spoiled Charles to some degree but that aside, he had offered no humility at any time in his life, seizing on the belief that his mother loved him far more than she loved her husband. His arrogance had caused him to treat his father with little respect. Following this night's events his mind was in turmoil. He walked straight passed Enid without another word and took himself up to bed, she followed soon after, her better sense told her to leave him be. Husband and wife lay in the bed each with their own ire, darkness had been known to still many battles, the ensuing hours of sleep would bring a calm to the morning and Sunday's visit to Saul, a respite to Charles' dilemma.

CHAPTER FOUR

Annie's Sunday had been a joyous revelation, she looked forward so much to her time with Harold, they held great discussions on life, he was so eager, although he had not once been beyond the city boundaries, Harold seemed able to see the great, wider world. Annie listened to him as he voiced his plans and dreams, the future had not concerned her before she met Harold, each day as it came presented enough to fill Annie's world, and looking further than that would have been a notion too frivolous. But now her thoughts bounded alongside his, confident, strong, completely at ease with their company. A dull sky became brighter, a weighty problem reduced in size to a manageable affair. He was a rock, a constant, Annie had found her soul mate. Harold had suddenly sprung to his feet, pulled Annie to hers with both hands saying, "Come on, mam wants to meet you."

From outside the house appeared quite small, a 'smiley' face had been etched into a brick by the side of the front door.

"I did that when I was about ten," he laughed at the image, a full round face, big round eyes, a nose and wide smiling mouth. "I scratched it into the brick with a piece of slate, mam said it was naughty but dad gave me a farthing and said I should be allowed to draw the old Queen."

Inside the house there were even more smiling faces, the room seemed to expand to accommodate them. Mrs.Boucher, Harold's mam, was a busy plump little woman, constantly producing food from an old stove which in spite of its shabby exterior, displayed an amazing capacity to oblige and the family happily munched away on her efforts. Their contentment seemed to be all the reward she sought, wiping her floury hand on her pinafore, she took Annie's hand warmly and said.

"Now you sit down dear and Nora will get you a cup of tea, help yourself to a bun, Father," she called loudly to the back yard, "Father, Annie's here."

Harold's dad appeared in the scullery doorway, a gentle giant of a man, he crossed to Annie.

"Eee lass you've really smitten our Harold, reckon 'e uses more soap 'an water than 'e's ever done afore." His laugh was so loud and full Annie felt she could hear it begin at his toes and gather momentum as it travelled, finally reaching an almighty crescendo at his tonsils.

"Leave off Father" said Harold.

The two men were obviously close, the big grin across both faces was a regular feature, the deep laughter lines at the corners of the eyes confirmed it. Frank was Harold's only brother, just eleven months younger than Harold. Nora was the eldest of all, she took care of the four youngest, all girls, Gertie, Jean, Mavis and Maggie. Frank kept the family continually amused by his roguishness, he worked for Cyril Lovatt the baker and besides working in the bake house, he delivered orders on a 'boneshaker' bicycle which had a large basket attached to the front. He had the art of mimicking Lovatt's customers and was really very good at it. The children's laughter filled the living room, even Mrs.Boucher who pretended to be shocked, chuckled behind the screen provided by the open oven door.

Maggie began the entreaty, soon to be joined by Mavis, "Please, please Frank, can we do it now?"

It was a regular event on a Sunday afternoon, Frank gave the little ones a ride in the basket of the bike, up and down Mitchell Street, one at a time. Maggie went first, an old belt of her father's placed around her middle and secured to the handlebars. Recognising the preparations their terrier, Eli, rose up from his place of rest by the dolly tub in the scullery and joined the excited group in the street.

"Now hold on tight," cautioned Frank.

The bicycle rattled and bounced its way across the cobbles, Frank peddling furiously, empowered by his recent consumption of three currant buns. Maggie squealed with glee, jumping up and down in the basket, reined only by the belt, her cheeks glowing like polished apples, her curly hair dancing about her face in total abandon. Eli competing with the bicycle for speed, yapping excitedly in unison with the delighted child. Annie felt her heart would burst from all the happiness. Harold had brought her to this place of love and contentment and the sights and sounds had bolstered her spirit more than the finest tonic.

He walked her back to Winchester Street where he gently took her hand and led her into the entry. Neither spoke, his lips found Annie's and such warmth overcame her that the usual chill of the entry was no more.

"Take care my Annie," he whispered.

She could feel the strength of his hands on her back and wished to stay in his hold forever but it was time to go in, time to go to Bella.

"You must meet aunt Bella soon Harold," she said.

He winked at her, "Don't look so worried, I'll be charmin', you'll see."

He waved and blew her a kiss and ran up to the corner, "charmin' I'll be I promise," he called back to her, then he was gone.

Annie wanted so much for aunt Bella to like Harold, to let him lift her spirits too.

Edna had almost completed Mrs.Wright's curtains, Saul had been summoned to The Park urgently when Davina Wright had quite suddenly decided that the heavy drapes in the drawing room were too worn to be on view to the cousins who would doubtless visit the house after the wedding. Annie had now all but finished the gown and both orders completed, an appointment to hang the drapes and finally fit the ensemble had been made for the following day.

The two young women were taking their short dinnertime break, "Did you see Billy yesterday?" Asked Annie.

Edna grinned and replied, "Yes we went fishin', Billy likes to sit by the Trent and try to outwit the fish, he says it's like catchin' a woman, you 'ave to be patient, just sit 'an look at 'em for a bit 'til they feel at home with yer, then give 'em summat sparkly that they can't resist, when you've got 'em well hooked, lift 'em up an' kiss 'em, then smack their tail ends an' put 'em back to save 'em 'til next week!" she giggled. "Anyways, it's alright by the river, there's nobody gawpin' at yer when yer fancy a cuddle."

Edna seemed happy and Annie felt pleased that Sunday had brought good things for both of them. She described the events in Mitchell Street, they shared the moment of laughter then returned to their machines. Saul was intent on his paperwork, he had been very quiet all morning. A few more minutes would secure the last three fasteners on Mrs.Wright's gown then Annie needed to gather up the cloth to take to May and check the bundle with Saul. He gave it but slight attention, his routine to reconcile the stock was, after all these years automated, he knew Annie presented no cause for doubt. There had been heavy rain the previous night and Peverell Street looked better for having had its face washed. Some of the dust and grime which had clogged its pores had been forced by the weight of rain to surrender its grip. The slabs and cobbles which made up the street's features, today seemed able to show a lighter complexion.

May's husband opened the door and Mabel appeared beside him the child gave Annie her usual welcome, taking Annie's hand and pulling her inside, the moist, sticky thumb adhered itself to Annie's palm. May sat quietly at the table wearing a troubled look.

"We have a problem Annie," Alfred said in his low weakened voice, "May has been stitching by night to give her attention to Mabel and Grace by day but the people on either side have complained harshly about the noise of the machine, the sound travels through the walls."

May's eyes filled with tears and she wrung her hands in despair. Annie persuaded May to do what she could through the day and not to worry.

"We will think of something before I come again on Wednesday, it's just lucky that I have something for you Mabel, look."

She pulled from her pocket a fat wax colouring stick saved from her own childhood. Aunt Bella had taught Annie at home and some of the wax sticks and chalks still sat in the old candle box in Annie's bedroom. Then she unwrapped the parcel of cloth to take from within two large pieces of card cut from the bottoms of thread boxes.

"Now when your mam is busy doing her stitching, you can draw some nice pictures for me, your dad will help you and you can surprise your Alfred when he gets home from school, draw something for him too."

"I used to be a carpenter Annie, I'm no good at drawing."

"Needs must Alfred," she replied and kissed his cheek.

Mabel's eyes had looked at the colouring stick and card and the little girl jumped up and down with excitement. Even May could not resist the child's enthusiasm and by the time Annie left them the mood in the house had been transformed, clutching the parcel of shirts she made her way back.

"Hello Shawcross," Annie paused in front of her canine friend, she needed to share her quandary and the docile dog offered a receptive ear.

"What can be done, there must be something, what would you do Shawcross?"

She patted the large furrowed brow and drew from her pocket a piece of crust which she had purposefully kept by from her dinner, he took it from her fingers so gently, Annie felt only the softness of his cascading cheeks. It reminded her of the texture of velvet which she had so many times turned into bonnets. A problem shared is a problem halved she told herself.

"Now you think about it Shawcross."

She continued on her way, it seemed like no time at all that she was back at the workshop.

Her mind had travelled wildly, desperately seeking a solution and her feet had followed the same pace as her thoughts. Edna looked up as Annie entered, Annie had no way of seeing how flushed her own face had become from the exertion.

"God almighty Annie what's up?"

Edna's remark surprised Annie.

"How do you know May has a problem?" Annie asked in her confusion.

Saul heard the two women talking and came through from the back office. Annie briefly explained the situation, not wanting to alarm Saul over the complaints, she added, "May is going to stitch by day until we can think of something."

The appointment in The Park was made for mid morning. Edward Meade pulled up outside and the boxes were placed in the carriage. Annie and Saul positioned themselves on the seat but were mindful of the need to restrain the boxes from any wayward intent, their contents were valuable both in money and reputation. Meade was asked to return for them in ninety minutes. All the boxes safely inside Ivy lead them to Mrs.Wright in the drawing room, in anticipation of their arrival a set of steps had been placed by the large window. Annie could see no reason to replace the existing drapes, she could not recall the curtains at the windows of aunt Bella's ever being changed, only being taken down to be washed in the spring and hung back up again when dried and ironed. They were of thick heavy cloth and fell full length from the pelmet to the floor.

Saul positioned the steps and told Annie to gather up the curtains as he released them. As the folds of material enveloped Annie's shoulder, she could smell furniture polish and faintly the odour of paraffin, used to clean the glass in the window. The old curtains finally down, Saul told Annie to support the weight of the new drapes as he secured them to the pole. Mrs.Wright's pleasure at the fresh soft furnishings bubbled over in her continuous chatter.

"Oh the colour is splendid and the ruched pelmet puts cousin Isobel's in the shade, she will be so envious, they are perfect, so elegant, I can't wait for the wedding." She clapped her hands in a gesture of triumph.

"Such heavily made up material too," she said "it makes such a difference you know, when the daylight fades and Ivy draws them across, a wonderful peace is brought to the room, not a sound from the street can be heard, it permits me total concentration at my reading and letter writing. Indeed when the Elliotts across the road had a chimney fire, I had no knowledge of it until the following morning when the builders arrived to repair the stack, it had apparently split from the heat down its entire length and could have collapsed and killed ...." Davina prattled on and on.

Annie's ears received no further than the words 'not a sound from the street can be heard', at that moment they lost function and repeated over and over again, like some solemn chant to be ingrained on the soul.

Annie had to attend Mrs.Wright in her dressing room for the final fitting of the gown. Davina, resplendent in her rich burgundy coloured satin and silk creation, paraded in front of her mirror like an Empress, her obvious delight reassured Annie and before her courage could fail her she asked.

"Mrs.Wright, what will you do with the old curtains?"

Still presiding over her empire in full regalia Davina didn't pause to ponder Annie's enquiry but almost sang a response in her happiness.

"They go to the Mission my dear, oh what joy, I feel ten years younger in this, you don't think the shade is too youthful for someone my age do you Annie?"

"You look wonderful ma'am, you will turn every head I feel sure."

Then Annie's earlier words seemed suddenly to register.

"Why do you ask about the curtains my dear?" Said Davina.

Annie was aware of the need to hurry, their task in the drawing room had taken some time, Saul was still downstairs perfecting the swags to match the folds exactly on both drapes. Meade had been instructed to return in ninety minutes but she could not allow this opportunity to pass and with Annie's engaging boldness she poured out the story of May's plight. Davina was a lady of comfortable means, her late husband Nathan had been the pit owner at Birchdale, a significant figure in the world of commerce, he had also been a director at Braithwaite's Bank. She had been a widow for close to twenty years and unfortunately no offspring had come from their union. In spite of being far removed from the trials of life in Peverell Street, she nevertheless had a mind which opened to the lives of others. Her surroundings displayed all the trappings of a sheltered background but her own characteristics were far from frivolous. Her response was immediate, Annie felt like hugging her.

"My dear, I cannot think of a better purpose for my old drapes, to be used for a practical solution to such an acute problem is a very good outcome, but Annie, how are we to transport them to May's, shall I arrange a carriage?"

"Oh no, that wouldn't do, you see, the cobbles are very rough in Peverell Street, it would not be appropriate!" Annie's anxious words imparted tactfully the actual circumstances to Davina.

"I really must go," Annie said, "Saul will be preparing to leave, Mr.Meade will be back very soon, I shall speak with my best friend Harold this evening, he will know what to do."

Realising Annie's need to return to the drawing room she patted Annie's hand and said quietly, "I will await your plan my dear, don't worry, we will manage somehow."

After the two had left the house, Davina reflected on the morning's events. Her excitement at the drapes and gown had now been tempered by desire to be involved to some degree in Annie's plan. The days could be long for Davina, she had many acquaintances and one or two friends but apart from cousins there was no immediate family. She had felt an instant liking for Annie and to be instrumental in relieving May's anxieties and to possibly meet Annie's best friend Harold brought an interest and purpose to her day.

Meanwhile, Saul and Annie travelled back to Winchester Street. Saul was pleased by the result of their time spent at the house, Mrs. Wright had been thoroughly satisfied with both drapes and gown and complimentary of the work involved, he felt relieved to have reached this final stage. Davina Wright intimidated him somewhat, he knew that while in her presence he was being scrutinized, now with the examination over and having achieved a commendable result, his body relaxed, mind and stomach untangled their knotted fibres and his eyes closed as he calmed. Annie on the other hand was employing her time in the carriage to come up with a scheme. It was not until they passed Cyril Lovatt's bake house that inspiration blossomed, of course she thought to herself, Frank's bicycle. If the curtains were wrapped separately, then one at a time they could be transported in the big bread basket, it might have to happen as darkness fell, I don't imagine Mr. Lovatt would object greatly but Frank might feel it wiser not to ask, just in case. She was deep in these thoughts when Saul asked.

"Are you alright Annie, you seem very quiet, are the walks to May's and the later evenings proving too much for you?"

"Oh no, not at all, I was just daydreaming. The house in The Park has so many things inside and I find some of them very interesting."

It was not an untruth, she could not answer falsely, it satisfied him and they journeyed on contentedly to the workshop.

The afternoon's work over, Annie hurried home, she must speak with Harold urgently. Aunt Bella was preparing a meal of brawn and boiled potatoes. Annie needed to explain to Bella that after the meal she must walk to Mitchell Street to see Harold, that May needed help and that Harold would know what to do. She felt tense, it was impossible to predict Bella's reaction. Annie filled the coal bucket, scrubbed her hands and laid the table for the two women to eat, placing the small glass dish which held the salt in the middle of the table. It had always been at the house, that salt dish, shaped almost like a coffin with a tiny silver shovel like spoon which had a pretty handle made from Mother of Pearl. Annie felt the old glass dish held within it not just salt but the story of aunt Bella's past too, each tiny grain bearing a secret, an iota of knowledge. If only they could speak Annie might then have an understanding of her aunt's moods.

The meal ready Annie and Bella sat down to eat.

"May was very distressed yesterday," said Annie, "her neighbours have complained about the noise the sewing machine makes. May has been working by night so as to allow herself time to look after the family by day, the sound travels through the walls. I think I can help her but Harold would need to fetch some heavy curtains from a lady who has no further use of them, he will have to use his brother's bicycle."

Bella looked confused and spoke sharply to Annie, "Hush child," she said, "tell me what it is you want to do."

Annie related the story of the old curtains, choosing at this stage not to declare from where the curtains were coming. She told of Frank's bicycle with the large basket, making only a fleeting reference to Cyril Lovatt, she dare not make it sound like a conspiracy but was aware a degree of caution concerning some details might be necessary, she must go to Harold's house as soon as she could.

"Eat your food then go right away," said Bella, "I will clear away the meal, you will not walk back here alone, you will promise me that."

It was a demand not a mere request, Annie sensed her aunt's resistance and quickly assured Bella that Harold would walk her home.

"You must meet Harold soon Aunt Bella," said Annie. "I thought I might bring him to see you next Sunday."

Annie's throat tightened with trepidation, for an instant she could not swallow, choked by the dread of Bella's words.

"You'll not be late home, the time it will take to Mitchell Street and back will be late enough, those curtains wherever they are won't be fetched tonight."

Annie's feet sped down the entry and up the street. At least aunt Bella had not said no. It felt wise not to pursue the conversation and to do what Bella had bidden, she would go to Harold's as quickly as she could.

The pan of water on the coals was now hot enough to wash the dishes, Bella poured it into the bowl and lowered the plates, knives and forks into the heat. Her fingers once so fine and slender now showing signs of age at the joints, some swollen from the early stages of arthritis. She remembered her mother's words spoken to her when she began work teaching. 'Those hands will achieve much Bella' she had said 'they will pass your brightness to others and hold their future in your keeping.'

Bella lay on her bed, anxious until Annie returned, she was tired but her mind had travelled back at the memory of her mother's words and it now determined to keep her awake.

She could see her mother's face, her gentle eyes and sweet smile, a good woman, daughter of a vicar, the Reverend Bundy. Bella's father was a steward at the Chapel, he worked at the printers. The two had met when her mother had been sent by her father to collect Hymnals for the Church. Bella had a younger sister, Ruby, not as gifted at her studies as Bella but a very pretty young woman. Their father was completely consumed by his belief and had become an Evangelist. His authority over the household had been severe, his interpretation of the faith being perfection in all things, no allowance for the frailties of human kind, no tolerance of the slightest error, no weakness in thought word or deed with the result that Bella, her sister Ruby and her mother, Clarice, had all become afraid of this, 'Steward of God's house', Sefton Pownall.

Bella was on her way home from her work in The Park, she had been employed by the Hemsleys to teach the two young children of the family, it took her half an hour to walk the distance home. The job suited her well, the Hemsleys were kind and considerate and had offered a position to Ruby, helping their cook. Ruby's work was not finished until after the family's evening meal and so she returned home later than Bella.

That evening Sefton had left to attend a meeting at the Chapel, Bella and her mother lightened in their spirits by his absence were chatting as they cleared away the dishes. They had settled down, Bella to mark the children's work and Clarice to her needlework, when the back door had burst violently open. Ruby collapsed into the scullery, her clothes were torn and filthy, her hair was entirely freed of pins and fell in tangled masses about her shoulders.

Her eyes could not be seen behind a wall of tears and her cries rent the air like those of some desperate, cornered animal. Bella's mother had become rooted to the spot by shock, it was Bella who gathered up the terrified Ruby and held her in her arms begging the girl to stop her fearful cries. Only sobs now persisted and between these eruptions Ruby spluttered out the words which sickened Bella's very being. The walk home, a man grabbing her from behind, stifling her screams with his hand, a big rough hand that reeked of beer and tobacco, he pulled at her clothes, ripped her underwear and in the gloom of a desolate alley, against a wall which stank of urine he raped her 'til her breath was almost at its last and her small frame near crushed between his lunging bulk and the merciless wall. Bella called to her mother.

"Quickly heat some water, we must clean Ruby."

Her fear was not now for the beast who had abused her sister, but for their father who would see this deed as Ruby's eternal damnation, her certain promise of hellfire.

They must work quickly to erase all evidence of the terrors of this night. The two women washed Ruby, desperately trying to comfort her as they did so. Bella wrapped the torn, dirty clothing in a piece of old paper and thrust the bundle into the bottom of the bag in which she carried her books to work, there they would be hidden overnight and she would dispose of them away from the house in the morning.

Ruby lay in her bed, Bella knelt on the floor beside her, smoothing her brow, over and over Bella's soft hand passed across Ruby's forehead inducing rest.

"We shall tell father that you came home from work feeling very unwell and that you shall stay in bed until you feel better. You understand why we must say this to father don't you Ruby?"

Ruby's voice was feeble but she replied faintly, "I know, I know why," then she gave into exhaustion and her tragic mind found a fitful sleep.

Bella and her mother agreed their story and sat as naturally as was possible to await Sefton's return, it was not long before the back door latch rattled, he had come and the plot was sealed.

Bella's memories were abruptly halted when she heard downstairs the sound of the scullery door, Annie was back and her relief swept away all other thoughts. Annie called up the stairs, "I am home Aunt Bella, Harold walked me to the back door, he said to say he hopes to meet you on Sunday."

Annie awaited Bella's reply with the deepest hope.

"Bolt the door and put out the lamp," came back the voice from Bella's room.

Annie sighed but did as aunt Bella had ordered calling, "Goodnight" as she took herself to bed. Her mind now turned to Harold and the errand he had agreed to undertake the following evening.

They had secured Frank's permission to use the bicycle but not at too late an hour, as Frank pointed out, to be on the streets in failing light could be dangerous. It was agreed that to go to May's via Connaught Street meant not having to pass Lovatt's bake house and was only a slightly longer route. Annie had assured Harold that Mrs.Wright would recognise his name and receive him and would permit him to take the curtains. The first endeavour was to be the following evening and the second on Thursday evening when Annie would go from her work straight to May's house. Tomorrow she would tell May and Alfred of the plan when she delivered the cloth, Annie had no way of contacting Davina Wright in advance of Harold's arrival and could only trust her instinct in believing Harold would be welcomed.

Sleep finally overtook her and she awoke next morning from a vivid dream, the few images of the dream she could remember before it all became lost in a haze of bewilderment she mentally recorded, so that she might recount it to Harold. Now however, she must be sure all was well with aunt Bella and make ready to leave for her work.

She raked the embers of the fire, sometimes if the old grate's contrary nature favoured her, there remained just enough red to win a response when teased with a fine stick of kindling. This morning its mood was unfriendly and offered not a single spark of co-operation. Resigned to her task Annie cleared all the spent embers and ash from the grate and laid paper and sticks, she took a measure of rancid fat from the stale dripping jar and tucked it into the middle of the kindlers to encourage the lifeless fire to stir. A small box of sulphurs sat on the mantelpiece, she struck one, allowed the flame to establish and then lowered it into the paper. Small blue flames crept around the edge of the grate, slowly bringing the fire back to life. It found the melting rancid fat and sizzled its annoyance at being disturbed. Now it was awake the fire demonstrated its authority and the flames leapt high up the chimney quickly sending Annie away from its heat. With a small shovel she carefully placed a few nubs of coal over the fire's angry belly, then put the kettle on top. It was her routine to take Bella some tea before leaving the house. Annie scrubbed her hands in the cold water on the scullery table and washed her face. Her fingers often became quite sore from all the necessary scrubbing and all she could do was apply a little zinc and castor just before she went to bed each night, 'baby's bum' ointment as Edna insisted on calling it. The kettle boiled and Annie warmed the teapot and put the tea to brew. Just as she was about to pour some, Bella appeared at the foot of the stairs, it made Annie jump.

"You gave me quite a start Aunt Bella" she said.

"I need to talk to you before you go, sit down for a moment. It is good that you help May, no one should be despairing and without help, but you shall promise me that you will never walk on your own after evening light and I will see this Harold on Sunday, you shall fetch him after dinner."

As Annie walked down the street to the workshop she could not decide whether to feel relieved or fearful but Monday would surely follow Sunday and by the time she walked to Saul's on that morning she would know her fate.

"Please God let it be alright", she whispered the words to the sky above and trusted her plea would reach the almighty in time.

The afternoon revealed a busy scene in the area about May's house. Wednesday was the turn of Peverell Street to have the tub waggon that collected the waste. The noise and the cocktail of odours were dire. As Annie approached the house where Shawcross lived, a tall heavily built man stepped into the street from the entry where the dog would normally be. The man had an awkward gait, a limp, but nevertheless carried the tub to the waggon. Annie heard him speak to the tubman, some sort of exchange took place between the two men, something passed from hand to hand, they nodded at each other as if to reaffirm an understanding, then the man disappeared back into the entry. Annie assumed that Shawcross would be in the way on these occasions and hoped she might see him returned to his usual place when she travelled back shortly.

May and her family were in reasonable spirits. Mabel immediately outstretched her arms to Annie, holding firmly with her eager fingers a piece of card so full of drawings, not a square inch of paper was left unused.

"We have been great artists since you were last here Annie," said Alfred.

"For you, it's for you," the excited child's voice rang about Annie's ears like a peal of bells, the same sequence of notes repeated over and over in a continuous summons to attend.

"Alright Mabel," said her mother, "Annie will look in a moment but let her put down her parcel first and catch her breath."

Annie produced a candy stick from her pocket, looking towards May to obtain the necessary agreement.

"Now you say thank you to aunty Annie Mabel."

The little girl's face was a delight, in its innocence it displayed nothing but love, Annie wanted to lift her up and carry her away to the arboretum, to put her down among the flowers where her prettiness could shine alongside theirs. It took several minutes to explain to Alfred and May the plan which she and Harold had put together.

"Now Alfred, I need you to help, you must think of a way for us to secure the curtains to the walls, they are very big, each drape will cover the whole of one wall."

Alfred looked up to the beams and boards above their heads.

"The only way is to nail them to the ceiling board as close to the wall as possible. We will need to pull out a few bits of furniture whilst we do it and put them back against the curtain afterwards. The nails will have to go through the cloth it will damage the curtains." Alfred was concerned.

"May is more than capable of cutting away the damaged strip of material and repairing them if the need of them is passed, the lady doesn't wish them to be returned, they will be yours to keep."

Everything arranged, the finished shirts collected and Mabel's precious drawing safely folded and lodged in her pocket, Annie made her way hastily along Peverell Street. The ongoing waste collection rendered the air so thick with odour that Annie felt nauseous. Shawcross was again at his post, whether his charge was to keep badness out of his territory or to hold it within, Annie was not quite sure but she was certain that in it all, her friend Shawcross was a totally innocent bystander, just as trapped amid this deprivation as dear little Mabel.

At her work that evening Annie's thoughts were constantly with Harold. What would Mrs.Wright say to him, surely she would be with Harold as she had been with her, warm and kindly. It was a daunting task for him not having ever met the lady before and on meeting her for the first time, needing to be receiving something and not to be giving. Annie was anxious for him but would know nothing until the following evening, it was a torment she must bear until then. Annie need not have worried, events at The Park were entirely harmonious.

Harold looked up at the grand house, Annie had described the tall railings and dense shrubbery, she had directed him to the far side of the house where, when he rang the bell by the heavy oak door, Ivy would answer. He propped the bicycle against the wall as best he could, a flower bed at its base held the root of a vigorous wisteria which had spread its cloak of delicate mauve blooms across the façade. They fell in perfect cascades and stirred softly with the breeze. Harold remarked to himself that it would be a hard job to find a cheerless brick on which to scratch a smiley face by this door. The catch rattled on the other side of the weathered oak panel and the door was opened by Ivy, just as Annie had said, she looked startled but quickly casting her eyes up and down his attire uttered.

"Not today thank you."

The intoned delivery reminded him of grandad Boucher's talking Jackdaw. The door was about to close when Harold said, "Excuse me Miss, but I'm 'ere to see Mrs.Wright, if you tell her it's Harold, Annie's friend."

"You had better wait there," said Ivy and closed the door.

The 'nobs' are a strange lot he thought, at home it took mam no more than a few seconds to open the door but in the time it took the gentry a man could have washed a vat o' tripe! Eventually Ivy returned and Harold was admitted.

"Follow me," she said.

He was not unnerved by these surroundings, in fact he was quite looking forward to meeting Davina Wright, partly from a natural curiosity but mainly because of Annie's obvious regard for the lady.

"Thank you Ivy," sang Davina with her usual aplomb.

Ivy retreated and closed the door behind her.

"Aah now, Harold, so you have stepped into the breach and agreed to be our knight in shining armour."

He gave a small bow, "tut, tut, tut," said Davina, "my dear, when a lady of my years finds herself before a young man, she is fully aware that the moment will be short lived, so you can believe it to be true that I much prefer to see your handsome face for those few precious seconds than to gaze upon the top of your head."

Harold's face broke into a generous smile, the two shook hands warmly, neither felt the slightest barrier of awkwardness.

"Now, what is the plan?" Asked Davina.

He explained he had the use of Frank's bicycle but that he could take only one curtain this evening and if convenient, the second tomorrow evening.

"Do you have other siblings?"

"Oh yes," replied Harold, "Frank is my only brother but I have five sisters, Nora, the eldest of all and four younger than Frank."

"What a wonderful household it must be," said Davina. Her words were tinged with envy, she rattled around in that large house like the last farthing in a money box.

"Your mother must be so proud of you all."

Harold laughed, "Poor mam, I don't think she ever has time to feel proud, she never stops baking, washing and cleaning up. She says she'd have it no other way, but it can't be right, she sees nothing of the world. I want it to be different for Annie, I would like to take her to beautiful places, the sea, mountains, lakes."

Davina liked him very much, she felt so pleased it was Annie to whom he wished to show these wonders.

"Would you like something to eat Harold?" She asked.

"Mam will plate up something for me to have when I get home but thank you anyway".

"Perhaps tomorrow evening you might have a bite to eat before you leave. If I have a curtain wrapped in readiness, then you would surely have enough time and it would save your mother," she said.

Harold sensed her loneliness and hadn't the heart to refuse her and so it was settled.

Davina rang for Ivy. "The curtains we took down from the drawing room, I need you to wrap one in a laundry bag Ivy and bring it to Harold at the side door."

Davina walked with him to the bicycle. "I shall see that the other curtain is ready for you tomorrow," she said.

Her eyes fell on the transport, it seemed very familiar but her sensitivity and discretion silenced her curiosity, Annie's plan was good enough and she found no need to question it.

Harold's journey along Connaught Street took him past The Nelson and this evening the brewery waggon was making a late delivery, four magnificent heavy grey horses made up the team. Wrenshaw's horses were a well known spectacle around the city, all the animals were greys and kept in splendid order. Harold stopped the bicycle for a minute to watch them as they drew up outside the pub yard. The brasses on their harness shone brilliantly, the leather blinkers so regularly waxed that they too caught the light and reflected the grandeur of the brightly coloured plumes that decorated the full bridles. Their manes and tails brushed so finely each hair waved free of the next in the light wind the horses created as they moved. The draymen in bowler hats and leather aprons worked their routine with precision, it was performed so often. The brewery was blessed with excellent health, no matter what market forces afflicted other trades and lowered performance, Wrenshaw's continued to glow with well being. If man had no work and lay depressed, it was beer he sought as his remedy. If he met with competition then he fired his resolve with goodly measures of ale and when his fortunes were fine, he celebrated with vast quantities of the rich brown nectar. Wrenshaw's success was surely guaranteed, only if man were to join the ranks of the 'Do-Do' would their empire ever be threatened.

A far cry from the old work horse and waggon that carried the ill fated beasts to Josiah's yard thought Harold. This reminded him of the need to press on, by the time he had delivered the curtain to Peverell Street and cycled home from there the day would be far spent.

Nora was sewing a patch onto the seat of Frank's trousers.

"I can understand how that situation came about," observed Harold, rubbing his backside as he crossed the room, "our Frank must 'ave a permanently sore arse. Where's mam?" He asked.

Nora looked up from her work and nodded towards the stairs, "Just saying goodnight to Gertie and Jean," she replied, "father and Frank have gone down the allotment, should be back soon, your supper's in the range."

Samuel Boucher had taken over the allotment from his father, it supplied the family with basic vegetables and a wealth of soft fruits which Sarah, his wife, turned into pies, jams and flavoured vinegar, the latter sprinkled onto generous helpings of batter pudding.

Most summer evenings Samuel spent much time and energy in cultivating and gathering this produce. He would say to Sarah as he laughed his way through the door, 'Got to put all this soot somewhere'. Dug into the ground he swore it made the small early spuds grow into 'men' as he proudly called the big wholesome looking potatoes he carried indoors for Sarah to bake. His father before him had done likewise, the tradition had simply continued as a matter of course. Grandad Boucher would sit under the shade of the Bramley apple, a fine old tree in the corner by the compost heap and before he had chance to make himself comfortable the Jackdaw would perch on his shoulder and pull at the hairs which grew from his ears. With the result that the bird had a limited vocabulary, just two words which it mimicked with considerable clarity. 'Bugger off, bugger off', it would say.

On starting school, Harold and Frank had been cautioned many times by their mother, 'You say that just once and I'll pull its old neck.'

The threat had worked well, both boys having a great liking for the bird, had dutifully complied until one day grandad had declared, 'The old bugger's dead'. After that Sarah had not a hope!

Next morning Harold made ready for work, Frank had already left. His job at Lovatt's demanding an early start but he was usually home by mid afternoon.

Josiah had been leaning more heavily on Harold of late. The years of hard work at the slaughter yard had taken their toll on Josiah's joints and arthritis was now restricting his movements and slowing him down. Billy Dodds had worked there for only a year or so and didn't have the experience that Harold had gained.

Josiah was at his books in what passed for an office, a small wooden shed tucked away at the back of the yard. In the summer the vats holding the waste needed to be collected at the end of every 'Kill', no matter how stoic the men's attempts at containing the smell with the heavy wooden covers, the flies travelled in droves from far and wide, the cutting shed had been made as secure against these wingéd armies as was humanly possible. The large meat hooks were suspended from chains, which Josiah had wound around the entire length of a trunk of oak that spanned the width of the shed at the far end. One corner of the yard held a 'lean to' where the wood used to fire the boiler was stacked. Pigs had to be dipped and scrubbed of bristles, sheep and cattle skinned. The work was brutal and yet carried out by men whose nature was gentle. It was a contradiction which would defy reason but for man's need to earn a living, and that vital requirement, food.

The bloodiest part of the routine was now done and the bodies of the sheep which had occupied the holding pen the previous night had been opened and now hung over the vats to drain down.

The men had a chance for a few minutes ease. Harold and Billy sat on an old bench with their backs against the wood pile for support, it was the lower back which ached most after such sessions. Billy pulled aside his thick apron and reached into his pocket for his tobacco tin. Harold didn't smoke, Samuel had always said, 'I can sweep a chimney 'til it's clean as a whistle, but I can't sweep me lungs,' and as a result had never used tobacco. Harold and Frank had accepted their father's philosophy and had not taken it up either. Billy made a thin roll up and held it in the corner of his mouth for a while before he lit it, he had an amazing ability to keep it there while talking, like a thing magnetised.

Harold had found himself a mint and leaned back on the logs with his eyes closed.

"Ere Harold," said Billy, "I was in the 'Nag's Head' last night just for a pint an' old Ned Tinkler's in there, like allus, playing the piana, no one takin' no notice of 'im as usual. He keeps on shoutin' at 'em, 'Sing yer bastards, sing, sing yer bastards, sing', then this posh lookin' geezer gets up from 'is seat and walks over to the piana, everythin' goes deathly still, 'e looks down at Ned an' in this deep grainy voice, all deliberate an' slow like, 'e says, 'I am not a bastard'. Well by now you could 'ave 'eard a man scratch 'is balls. Ned looks straight back at 'im and gives this almighty sniff, then says, 'Well you won't 'ave to sing then will yer'. God Almighty, the place was a riot 'an that bloke's face, what a picture."

The two men laughed heartily. Billy had come to Josiah's to replace Elliot Darch who had simply got too old for the work, Elliot was a decent enough chap but very sober, not given to inspiring mirth. Billy however was the opposite. Never a day went by that some remark didn't result in real gut laughter and given the surroundings in which the men worked, it was sorely needed.

They had put in long hours and both Harold and Billy were glad to be hanging up their aprons. For the first ten minutes their walk home followed the same route, then Billy turned into Ainsley Road and Harold carried on to the next corner where he cut through to Mitchell Street. He was in a hurry this evening, it would have to be a quick wash and then his errand on the bicycle to The Park. In spite of his tiredness he had a lighter tread today, when he finally reached May's house he would see his Annie.

"Don't forget Mam, I'm takin' refreshment with me new lady friend so I shan't need anythin' keeping warm," he winked at Nora.

"You mind your manners an' don't you eat that good lady out 'o sight 'an 'earin' neither, you can 'ave supper when you get 'ome. What time will that be Harold?" She asked.

"Not sure Mam, I shall 'ave to take Annie back to Winchester Street then come straight back 'ere but we've got to fix these curtains up for May somehow."

"I shall be glad when all this is done an' Lovatt's bicycle is back in the yard," she said, letting out a long sigh.

"Oh, wait a minute Harold," Sarah went to the cupboard and took out a jar of gooseberry jam, "put this in the basket and give it to Mrs. Wright."

Harold chuckled as he wheeled the bicycle through the back yard and into the street. Dear mam she never had an ill thought for anyone, she only ever wanted everything to be alright.

Knowing the cobbles would shake the basket he took off his cap and placed the jar of jam inside it, that should cushion it a bit he thought. It was now nearly six o'clock, the journey was uneventful and on his arrival Ivy ushered him straight through to Davina. He noticed a parcel, placed on a low table just inside the door, obviously the curtain made ready as promised.

"Now Harold, do sit down and rest for just a minute or two."

Davina was openly delighted at seeing him again. Harold was clutching his cap, waiting for the right moment to produce Sarah's jam.

"Ivy will bring a tray and we shall have a bite to eat," said Davina.

"Mam has sent you this," Harold held out the gift proudly.

"Oh, how splendid, my dear you must give your mother my kindest regards."

The door opened and Ivy appeared with a laden tray. Harold jumped to his feet to take it from her. Davina smiled, his natural courtesy endeared him to her. Ivy was taken by surprise but warmly flattered by his thoughtfulness. He was so insistent on relieving her of the weighty tray that she had no option but to let it pass to him, she looked towards Davina hoping to be pardoned any misdemeanour.

"That's alright Ivy," she said, "we will manage nicely, if you would just bring a beer for Harold and a glass of my sherry."

Harold put the tray down on the table.

"I hope you like raised pork pie Harold, it was one of Nathan's favourites."

"It looks grand ma'am," he said, as indeed it did.

There was a large wedge of cheese, a dish of pickled onions, some crusty bread and a pot of mustard.

"Come now my dear, help yourself, I shall take just a little bread and butter, I ate handsomely at lunchtime, it is not wise, at my age, to indulge too late in the day."

The beer was refreshingly cold, it revived him.

"Do try some of Mr.Lovatt's excellent bread Harold," she said giving him a very old fashioned look as she offered him the platter. The understanding between the two was complete.

"Such a distance on that bicycle must have made you hungry."

Harold took a piece of bread and spread it liberally with butter, he took a bite and looking directly at Davina, gave a knowing wink! She took another sip of sherry and began to chuckle, it set Harold off too, bound together by conspiracy they united in a toast to Cyril Lovatt and his excellent bread.

The parcel safely packed into the basket, Harold turned to Davina and spoke quietly, "Thank you, I know it means a lot to Annie."

She took his hand and said, "It has given me nothing but pleasure, please give Annie my fond wishes and of course my regards to May. I do hope she will find some relief."

He wheeled the bicycle to the corner of the house and before disappearing, he looked back and waved. Davina felt her eyes watering and a great emptiness inside her, she wondered when she might see Annie and Harold again. 'Come, come now woman' she cautioned herself, this won't do, you have a wedding to think about and cousin Isobel's visit to attend to. Now there indeed lay a distraction, cousin Isobel.

"Oh my dear soul" said Davina. She spoke the words out loud, then took a deep breath and turned back into the house, the heavy oak door closed once more on her solitude.

May sat upstairs with Grace and Mabel. It was fortunate that they occupied the bedroom above the small sitting room where young Alfred slept. The living room furniture had already been pulled into the middle of the floor by Annie and May. Alfred had retrieved his tool box from the privy shelf where it had lain in abeyance since his last day of work. Fate had proved kindly and the box had yielded sufficient nails to secure the curtains to the boards above. The task could not be achieved without a period of noise so needed to be completed swiftly. May was to cushion her mother's ears with the pillow and Annie had been to the doors of both neighbours to advise them that just for a little while there would be some hammering but thereafter they should experience no further disturbance. On the one side Annie had received a reasonably gracious response but at the door of the other had been told, 'It better be bloody quick or else'. Harold stood on a chair and Annie fed the material to him as he hammered it to the boarding. The rooms at the house in The Park were very much higher than the modest accommodation at No.28 Peverell Street and Alfred rolled up the surplus curtain and pushed it to the base of the wall. The furniture was set back in position against the newly adorned walls and they surveyed their efforts.

"Blimey," said Harold, "you'll need to get out the best china now Alfred." They chuckled.

Annie fetched May to see what they had done.

"What is the first thing you notice?" Annie asked her looking amused.

"Beeswax," replied May, "I can smell beeswax."

The two women laughed at the unlikeliness of it all, this plain dwelling now wearing an elegant gown befitting of the gentry and even smelling of richness!

Harold made a small bow and giving May a roguish wink said, "If you please ma'am we'll be on our way."

Alfred Watkinson had taken on a much improved pallor. Annie had noticed this over the past few weeks and felt that Josiah's help had contributed greatly but she was quite sure that more than any other factor, the company of his wife in the home had brought about this change. Whilst Josiah's 'tit bits' had fed Alfred bodily, May's presence and quiet strength had nourished his spirit. Alfred shook Harold's hand with a firmness previously not possible through weakness and thanked him sincerely, he then went to the sitting room where his son lay in bed and returned with a small picture. With one hand on Annie's shoulder he kissed her forehead.

"This was my mother's, I want you to have it Annie, keep it always and remember the friendship we all share."

Annie took the little framed picture, it had in one corner embroidered in silks, the image of a window, opened to a blue sky and on the ledge of the window sat a bowl of brightly coloured roses that matched the summery patterned curtains on either side.

She read the words of a verse printed below;

    May every window open to the sun

    and life for you be full of pleasant ways,

    So that you may, as the seasons run,

    Look out upon a world of happy days.

She felt the warm moisture of tears in her eyes and saw the same emotion in May's eyes too.

It was getting late and Harold had to take Annie back to Winchester Street before he could go home. He walked the bicycle up Peverell Street with Annie by his side, Shawcross barked sharply as they approached.

"Why my dear Shawcross, I do believe you are jealous," said Annie, "meet my other friend Harold."

"Pleased to make your acquaintance old chap," said Harold and tipped his cap. As they progressed slowly up the street the sound of some domestic altercation became louder until alongside them, an open door allowed a barrage of obscenities to escape the dwelling and engulf them in its volley. Annie quickened her step, "Come on Harold, lets get to the corner." They put several yards behind them and peace finally prevailed.

It was at that moment that Annie remembered her dream. "I had a strange dream the other night," she said, "I was outside the Mission Hall, a young woman stood by the gates, she was very pretty but she was crying bitterly. I went to her and asked what was the matter, all she would say was 'They won't let me in'. I can't remember much of the rest, it faded too quickly, what could it mean?"

"Dreams seldom mean anything," replied Harold, "they are just a jumble of things you've seen, done or heard. I usually dream about sheep and pigs or Billy Dodds," Harold laughed.

They had reached the corner, "Now sit on the bar in front of me," he said "tuck your skirts up or they'll catch, hold onto the handlebars, I won't let you fall."

Annie felt anxious, not only was her position precarious but she knew aunt Bella would be dismayed at the lack of decorum. It was however necessary to make haste, Harold still had to ride the bicycle back to Mitchell Street and the light was fast fading. The bicycle offered the only means of travelling home more swiftly. Harold's arms steadied her balance and his hands overlaid hers on the bars as he steered them along. He briefly buried his face in the hair below her hat and kissed the nape of her neck. He began to sing;

"Annie - Annie - give me your answer do,

I'm half crazy all for the love of you,

It won't be a stylish marriage,

For I can't afford a carriage,

But you'll look sweet upon the seat,

Of a bicycle made for two!"

Annie's heart beat faster than she was able to think, Harold's breath glanced her cheek as they travelled. The bicycle jolted and shook over every cobble, something deep within her womanhood was aroused. It was glorious and yet alarming. They reached aunt Bella's. Annie untucked her skirts and slid down from the bar, she gave Harold a brief kiss, all that she dare and turned to the back door.

"Is that all the goodnight kiss I get?" He said teasingly.

Her face was brightly flushed, her breathing short and tense, whether the vibration of the bicycle or the closeness of Harold's body had found her inner desires she knew not, but at that moment she needed the sanctuary of her room urgently.

"Love you Annie, Harold turned to walk away, "you will marry me won't you?" He spoke softly.

"Be careful riding home Harold, yes, yes I will." Annie's voice trembled, the door latch rattled into the clasp and Harold heard the bolt slide across.

"Goodnight my Annie," he whispered.

Bella called out, "Its alright Aunt Bella, I've bolted the door and put out the lamp".

Annie sat on the edge of her bed, she lit the candle on the shelf and took the small framed picture from her pocket. Her body now quieted, her fingers moved over the words and she read again the verse.

"Happy days, dear Harold, let there be a world of happy days." She uttered the words quietly to herself, she placed the picture on the shelf by her box of chalks. Sunday loomed very close, the verse somehow reassured her and the night brought not a troubled dream but a deep and restful sleep.

Annie had remembered to collect Mrs.Wright's laundry bag from May's on the Friday afternoon. She felt she must walk to The Park and return it and thank her for the kindness she had shown to Harold and for her great help in solving May's dilemma. This Sunday morning she would abandon the congregation at the Mission Hall to their fate and to Mr.Shawcross. If she walked briskly she could spend just a few minutes with Davina Wright and be home in time for dinner with aunt Bella before going to fetch Harold.

Ivy answered the door and greeted Annie with a ready smile. "Come in," said Ivy, "if you would wait here for just a moment." Ivy went along the hall to the drawing room and Annie could hear Davina's voice say.

"Oh yes."

Ivy hadn't time to return before Davina caught up with her and stood in front of Annie, her face beaming with delight and her arms outstretched.

"Come my dear, come and tell me all about it." Davina took Annie's arm and propelled her to the drawing room.

Annie explained she had returned the laundry bag and related the events at May's. "Everyone is so grateful to you," she said.

"Oh nonsense my dear, I did nothing but relish the company of your young man for a few precious moments." She clapped her hands in a gesture of appreciation, it amused Annie and she couldn't hold back her laughter.

"I'm so pleased you like Harold," she said, inwardly hoping that aunt Bella would share just a little of Davina's enthusiasm. "I have something for you." Annie took a piece of card from within the folded laundry bag. "May's little girl Mabel has drawn some pictures for you, I'm sure you will like them,

Mabel has done them with much love."

Annie handed the card to Davina who gazed down at the child's work and in an emotional voice said.

"You must tell Mabel that it is quite the nicest picture I have in the house and I shall put it by my chair so that I might see it all times of the day."

Annie leaned forward and kissed Davina lightly on the cheek, it seemed entirely correct and Annie felt no sense of impropriety. No voice rebuked her, 'You remember what you are my girl'. It echoed somewhere afar off but too far for Annie to be mindful. The two women were at ease in one another's company. Annie explained her need to be going.

"Are you sure you will be alright walking all that way back, I could call a carriage," said Davina.

"Yes I'm quite sure," replied Annie.

"Do not fret my dear, your aunt Bella has more heart than you could know, it will embrace your Harold just as mine has, you'll see. Now off you go but promise you will visit again soon."

Annie had reached the corner of Sherwood Road and heard a voice she instantly recognised, it was Charles Eddowes. He and another man appeared to have just come out of The Standard pub, the exchange of words was surely acrimonious. Annie held no intent to overhear but Charles' tone was harsh, his voice raised.

"You'll get it next week, now leave me be." Charles strode angrily away from the man tossing back his hand in a gesture of dismissal. He had not noticed Annie, she hurried on.

As she turned into the yard from the entry she could smell mutton cooking. Aunt Bella stood by the table in the scullery with a bowl of vegetable peelings and apple cores in her hand.

"Tip these on the heap," she said to Annie.

At the end of the yard was a small wooden gate and two steps led down to an area just big enough to accommodate an apple tree, one blackcurrant bush, a clump of golden rod and a compost heap on which the kitchen waste and soot from the fire were tipped.

Annie filled the coal bucket, the confidence she had found since meeting Harold had enabled her to display to the contrary old coal shed door a greater degree of determination and now her stronger tactics usually resulted in a quick submission. She washed her hands and took the cloth and cutlery from the drawer, laid the table and placed the salt dish in the middle. Two plates sat warming in the hearth by the old charred saucepan. Bella handed the thick towelling cloth to Annie, she wrapped it around the handle and lifted the pan to the trivet, Sunday dinner was either mutton or knuckle of pork, through the week they ate meals made from offal. Sundays did bring a treat though, Bella baked apples for pudding. This day Annie had escaped the overbearing Minister but normally the soft flesh of the fruit basted as it was in syrup and raisins would be blesséd 'post Shawcross' comforter. Annie genuinely believed that the sweet goodness it imbued would 'deliver her from evil' ever before the rantings of Mr. Shawcross! Thankfully aunt Bella did not ask about the Mission, Annie would tell her later of her visit to The Park but for now it seemed easier not to mention it.

"Harold is looking forward to meeting you Aunt Bella, I'm sure you will find him interesting to talk to, he knows about such a lot of things."

Bella's directness took Annie by surprise, "You have feelings for this young man?"

It was spoken as a question and Annie felt obliged to answer truthfully.

"Yes I do, I can't explain how I feel, I only know that since meeting Harold I have felt different, more of a person." She awaited some barbed reply from her aunt but Bella was strangely subdued.

"I've made a boiled fruit cake, you can cut that and there's a jar of redcurrant jelly Mrs.Bacon gave us."

Annie was amused by Bella's concern over tea. Any visitor to the house was rare, indeed it hadn't occurred to Annie until this moment how much of an ordeal it probably was for Bella, she saw so few people, but if anyone could bring a little mirth to Bella's soul it would be Harold, Annie felt quite sure of that.

The meal over Annie hurriedly cleared away the dishes. Bella sat quietly in her chair, Annie expected her to take a nap for a while and knew it would be much later in the afternoon before she arrived back with Harold, so Bella could be quiet until then. There was plenty of coal in and water. Annie gathered up her jacket and hat.

"I'll be off now, she said.

Bella's eyes were already closed but Annie sensed she was not asleep, this pretence was Bella's refuge. Annie closed the door gently, soon she would see Harold, the thought inspired her and her steps were fleet.

Annie could hear Maggie's gleeful laughter even before she reached Mitchell Street, the delighted child, Frank and bicycle intent on the usual Sunday activity. Harold saw Annie turn the corner and hurried to meet her.

"Just in time for your turn in the basket," he said teasingly. He took her hand, his fingers seemed to brush away all anxieties before closing tightly around hers, there to hold secure a blissful contentment.

"Mam is making blackberry and apple pie," he said. "Gertie and Jean picked the berries yesterday down 'The Meadows'."

Sarah greeted Annie warmly, the smell of cooking and baking filled the house. Samuel got up from his chair where he had rewarded himself with forty winks. His morning at the allotment had yielded a handsome harvest of produce and Sarah now transformed it into a wealth of store for her larder with the most cheerful zeal.

"Look at my old clucky hen," said Samuel fondly of his wife and planted a kiss on her lips, then he turned to Annie and mimed the words he knew surely, that Sarah would speak.

"Children and chicken should always be pickin'," said Sarah. Annie giggled, husband and wife were as one, completely in tune with each other.

Nora was pressing clothes, the heavy flat iron sat on top the range whilst she took another shirt from the basket and spread it across the old blanket on the table.

Eli, exhausted from his pursuit of the bicycle, very slowly wobbled across the scullery floor and flopped down by the dolly tub. His tongue lapped the air, water dripped from his mouth, the old enamel dish from which he drank now empty. He panted his way to recovery and within minutes lay fast asleep.

"Silly fool," said Sarah, "'e never learns, one day 'e'll go to sleep an' not wake up."

Mavis had just come in and overheard, the child could not bear the thought and rushed over to Eli, threw her arms around him and poured out words of deepest devotion. Allowing himself only slight disturbance, he licked Mavis's cheek and returned to his slumbers.

Frank lifted Maggie down from his shoulders and she scampered inside, followed by Gertie and Jean. A plate of jam tarts disappeared without trace. Sarah sighed and proceeded to roll out more of the dough. It was a pattern of events as familiar to Sarah as breathing. Every day she satisfied their eager appetites until each belly was filled and at rest, then the whole process would begin again with the morning light. Captains of industry would have envied her achievements, a growth rate sound and steady, proven over many years, her return beyond price. Now this amazing 'executive' wiped her fingers on her pinafore and closed the oven door on another batch of success.

Annie was quite determined, "I shall help you clear away Mrs. Boucher," she said. Sarah could see that it was pointless to protest and the two women chatted happily as the work was done.

"I 'ear that Harold is to meet your aunt Bella today," said Sarah, she chuckled, "she'll 'ave to put up wi' his tongue 'cause it 'ardly stops, you make 'im behave 'isself Annie dear or your aunt Bella will think I've not reared 'im right."

Samuel, Harold and Frank were in the back yard chopping and stacking wood. An old elm tree in the hedge at the allotment had succumbed to the strangling grip of ivy and now offered up a quantity of valuable burning for the range. The men's task completed, Harold went to the scullery to wash.

"Suppose I better do me neck and behind me ears in case your aunt Bella gives me an inspection," he said teasing Annie. Sarah winked at Annie and called out.

"You'll 'ave to pass my inspection first, I'll not 'ave any son of mine visiting folk wi' a tide mark round his neck."

Harold stripped to the waist and bowed over the bowl of water. Annie watched the muscles across his shoulders flex with every movement, his back lean but strong, seemed to lure her thoughts 'til she imagined her fingers smoothing away any weariness from his body and then wrapping it around in softness as only a wife may. Sarah observed Annie's gaze. Many years had passed, many babies birthed but she recognised 'that look'. Her own beloved Samuel stirred her longings still, she patted Annie's hand and whispered softly.

"It shall be Annie, it shall be."

The arboretum had taken on a look of faded summer, a few petunia and nemesia flowers stubbornly refused to make way for the autumn ferns but even their blooms had become smaller under the light of the shortening days, their stems less determined to grow taller than their neighbour as the cooler winds explored the flower beds searching for any tired leaves or petals they might unloose and carry with them to the pathways, there to deposit in deep accumulations for the children to shuffle through.

"What's in the package Harold?" Asked Annie.

He had picked it up from the shelf just before leaving home and held it tightly as they walked.

"Ah bein' nosey now," he replied taunting her. "It's not for you so you'll just 'ave to wait and see."

Annie could tell he was quite resolute, it appeared an odd shape and it made her curious but wait she must.

"One day we shall ' ave a garden," he said, "I shall fill it wi' flowers for you Annie, even when it is the darkest, coldest of winters I shall make sure there will always be a flower."

He picked a petunia and tucked it under the edge of her collar.

"We shall be told off," she said worriedly.

"Will you visit me in prison then Annie Bundy?" He laughed and kissed her cheek.

They had walked happily from the arboretum and now turned from the entry into the yard. Annie's heart raced, the moment had come, inside waiting for them was aunt Bella. Harold sensed her anxiety, he whispered.

"Soon you'll find out what's in the package."

It was enough to propel her over the threshold and to announce in a faltering voice, "We're here Aunt Bella."

Annie's eyes were drawn to the corner of the room where Bella sat in her chair. The fire crackled animatedly, evidence of sticks and fresh coals lay between the flames. The kettle sat on the trivet in the hearth, Bella's hands, free of the gloves that would normally encase them rested in her lap, the bootees she wore to keep the chill from her feet by the idle fire that prevailed all other days had been replaced by neat black shoes that peeped out shyly from beneath a long grey skirt which Annie had not seen for so long she had forgotten of its existence. A bodice of black satin with smocked sleeves underlaid a deep collar of white cotton Broderie Anglaise that came down to a v at the front. At the neck, a small silver brooch caught the light of the fire and glinted across the room to where Annie and Harold stood. Bella's face freed of shadow normally created by her bonnet now dared to show a faint smile.

Harold stood before her and with the charm of a seasoned diplomat lifted her hand from its resting place, shook it firmly and declared.

"I'm so glad to meet you Miss Pownall, Annie has told me you are a wonderful teacher. Dad wishes he could ave had more learnin', he says a good teacher makes for a good student an' if he'd had better teachin' then he might ave' run the pit that produced the coal that made the soot that clogged the chimney instead of bein' the man that had to sweep it!"

A big grin straddled his face and unable to resist it, the faint smile that at any second could have retreated behind one of aunt Bella's frowns now ventured across her cheeks and Annie heard her say.

"Then tell your father he cannot be blamed for the smoke and fog which choke our lungs, we must lay the fault at the feet of our teachers."

Annie believed that from this moment everything would be alright, aunt Bella's nervousness had melted away under the warmth of Harold's charm. She had responded to his open nature, there would no doubt be a rigorous examination of his character and prospects over the coming weeks but Annie felt able to set about preparing tea, content to leave Bella and Harold to themselves whilst she laid the table and cut the bread. Their conversation flowed freely, Harold had a thirst for knowledge, in his talks with Annie he had surprised her with his inquiry and reasoning.

"Surely it wouldn't be fair to blame teachers for the poor air, without coal we would struggle to keep warm, to cook, to power industry." Annie overhead passages of their debate.

"That is true," replied Bella, "so whom should we fault and whom should we credit?"

Annie poured the tea, "Come on now I've cut the cake," she said.

Harold's package still sat at the edge of the table, if aunt Bella held any curiosity, she didn't show it.

"It's a grand cake," declared Harold.

"Have another piece," prompted Bella.

"If Annie promises not to tell mam then I won't say no, but it mam knew I'd taken a second piece at someone else's table, she'd likely clip me round the ear for not mindin' me manners!"

Annie busied herself clearing away, Harold carried the dishes to the scullery and the two young people worked happily together. Bella lifted some coals onto the fire, the room was pleasantly warm, feeling no chill from the air her skin had found an attractive blush.

"I 'ave something' for you Miss Pownall," said Harold. He handed her the package, Bella seemed hesitant. "I made one for mam a while back."

Bella carefully untied the twine and unfolded the paper. Annie had waited since leaving Mitchell Street to discover the contents of the package.

"I like to carve pieces of wood," said Harold, "the soft colours of the grain and the smoothness of the finish, almost like Maggie's skin, it's calmin', clears me 'ead of all troubles."

Bella held up a figure of a horse, expertly crafted, the detail fine.

"I try to remember Wrenshaw's horses and copy them," he said.

She stood it on the mantelpiece and ran her fingers slowly along its back.   "It is beautiful work, quite beautiful, thank you Harold."

"Well I reckon it's time I was on me way, work starts early at the yard tomorrow. Thank you for that grand tea Miss. Pownall."

"Shall I walk part of the way with you?" Asked Annie.

Aunt Bella gave her a hard look.

"No," replied Harold, "you've already walked a long way today, you rest now."

Annie went with him to the entry, her arms slipped around his neck and she kissed him with a love which knew no limit.

"My Annie," he whispered.

"Yes, I shall always be your Annie," she uttered the words as an oath.

Bella stared at the fire. "You look different Aunt Bella, your collar is really lovely, you should wear it more often." Annie had realised as soon as she stepped into the room with Harold earlier in the evening that aunt Bella had not, as she supposed, spent time in sleep but in preparing herself as best she could for Harold's first visit. Bella continued to gaze at the dying flames.

"It is too late now," she said.

"What is too late, what do you mean Aunt Bella?" Annie said.

"Fill the bucket before you lose the light," came back the reply.

Annie picked up the old pail, the subject was obviously now to be closed. As she did battle with the coal shed door, a mouse scuttled across the cobbles towards the garden gate, frantic to be undercover, out of view. Aunt Bella would doubtless run for cover now too, back to her corner, hidden behind layers of camouflage, blending with the dark walls and curtains.

Harold must come again soon she thought, he had found Bella's refuge and she had allowed him to share with her for a while. For this, Annie would be ever grateful. She placed the filled bucket in the hearth.

"I'm tired now, I shall go to bed," said Bella.

Annie knew she must tell of her visit to The Park, confess she had not been to the Mission.

"I walked to The Park this morning, I didn't go to the Mission. I thought it would be very rude not to thank Mrs.Wright for letting May have her old curtains, so I went to see her instead. I took her a picture Mabel had drawn."

Bella's stare had left the fire and now turned to Annie.

'What is your name my dear?' 'Annie Bundy ma'am .....' Annie remembered that look in Davina's eyes which had alarmed her on their first meeting. She saw that very same look now in aunt Bella's eyes.

"Do you know Davina Wright?" Annie asked.

Bella's voice was stern. "How do you suppose I would know any lady in The Park."

She rose from the chair, Annie clung desperately to the happiness the last few hours had given them.

"It was kind of Harold to bring the horse wasn't it?"

Bella again smoothed her fingers along the back of the small wooden figure.

"Yes, that was kind." She made her way up the stairs calling back to Annie, "Bolt the door and see to the lamp."

Annie lay in bed, she had seen recognition in both Davina and Bella but neither offered any explanation. Why did they react in that way? Whatever the explanation might be she would drive all thought of it from her mind this night.

Today had been a good day and in the morning, when she and Edna exchanged accounts of their Sunday activities, she would have only happy events to report, anything else would keep.

Annie heard the sound of the heavy drawers in aunt Bella's dressing table being pushed back in place, the rare glimpse of finery gone, its brightness now concealed. Harold would make everything right, with this as comforter she found sleep.

CHAPTER FIVE

Isobel's words suddenly became stifled and she gave an almighty sneeze, just at the moment their carriage had found an uneven patch of road. Davina caught hold of her arm to steady her on the seat.

"Cousin Henry should have paid far more attention to the seating arrangements, he knows I have a delicate constitution but young Thomas ushered me into the draughtiest seat in the Church, the cold air on my neck was enough to prove fatal. I fear I've started ....," another sneeze managed somehow to expel itself between Isobel's wearing commentary. Davina retrieved Isobel's purse from the floor and restored it to her lap.

"There, you see, now I have a chill. It wouldn't have been so bad if we'd been given some warming sherry when we arrived at Hermione's but the maid took so long to collect our top clothes before she could carry around even a hint of sustenance, I declare I had already suffered irreversible effect. Henry should have taken on more staff, it is too bad."

Davina tried earnestly to lighten the situation, "I thought Daphne looked very nice didn't you Isobel?"

"Well given the size of the poor girl's nose and all the excess weight she bears about her hips then I suppose Hermione made a valiant effort."

Davina sighed, determined to have one last attempt she said, "I did enjoy the meal, it was all very generous, Hermione had gone to a lot of trouble making sure there was something to please everyone."

"The syllabub was cloying," said Isobel, "I wished afterwards I'd chosen the custard tart but doubted the eggs would be as fresh as they should be and my word! Who made the cake? I am quite convinced that not a single drop of brandy had found that confection, more than likely gone down their cook's neck. I never did approve of her appointment, far too quiet and still waters run deep my dear."

"Whatever you say Isobel, we are home now."

The carriage drew up outside Davina's front gates. In spite of her cousin's contrariness, Davina had enjoyed the family wedding, she had been complimented several times on her elegance. Now as she divested herself of her new gown she thought of Annie, how those hard worked fingers had accomplished such fine stitching. Davina had despatched Ivy to Isobel's room and could hear the forceful voice delivering a host of instructions to the unfortunate young woman.

Isobel's visits had numbered two a year since Owen's death. He had treated his wife like a Queen Bee, pampering her every whim, ensuring that she was continually waited upon. Their only child, Lawrence, a very bright young man, had fled the 'hive' at the earliest possible opportunity and now lived with his wife and two children in Durham, where he taught mathematics at a Public School. Owen, it could be said, had allowed his Queen to work him to death, one day he literally collapsed at the mouth of the hive. Exhaustion had overwhelmed him, but not, one could only trust, before his satisfaction was complete, his store of honey robustly adequate, he had ensured the Queen's future well-being and expired, hopefully knowing this worker's task was done. As a result Isobel was a considerably wealthy woman. Owen had prospered through his work at the collieries in Derby, rising quickly to management and then ownership. It had been he who directed Nathan along a similar course and he who had helped and advised Davina on the sale of Birchdale following Nathan's death.

Isobel had taken it upon herself to visit Davina as frequently as she could over the years, always reminding Davina that she, sadly had no offspring, unlike herself who had produced the eighth wonder of the world! Poor Lawrence, his mother's endless declaration to all and sundry of her son's genius had embarrassed him greatly. Davina liked the boy very much and had been saddened at never seeing him through latter years but could fully understand his retreat.

She placed the gown on a hanger and smoothed it gently with her hand. In those early days with Nathan she had felt so proud to be on his arm. He was very good looking and drew much attention from any female company he had about him. Yet she could truthfully say that she had never felt jealous. It had always been some kind of silly game, an entertainment to Nathan. As some men played cards and wagered bets, so Nathan used the attentions of young women to distract him from the daily routine, but it was Dee, his Dee as he affectionately called her, to whom he came home and genuinely loved.

Davina could hear Isobel leaving her room, she quickly closed the door of the wardrobe and made sure her buttonhole had sufficient water in the small cut glass vase on her table. She popped a little piece of candy into her mouth, the ensuing hours would require much fortitude and an intake of sugar might strengthen and comfort at the same time. Davina took a deep breath and went forth to face her challenge.

The two sat in the drawing room, Davina could tell that Isobel had noticed the new drapes, but to induce any complimentary remark from her cousin with regard to anything other than herself took a degree of craft at the best of times.

"I think they meet this season's fashionable shade admirably, don't you Isobel?" Asked Davina.

"What's that dear?" Came back the reply.

"My new drapes, have you felt the weight of the material?" Davina persisted.

She knew full well that long before this moment Isobel would have scrutinized not only the weight, colour and design but every stitch and fold.

"Yes, very nice dear."

The subject was dismissed immediately with a hasty, "I shall require another blanket on my bed tonight, I have definitely taken a chill. Have Ivy bring me up a 'hot toddy' when I am ready for sleep. Cloves and whisky have excellent medicinal properties. Has Daphne's husband any real prospects or will he always be on wages? Redmond's is doing so well, it can't be long before Lawrence is made headmaster, he has truly established that school you know. So many of the very best people enrol their sons, he has made it so popular that I'm sure there must be a waiting list. I know for a fact that Emmeline Campbell-Carterton has placed her boy there and they are real aristocracy Davina. The only meat they eat is from their own estate and I'm told they have a wine cellar bigger than Burton's entire store. If Owen had just kept going a bit longer we would surely have been invited to take dinner with them, but a lady on her own, even if it is the future headmaster's mother, only complicates the seating arrangements. My dear, life has been a series of sacrifices since Owen gave in, I'm afraid his constitution failed him. He was never one to eat 'greens', I told him tirelessly that he should, that for my sake he should but no, he knew better and now I get asked nowhere. If dear Lawrence had not been so committed to Redmond's he would have visited us more often and admonished his father, but with no one to remind Owen of his duty to me, I am left on the wings of the world, a forgotten widow. That is why I resolve not to allow you to become so abandoned Davina, at least you will always have me to lift your spirits and keep you from melancholy."

A knock came at the door, "Come in Ivy," called Davina, Ivy's arrival was welcome indeed. The girl stood with a tray of tea, "Isobel, you will need to make a little space for Ivy."

Books, spectacles, smelling salts and purse all littered the small table. Isobel tutted and grudgingly removed the items to enable Ivy to place the tray. Davina recalled Harold's visit, his thoughtfulness and good manners.

"Thank you Ivy," said Davina. "Would you put another blanket on Mrs. Hardwick's bed and tonight we shall take a 'hot toddy' just before we retire."

Isobel looked sharply at Davina but before she had chance to speak Davina said, "We shall drink it here, Ivy needs also to rest, her days are long enough."

"Well you mark my words I shall be quite unwell through this chill, I feel my chest tightening already." Isobel produced a loud cough to endorse her claim.

The evening continued with Isobel's monologue. When Davina finally obtained release, the peace of her own bedroom seemed to her like the offer of ether to remove a blight!

Poor dear Owen, his loyalty and devotion scarcely acknowledged by Isobel and yet she had been bestowed these blessings without any failing all the years they were together. Nathan had taken instruction from Owen on many issues but sadly, his character had not followed Owen's guide. Nathan's dalliances had caused Davina many hours of anxiety though his kindness to her, his warmth and moments of wonderful love had never ceased. She could forget all doubts, overlook all shortcomings when his lips joined hers, when his softly spoken words played joyfully with her emotions.

Jack and Constance Braithwaite were highly respected. Braithwaite's Bank had been considered a cornerstone of Nottingham's industrial base and Nathan, as one of the directors had secured a favoured position.

Jack was a conscientious, upstanding figure, he and his wife took delight in their daughter Hilda, sadly Constance had miscarried twice since Hilda's birth, now husband and wife showered all their attentions on this young woman.

Hilda held a great fondness for her father and pleaded with him to allow her to come to him at his work from time to time to help in his office. In fact she was quite able and learned much of the bank's management and day to day operations.

A sweet natured young woman, she was affectionate and innocently charming. Jack had been working long hours, the commercial life of the city had prospered and expanded, business at the bank had been brisk, his integrity kept him at his desk on some days until evening.

"Don't be too late tonight dear, said Constance. He had developed a troublesome cough and his pallor was grey and tired.

"I shall go with you Father," said Hilda.

"No my dear, not today, the weather has clamped down very cold, you must stay here with your mother, I won't be late home."

That night Jack's breathing became laboured, Constance propped him up with extra pillows but his condition caused her alarm, his cough and shortness of breath persisted through the early hours. The doctor was sent for and his diagnosis quickly arrived at.

"I am afraid your husband has Pleurisy Mrs.Braithwaite, he will need careful nursing and bed rest for several weeks."

Jack spoke slowly, bidding Constance and Hilda to listen intently. "You must speak to Nathan Wright, ask him to act for me at the bank, he has the knowledge and ability."

"I can help him Father," said Hilda, genuinely wanting to reassure him that everything would be alright, "I know quite a lot about the office."

"No my dear," replied Jack in a weary voice, "that isn't possible."

Hilda tried again to persuade him but her mother, concerned by Jack's weakness, told her to leave the matter and let her father sleep.

Nathan raised no objection to 'holding the fort' for Jack. He was, as Jack had considered him, perfectly capable and honest in business.

A week of her father's illness had passed, he was tended devotedly by Constance, his health was not good but had improved slightly. Hilda felt a pressing need to do something for her beloved father, she had been to visit a friend but purposefully left early to allow herself time to call at the bank.

Nathan sat deep in paperwork, he rose immediately to his feet and greeted Hilda with genuine delight.

"How is your father today?" He asked.

"A little better I believe thank you," replied Hilda.

Nathan, without ever really intending, could find that vulnerable loose thread in a woman's thoughts and momentarily suspend it. Hilda's naivety and innate sweetness set her aside from the women who normally received Nathan's flirtations.

She said nothing to her mother of her visit to the bank, she had helped Nathan reconcile some figures and prepare some statements of account. The episode had been pleasant and she felt her time had been spent usefully, but given her father's view on the subject she decided to keep it to herself, until he was better at least.

Hilda continued to call at the bank, once, twice a week, she arrived one afternoon.

"Ah just the right time," said Nathan, "I am going over to Birchdale to attend to a matter there, the weather has lightened, the sun has real warmth today, come along it will be a change."

Hilda hesitated, Nathan had found that loose thread.

Jack had been back at his desk for two months. He had noticed Hilda's desire to help in the office had become much less of late, he assumed she was now catching up on all the time she had been denied her mother whilst he had demanded so much of Constance. When he arrived home that evening, he found his wife in a tearful state of woe and Hilda, laying on her bed, clutching a doll from childhood. She had told her mother she was pregnant. The situation was wretched and would leaden the lives of more than they could know.

Davina's memories had eventually donned the mantle of sleep and it was a tap, tap, tap on her door which woke her.

"Come in."

She was surprised to see Ivy, it was still early.

"Please ma'am, Mrs.Hardwick has called me, she says it is quite autumnal and she wants me to light the grate in her room, she is too unwell to dress today so would like me to bring her some hot porridge, a lightly boiled egg with some thin bread and butter, some honey and a jug of boiled milk with a large measure of brandy in it."

"Would she indeed," said Davina. "I will come down right away Ivy, prepare the breakfast tray and we will light the fire presently."

Davina sighed, this will be a long day she told herself.

Isobel had consumed ample breakfast and the fire was now crackling in the grate.

"I thought you might read to me Davina, it would be soothing as I am so poorly but before you fetch my book, I think I should take another measure of brandy to warm me through as it will be some time before that small grate makes any impression on my feet."

Davina began to read aloud from Isobel's book, which was titled, 'Mrs.Deakin's Day Out', she had uttered only five words when Isobel interrupted.

"How long has Ivy been with you dear? She is a little slow don't you think? It wouldn't hurt for you to gee her up a bit now and again. I found my maid, Mary, taking time to look at herself in the mirror in the hall, I told her it would be altogether more sensible to polish the brass coal scuttle and view herself in that. The distorted image that gave would be very much more desirable than the real thing! She has dreadful skin you know, too greasy, it's impossible to tell the blackheads from the pimples, a good scrub with a pumice stone and coal tar wouldn't come amiss, I told her so. She has two evenings off each month, doubtless pursues every chance to find a man, not a hope I'm afraid. I've seen her reaching up to the top shelves with the feather duster, her ankles are far too thick, Ned Fowler's horse has a daintier gait!"

At last Isobel drew breath and seizing the opportunity Davina tried again, she managed just two words before, "Poke that fire a bit dear, get some flame going, it's cold as charity in here."

Davina put Mrs.Deakin down on the chair and tended the fire, in fact the room felt warm but Isobel was proving true to form and any effort made on her behalf would have fallen short of her expectations.

Davina heard the doorbell. "You must excuse me Isobel, but I need to go downstairs for a moment."

Ivy was already on her way to call Davina.

"I'm coming Ivy dear."

Davina felt liberated, she had no idea who was at the door but

Sweeney Todd would be preferable to cousin Isobel.

"Good morning Mrs.Wright," said the young man. "I have brought you papers from the bank, they contain details of your quarterly dividends. I wonder could you agree them and write your signature at the bottom of each sheet?"

Davina took the envelope from him, "Yes, of course, would you come through to the drawing room, my writing desk is there."

Davina rarely saw Charles Eddowes other than when he came with bank documents. "Your father was here a little while ago, he fitted the new drapes for me, is he well?"

She looked at the young Charles intently, he shuffled awkwardly, there was something about the house that made him uneasy, Mrs.Wright had never been anything other than pleasant and polite but he felt out of place and could find no explanation.

"Yes, thank you, father is quite well, I shall tell him that you asked," said Charles.

The business attended to, he left. Davina watched him from the window as he walked down the path.

"Are you alright ma'am?" Asked Ivy.

Davina was deep in thought and didn't hear. Ivy tried again, "Would you like me to make you some tea?"

This time Davina turned to look at Ivy and said, "Thank you, that would be very nice. Ivy do you know that you have a lovely complexion and very dainty ankles."

Feeling somewhat bewildered Ivy withdrew to the kitchen where her familiar duties reassured her. Mrs.Hardwick's demands and Davina's vagueness were not the normal routine, boiling the kettle and laying a tray were, with the latter she felt safe.

Davina returned to the bedroom to find Isobel disgruntled.

"A body could die here entirely alone, you have been gone hours," she said harshly, "who was that?"

"Just a little business of the bank, it is all seen to, I shall read your book to you now," said Davina.

She opened the page and began a sentence but Isobel's interest seemed to have deserted Mrs.Deakin and transferred to Davina's finances.

"I hope you are investing wisely my dear, you really should spend some time studying these things. Nathan's life was sadly so short, you owe it to him Davina to make the very most of what he left you."

Davina had crossed to the grate and now prodded at the fire with such force that the poker struck the fire dog and clattered loudly.

"Gracious me Davina, you make no allowance for my poor head, I have suffered a dreadful headache since I ate that porridge. Ivy makes it too stiff, in my frail condition the effort required to swallow it quite upset my equilibrium. I think I shall comfort myself by writing a letter to Lawrence, I'm sure my regular correspondence has encouraged and inspired him over the years and at this important time it is even more crucial. I suppose I should be putting my thoughts to what I shall say at the assembly. There will be a special assembly you know when he is made headmaster. They are sure to ask me to speak don't you think my dear? Oh yes, I must make the effort, perhaps you would let me have some items from your bureau. Send Ivy up with them, and something to lubricate my throat too, it is so dry, have you any butterscotch Davina? I always keep butterscotch at home. Yes, send Ivy up with some writing materials and butterscotch."

Davina made her way downstairs once more, at least Isobel had settled on some occupation which should allow the household a little peace and quiet. Providing the required stationery and sweets was a small price to pay for such bliss!

"Would you take these to Mrs.Hardwick Ivy and place just a little more coal on the fire in her room whilst you are there."

Ivy knocked at the bedroom door, "Enter," Isobel summoned.

She surveyed the tray, "Yes, very good," she said, "but I shall need two more pillows, I cannot achieve the correct position for writing without two more pillows."

Ivy went to the linen cupboard and returned to Isobel.

"That's right my dear, place them at my back, now hand me my wrap or I shall feel the cold across my shoulders."

"Will that be all ma'am?" Asked Ivy.

Isobel was busily unwrapping a butterscotch, "What is for lunch, I shall need something hot and substantial, one must feed a chill but starve a fever. I am definitely afflicted by the former. I think some more coal on the grate Ivy, my wonderful Owen, I think of him every time Mary poke's the fire. I will call you when my letter is ready for the post."

The day continued to be a stream of requests and demands with just the briefest interval of nervous anticipation. Davina was concerned for Ivy who had been up and down the stairs more times than she could remember. When at 5 o'clock Ivy returned from Isobel's room with a written menu for the evening meal, Davina felt enough was enough.

Isobel was sitting up in bed flushed from the effects of too much heat and more brandy than could be deemed medicinal! Davina sat on the side of the bed and put her palm to Isobel's brow.

"Oh my dear, I do believe you have a slight temperature, yes you definitely feel hot. I cannot sit by and do nothing to relieve your distress when I know just the thing to make you feel so much more comfortable. You shall not eat anything this evening, we must not allow the fever to take hold. I shall be back in a few minutes dear."

Davina ignored Isobel's protestations and went downstairs to the kitchen. "Ivy would you prepare a small silver tray for me. I need you to find one of those pretty crocheted mats to place on it, also a fine glass tumbler and a teaspoon. Fill the tumbler with water to just above the half then bring the tray to me, I shall be in my bedroom."

Davina took the tray from Ivy, "Thank you dear, I shall be down very soon, Mrs.Hardwick won't be taking a meal this evening and I shall have something simple, a bowl of soup and some bread will be all I need."

Davina placed the tray on her dressing table. From the side drawer, she took a small jar of Epsom Salts.   Very carefully she put two level teaspoons of salts into the water and stirred briskly, it effervesced for several minutes before finally becoming clear and still again. She wiped the teaspoon dry and placed it back on the tray along with the jar of salts.

"Isobel dear, I find that when my temperature is raised, even slightly, a small dose of purifying salts lowers it immediately and cools the system, restoring the desired balance. It never fails me. However we are all different in our make up so I have brought the water and salts to you as you will judge best how much will benefit yourself, I usually take just one level teaspoon."

Davina held the tray for Isobel who had resigned herself to her cousin's ministrations, she still had one or two butterscotch under her pillow and if she were to be denied a scrap of supper then so be it. Isobel took the spoon, dipped it into the jar and lifted it, just comfortably filled with salts, into the tumbler, it fizzed its way up the glass.

"Drink it down quickly Isobel whilst it has a head, it's most pleasant taken that way."

The glass emptied, Davina gathered up the tray, making no comment at Isobel's expression of distaste.

"Now dear, take a little rest, you should relax, let yourself be totally calm, I shall look in on you later."

Davina put the small glass jar of salts in the drawer and returned the tray to Ivy in the kitchen.

"Shall I bring your soup now?" Asked Ivy.

"Yes dear, I shall take my meal whilst Mrs. Hardwick is resting."

Ivy brought the soup and bread and was about to close the door as she left the room when Davina said.

"Leave the door ajar please Ivy, if you hear activity upstairs in Mrs. Hardwick's room don't disturb yourself, I shall go to her."

"If you are sure ma'am" said Ivy.

It was not very long before Davina heard urgent movement on the landing, indeed with just a few minutes of interval between, there were several movements along the landing. Eventually a longer period of calm prevailed. Davina waited until Ivy had cleared away her supper dishes and then made her way up to Isobel's room.

"How are you dear? You look much less hot and flushed, in fact your cheeks are now quite pale. I am convinced that your temperature is back to normal."

Isobel spoke very slowly, subdued could quite well describe her.

"I fear Davina that the change of water has affected me. I am sorry to disappoint you, I know how much you look forward to my visits but I am afraid I must return to Derby tomorrow, on the noon train, I think it for the best."

"Oh so soon dear, what a shame," replied Davina. "Perhaps you might feel differently in the morning after a hearty breakfast."

Isobel, trying desperately not to move a single muscle, declared herself to be in total denial with regard to food.

"I shall travel on an empty stomach with just a little boiled water in my flask," she said feebly.

"Well, I'll see you in the morning dear, I shall be off to bed myself very shortly unless you would like me to read Mrs.Deakin's Day Out."

"I think I am just too tired to listen now Davina," said Isobel.

The night had brought a sleep of weariness to all three women. Isobel had asked Davina to arrange a carriage to take her to the station.

"Are you quite sure of your need to travel today Isobel?" Asked Davina.

"Yes dear, I shall go home and make preparation for Lawrence's elevated position, one must put duty first."

Ivy knocked on the drawing room door. "The carriage is here ma'am, I have brought Mrs.Hardwick's travelling bag downstairs in readiness."

"Thank you Ivy," said Davina. "I won't come to the station if you don't mind Isobel," she said as they walked to the front door. "I feel not quite myself, probably all the excitement of the wedding now catching up with me."

Isobel safely ensconced in the carriage Davina blew her a kiss and called out, "Do give my love to Lawrence."

The carriage drew away, Davina turned to go back into the house. Ivy stood at the foot of the stairs holding her basket of cleaning utensils.

"Shall I strip the bedding and clean the grate now?"

"Ivy, I am a wicked woman," said Davina.

"Oh no ma'am, you could never be that," replied Ivy with sincere loyalty.

"Well, perhaps not truly wicked, nonetheless, I shall need tonight to pray for a degree of forgiveness, I do hope the good Lord will take account of the extenuating circumstances".

Davina sat back in her chair in quiet contemplation. A feeling of guilt had not fully escaped her. I did it for Ivy she told herself but this notion only achieved to weight the guilt.

Just then Ivy appeared, "It is too late to catch Mrs.Hardwick now but she has forgotten her book, it had slipped to the floor and lay hidden by the edge of the counterpane."

Davina could hear Ivy busily cleaning the grate upstairs, the house had found once again its usual routine. Back to her solitude, Davina sighed, her eyes caught sight of the book laying on the table beside her, she picked it up and opened it at the first chapter. Today she would not be alone after all, she would embark on a journey and travel with Mrs.Deakin on her day out.

CHAPTER SIX

Charles' visits to the workshop had become more frequent of late, Annie could hear Saul's voice as he spoke with Charles in the office, their exchange was not harmonious and Annie wished she could dismiss herself but the fine embroidery on the christening gown, which presented this evening's task, could not be delayed. She hummed one of the tunes which Harold regularly sang as they walked together in an attempt at veiling the men's conversation, she felt awkward at being present on these occasions.

At last Charles left his father and crossed the floor of the workshop. His mood was sullen, he ignored Annie as if she wasn't there. The heavy door slammed shut behind him with such force that it dislodged Saul's walking cane which had rested against the wall in the corner below his jacket. Annie put down her sewing and went to pick it up, as she turned to walk back to her table she could see Saul, his elbows on the desk, his hands cradling his head, she felt compelled to speak.

Annie went to the doorway of the back room and in a gentle voice said. "Charles seems troubled, is there anything I can do?"

Saul raised his face to look at her, he said nothing for a moment then, "Money, always money, that is all I am to him, all I have ever been."

Annie recalled that Sunday when she had seen Charles outside The Standard.

" 'Enid has many wants father', that's what he tells me Annie, now Enid is soon to have a baby and the wants have become even more, I pity that child, it will need to be made of stone."

Annie now stood by his desk, alarmed by the severity of Saul's remarks. "When is the baby due?" She asked, "I'm sure that when they hold their baby, all will be well, to look down on your own child asleep in your arms must fill the heart with only good, Enid will be content then, I'm sure she will."

Saul fired his words at Annie with intense resentment. "So that's what you think is it Annie? Just hold your own baby and all troubles disappear, just cradle it in your arms and everything will be sweetness and light. Is that what happens Annie, is it?"

Annie stepped back, his tone was bitter, his words harsh and delivered with real anger, she had never before seen Saul behave in this way.

"I have almost finished the robe, I'm sorry, it wasn't my place to speak, please don't be angry, aunt Bella couldn't manage without my wages. I won't ever say anything again, really I won't."

She turned and went back to her work.

Saul could see that she was trembling, her fingers could scarce hold the needle steady. He had done her a dreadful wrong, twenty one years of wrong doing, of all the people in the world Annie had shown him most loyalty, most decency. He could have wept at his own miserable weakness.

"Forgive me Annie," he said, "I am thoroughly ashamed, I vent my anger and frustration on you yet you did nothing to warrant it, you spoke only from concern, I apologise Annie."

She looked at his eyes, they were heavy with regret, his shoulders hung with despair.

"We have quite a number of remnants in the stockroom, I know there is some brushed cotton, perhaps Edna and myself could sew one or two items for the new baby, in our own time of course," said Annie.

This caused Saul to smile, only Annie could have thought of such a positive approach to it all.

"I think that would be a good and sensible thing to do," he said. As he returned to his office he called back to her, "Bella is blessed to have you Annie."

He made the words sound cheerful and bright but inwardly his soul ached. He felt actual physical pain, as he sank down on his chair his body seemed almost to fail him. His fingers gripped the wooden arms until his knuckles turned white, the skin so taut across the bone it became near invisible under the pressure. The moment passed. Saul wearily picked up the pen to finish his bookwork and gave an involuntary shudder as he underlined the words 'Final Account'.

The evenings had drawn in and Annie now left the workshop in darkness. Aunt Bella insisted she walk straight home, at least it was only a short distance. They had not always lived in Winchester Street. Just before Annie began her work at Saul's, Bella decided to move from Lenton on the opposite side of The Park, to Sherwood. Annie had taken her lessons at home with aunt Bella and had no close friends at Lenton so the move had been almost an excitement, somewhere new and different. Annie had come to know only the Hemsleys who called to see aunt Bella quite frequently but they had to move to Sheffield. Mrs.Hemsley's mother lived there and she had deteriorated in health. Alice Hemsley had been spending longer spells away from Walter and the children in order to look after her mother, being such a devoted couple, Alice and Walter could not bear these periods of separation. The only solution had been to relocate to Sheffield. Walter, an accountant, was very good at his work and set up an office there, he gradually built up a satisfactory list of new clients. They wrote to Bella from time to time. Annie as she grew old enough to understand, felt grateful to them for their continued friendship with aunt Bella, it seemed the only communication her aunt pursued.

Bella had a pan of broth resting on the trivet in the hearth. "I've had mine," she said, "you are later tonight, he shouldn't keep you 'til now, it's not right."

Annie could tell that Bella was annoyed, the recent weeks had been mellowed by Harold's visits, he would call occasionally for just a little while on an evening when Annie didn't work. The previous Sunday he had brought his favourite book to show aunt Bella it was, 'The Encyclopaedia of the Natural World'.

Harold would gaze at the illustrations and read passages, asking Bella to explain the meaning of the words he didn't understand. Annie had felt quite anxious at the outset but Harold's desire to learn and Bella's aptitude for teaching, produced a remarkable union of minds which Annie had found delightful to witness.

She must steer aunt Bella away from ill temper Annie told herself.

"Saul has been telling me about the baby, I couldn't be rude and appear disinterested when he chose to let me know that Enid and Charles are expecting a baby, I suppose he wanted to share the good news."

Annie had no intention of divulging any of the unhappy circumstances of which Saul had spoken, she doubted he had ever meant to utter these confidences to her at all. Bella seemed strangely quiet. Annie was glad of the broth, the air was fast becoming chill and the hot goodness soothed away any shiveriness. She wiped the inside of the bowl with the last piece of bread and said, "That was really tasty Aunt Bella,"

"This time of year always improves broth," replied Bella, "Nobby had parsnips and flat poll cabbage on the barrow today."

Mr.Green who came around selling vegetables had always been known as 'Nobby', Annie presumed it was because among the variety of produce, he carried brussels sprouts and everyone referred to them as 'nobby greens'. "Winter vegetables stick to the ribs much longer than summer leaves and beans," declared Bella.

"I'm sure Saul will tell us at the workshop just as soon as it happens, I believe the baby is due very soon," prompted Annie.

Aunt Bella, however, showed no emotion on the subject, not surprise, not pleasure nor displeasure. In fact Annie thought the arrival of parsnips and flat poll cabbage had created a much greater interest! It was impossible to fathom Bella's moods, Annie was simply thankful that the annoyance her aunt had displayed at her lateness home did not persist and the two had bid each other 'goodnight' without sharp words to hinder sleep. Annie dwelt for a few minutes on the incident at the workshop but she turned her mind to remnants of brushed cotton and the clothes she and Edna could create from them for Saul's grandchild. Her planning efforts induced sleep.

Bella's thoughts were far from soporific, she had travelled back in time to her mother and Ruby.

It had been necessary to confide in the Hemsleys, they were truly, good kind people and had shown complete understanding and genuine concern. Ruby needed to return to some duties, to try to recover some degree of normality but her nerves were still raw. Alice Hemsley had arranged for Ruby to work the same hours as Bella, she could help their cook as before, but spend time through the day helping with general housework. This would enable the two women to walk together both to and from their tasks. They had been on their way home, the November day was damp, the sky heavy and grey.

"Come on Ruby, let's hurry, mother will have the kettle on the coals."
Ruby had stopped walking, she stood quite still.

"What is it? Bella asked, "Ruby talk to me."

Bella held her sister's shoulders and looked directly into her face. Ruby didn't cry but her words shook from the dread that had consumed her young mind.

"I haven't bled." She spoke the words like a confession, as though she now declared her mortal sin.

"Haven't you bled since that night?"

Bella's voice was anguished, only then did the tears pour from Ruby like a flood. Bella had not meant to sound stern and Ruby's distress pained her greatly. She held her young sister in her arms and comforted her with kisses of reassurance. "Come now, we will go home and talk to mother, it will be alright."

Bella grasped Ruby's hand as if in doing so, some of her own strength would pass to her sister, she would not let her down, if it took all the strength she could muster, she Bella, would see everything came right.

Clarice was mending stockings, the room felt warm. Bella took Ruby's coat and hung it with her own behind the door. The kettle was hot, she made some tea and put a mug in Ruby's hand.

"Wrap your fingers around this Ruby, let it warm you. Mother there is something we must tell you," said Bella.

Ruby had sat in total silence, staring into her mug of tea whilst Bella had imparted the devastating news to their mother. Poor Clarice was distraught, Ruby began to cry again and carried on crying until her slight frame was close to collapse under the severity of her sobbing. Bella pleaded with them to be calm. Finally her capable authority found their trust and exhausted from fear and despair, they allowed Bella's assurance that it would be alright, to still their cries and dry their tears.

It was agreed that they would not tell Sefton until it became no longer possible to hide Ruby's condition from him. Whatever his reaction, they would support each other, Ruby had done no wrong.

The weeks passed in the accepted routine. Bella and Ruby worked in The Park at the Hemsley's as normal and Clarice survived by convincing herself that Sefton would control his tyranny and somehow force himself to show his young daughter some compassion.

In spite of letting out Ruby's skirts and introducing loose cardigans to her appearance, the situation could not continue without Sefton being aware.

Bella knew her father well, his supposed strength of character she held no regard for. He was a bully who enjoyed playing the role of master over his female household. In any circumstance where his strength might be pitted against other men, he would yield at the first feel of pressure. Sefton had come to know Bella's spirit over the years, she had stood up to him more than once and her steel had each time dominated his own.

The supper over, Ruby and Clarice were finishing the chores in the scullery. Sefton sat by the fire, his face hidden behind the pages of the Gazette.

"Father I need you to listen to what I am actually saying and not to what you suppose you are hearing," said Bella.

Her tone was clear and deliberate. "This family has been served a great injustice, the act of one evil man has brought a trial to us which is so cruel, we will need all our strength to bear it."

He had put down his paper and stared at Bella but did not speak. She told him the events of that fateful night, how they had chosen to spare him the intense distress it had caused them, but now the worst of it he could not be shielded from any longer.

"Ruby is with child."

Bella had barely uttered these last four words when he rose from his chair like a beast which had just sighted prey. He pushed Bella aside, the bottom of his jacket caught on the edge of the chair, no obstacle could impede his stride. The chair toppled to the floor, just outside the salvation of the rug, it came to rest on the planking with a resounding thud.

Clarice cried out, "Let her alone Sefton, let her alone!"

Her tortured, heart rending despair drove her emotion to its limit. Now she pulled at his sleeve, her fingers franticly twisting the cloth for grip. His arm lashed out and she fell back against the scullery table, the force propelled it across the flags and the harsh grating sound it made echoed through Bella's head like thunder. He had reached Ruby, her eyes revealed terror, a torment of mind beyond human endurance.

"So, you would have me let her alone would you, see what happens when I let her alone, you are damned girl, you will never pass through the gates of heaven. You shall be cast into the wilderness, there to wander the barren plains with all other sinners, but you shall not bring damnation down on us all."

Ruby's cries rent the air, her tears fell over Sefton's hands where he held tight the front of her cardigan. He wiped his hand across her hair and stung the side of her face with his palm. Clarice was hysterical and Bella tried desperately to hush her screams. Sefton opened the back door and pushed Ruby into the darkness of the yard, he closed it again and rammed the bolts home. Bella could hear Ruby's weakening plea.

"Let me in Father, let me in."

If there is a God then I know He is on my side thought Bella. She could bear it no more. She stood in front of Sefton and before he had chance to raise his hand, her words fell on him with such force they might have been delivered by the Almighty Himself.

"You lay a finger on me Father and you will, oh you surely will know God's wrath. I shall go to your 'blesséd' Chapel, I will stand in the 'blesséd' pulpit and I shall preach of this night to your 'blesséd' congregation. I shall deliver the sermon of all sermons, they shall learn every word of every verse of every chapter of the book of Sefton. They shall come to know his evil, his unfettered wickedness. How he struck his wife then smote his innocent child and this he did in the name of 'The Father', that Father of all mankind who loves with an everlasting love. You will leave this house, you will leave this very night and you shall not return. If you ever show your face in this street again, I shall shame you before all Chapels, all Churches, all congregations and peoples across the city. You would never lift your head from the miserable, wretched sentence of infinite Hell. Go Father, go upstairs and gather your things."

Sefton stood transfixed, his hands now lay inert at his sides, his enflamed, bloody red face turned to an ashen image of dread.

"Now, Father, now!" Bella's might could have dominated any field of battle, she had taken her command from the highest order there is. He crossed the room and disappeared up the stairs. Bella unbolted the back door. Ruby sat on the ground, her head between her knees, her shoulders racked with cold. Bella lifted her to her feet, "Come on Ruby, come and sit with mother by the fire, you are safe now. Mother, stir the coals."

Clarice was rendered immobile with trauma. Bella took her mother gently by the hand and led both women to the fireside, she sat Ruby in the big chair and spoke slowly but firmly to Clarice.

"Stir the fire Mother."

Bella picked up the fallen chair and placed it by Clarice then stood between the foot of the stairs and her sister and mother. Sefton's tread now descended.

"Have no alarm," said Bella with not the slightest waver in her voice. He gripped the handles of a bag in one hand and as if in one last act of defiance, he held his Bible in the other, but he did not speak. Bella followed him to the back door.

"Pray Father, pray very hard for that wilderness not to be yours but remember my words, for they are the gospel you must now abide by, or be damned!"

Bella listened to his tread across the cobbles of the yard until they faded to silence, she put the bolts in place and leaned back against the door. Just for a second she felt the threat of approaching weakness, before it could have any chance of finding her she crossed to the table and pulled it back into position, she poured water from the jug into the kettle and carried it to the hearth.

"Put this on the coals Mother, we shall have some tea, Ruby, there is mending to do. Mother, you need to complete your embroidery, soon we shall be busy with other things. I have lessons to mark."

The fire crackled as flames reached moisture on the side of the kettle. Bella fetched her case from the sideboard, put the mending box in Ruby's lap and her mother's embroidery frame and silks by the chair.

"When we have drunk our tea we shall do our work," declared Bella, and so it was.

*

Bella's mind would not be still, she heard the mantel clock strike two. A coldness tormented her, in spite of ample bedcovers, her toes stung with chill. She lit her candle, pulled on her heavy wrap and forced her numbed feet into her slippers. There was no sound from Annie's room. Bella crept down the stairs, breathing in sharply as if she believed this would lighten her weight when she reached the sixth tread, which always creaked underfoot.

The fire still had a glow of red. She put some lengths of kindling into the patch of brightest colour, it responded with a ready flicker that quickly grew to a flame. She put just a few nubs of coal at its heart and rubbed the tips of her fingers together to shed the loose particles of coal dust that had found the lines and chaps of her aged skin. The candle light caught in its beam Harold's small wooden horse. Bella smiled to herself. In the midst of all those troubled memories it was Harold's influence that effected the smile. She could have hoped for no one better than Harold to care for Annie. Life's demands had made Bella stern, the need to be ever strong had entirely overwhelmed her humour. Now perhaps the belief that Harold would soon take Annie to his charge might relieve the concerns which increased with the passing years.

The fire now offered enough heat to warm some milk. Bella put a small pan on the coals and watched as the edge of the milk began to bubble and rise slightly up the side of the saucepan. With the old towelling cloth she gripped the handle and poured the steaming milk into her cup. She sat back in her chair and sipped it. It began to warm her and the heat of the hearth comforted her restless toes. Her mind had now freed itself of the past and seemed ready to concede to sleep, her eyes felt heavy, she made safe the fire, took up the candle, drew in a deep breath to once more lighten her tread and returned to bed. At last deep, peaceful sleep, ordered the early hours to, 'Let Bella alone'.

CHAPTER SEVEN

It had been a hard morning at the yard, Harold and Billy had earned their few minutes of respite and sat with their backs to the wood pile. Josiah had gone to the tannery and had taken with him a small parcel of ox liver to drop into May and Alfred on his way up Peverell Street.

"It 'appens the same every year," said Harold, "as soon as the air begins to bite, folks eat more meat."

"Well," replied Billy, "stands to reason, a few green leaves an' beetroot barely fills a 'Toff's' belly, even they have to top up with their hams and pheasants and stuff, but your workin' man, if 'e's goin' to 'ave any chance o' keepin' the tallow on 'is bones, then 'e's got to 'ave a good plate 'o stew wi' a pile 'o dumplin's, a basin 'o steak an' kidney wi' a thick suet crust, liver wi' loads o' soft fried onions, wintertime 'e'd go down wi' pneumonia else!"

Harold smiled, just a few minutes earlier he and Billy had been loading the hides onto Josiah's waggon, Billy had a favourite ditty he always sang to accompany this particular task and today had been no exception. Billy had thrown the last hide up onto the waggon and delivered his usual rendition .....

"What fun we had when grandma died,

Skin of her arse with onions fried.

We rubbed our bellies and grandad sighed,

T'would have been a waste to tan her hide."

Harold found a mint in his pocket.

"'Ere Harold, Edna's been goin' on at me to take 'er to the fair, 'tis the last night on Saturday, why don't you bring Annie an' we can all go together, just for an hour, it don't need to be for long, a man could spend 'is wages very quick if 'e stayed there for too long but 'twould be a bit 'o fun, what do you think?" Asked Billy.

"I'll have to ask Annie, I shall see her tonight," replied Harold.

"Course 'er aunt's a bit of a witch isn't she?" Said Billy.

"No that's not true, she can be a bit stern can Miss Pownall, but when you get used to her she's alright really. She's knowing about a lot of things, she is a teacher, she gave Annie all her lessons," said Harold. "I'll tell you tomorro' whether we can go or not."

Billy stubbed out his rollup with the heel of his boot. "Heard a bit 'o news yesterday," he said, "Enid Eddowes is about to 'ave a kid, hope it 'as more mirth than its father, miserable bugger 'e is, allus tetchy, like our mam says when me dad's in a grump, 'been out and widdled on nettles again'. That Enid's a looker though, only ever seen 'er a couple 'o times but she was at the 'ead 'o the queue when looks wer' give out."

Billy chatted on and Harold listened passively as he sucked on a mint. Billy's tongue finally took a rest break and Harold said, "I'd like children, lots of 'em like at 'ome, but I shall make some money first, establish meself so Annie can 'ave some 'elp. Mam never stops, she's 'appy enough I think but some days I look at 'er and 'er face seems old, 'er 'ands are worn an' rough, she never 'as any time to tend 'erself. I want it to be better for Annie."

"I reckon me 'an Edna might 'ave a long period 'o practise first," said Billy and gave a roguish laugh. "Besides, God knows what Edna'll make of our family. It wer' only last night when I was talkin' to dad that 'e told me we got a relative works on a fairground somewhere, so I asked 'im if it wer' the bearded lady. 'Don't be daft lad', 'e said, 'you know your aunt Jessie works full time at Clark and Brown's stuffin' 'orse 'air into upholstery'. You should see our aunt Jessie Harold, when we wer' little an' mam told us, 'Give your aunt a kiss', it was awful, we didn't mind grandad's whiskers, they felt alright but aunt Jessie's, ugh," Billy shuddered. "Strange really 'cause she 'ad 'ardly any 'air on 'er 'ead, they reckon she 'ad that 'Allo Peachy' thing."

Harold chuckled then got to his feet, stretched his back and said, "Come on Billy Dodds or we shall 'ave beards longer than your aunt Jessie's before we finish strippin' that flare fat."

The two men were glad to reach the end of their work.

Josiah had returned from the tannery and retired to his makeshift office. It became more noticeable to Harold how much slower Josiah's movements had become, his aching joints forced him to leave a lot of the gruelling work to the younger men. Josiah still stoically helped with the unloading of animals and the penning, he did all the deliveries and the paperwork but his reliance on Harold to oversee the 'Kill' and processing had increased considerably. Josiah was an honest man and had already told Harold he would be putting up his pay accordingly. It was this knowledge that set Harold to thinking about marriage. He knew Annie was the girl he wanted, if Annie agreed they would be married in the spring.

When he reached home and turned into the back yard he could smell Sarah's stew, the savoury aroma of onions quickened his step.

"'Ow are yer Mam?" He asked and produced a small newspaper wrapped package from his jacket pocket. "With love from Josiah, to render down for drippin'," he said with obvious pleasure.

"Bless that man," said Sarah as she undid the paper to reveal a nice piece of 'flare fat'. "I'll cut some up for the dumplin's."

Her skills in the kitchen never failed to amaze Harold, all the years he could recall since infancy had been filled with images of his mam at her work table in the kitchen. Frank had once said to their father, 'When you think of mam you think of food'. Samuel with his usual quick humour had replied by telling Frank, 'Tis a wonderful thing son when your children are small to see them suckin' on mother, brings joy to a man's 'eart. Then when they get big they begin to suck on father an' that isn't so good, which reminds me, what's happened to my oil can that you borrowed for the bike? I need it for the wheels on me barro'.

Samuel had a quick wit and the wisdom of Solomon, it made for a glorious combination.

"I'm goin' to see Annie after supper Mam, Billy and Edna are goin' to the fair for an hour on Saturday night and want Annie and me to go with them," said Harold.

"There can be some rough characters down that fairground, I don't know what Miss Pownall will think of that notion, don't you cross 'er Harold, I don't want no upset."

Sarah sighed as she stirred her pan of stew. Harold planted a kiss on her cheek and said, "Dear Mam," he dipped his finger in the pan, licked it and grinned at her, "lovely Mam, just like you."

"Get away you great dough ball," she said and made like she would wallop him with the spoon.

He ran into the scullery laughing, "Do you need any wood or coal bringing in Mam?"

"Yes, bring them in before your father comes, 'e should be 'ere soon, 'e can sit down for a bit before supper then. Frank's gone to the allotment with Gertie and Jean to fetch apples and Nora's upstairs with Mavis and Maggie putting the clean beddin' on."

The house seemed to burst at the seams, yet everyone was clean and fed and went to their bed happy.

To Harold it represented everything good, it had made him what he was. His little face by the front door, smiled the happy nature of the house proudly to the world. He couldn't build a Pyramid or a Taj Mahal to be his lasting monument but his engraving on the brick at the front of 69 Mitchell Street made their house different, it had an identity that would always remain. It may only be a small endeavour but it was unique and Harold's own creation, the thought satisfied him. He made haste through supper and promised Sarah that he would abide by Miss Pownall's wishes with regard to the fair. Samuel called to him. "You give that lass a kiss from me."

"If you want to kiss Bella Pownall Father, you'll 'ave to do it yourself!" Harold laughed wickedly.

"You cheeky whipper-snapper," said Samuel with a big grin across his face. Sarah observed the banter between father and son, it pleased her greatly, their understanding of each other came entirely without effort. She had known families where the father could not bond with the first born son, jealousy, the threat of a second male within the household among some of the theories for this behaviour. Thankfully Sarah had no such concerns, her own men were at peace with each other, father and son, she was wholly content in the knowledge.

As Harold approached the back door of Bella's house he could see, through a chink in the curtains, Annie moving busily about inside. He knocked quietly on the door, Annie appeared with her pinafore on proudly announcing, "We've made apple jelly with the windfalls, look it's as clear as glass and it's started to set already." She pointed to six jars of jelly on the scullery table.

"Aunt Bella says it should be crystal clear, if it's cloudy then it won't keep."

"Looks good to me," said Harold.

The kettle sang gently on the coals, Bella warmed the teapot and prepared three cups. Harold felt quite at home with Bella, her initial coolness he'd considered a sign of intelligence, after all she had no real knowledge of him he might have been the worst kind of bounder, highly unsuitable for Annie. The fact that Bella invited him to visit so that she might judge his character for herself was good policy in Harold's book. After some time of general conversation he felt the moment was right for the subject of the fair.

"I've never seen a real fair," said Annie, "only on the posters. It is alright for me to go isn't it Aunt Bella, please?"

The response was delivered only after much thought, "Provided you go in the early evening and be home no later than 10 o'clock. You know without my telling you that some folk will spend time in the pubs first then stumble into the fairground with little of their senses. It's no place for anyone decent by then. You will stay together Harold, you and Billy Dodds will not take your eyes off Annie and Edna."

"You have my word Miss Pownall, Annie will be here by ten, I shall bring her right to the door. That will be plenty time enough at the fair for all of us, as Billy said, 'too long there could eat up a man's wages', a bit of fun is alright but there are more important things to consider."

Bella turned to stir the fire, a faint smile on her face. So Harold did have plans for the future, she had no doubt at all that these plans would include Annie.

So it was agreed. Annie couldn't sleep for excitement at the prospect of seeing a real fairground, she would tell May and Alfred about it the next day, and Edna, well she would buy something nice for Edna at the fair, a thank you for suggesting it. They were to meet Billy and Edna at half past seven by the corner of Waverly Street, it was only twenty minutes walk from there to the Forest Ground where the fair was held each year.

"Come on you two," called out Edna when she saw Harold and Annie approaching, "I can smell the cockles from 'ere."

"Now stay close to me Annie," said Harold, "there will be a lot of people there, don't want you gettin' lost. I've got only a sensible amount of money on me, no good puttin' anything in a back pocket, I shall have to keep it inside the front of me jacket where I can watch it. The crowd will hold a lot of pickpockets, slick as monkeys they are, whip the sugar out of yer tea while you stir it!"

Annie's excitement had suddenly become tempered by apprehension, it did present an alarming place but the sounds and smells as they drew close intrigued her. Edna and Billy had picked up the strains of a barrel organ and began to sing and dance like a music hall turn. Edna put her arm through Annie's and drew her into the merriment.

"Come on, join in Harold," she cried.

Edna sang loudly and kicked her skirts up unashamedly in front of her in time to the music, her laughter was irresistible and the four young people promenaded along the street with abandon. By the time they reached the fairground Annie's cheeks were as red as Maggie's when she bounced her way over the cobbles in Frank's big basket, but now the ground beneath Annie's feet was as smooth as glass, worn so by the countless number of folk who had walked between the booths and side-shows over the past two nights. The noise filled the air along with the smell of cockles, vinegar, toffee apples and stale body odour. Even the exchange of coins, constantly taking place at all the stalls released a strange metallic smell that fought with the oily vapours of the steam engines for dominance. Annie clung to Harold's arm fascinated by this diversity of human kind and its accompaniments but making sure she did not become lost in it.

"Lets go in there Harold," said Billy, "its always a laugh," he pointed to a side-show called 'Hall of Mirrors'.

Harold and Billy handed their money to a large colourful woman, her outfit was like nothing Annie had ever sewn. It revealed a bosom that should it have been forced entirely below the bodice, might have resulted in crushed ribs and asphyxia, indeed the amount of rouge applied to her face made it difficult to tell if she might actually be stifling. Her open palm held out to receive the money, appeared to Annie as big as that of the tub man as he locked his palm to the base of each tub when he tipped it. To imagine such a woman cradling a child was near impossible. Annie had once heard two men outside the Mission in conversation, she had quite unintentionally overhead the one say, 'She's been behind the bar at The Highwayman for years', the other had replied, 'Eats her young she does.' It had been a great puzzlement to Annie, she could not possibly ask aunt Bella the meaning of their remarks. Perhaps this was the very woman who spent years at The Highwayman but now chose a different vocation. It offered an explanation which prior to now Annie could not have dreamt of.

They followed a line of people into the booth, Edna caught hold Annie's hand and pulled her alongside a large mirror, the two women squealed with laughter at the image. Harold and Billy standing in front of the mirror on the other wall, had suddenly become as round as the dome on the Civic Hall. They grew from short to tall then swelled from thin to fat but it was the contortions achieved by the girls' hats which caused most hilarity. Annie's sides ached. Outside in the air once more, the happy mood continued and Edna pleaded with Billy.

"Lets go in the swing boats".

As soon as two emptied, Harold and Billy lifted the girls in and climbed in beside them. Harold teased Annie, "Don't worry gravity keeps you in when we go right over the top, only raggin'" he said quickly when her face showed alarm. He blew her a kiss and cast his all comforting smile, with the motion of the swing boat Harold began to sing;

"Swing me just a little bit higher Annie Bundy do,

Swing me just a little bit higher and I'll love you."

Annie could feel the night air stroke her cheeks in the draught the swing boat created as it travelled to and fro. It began to lighten her head, she felt truly airborne and Harold was flying with her. The sensation aroused her, coming down to earth was made only more difficult when Harold took her hands to help her alight and drew her to him, he whispered in her ear.

"Marry me next spring Annie."

Billy called out, "I'll wager tuppence I can beat you at the coconut shy Harold."

"Alright yer on," replied Harold. "Come on Annie, we'll show old loud mouth over there." He grinned at Billy and Edna.

Annie was still turning his words about in her head. Marry in the spring, but what about Bella? Her dilemma was profound. She would allow fate to determine her answer. If Harold missed all the targets then she would say no, if he toppled one, then she would accept it as destined and say yes. Whatever fate decided must surely be for the best. The men handed over their money and were given three balls each. Edna gave Billy a big kiss on the cheek and said, "You go first Billy."

His first throw just grazed the side and the coconut trembled but stayed on the stand. Edna tugged at his arm with excitement. He threw again but the ball fell short. Billy took aim at the last coconut as if it were an opposing warrior. The ball glanced the top of the warrior's head but Billy had failed to bring his opponent down.

"Bugger," he said, disgusted at himself.

He reached into his pocket for consolation, he would make himself a rollup while Harold took up the challenge. The man had put the coconuts back in place and given Harold the signal that all was ready. Annie drew her toes up inside her boots, she could feel her stomach tightening. Harold turned his head and gave her a wink. He threw the first ball and it brushed the stand but caused no threat to the coconut. Annie's insides were in knots. Billy had positioned his rollup in the corner of his mouth where it clung as he spoke.

"Come on Harold, pretend it's that bugger Arnold as used to pinch your mint in school."

The second ball left Harold's hand but fell wide, Annie felt sick. He turned to her.

"Not all is lost yet young Annie," he chuckled, "father says it's never all over til' the fat lady sings."

He launched the last ball, fate plotted its course, it struck the target plumb on and the coconut fell to the ground with a deep thud.

"You lucky devil," said Billy, and slapped him on the back.

Harold looked at Annie and said "Aren't I good?" With a huge grin of satisfaction.

"Yes," she replied, "Yes I will."

The man gave Harold his prize, a large coconut from the shelf at the side of the booth. Billy immediately grabbed it from Harold's hand, turned it upside down, removed Edna's hat and held it over the upturned coconut. Then he announced.

"Meet my dear aunt Jessie!"

"You silly sod Billy," said Harold with a chuckle.

Edna wanted to know more. "What's your aunt Jessie got to do with a coconut?" She asked Billy.

"Ah well, now the story goes."

Harold gave a loud laugh. "If you thought the mirrors made Billy tall you must listen to this tale."

Undaunted Billy continued, "Grandma had a younger brother, sailed the seas he did. One time he came home from his adventures and brought his sister back a coconut, they were rare then. Well grandma were carrying aunt Jessie at the time and when he left and grandma an' grandad went up to bed, the coconut wer' still sittin' on the scullery table. Grandma came down first thing and saw this creature in the half light, she'd forgot all about the coconut from the night before, poor soul near died of apoplexy wi' the shock. Grandad allus maintained that it wer' the fright made aunt Jessie so hairy."

Harold roared with laughter. "Billy, if that gipsy fortune teller over there ever retires you could take over his booth an' do bloody well for yourself. Talk about spin a yarn."

"You're a proper doubting Thomas, Harold Boucher," said Billy and lit his rollup which had miraculously stayed in the corner of his mouth throughout. Annie had espied a stand of beads and bangles.

"O look Edna, which do you think is the prettiest?"

Edna surveyed the items then pointed to a bangle, "that's nice," she said "see how it sparkles."

"Very well, that is the one I shall buy," said Annie.

She had heeded Harold's words and wedged her soft purse of coins up the sleeve of her jacket. She paid the stall holder and carefully deposited the purse back up her sleeve, then she took Edna's hand and slipped the bangle onto Edna's wrist.

"What's that for?" Said a surprised Edna.

"It's just a present," said Annie.

Edna was delighted, it gave Annie genuine pleasure.

"Women and jewellery," said Billy.

Harold didn't speak. It was Annie's way to gladden the lives of others whenever she could. Next spring he would give her the happiest day any woman could have. All the gladness Annie made for others, he would make for her. Just as the words on Alfred's little picture said, he would create for Annie a world of happy days.

CHAPTER EIGHT

Charles had reached home just as soon as he could. The fog was so thick it enveloped the city early in the afternoon and now held all captive in a dense blanket of thick smoke filled smog. Curbs and railings had been rendered invisible, attempts at locating street name plates proved almost impossible. Even the sounds of the city were distorted with no movement of air to carry them. The Church clock, the school bell, the creaking pub sign, all lay mute under the veil in which winter so often shrouded Nottingham. Bertha Duffin had sent a messenger to the bank, Enid's pain had begun, Charles must leave his work and come home. Bertha had been spending much of the previous week with Enid, she was probably closer to her than any other of the women with whom the young Enid associated. At sixteen Enid had moved across the city and taken work in a bookshop, she had answered an advert for a single female lodger to rent a room at the house of Bertha Duffin, widow. The two women had warmed to each other right away, the rent had been more than reasonable, an important consideration for the vulnerable young Enid. Bertha had welcomed the small financial bonus which her lodger provided but her pleasure, first and foremost had been in securing company through the long night hours when the house had unnerved her by its emptiness. Bertha, Enid had very soon discovered, was the reassuring presence sought by most of the neighbourhood in any time of difficulty. For her own part Enid felt comfortable and happy while under the roof of Bertha Duffin, the arrangement had worked entirely well.

Bertha's words tumbled over each other in her haste to inform Charles.

"I cannot pacify her," she said.

He was trying to shed his coat but Bertha was so animated he could find no interlude long enough to avoid her flailing arms.

"Go to her, see if you can calm her, I have tried but she is so frightened."

Charles could hear Enid's distress as he climbed the stairs, she lay on the bed, her eyes fixed on him as he stood in the doorway. Her hands gripped at the edge of the bed frame, even Charles, who more often than not considered only his own anxieties recognised fear in the shaking, whimpering Enid. He didn't know what to say to her, their's was not a marriage of tenderness, their disagreements and often full blown arguments could become volatile. The intensity of feeling producing a friction powerful enough to make fire between them. It would burn with the searing heat of passion, then smoulder, not ever fully extinguished, but in waiting for that tantalising lift of air to inflame it once more. Their's was not a love which sought comfortable, soothing unity, their's was a love which created devils and demons to continually challenge emotion. The fighting could be severe, sometimes cruel but emotion always triumphed and the retreating demons would take refuge under the smouldering embers until the next lift of air. Charles crossed to the bed and not without some difficulty, prised her fingers from the bed frame, her grip tightened on his hand like a vice, "I'll fetch the doctor," he said.

Enid's whimpering became a cry, "No, send Bertha."

She pulled urgently at his hand. Charles felt threatened by circumstances around him. He had little knowledge of childbirth, only a slight grasp of gentleness and a smog over the city as to make it impossible to send Bertha from the house.

"Bertha will stay here with you, I must go myself, the fog is very bad, I will bring the doctor. Do as Bertha tells you, I won't be long."

Her cries were pitiful and filled the room as he forced her fingers to release his.

Bertha was anxious, "I don't know what is the matter, I can't understand why she is so pained." She wrung her hands, "Bring the doctor as quickly as you can Charles."

He gathered his coat and hat, opened the door to the thickening gloom and in seconds had disappeared from view. Bertha closed the door with such a weight of concern at her chest that she felt unsteady and clung to the stair rail for support. Enid's breathing was short and frantic.

"Charles has gone for the doctor, I know he will hurry," said Bertha, inwardly afraid he might become lost, the visibility was dire. She sat on the edge of the bed and chatted to Enid as naturally as she could, as much for her own sake as for Enid's. The room had become quite darkened, Bertha lit the lamp, she lifted the covers around Enid, the air grew chill, she felt the need of a wrap around her own shoulders.

"Have you thought of names for your baby Enid?" She asked.

It felt as though time too could go nowhere, marooned in the fog as herself.

Enid did not answer, she had again clenched her fingers around the bed frame and locked her lips in silence since Charles left. Her eyes moved across the walls of the room as if she expected to see the fiend which tormented her. The shadows seemed to taunt her as they strengthened with the fast fading light, soon it would be dark and the fog even more threatening.

At last Bertha heard the door downstairs and Charles speaking to the doctor as they made their way to the bedroom. Her relief was so plain to see that the doctor spoke first to Bertha.

"Hello Mrs.Duffin, I think you would benefit greatly from a cup of tea, in fact I think we all would. Perhaps you would go downstairs and put the kettle on, whilst we are here with Enid."

He spoke softly to Enid as he examined her, "For how long have you felt so distressed my dear?" He asked.

Enid's voice shook with emotion as she answered him, "Hours, for hours," she said.

"What is it?" Asked Charles, "Why isn't the baby coming?"

Bertha came into the room with a tray, the doctor turned to Charles and in a voice too low for Enid to hear said, "We will talk downstairs presently, leave it for now." Bertha very shakily poured the tea.

"Now Enid you must sip a little warm drink. Charles, prop your wife up against the pillows, she has slipped too far down the bed. Come on my dear, take just a small measure, it will make you feel better." He patted her hand and held out the cup for her to take it from him, "Just a few swallows."

She finally obliged him and took several sips.

"There, you were quite thirsty weren't you?"

The doctor's authority began to calm her, "Take deeper, longer breaths Enid," he said. "Charles, bring another lamp to lighten the room, Mrs Duffin, perhaps you could find a book of Enid's and read to her for a little while."

Charles positioned the lamp by Bertha's side and she began to read aloud. The doctor indicated to Charles to follow him downstairs, he took Enid's hand and said.

"I shall be back in just a moment, until then breathe deeply, allow your eyes to close and concentrate on Mrs.Duffin's words".

Downstairs in the living room Charles asked again, "What's happening, why is the baby not coming?"

The doctor sighed and put a reassuring hand on Charles' shoulder. "The baby will come before morning, I am confident of that, but Enid will not give birth just yet. Your wife is among a small number of people who unfortunately feel pain before actually experiencing it. She cannot help herself, it comes from an irrational fear of pain, it instils dread, it causes intense panic, tightens breathing and cramps muscles. She is imagining the worst for no real reason. You must be patient with her, it merits sympathy just as any other medical condition. Stay with her as much as you possibly can, comfort her, distract her, she needs you to be caring and gentle. Your calmness is all important, that will influence her own control. I rather think Mrs.Duffin will be here for the night too, as yet, the visibility shows no improvement, I will go up and sit with Enid for a little while. Explain to Mrs.Duffin what I have just told you, I will send her down."

Charles felt very nervous, he wished the doctor could stay but if it was to be several hours and if Enid was in no real danger then the fee for his attendance so far might be manageable at least, his presence throughout the night hours would be another matter. Charles' finances were already in trouble, Saul had kept him afloat but in spite of his visits to the workshop and to his father's home, his head was barely above water. He wished for someone to take this demanding situation from him but he could not leave Bertha Duffin to face it alone. Charles was trapped, his wife, the fog, finances, the arrival of a baby, all moved in on him. Suddenly he felt very beleaguered, he thought of his mother, and in his despair at finding himself at this time without her unfailing love, wished he had shown his father more kindness. The doctor had settled Enid as much as he could.

"Your wife is a strong young woman, the baby is well I feel sure, it is Enid's emotional state which causes me concern. Be very supportive of her Charles." He took his watch from the pocket of his waistcoat. "It is now seven thirty, I shall return around midnight. Fear not Charles, by first light you will be a father."

Charles opened the door and a rush of air came over them. "There, even the fog is lifting, the wind is picking up, I can now make out the building across the street. Very soon it will be much improved and so too will be your spirits Charles." The doctor shook his hand. "Relieve Mrs.Duffin for a couple of hours, the woman needs to rest."

With that he was gone. Charles closed the door, as the latch fell into place he felt overwhelmed by uncertainty. A father by first light, he wanted his mother, to feel safe in her arms, to know he was loved more than anyone. He drew his sleeve across his face to wipe away tears and made his way to the bedroom. Enid held out her hand, he sat on the bed and stared at his wife, even in her present agitated state she was truly beautiful.

"You go downstairs for a while Bertha," he said, "Try to rest in the chair by the fire, I'll call you if I need you."

He lay beside Enid and kissed her, for a few precious minutes, husband and wife found unity. Lull before the storm, ember over demon, it mattered not, this was their love and so be it. Charles' presence and the brighter light of the room temporarily calmed the frightened Enid. A spell of quietness followed until pain, real pain now stirred her, she gripped Charles' fingers with a strength that made his hand numb. He pacified her between contractions but they occurred more frequently and her agitation deepened.

"I must fetch Bertha," he said.

Enid cast a look at him which held fear and anger, "Damn you, damn all men, damn fathers, damn fathers to be," she spewed out the words over them both, like shedding a poison that had festered inside until her being finally retched it up! Bertha, restored by the chance to sleep, instructed Charles to fill the kettle and make ready clean towels. She had birthed many babies in the past but Enid's behaviour had been outside all previous experience. The doctor's explanation however had bolstered her confidence, if she had to deliver Enid's baby then she would bring this little one into the world just as she had all the others. The fog had cleared. Charles had opened the back door to take a breath of night air, the eyes of a cat shone out from the corner of the yard, he stamped his foot and growled like a dog. The disturbed creature now disappeared over the wall but without making the slightest sound.

Charles and Enid had been married for a little over twelve months. Enid's mother was an invalid, had been so since Enid's childhood. There were two boys, both older than Enid, the elder now lived in America, the younger lived with his wife and child on the opposite side of Nottingham close by his parents. Enid did not get on with her father, she had never told Charles why. Whenever he pressed her on the subject her mood had become difficult, sullen, he could manage her wild mood, at times she became charged and the danger aroused him but sullen, silent periods left him vulnerable, with no strategy to achieve her surrender. Enid visited her mother infrequently, over the past year she had crossed the city to see her only four times and then only for an hour of an afternoon. Given these circumstances, he supposed Bertha was as good a substitute as he could hope for in Enid's present condition.

Upstairs, Bertha had established a regime. "Breathe with me Enid, long deep breaths, breathe over the pain."

"God Almighty, what do you think I'm doing." Enid shrieked back at her.

The pitiful, whimpering hours had passed and just as the doctor had predicted, actual pain now concentrated her mind, it drove away fear and enabled Enid's true self to take charge of her emotions.

"Where is he, where is my miserable bank clerk?" She delivered the question to Bertha with the tone and volume of a drunken harlot.

"Do you want me to fetch him?" Said Bertha.

"Keep the bastard away from me, if I see him before me I shall damn him to hell."

Enid's hurt was now as Bertha would expect, this was normal, this was Enid. The contractions were now regular, Bertha wiped Enid's brow.

"Push with the pain Enid."

The room echoed with Enid's curses but no screams, no cries, not a single breath wasted on empty sounds but a verbal bombardment of obscenities and with every one an intensity of effort. Enid's baby came into the world just as he had been conceived, through a depth of passion that rocked humanity, the infant's first cry as robust and forceful as his mother's.

Bertha, with the skill of years, cut the cord and tied off. He was a lovely fleshy baby and as she wrapped him and put him in Enid's arms, she felt content at his weight and well being. Bertha went to the top of the stairs and called to Charles. He looked nervous as he stood in the doorway, his gaze went to Enid and the baby in her arms. Her eyes exhausted, spent from her exertions still held the strength to lure, her kiss was as powerful as any she had ever used to win him. She put one arm around his neck and pulled him down to their baby son.

"I hate you" she said and pinched the skin on the back of Charles' neck with real intent.

"That hurt," he cried out.

"Good," replied Enid, "I do love you as well." Her words teased him but Charles was completely in awe of the infant, the slightly mottled skin, so new to the world it had not yet adjusted to light and air. The double chins so soft to his touch, a little mouth which pursed and puckered, tiny fingers reaching, searching for security.

"Our son," said Enid. Her voice had given in to tiredness and the words trembled.

Bertha heard a knock at the front door, it was half past midnight. The doctor looked at Bertha with an enquiring expression.

"Yes," she said, "all is well, the little chap is quite plump, I am glad you have come, I shall let you see for yourself."

The doctor felt Enid's brow, "You have a very fine young son my dear, if he displays his mother's will and bears the look of his mother, then he will do well."

Her weariness rendered Enid submissive, her eyelids closed as a faint smile of acknowledgement passed to the doctor.

"Allow her a little spell of rest whilst we clean up young master Eddowes here, then put the infant to feed Mrs.Duffin."

Charles handed the doctor his coat and hat, "Thank you Dr Baragruy" he said.

"Your debt to me is comparatively small Charles, however your indebtedness to Mrs.Duffin is immense."

Charles shook the doctor's hand, "I shall show my appreciation as will Enid," replied Charles.

The street was quiet, somewhere in the distance a dog barked. Just two or three hours and first light would arrive to relieve the night of its command. He would need to arrange some time from his work to be with Enid whilst Bertha went home for a little while. He must tell Saul. A pang of guilt struck him, he had taken much from his father but given nothing. Now he gave a grandson, he could only hope that this new life might compensate to some degree for his own lack of interest. That Enid would find satisfaction in her baby and demand less. That in his mother's memory they might all learn to care.

This night had taken Charles across the threshold to manhood. As he climbed the stairs to his family he promised himself to do better.

Annie and Edna had been occupied on an order for Blackmore's School, the new intake of pupils had created a need for more uniforms. Their machines were now still for the women to have their dinner. Saul appeared at the doorway to the back room.

"I have something to tell you," he said, "Enid had her baby last night, it's a boy, I don't know any more than that. Charles called at home early this morning but could stay only a few minutes, he needs to arrange leave from the bank to be with Enid for a couple of days."

"I'm so pleased for you Mr.Eddowes," said Annie.

His expression showed surprise. "You are a grandfather now." Annie's voice held genuine delight.

Saul smiled, "A grandfather," he said, "yes Annie, of course, now I am a grandfather."

"We have made four gowns for the baby haven't we Edna?"

Edna still with a mouthful of bread and dripping, nodded agreement.

"We'll wrap them and when you go to see Enid you can give them to her," said Annie eagerly.

"I think it would be a good thing if you and Edna took them yourselves. Give Enid a few days to recover her strength and then, one afternoon, you can both leave the workshop earlier than usual to visit her."

The mood in the workshop was light. Annie looked forward to seeing the baby, Edna was saying nothing yet but she hoped when the day came, Annie might be happy to go alone, an opportunity to meet with Billy earlier in the evening Edna considered a much better prospect than Enid Eddowes, baby or no baby. Saul, in spite of showing age and weariness, moved about his office with an easy tread.

It was soon time for Annie to make her way to May's with the cloth, she tried to run a few yards where she could, the light was now quite poor when she left May and a quicker time there gave her chance to leave sooner. She had been relieved yesterday as the fog advanced, not to be due at May's, Peverell Street in fog or darkness would be a daunting place even for Annie. Her hastened pace helped warm her, the winter air now confirmed its arrival by the vapour which danced ahead of her breath.

"I'm sure it must feel draughty there Shawcross." She stopped by the gate and smoothed his head, he has intelligent eyes she thought to herself. In her pocket she had a soft mint. "Here you are, this will make you feel all nice and warm inside." The dog took the small sweet from Annie's fingers with such delicacy. "You're a big softy aren't you Shawcross?" She said.

As she walked on to No.28 she daydreamed, perhaps she and Harold would have a dog, something between Eli and Shawcross. The thought made her laugh, little Eli alongside big Shawcross. People used to laugh at the Waterfords when they first took over the hardware shop. Liza Waterford was an enormous woman, tall as well as broad, yet Calib could scarce see over the counter and Mrs.Marsh from the house next door claimed he wore schoolboys' nightshirts, she could read the labels when they hung on the clothes line. It was Wednesday so the tubman was doing his round, it appeared that he had nearly finished. Annie supposed he now started earlier to allow for the fading light of winter. If the fog had decided to veil Peverell Street today it would be unbearable thought Annie. The present combination of tannery and tubbery could at least be persuaded to disperse by the determined wind which teased her hat and carried a crumpled paper swiftly past her skirts and down the street, where she could see it clinging to the bottom of a gutter pipe. May, Alfred and Mabel were in good heart, Grace however clung to life rather like the crumpled paper outside in the street, when fate decided, both in turn would lose their grip.

Annie told them of Charles' and Enid's good news. "I have made something for the baby," said May, "over the months quite a few off-cuts have gathered, I had some narrow lace upstairs, left over from the children's christening robe. I managed to find it although it has been packed away for years. It is only big enough for a Moses basket but the remnants have made a nice little quilt."

Annie had no idea May was sewing for the baby, she hadn't suggested it as she felt May had quite enough to do.

"The quilt is beautiful," said Annie, "look Mabel, see what your mam has made."

Mabel's little fingers explored the surface of the material, "Pretty, I like this bit," she said holding her finger very carefully over a strip of lace.

"When you grow up into a lady, I shall make for you the prettiest gown you have ever seen. It shall have rows and rows of lovely lace, satin ribbons and pearl buttons. Mabel shall look like a Queen."

Annie tickled her tiny waist and the child chuckled with glee. "If you feel in my pocket," said Annie, "you might find something nice".

Annie swivelled about to position the pocket in front of Mabel and the eager little hand delved in. With a triumphant cry of delight she held aloft an orange. "Now," said Annie, "If you feel into my other pocket you will find something nice for your Alfred."

In went the hand once more with the speed of a shuttle across the loom. Annie had picked the reddest apple she could find. The motion as she walked had rolled the apple from side to side in her pocket, now it emerged in Mabel's hand, so highly polished that it glowed. The child's eyes sparkled with excitement at her prize.

"Now I think it would be a good idea if you shared your orange with Alfred and he shared his apple with you, that way you each have two treats," said Annie.

Mabel agreed the transaction and placed the fruit on the table to await Alfred's return from the shop where he had been sent to buy three bundles of kindlers.

Alfred senior continued to improve a little and appeared with more coal for the fire, his face now bearing sufficient flesh to enable his smile to grow without depriving his cheeks.

"'Tis getting nippy out there now Annie," he said, "will you have a cup of hot before you go?"

"Oh no thank you Alfred," replied Annie, "I shall get back to the workshop as quickly as I can, if Mr.Eddowes remembers to put some logs on the stove it will be warm in the workshop. Edna will probably stoke it before she leaves."

Annie had the shirts and quilt under her arm, she pulled up her collar around her neck and travelled up the street with urgency.

Shawcross had obviously adopted his evening position, he lay full length with his abundant chins resting over his big front paws, he raised his eyes to Annie and made a low, lazy grunt. She felt quite convinced that his communication was no other than, "good evening Miss Bundy". Annie responded accordingly and called out to him, "likewise to you good friend", but she did not slow her pace, anxious to reach Winchester Street before dusk.

The workshop lamps cast shafts of light across the cobbles. Annie opened the door, the smell of wood smoke greeted her, it was a good, safe feeling as she closed the door behind her and taking off her hat and coat she felt a gentle warmth inside the room. The old pot-bellied stove in the corner had been a silent observer of the proceedings ever since Annie began her work at Saul's. In fact, she had stood only an inch or two taller than the stove in those days.

"How is May?" Asked Saul from his chair in the office.

Annie crossed the floor to his doorway, the package in her hands, she paused, "Come in Annie," he said.

"Dear May has made something for your little grandson, look," her fingers worked quickly to unwrap the quilt. She spread it carefully at one end of his desk. Saul checked his fingers for ink and satisfied they held no threat to May's work, just as Mabel had done, he passed his hand over the linen cloth and brought his fingers to rest on the fine lace. He did not speak, his concentration was so deep Annie felt he had lost all awareness of her presence.

"Hilda had this pattern of lace on her wedding dress." His words held a sadness. Annie put her hand gently on his arm.

"Then what a wonderful thing it is that the baby will sleep with something of his grandmother to keep him warm."

Saul lifted his face to Annie, "Are you happy Annie?"

His question took her by surprise.

"Harold has asked me to marry him in the spring, he makes me very happy, I have said yes but I am all the company aunt Bella has. She does like Harold, they chat together about all manner of things and I would see her every day."

"Bella Pownall is the strongest woman I have ever known, and the finest, she will want only what is best for you Annie. If Bella believes Harold worthy of you then you have no cause to fret. Talk with her, as we grow older we need to know that everything is in order. Some mistakes we cannot rectify but the desire to feel that we are understood at the last becomes the force which drives us. Enough of work today Annie, go home. I shall lock up and go home too."

Saul looked very tired, Annie felt they had allowed each other a rare confidence to hold in trust.

"Goodnight Mr.Eddowes," she said as she pulled up her collar to face the outdoors. "Don't forget to close the damper on the stove, God bless."

Saul sat back in his chair. Annie had pulled the door to firmly behind her and the sound of the heavy latch echoed around the empty workshop, it stirred his memory.

All those years ago a door had closed on his plans abruptly but almost immediately another had opened. In his selfish feeble way he had crossed the threshold without a backward glance. A messenger had delivered to him an envelope from Braithwaite's Bank. He could recall the text exactly.

Dear Mr.Eddowes,

I believe it would be in your best interests to attend

a meeting at my office tomorrow at 9.30 am.

It was signed Jack Braithwaite.

Saul had been shown into the office to find Jack Braithwaite and Nathan Wright, the latter looked awkward as though he would have preferred not to be there.

"We understand you are a free agent, no family ties," said Jack.

Saul recognised the inference, how quickly news travels he had thought to himself.

"It is well known that you are an ambitious man Mr.Eddowes, with a good eye to business." Jack Braithwaite spoke only, Nathan Wright listened but made no comment.

"We have a business proposition to put to you, it is of a somewhat delicate nature and your discretion in this matter is crucial if the immense financial benefit offered is to be yours. We will pay you a very considerable sum of money which will enable you to establish and expand your business if you will agree to marry my daughter Hilda within two months."

Saul had been bewildered and his initial response had been to laugh but their expressions had remained totally sober.

"You wish to make your mark on this city Saul. If you are a man able to keep his silence and honour an agreement, then we will provide sufficient funds for your future success. My daughter is with child."

Saul had automatically cast his gaze at Nathan, he however remained silent.

"Marry Hilda, accept the child as your own, never speak of this to anyone and we will pay money into your account regularly throughout the next ten years. Fail to honour the agreement at any time and we will withdraw funding immediately."

Jack Braithwaite knew of Saul's selfishness, indeed he was relying upon it to dominate Saul's thinking and influence his decision.

The bank's face was saved, Nathan's adultery had escaped public knowledge, Hilda raised no objection. From the day she had confessed her condition to poor Constance, all Hilda had pleaded for was her baby. She had vowed to her parents and to God to be a good wife, for herself she had sought only one thing, motherhood. Constance and Jack had decided that to prevent all scandal the marriage ceremony must take place in Church as would be expected of the family. The good Lord would know their torment and in his mercy would surely forgive their sin. Saul and Hilda were married at St. Saviours on the 4th day of May 1881, so it was done.

Saul took the quilt from his desk and wrapped it, just as the years had wrapped his dreams. He closed the damper on the stove, took his coat down from the hook, picked up his cane, put out the lamps and locked the door on Saul Eddowes' 'great success'. He had kept his silence, honoured the agreement with credit to spare but would he be understood at the last? Saul made his way home, alone, very alone.

CHAPTER NINE

"The baby is a week old today," said Annie as she and Edna left the workshop with the parcel of gowns and May's quilt. They had turned into Sherwood Road when Edna declared,.

"Yer don't need me to go with yer Annie, Enid's sure to be findin' things difficult, babies bring a lot o' work, she'll be glad it's just you, she probably don't feel up to many callers yet."

"Oh, but I think you should come, Saul will be expecting you to," replied Annie.

"He won't know, Enid won't say anythin' she'll be too occupied persuadin' grandad to buy the kid a pram, besides, Billy says they're havin' a big bonfire down 'The Meadows' tonight, if I get 'ome early I can help mam with the chores and meet Billy, they're havin' fireworks an'all."

"I see, so that's what you are up to, well if Saul finds out you will have to own up 'cause I won't tell fibs for you."

Annie tried to sound vexed but she had to smile at Edna's attempt at being devious. A simple honesty dwelt within Edna, she could never master the complexities of subterfuge. It was easy logic in Edna's mind, she loved Billy, she did not love Enid and that was that. Annie began to laugh, the happy Edna had skipped along a few yards and now turned around to look back at Annie. In a moment of mischief she made like she was pushing a pram, Edna put her nose in the air and in a very 'lar-de-dar' voice called out.

"There, there, my precious, we shall return to the big house to see your dearest papa!" Then she blew a kiss to Annie and was gone.

Annie was still chuckling to herself as she walked past The Standard. She had not been to Charles' house before, she knew where it was but no errand in the past had taken her there. Annie walked around to the back door, nappies hung on the line across the yard, a bucket outside the privy door held more of the same but at the soaking stage. Perhaps Edna was right after all, Enid wouldn't be wanting callers. She knocked gently, not wishing to disturb the baby, she could hear no crying so thought the child to be sleeping. Enid opened the door looking a little perplexed.

"Yes," she said sharply.

"It's Annie from the workshop, I have something for the baby."

For a moment Annie felt Enid would take the parcel from her and close the door but Enid's tiredness and sense of insecurity clutched at Annie.

"You'd better come in a minute," she said.

The living room certainly displayed much evidence of a new baby, garments hung from the backs of chairs, the table still held dishes from a meal and laying open at one end of the table a large book revealed its subject through an illustration of an infant having a change of nappy.

Enid's hair was barely contained by the pins and her cheeks, normally blushed by a light application of rouge, now appeared pale and wan. In the corner resting on two chairs positioned side by side lay a Moses basket.

"May I look at the baby?" Asked Annie.

"You can have him if you like," said Enid despairingly, "he's only just gone off, all he wants to do is feed, my breasts are like udders, I haven't had a chance to do my hair, look at me."

Enid was close to tears. Annie peeped quickly into the basket, turned back to Enid and said.

"Lets see what we can do whilst he sleeps, go upstairs and fetch your brush and combs."

Annie cleared the dishes into the scullery, folded the clothes and put them into a pile at the side of the book.

"Now sit on this chair," she said to Enid.

Annie removed all the loose pins and brushed Enid's hair until it fell free of tangles, she pinned it up and fixed the combs.

"Open the parcel whilst I make us some tea," she said.

Annie could hear the rustle of paper as Enid undid the wrapping. Annie stirred the coals in the grate and put the kettle over the flames. The nappies on the line outside felt quite dry so she took them down and lay them to air over the arm of the fireside chair. The kettle soon boiled, Annie put a pot of tea to brew then poured the remaining boiled water into the enamel bowl on the scullery table, the dishes now soaking, she poured two cups of tea and put one in Enid's hand.

"What did you have for your dinner?" asked Annie.

"I haven't eaten since porridge this morning," replied Enid, "but I shall have to make a small meal for Charles later, I'll have something then."

Annie disappeared into the scullery and returned with a plate of bread and cheese, "You must have something or you won't make milk, eat this for now."

"I don't want to make milk, I want to be human again," said Enid, "I want a tiny waist, a flat belly and breasts which look normal."

Annie began to laugh, she had taken her cup of tea to the scullery and sipped it between washing the dishes. After a few minutes she returned to the living room to admire the baby.

"What have you called him Enid?" She asked.

"William" said Enid, "William Charles Eddowes."

"That's a good strong name for a man," said Annie, "is William your father's name?"

Enid's demeanour changed instantly. "No," she replied. Nothing more, just that one stern word.

Young William's cheeks were fleshy and full, his hands lay back at either side of his face, the little palms pink and wrinkled. Annie thought the child beautiful.

"I'd better be going," she said. Just at that moment the latch lifted and Charles entered the scullery. "Hello Mr.Eddowes," said Annie, "I am just about to leave."

His arrival had made her anxious. "You have a lovely little boy." She hesitated, "I think perhaps his mother is feeling tired."

Charles' response surprised her, "I have told her to let Bertha Duffin help more, you tell her Annie, she might listen to you." He gave her a smile before crossing the room to look at his son, the pride and pleasure in his face transformed his usual cold expression to one of refreshing warmth.

"Don't wake him," said Enid, her voice was tetchy, "my nipples are only just hanging on, they'll disappear down your son's throat if he sucks much harder. Bertha is coming tomorrow, she's spent the last two days looking after somebody's old mother." Enid's tone was almost scornful, Annie however felt a great respect for this Bertha. She was not acquainted with her but the ability and furthermore the inclination to look after old mothers and young mothers must surely be to her credit. Annie picked her coat from the hook on the scullery door.

"Look what Annie has brought," said Enid and held up the gowns for Charles to see.

Annie looked at Charles and said "May has made the quilt for you."

"They are all lovely Annie," said Charles, "thank you, give our thanks to May and Edna too."

He seemed changed, in the past Annie, at times, had felt him to be almost hostile as though he considered Edna and herself to be lesser mortals, worthy of only scant recognition. If William at just one week of age could influence his father so significantly then perhaps it augured well for the family. Annie thought of Saul, Charles' visits to the workshop, Enid's wants. As she walked away from the house the sound of a baby's cry filtered through the aged sash windows. Poor Enid, tired and fraught, but Bertha Duffin would no doubt rescue her tomorrow.

Now Annie would hurry home to tell aunt Bella all about William, for he had certainly made his mark. It seemed hard to imagine that such a tiny human being could change a household so much.

Bella sat quietly watching a pan of potatoes cooking over the fire. Some brussels sprouts, leeks and carrots sat on the scullery table.

"I've just come from Enid Eddowes' house," said Annie, "I took the gowns we made for the baby, he was asleep but I saw him in his basket, he has plenty of hair, a lovely plump face and strong hands. Enid looked tired but someone called Bertha Duffin is going there to help tomorrow. Charles arrived just as I was leaving, I could tell he is delighted by his little boy, they have called him William. I do believe the infant has brought a change to Charles' nature, he seemed softer, more gentle. Enid is pining for a slender figure but I think her weariness will soon pass and then she will find nothing but pleasure in her baby and concern for herself will fade. I'm sure Saul will enjoy the child too, he has been low in spirits ever since Mrs.Eddowes died, this will cheer him don't you think Aunt Bella?"

"For every birth there is a death," said Bella not taking her eyes from the fire.

"But it has been more than three years since Charles' mother died," said Annie, trying to hold on to the present happiness.

Bella turned her face to Annie, "Nobby came today, he was in Peverell Street this morning, Grace Hickling died in the night."

"Oh poor May, I should go there," cried Annie worriedly.

"Leave them be tonight, you will go tomorrow as usual, familiar routine is what will get May through the coming days. They will need practical help more than soft words, she still has to feed the living, there is nothing more she can do for the dead."

Bella's words seemed cold and harsh. Annie wanted desperately to run to Peverell Street and hold May and Mabel, to comfort them but Bella's mood was severe, it would not do to cross her.

Their meal passed in quietness, both were subdued, Annie had forced herself to eat just a little, afraid to vex aunt Bella. She cleared away the dishes, the coal bucket needed to be filled, as she opened the back door the sound of fireworks made Annie shudder. Edna, Billy and many others would be down The Meadows having fun, while just a short distance away, May and her family were facing the worst of times. Bella was silent, she sat in her chair by the fire. Annie sensed Bella's mind was elsewhere, she gazed into the grate as though it were a stage, the flickering flames playing out a scene of drama, the darker coals portraying tragedy, the ashes and debris which littered the hearth representing the sad remains of what used to be.

Bella's thoughts had taken her back to Lenton. After Sefton had left she and Ruby had resumed their work at the Hemsleys but the events of that dreadful night were to dominate the following winter. Ruby took a chill and despite Clarice nourishing her with beef tea and malted milk, Ruby's appetite became feeble. She had no strength, the walk to 'The Park' and her duties could be no longer. The Hemsleys had been good kind people, Bella could not lie to them, she must tell them the truth and trust their understanding would not diminish. So Ruby began her confinement, cared for by her mother with the greatest love. Bella worked hard adding some domestic duties to her employment in order to bring into the household sufficient funds to support them and to prepare for the baby. The weather had been very unkind but Bella told herself the worst of winter would soon be behind them, it was now February, a shorter month. There had been a light snowfall, but the frost of the previous night had barely lifted, now the street stretched treacherously ahead of her. Each step cautious, hampered by the slippery surface she was relieved to turn into their own yard. It had taken her longer than usual to reach home but at least she had done so without falling. Clarice heard the latch, she had been listening from the top of the stairs, afraid to leave Ruby alone even for a minute, pacing from bed to landing and back again constantly over the previous ten minutes, waiting for Bella's arrival. Clarice called out, her tone revealed her distress. Bella kicked the snow from her boots, cast her hat and coat across the scullery table and hurried up to her mother. Ruby lay on the bed, her face flushed, she murmured words too faint to be audible.

"The baby has started, it shouldn't be yet" said Clarice, "I know it's early, she can't eat, even drinking is taxing her, I'm sure she's feverish, God help us Bella, she'll be too weak to stand the pain soon, let alone bear the child."

Clarice lost her breath through panic, her eyes filled with tears. Bella felt Ruby's head and held one hand.

She knew right away what she must do, "Mother, I have to fetch the doctor, I shall be as quick as I can, sit with Ruby, stay with her, rub her hands, talk to her."

Bella near flew down the stairs, she could not leave the fire without coals, the house had to be warm this night. She tipped the contents of the bucket into the grate and put on her hat and coat, she would refill the pail later but now she must conquer the weather and bring help to Ruby. Placing her feet on the clean snow enabled her the best grip, the hollows she had made just a few minutes earlier as she walked home, now felt crisp and icy. Bella stayed close to the walls of the houses as she made her way up the street. Others, negotiating the perilous conditions paused to catch their breath and spoke of their progress from whichever direction they had begun but Bella, intent on her mission, gave them little response. Every moment was vital, the night was dark, if a curtain allowed a narrow shaft of light to escape a house its illumination, however slight offered the chance of a safer tread. Bella wasted no opportunity to hasten her pace.

Eventually she turned the corner of Cromwell Street. The doctor's house was half way along, please God let him be there thought Bella. She rang the old brass bell that hung from a bracket by the front door, in her anxiety she lifted the heavy lion's head to knock, just for good measure but her fingers were so numb with the cold that her first attempt failed, she tried again and this time her driven strength created such a pounding blow that inside the house it sounded like gunfire. She could hear footsteps, a middle aged woman opened the door and flinched violently at the icy blast which engulfed her. Bella spoke as clearly as she could, chill and emotion challenged her ability to deliver the words. The woman called out to someone in a room beside her, the doctor appeared. He looked briefly toward Bella, donned a thick coat, picked up a bag, turned to the woman who was obviously his wife and said.

"Don't wait up, I shall be some time, if anyone else calls direct them to young Dr. Twomey. Now young lady, I heard what you said, no need to repeat it, keep your mouth closed to repel the chill, stay close to me."

Their steps held firm and by some miracle they reached the yard without incident. Bella opened the door and felt relieved at the temperature within, she took the doctor's coat and directed him upstairs. Whilst she still had her top clothes on she filled the coal bucket, made good the fire and placed a large pan of water over the heat. Bella could hear her mother's tired voice as she made her way to Ruby's bedroom. The doctor sat on the side of Ruby's bed, within seconds Ruby's frail body contorted with pain and her cry grew agonised.

"Has Ruby taken anything to drink?" He asked Clarice.

"I have tried to put water past her lips but she swallows scarcely any," she replied, her shoulders shook from fear and fatigue. The pain came again and Ruby searched for her mother's hand.

The doctor lowered his face to Ruby's and with the gentlest of voices told her that her baby wanted to enter the world.

"We are all here Ruby, don't be afraid."

Bella had brought some clean towels, he took the largest, folded it double and lay it on the bed underneath Ruby's bottom, lifting her was effortless, Bella could tell he was alarmed by her frailty.

"You are to be a mother Ruby," he said, "when the pain comes, squeeze your mother's hand and push down to help your baby."

She did not complain but every effort seemed to take a little more of her away. Her cries became weaker but at last her baby girl was born. A very small, early baby, covered in the 'soft cheese' like substance which is indicative of premature birth. The doctor worked quickly, he made safe the cord, wrapped the infant in a soft sheet and blanket, "Miss Pownall, I need you to sterilise this bottle and teat. You have some fresh milk in the house?"

It was an anxious question. "Yes, we have fresh milk," said Bella.

"Fill a clean bowl with boiled water, immerse the bottle and teat whilst you rinse a small pan with boiling water. Heat just a small cupful of milk to tepid, when the milk is warm enough pour it into the feeding bottle."

Bella had just completed her task when the doctor appeared at the foot of the stairs with the baby in his arms. Tiny as she was, her strength of lungs produced a demanding cry. He indicated to Bella to sit by the fire.

"Put the teat to her mouth, pray to God she will suckle."

Bella could not hear a sound from upstairs.

"I need to go to your mother," he said.

Bella looked at him, not in hope, she knew that Ruby was gone, but for confirmation it was so, he nodded. Bella's tears fell over the baby but undaunted the little mouth pursed tightly around the teat and sucked the warm milk. Bella remembered the story of an orphaned baby in a book she had read some years before, 'Orphan Annie'. As she looked down at the remarkable bundle in her arms she whispered, "Hello little Annie, aunt Bella will keep you safe."

That night when she and Ruby had walked home from the Hemsleys and Ruby had declared 'I haven't bled', Bella had wiped her eyes and promised 'I will make everything alright'. Bella now held that promise in her arms and while she lived and breathed she would keep Annie safe.

The doctor lead Clarice downstairs, she had cried herself to exhaustion, he pulled a chair to the fire and lowered her to it, the kettle was hot on the trivet.

"Hold your grandchild Mrs.Pownall, I need Bella's help for a few minutes."

They washed Ruby and put on a clean nightgown, Bella brushed her hair and pinned it, they lay her on clean bedding.

"I shall wash the baby now," said the doctor, "down by the fire in the warmth, make some tea Bella give a cup to your mother, put sugar in it, see that she drinks it all. Who can help you?"

"I work for the Hemsleys in The Park, if you could get word to them I would be very grateful, I believe Alice Hemsley would come to see mother, perhaps you could ask her to bring some fresh milk."

"We need to inform an undertaker Bella," he said softly.

"Yes, could you ask Mr.Gilbert to come?" Bella was calm, her mind had to be ordered, her mother was in no fit state to act, Bella herself must do whatever became necessary. The doctor gathered up his bag and donned his coat, as Bella opened the door to see him out he said in a low voice, so as not to alarm Clarice.

"The infant is very small Bella and I fear undernourished due to Ruby's poor health, she will need feeding frequently, at least every two hours and if she demands it, then even more often. If she survives then in my experience you will find she thrives quickly, her strength will become evident, but you must be prepared for the possibility that will not be the case. I will call on the Hemsleys first thing in the morning and inform Mr.Gilbert also. I shall return to see you sometime tomorrow afternoon, indeed it is almost tomorrow already. Persuade your mother to take some rest."

With that he was gone into the darkness, Bella could hear his tread on the icy ground growing fainter, she closed the door quickly to keep in the warmth. The few hours between that moment and the morning light were so charged with emotion that even Bella found the arrival of Alice Hemsley a relief which reduced her legs to jelly. Mr.Gilbert had already been to the house and was to return late morning. Bella needed someone to bolster her resolve, the weight of responsibility seemed so great, in her tiredness she had begun to doubt herself. Alice Hemsley proved to be a 'stay' and support. Outside the temperature had risen above freezing and the snow and ice was now transformed to a grey slush which displayed no real urgency to leave the yard.

Alice asked the carriage driver to bring two large cases into the house, then she instructed him to return for her in one hour. She had crossed the room immediately to look at Annie in her basket, with a voice quite steady she said, "You have a beautiful granddaughter Mrs.Pownall."

Clarice sat by the hearth, too overcome by the events of the previous night to respond. Alice knelt in front of her, took both hands in her own and said without waver.

"We live through our children, Ruby lives within this child." Then she opened one of the cases, "Come Bella," she said "we must organise life for *young Annie." She produced gowns, bonnets, sheets, blankets, nappies and all manner of items for the baby's needs. "I have kept these all this time, I just knew that one day someone would tell me I had not been a foolish sentimental old woman."*

Then the second case, which still sat on the scullery table, she opened to reveal, bread, butter, eggs, flour, jam - so much food. From the floor by the back door, where she had carefully placed it when she arrived, she lifted up a bag and took from it the precious milk.

"It is fresh this morning, I got it on the way here, Mr.Smithers was very kind. I sterilised some empty bottles at home and asked him to pour the milk into those. I have kept a clean cloth over the tops and they have travelled safely so the milk is quite pure. Doctor Young stressed the importance of clean fresh milk. "Now Bella," she lowered her voice but the nature of it remained firm, "What about funeral arrangements? If you need any sort of help, then say so."

At that moment Bella felt Alice Hemsley must have been despatched by God Himself, she answered as only Bella could.

"I am so grateful to you for coming and bringing milk. I shall pay you for everything and I have spoken with Mr.Gilbert, I believe we will be in a position to settle his account, it will be a simple burial. However, there will in due course be a bill from Dr.Young. I trust he will agree to my paying over a period of a few weeks by instalments. After the funeral, if mother is able to care for Annie by day I shall return to my work and relieve mother when I come home in the evening, we must establish a routine and be positive in our thinking."

Alice Hemsley almost matched Bella in strength of character and with a degree of intent which surprised Bella declared.

"You teach my children their lessons and for that I pay you as is entirely proper, however, it is my earnest belief and indeed hope that we, as two women doing our best in this world, share a friendship above and beyond a mere business agreement. These things I bring are from friendship alone, if you are able to return to The Park for the children's lessons we shall all be

delighted, if I am to leave this house knowing that all we have is some cold financial contract then we shall all despair.

Recognising the stubbornness in each other, a smile came to their faces and the embrace which followed locked them in abiding friendship.

Annie defied all obstacles, premature birth, the cold temperatures, cows milk and over the course of the days she suckled and slept, oblivious to the doctor's concerns and mercifully oblivious to the funeral of her mother. Bella had managed to convince Clarice that the weather posed too great a threat, Annie's grandma must stay and look after her whilst Bella and Alice Hemsley lay Ruby to rest. The cemetery was bitter, the grey sky determined itself to hold back any attempt by the sun to oppose its dominance. The two women stood in silence as Ruby's plain coffin was lowered into the earth. It was not the cold wind stinging their faces that delivered their pain, nor the icy ground on which they stood that chilled their feet 'til their toes burned, it was the desolation of heart and soul which so drove their hurt. Without Alice, Bella would have faltered and were it not for Bella's courage Alice would have lost her hold. They had lived through that moment by the strength of each other. Bella would never forget what Alice had done, she had not once brought tears and enfeebling pity, Alice had brought actual help and support.

There was a sudden thud, Bella looked up from the fire, Annie had dropped the book she had been reading, it struck the slate fender as it fell.

"Are you alright Aunt Bella?" She asked. "You are very quiet."

Bella shivered, "I am tired and it is growing chill, I shall go up to bed now."

She paused at the foot of the stairs, "When you go to work in the morning, take a pot of apple jelly with you and the knuckle of bacon from the meat safe. Take them to May when you go with the cloth. Ask Saul if May might have more work, now Grace has gone she will have more time."

Bella disappeared up the stairs, Annie didn't understand Bella's detachment. Surely her aunt didn't think May would be concerned about her work at such a time. Annie made safe the fire, banking it up for the night. Whatever aunt Bella had seen in the flames was now gone. She put out the lamp, sighed and followed Bella to bed.

The following morning Annie had carried out her chores with urgency and left for the workshop with the bag of items for May. Saul had heard of Grace's death and told Annie to leave her machine at midday and go to Peverell Street a little earlier than usual. Edna knew nothing of May's loss until arriving at work, she had been looking forward to relating events at The Meadows but even Edna felt concern for May, her humorous report of bonfire night was pigeon holed until the gravity of the present time was passed.

Annie had covered the distance between the workshop and No.28 Peverell Street faster than at any time before. She knocked quietly at the door, Alfred senior answered.

"Come in Annie," he said.

May sat by the table with Mabel on her knee, that all comforting thumb firmly lodged in the child's mouth. Young Alfred sat in the corner, he held a length of twine which he wound round his wrist, then unwound it, over and over again, like some mechanical movement counting seconds as they passed into minutes. There was no evidence to suggest that the family had taken even the simplest of meals. Annie crossed to the scullery, she filled the kettle and put it over the coals. All the bread she could find was half a small loaf. Annie worked quickly, she sliced the bread as thinly as she could, there was a small amount of butter in a dish but the cold air of the scullery rendered it too hard to spread, the apple jelly alone would have to do. The kettle began to sing its readiness, she put some tea to brew and carried a plate of bread and fruit jelly to the table. Taking young Alfred's hand, she led him to a chair by May, she spoke quietly to his father.

"Alfred, you must make them eat, I will pour some hot tea."

Annie, with the gentlest of gestures, persuaded the little thumb to vacate Mabel's mouth and before it had chance to take up lodging once more she put a piece of bread with the sweet tasting apply jelly to Mabel's lips. She stroked the little girl's hair and whispered, "To please aunty Annie." Then she turned to young Alfred, "In a moment I shall need you to run an important errand for me Alfred so you must eat a little something if you are to be strong enough to go in this cold weather. Now May, aunt Bella says you must try her apple jelly and let her know if it is a good set."

With Annie's coaxing, she achieved to persuade them all to accept some nourishment. She took young Alfred to the scullery, pressed some coins into his hand and said, "Go to the shop, buy a loaf, some cheese and some potatoes, show the lady at the shop your money, she will give you as many potatoes as she can."

Annie cleared away the dishes and asked Mabel to crayon a picture for her to give to Mr.Eddowes' new baby.

"May, how will you manage the funeral?" Her words were kind but purposeful.

"I don't know Annie, we don't have anything by." She began to weep tears of desperation.

"We are so busy at the workshop with orders for Blackmore's School, if you could manage some extra work I know Mr.Eddowes would be grateful and it would take the pressure off Edna and me, you know how Oliver Blackmore becomes so annoyed if we don't have the uniforms ready on time."

Annie could not leave May and her family without hope. If all else failed then Saul must take some of her own wages to pay May. She instructed Alfred senior to boil potatoes and cut the bacon from the knuckle.

"See that you all have a hot meal this evening," she said, "you cannot bear grief if body and soul are starved Alfred."

Her words were firm and she delivered them with authority which reassured him. "I shall come again on Friday May and whichever day the burial takes place I shall go with you. It is too cold to risk Alfred taking bronchitis, he should stay here and distract the children. Grace would want you to think of them first, she has at last found her Joseph again, be pleased for her May, she has longed for him all these past months."

As Annie made her way back up the street she rehearsed the plea she would make to Saul, she felt nervous but her anxieties were as nothing alongside May's. "Hello Shawcross," his soft warm ears nodded back at her and as she stroked him, she felt a curious devotion to this peaceful creature. Always there ready to listen to her problems, never causing her alarm, just quietly present, a constant bystander to all life's events. She leaned over the gate and planted a kiss on his head. "Lots of love Shawcross," she said and hurried on up the street.

Later that afternoon when Edna had left the workshop, she knocked on the side of the open doorway to Saul's office.

"Come in Annie," he said, "how is May coping?"

Annie described the scene at No.28 and before her courage could retreat, she asked him if May might have extra work.

"I cannot give May extra work if it takes away from you and Edna. I know you would tell me to let May have your work if that were the only way but your aunt Bella is reliant on the income your work generates."

Saul was not without sympathy for May but he was after all running a business.

"Soon, people in the big houses will be preparing for Christmas, we could create some special things, festive table-cloths and napkins, yuletide stockings for children to hang by the hearth, warm wraps for the carol singers. We could persuade the outfitters on Castle Road to stock them, it would prove good business for them too. I'm quite sure such items would sell well. It isn't too late to take delivery of the fabric, we already have gold braids, we would need some dark green too and rich red felt."

Annie scarcely drew breath, her vision of the workshop with the increased productivity had been conveyed to Saul through her enthusiasm and confidence.

"Do you truly believe this Annie?" He asked, "Do you have sufficient commitment to make it all happen?"

"Oh yes, I really do, I would make it happen I promise," she said.

Her determination to achieve filled him with hope. He had failed to live even a small part of his ambitious dream, could Annie, this endearing young woman who had haunted his past grant him a ray of hope before he left this world? He could not deny her plea, May would be given extra work, he would order the necessary fabrics and Annie would oversee the production of the special Christmas items. Provided he offered an attractive price to Drew's outfitters, he felt confident they would agree to expand their variety of stock over the seasonal period. The plan lifted his spirits, new grandchild, new business, approaching new year, he found a feeling of contentment he had not experienced in a very long time, and so it was all agreed. Annie, without realising it had done as aunt Bella had said, given practical help, strengthened spirits, honoured the dead but nourished the living. It was another lesson taught her by Bella, one day she would recognise its worth but for now Annie was simply happy to have secured hope and support for May.

CHAPTER TEN

Annie took May's arm to steady her as they followed the pall-bearers along the path to a corner of the cemetery which Annie felt must have been set aside for families such as May's. It was on the highest ground at Witford. The wind searched every bone for marrow, the faces of both women, tinged with blue, stared at the granite and slate memorials which flanked them at either side. Annie recalled her history book, the offender, wrongly accused, made to walk to her doom surrounded by onlookers feeding themselves on her misery until their ghastly appetites were finally sated, when the axe man dealt his blow and the poor mortal was no more!

Annie tightened her grip around May, if Alfred had ventured here alive then he would most surely have very soon returned dead. The bleakest, harshest, greyest part of Witford hill cemetery was definitely kept for those people whose lives matched it the most. The authority obviously believed the people who dwelt in genteel surroundings, behind soft warm drapes could not bear this sentence. It was done.

"Come on May, we should get back to Alfred and the children."

Annie feared for May's health, she had such a slight frame and little had passed her lips. As they left the gates of the cemetery a familiar voice called from a carriage standing in the road. Edward Meade removed his hat and said "I'm to take you to the corner of Peverell Street Miss Bundy." He helped the two women into the carriage, Annie's expression asked the question for her, "Saul Eddowes Miss," said Meade.

They travelled quickly, a better colour now brought their faces back to life, their features again found movement, just a few minutes earlier, eyes, mouth, cheeks, all had been paralysed by cold and desolation. Now the shelter of the carriage, the earthy smell of the leather, the comforting rhythm of the horses hooves soon transported them to the corner. Meade pulled up and helped them down to the cobbles.

"Thank you Mr.Meade," said Annie, she lowered her voice, "Is there any ....," before she could complete the sentence he whispered back.

"No Miss, all done."

In Winchester Street Bella had sat watching the clock thinking of May and Annie, as the hand reached the two she pictured the scene but the characters had changed, her mind was back at Lenton.

After Ruby's funeral, Bella had resolved to bring routine to the home. Annie fed on the warm milk and slept until her next bottle was due, she had struggled her way into the world but now lay in her basket, causing little disturbance, opening her eyes to Bella and Clarice when they lifted her to them and taking the milk readily as if she knew each measure of nourishment gave life.

The clothes and food Alice Hemsley had brought reinforced Bella's will. Clarice loved the child dearly, she would cope by day but Bella must take over responsibility by night, and so the routine was established. Bella returned to her work in The Park plied almost daily with items from the kitchen which Alice Hemsley declared 'Will go to waste if you don't take them Bella and I cannot bear waste'. Dear Alice.

Bella had been feeling guilty, she had found little time to spend with Saul over the past few weeks. They had been courting for two years, he was so ambitious, so occupied by his schemes and plans that Bella felt he would not have missed her too badly but she always tried to help him with his paperwork and encourage his enthusiasm.

'We shall have factories and workshops throughout the Midlands Bella', he would say, 'Your bright mind and my head for business will create an empire, our children shall inherit a fortune'.

Bella would laugh and tease him, 'We have to marry and make babies first', she would tell him.

Almost four weeks had now passed since Ruby's death and Annie's birth. She had managed to spend some time with Saul on the last two

Sunday afternoons. He asked little about Annie but he was after all a man Bella told herself, she imagined it not unusual. One day they would marry and Annie would simply be a sister to their own offspring. Bella had been walking home with the Hemsley children's lesson books in her bag, along with the 'raggedy end' of boiled beef as Alice had described it. Her spirits had lifted with Annie's progress and the first brief signs of spring, she found herself humming the tune of a song Clarice sang to Annie when she put her to sleep. She would have a cup of tea with her mother then set about marking the lessons.

Bella lifted the latch on the door but it resisted her attempts at opening it. The latch was undone and it wasn't bolted but something prevented the door moving. She called out, if Clarice was upstairs then she wouldn't have heard movement below, Bella thought she could hear Annie murmuring, with more weight behind her effort she pushed her shoulder hard against the top of the door, it opened just enough to allow her to see her mother's hand and the dark blue wristband of Clarice's cardigan laying on the floor.

Bella cried out, "Mother, Mother," the hand had not moved. Annie now cried hungrily, Bella must fetch help.

Next door Stanley Copeland might be at home, he worked shifts. She rapped at his door with her knuckles 'til they stung with pain. Agnes Copeland came to the door with a comb and scissors in her hand.

"Why my dear Bella, whatever's the matter?" She asked.

"Is Mr.Copeland there, it's mother, she's collapsed behind the door."

"Yes dear, I was just cutting his hair, Stanley you're needed, make haste."

He appeared at the door with an inside out apron around his neck and shoulders.

"Please Mr.Copeland can you help me open the door." Bella led him across the yard, he pushed and like Bella could see the hand.

"I'm goin' to 'ave to put all me weight behind it lass," he said.

He managed to force a gap wide enough for Bella's small figure to pass through.

"Please Mr. Copeland can you get word to Dr Young?"

Stanley could hear Annie crying and Bella frantically begging her mother to wake.

"Don't worry lass, I'll fetch him right away."

Clarice did not respond, her hand and arm were flaccid. Bella took down the mirror which hung on the wall by the wash bowl and held it to her mother's nose and mouth, she felt barely warm. The mirror was clear, there was no breath. Annie's cries grew more demanding, Bella could see that Clarice had been about to warm some milk, the small pan sat on the table the jug of milk beside it, the feeding bottle had been removed from the bowl of boiled water where it lay between feeds. Thankfully there was fire in the grate, Bella poked at the coals to get some red and placed the pan over the heat.

She spoke to Annie, "Hush now, just wait one minute." The child was hungry, Bella poured the milk into the bottle, secured the teat and lifted Annie from her basket. She popped the teat into the desperate little mouth and quickly went through to the front of the house to unbolt the front door. Annie sucked the milk so fast Bella had to pull the bottle back.

"You'll be sick, and I've mother to see to, don't be so greedy." In her turmoil Bella addressed Annie as if she were at least ten years old.

"You need changing." Bella took a nappy from the pile on the table, with more haste than she would have believed possible, Bella cleaned the tiny pink bottom and wrapped it once more in a warm soft nappy. Annie's eyes had fixed on her as she did so, but the crying had stopped and the little hands brushed Bella's wrists as she fastened the pins.

"Please come, please come soon," Bella thought aloud.

She had not to wait long, as the voices approached the back door she called out, "Go to the front, I've undone the front door."

Dr. Young and Stanley Copeland walked through to the living room, Stanley held Bella's bag which she had dropped outside in her panic.

The doctor knelt beside Clarice and passed a look to Stanley which confirmed what Bella already knew.

"I'll fetch Agnes," said Stanley, the doctor nodded.

"I am so sorry Bella, the strain of the past few weeks must have taken a heavy toll. Whatever happened was very sudden I feel sure."

The doctor sat her on the fireside chair, Annie was still in her arms but already the tiny eyelids had closed and the infant slept peacefully. Agnes came into the room out of breath from rushing, she put her arm around Bella's shoulder.

"Just look at that little baby," she said, "bless 'er 'eart."

"Would you make a cup of tea for us all Mrs. Copeland?" The doctor asked. "It might be best if you made a pot at your house and brought it round."

Agnes cast her eyes to the scullery, "Oh yes, course it would, I won't be long." Agnes patted Bella's arm and left them.

"Bella, who do you want me to call to help you?" The doctor spoke softly.

"Saul Eddowes, he'll probably still be at his workshop on Bullwell Road, he's often there 'til quite late."

Bella could not hold them back any longer, the tears began to fall and her voice faltered, "Tell him it's urgent doctor, he's always so wrapped up in his work."

The doctor lifted Annie from her arms and laid her in the basket.

"The child has gained weight, she is much stronger than I dared hope." He placed the blanket lightly over Annie and smiled at her contentedness. "I will inform Mr. Gilbert. What of Alice Hemsley, would you like me to let her know?"

"I suppose you should," replied Bella, "otherwise she will wonder why I'm not at work in the morning, although Saul could call on her later. If it's not too much trouble doctor then perhaps you should tell her just in case."

Her sobs had eased and by the time Agnes arrived with a large pot of tea Bella was calm. The doctor quickly drank a small cup then picked up his bag to leave.

"I shall go now Bella and fetch some company for you, I'm sure

Mrs. Copeland will be here for a few minutes yet."

"Oh yes doctor," said Agnes, "I'll look after them, sip your tea now Bella, Stanley said to tell you if you need anythin' just you let him know, mind you tell that lass he said."

Agnes meant well but Bella wanted to be alone with Annie 'til Saul arrived. Eventually she persuaded Agnes to return to Stanley's haircut, she would be alright, Mr. Gilbert would likely be there at any minute. Indeed, the undertaker came as soon as Dr. Young informed him. Mr. Gilbert was usually so highly composed but the tragedies of this house had affected even him, he struggled to find words which he deemed appropriate in Bella's situation.

"Would you like us to carry your mother upstairs Miss Pownall, or would you rather we laid her in the chapel of rest?" His man stood in the doorway awaiting instruction.

Bella thought as quickly as she could, it would be easier on Saul if her mother's body lay at the Chapel, he or Alice Hemsley would take her there to see Clarice she felt sure. Mr. Gilbert and his man did what was necessary and left.

Still Saul had not come, more than an hour had passed before a knock came to the back door, Bella flew to the scullery to let him in. She had sat gazing into the fire consoling herself with the thought that as she and Annie were now alone, it would be entirely possible for her and Saul to marry. It would be sooner than they had planned but Annie was no bother and she could do his books and care for both him and Annie at the same time. Caring for Saul would be no hardship, Bella loved him sincerely, she understood his ambitions and saw his gentler side in a way few others did. She fell onto his chest and let her weary head lose all reality as she pulled the lapel of his top coat about her face. It smelled of machine oil, calico and French chalk, she wrapped herself in Saul's world for a few precious minutes until she must return to her own.

She led him into the living room, he made no move to look at Annie in spite of the child's gentle murmurs.

"I'm sorry about your mother Bella," he said, "but perhaps it is fate, sometimes these things are ordained to be."

"After mother's funeral," Bella paused and took his hand into hers, "we must be positive, mother and Ruby would want us to be strong and positive, I know we hadn't intended being wed just yet but we can begin your empire a little earlier." She squeezed his hand.

"You shall be my second in command," said Saul, "I will make you my Empress Bella." He kissed her.

"Annie will know the business too, as will all our children, I shall teach them well," declared Bella.

Saul pulled back his hand, "There will be no time for a baby yet, we must devote ourselves to building the business, then we shall think of children but not until then." Saul's words were stern.

"But what about Annie?" Bella's eyes crossed the room to the Moses basket on the chair in the corner.

"You'll have to place her with the authorities, she'll be cared for, she's not your responsibility Bella, an infant would be in the way of everything we have planned, best to get it over with sooner rather than later."

Bella stepped back from him. "I think that our plans do not coincide at all, I must have been mistaken." She walked to the back door and held it open for him.

"Don't be foolish Bella," he said.

"Goodbye Saul, leave now, the open door is letting out the warmth."

Her face set firm, her voice wavered not the slightest. He put on his hat and left. Bella slammed the door with such force it woke Annie.

The cries became hungry, Bella took the pan, the milk and feeding bottle. As she sat with the baby in her arms sucking the teat, listening to the gentle gurgling sounds Annie made as she swallowed, Bella spoke to her not as an infant but as if she were a solemn 'happening'.

"Always remember what you are. I believed God would be on my side but he is not, you are my sentence, Sefton Pownall knew God better than I after all."

The night was long but Bella now heard footsteps outside, it was still early but well light. Alice Hemsley stood at the back door, as she entered she squeezed Bella's hand, crossing to Annie's basket she spoke softly so not to wake her but clearly as to let Bella hear.

"Walter and myself are completely agreed he has far too much work, I barely see him most days and he is getting older after all, he needs to reduce his workload. He has told me to ask you most earnestly if you will please consider assisting him. He has a number of clients whose files are not too heavy to be sensibly transported, he would be eternally grateful if you would balance the books of these clients for him, whilst you are at home looking after Annie. He trusts your discretion totally and your capabilities, he knows, are as good as his own. Please say yes Bella, I would so much like to see more of my husband and you could make that happen."

Dear Alice, always there with a practical solution, Bella accepted the arrangement graciously.

"I need to ask a very big favour Alice," she said, "when it is mother's funeral I cannot leave Annie on her own, would you sit with her whilst I lay mother to rest?"

"Of course my dear," said Alice, "but you cannot possibly go alone to the cemetery, Walter shall go with you."

"No, leave the man at his work, I would rather be on my own, truly I would."

Alice knew Bella well enough to be quite sure that it was Bella's wish.

"Very well, I understand. I shall call again late tomorrow with some fresh milk, by then you may know when you need me to sit with Annie. Make a meal for yourself Bella, while she sleeps. I have put some things on the table in the scullery, they would only be wasted if you didn't have them, I cannot bear waste. The children send their love, I have told them you enabled them to live far too sheltered a life. I think we shall put them to attend Harrow Road School, it has a good reputation and the walk each day would grant them some fortitude. I do believe they need to be prepared for the harshness of this world Bella, I really do. I shall let myself out."

Alice pulled the door closed behind her and hurried across the yard and into the street to the waiting carriage before her tears could be seen by Bella.

The day of Clarice's funeral had broken clear but cold. Alice had arrived as agreed to sit with Annie.

Bella followed the pall-bearers, her eyes looking ahead, not turning to glance at anything around her but fixed on the coffin, she watched as they lowered Clarice's remains into the grave. Since Ruby's interment there had been just two other burials, Bella now looked from her sister to her mother with barely the width of a bed between the two and less than five weeks in time. She did not weep, she felt no chill, her entire being was numb. Bella Pownall had turned into impenetrable stone.

Alice heard the door, "Annie has taken her milk and gone straight back to sleep," she said as Bella entered the living room.

"Yes" replied Bella, "She always does."

"I have some hot soup on the hearth, my carriage won't be here for another half an hour, I think I shall have some, you'll take some with me won't you Bella?"

She carried two bowls and spoons to the table, Bella had answered neither yes nor no, she had removed her top clothes and stood quietly by Annie's basket. The two women drank the soup, Alice realised Bella's quietness was not maudlin, it was a dignified acceptance of what must be.

"I shall bring more files in a day or two Bella, if you need anything in the meantime then send word."

Alice blew a kiss into Annie's basket, squeezed Bella's arm and left them in peace.

The fire needed coal. Bella went to the shed to fill the bucket, built up the grate, scrubbed her hands clean and checked the feeding bottle lay in the *boiled water ready for the next use. Then she closed the scullery door, crossed to Annie and pulled the blanket lightly over the child's legs.*

"Orphan Annie," she spoke the words slowly, "orphan Bella, we are without family except for each other."

She sat at the end of the table where the light was best, took the top file from a stack of six, opened it and began her task. Bella was to balance the books of Hector Hargreaves, Candle maker.

There was a sudden rattle, Bella had been so deep in thought that she had forgotten the time. Annie's voice called out, "I'm home, ooh warmth." Annie took off her hat and rubbed her hands before the fire.

"It was so cold, there was no one else at the cemetery, just May and me. You couldn't imagine how awful it was Aunt Bella, but when we reached the cemetery gates Edward Meade was there, Saul had sent him to take us back to the corner of Peverell Street, wasn't that kind?"

Bella's eyes turned on Annie with such steel they cut like a blade. "The bucket needs filling." She rattled it against the grate to enforce the fact.

Annie's stomach turned and tumbled like the cart wheels that resisted being stilled on the sloping streets of Witford Hill. She took the pail and fought with the shed door and the old shovel. Why was everything such a battle? Why were aunt Bella's moods so extreme and unpredictable? Annie had tried so hard to understand, Bella's words could be so hurtful, too harsh, yet throughout the years it was only when Annie was with aunt Bella that she had felt truly safe. Now Harold wanted them to marry in the spring, she loved Harold very much, perhaps it was time to take a step back from Bella, some distance might enable her to see the reason for her aunt's difficult moods, perhaps she, Annie caused them.

Annie needed to find out what she was, who she was, it was time she did so.

CHAPTER ELEVEN

The workshop had become a hive of activity, Annie's plan had inspired everyone. Saul had organised the fabrics and May had been appointed yuletide stocking expert. Annie and Saul had agreed the templates which Annie had cut from card. Rich red and green felt, gold cord, had all been despatched to No.28 Peverell Street via Annie.

May had skilfully produced the stockings on her machine, the holly leaves Alfred senior cut from the green felt and when May had finished all the required stitching, Alfred completed the work by threading gold cord through the tops of the stockings to create a drawstring. Mabel had been filled with such excitement, her little being could not contain it all, she bubbled over with glee at the sight of each one.

Edna had been assigned the table-cloths and napkins.

'We should use a coarse red linen', Annie told Saul, 'If we border it with gold braid, the cloths will look very festive and the napkins need only be a plain red square. Even people from the big houses will limit what they spend on something they'll use for just two days a year, so richer materials would make the stock too expensive'.

Saul listened to Annie's reasoning, she was quite right, her quick mind and sound logic heartened him. The warm capes for the carol singers Annie herself would sew. She made pattern pieces from brown paper and cut the red felt to shape with virtually no waste of fabric by laying her pattern alternately up, then down along the length of material to produce sections of the cape which, when sewn together, fell full at the bottom and narrowed at the top to fit neatly around the neck. The bottom she decorated with rich green braid and the top fastened with a large hook and eye which, when in place, lay completely hidden by three green holly leaves sewn to one side of the cape at the neckline.

Edna was eager to model the first one Annie completed. Annie positioned the cape around Edna's shoulders and secured the hook and eye. Edna dashed across the room, took Saul's cane from the corner, hung her small hand bag from the top like a lantern, picked up a notepad from Annie's table, held it out like a songbook and burst into a dire rendition of 'God rest ye merry gentlemen' Annie could not resist Edna's mischief and laughed heartily.

From his office Saul called out, "What are you up to?"

He appeared at the door to the back room and at the sight of Edna joined in their unfettered laugher. It was a rare moment, Annie had seen Saul smile only seldom and free, open, laughter she could not ever recall witnessing.

A box of samples was now ready and Saul's task was to sell the new stock to Drew's on Castle Road. He had left Annie and Edna to pack the order for Blackmore's School, which thankfully was now complete and left the machines available for the Christmas items.

"What are you and Harold doin' at Christmas Annie?" Asked Edna.

Christmas as yet, felt a long way off, whilst Annie's thoughts had been engaged in creating increased work for them all and their sewing was very seasonal in its design, Christmas as it related to herself, had not entered her mind at all.

"I suppose I shall have dinner with aunt Bella and see Harold in the afternoon," said Annie.

"Well that's alright but you got to 'ave some fun as well, Billy says we might go down the embankment and watch the silly buggers swim across the river. 'Twas rumoured last year that Hannibal Burton took that long speachifyin' when 'e come out o' the water, that 'is costume froze to 'is 'John Thomas' and 'is missus 'ad to thaw it, ever so slow, over a candle flame else 'e'd 'ave lost it wi' frost bite. They reckon 'e's one o' the wealthiest men in the city, that store of 'is supplies all the nobs wi' their booze an' fancy meat an' game birds. I've 'eard me mam tell that 'is brother wer' born wi' out balls but 'e did well for 'isself, made money abroad, become a noble gent as the paper called 'im but mam said the paper got it wrong, it wer' s'posed to be 'no ball' gent."

Edna laughed wickedly and Annie, no longer shocked at anything Edna revealed, chuckled at the nonsense of it all.

It was an anxious time for Annie, the samples Saul had taken to Drew's were good, the women stitched well, the colours and designs were attractive but at the back of her mind she harboured a small doubt. It was getting too close to Christmas to take the samples around a wider area, the large houses in The Park presented the best possible market and Drew's outfitters enjoyed the patronage of most residing there.

Annie had visited Davina Wright very briefly a couple of times during the recent weeks, as she had been leaving at her last visit, Davina had made Annie promise to bring Harold soon. It was something she must arrange with him in coming days. The slaughter yard too had experienced an increase in activity as the butchers began to gather orders for the season. Harold and Billy had worked late twice in the previous week. Harold's head was filled with plans, the wedding, a home, 'We have to tell your family and aunt Bella', Annie had said.

'We shall tell them at Christmas', declared Harold. 'Mam will be all excited and father will be off sweepin' every chimney this side of Macclesfield to pay for a 'do'. That's what bothers me Annie, there are too many mouths to feed in our house for mam and dad to be thinking about that sort o' thing'.

Annie didn't want a 'do', all she wanted was to marry Harold, to go straight home, wherever that may be, there to begin the lifetime of Mr. and Mrs.Boucher. It was the reaction of aunt Bella which worried Annie. Bella's mood lightened noticeably in Harold's company, she enjoyed his lively chatter. Annie saw more evidence of a smile when Harold sat with Bella, studying some book which held his curiosity, endlessly seeking more knowledge through his questions which Bella answered with genuine pleasure. But a marriage, their marriage, would aunt Bella find pleasure in that?

At that moment the gate rattled and Saul opened the door with a look of satisfaction across his face. The box of samples was no longer under his arm.

"Better get sewing young ladies," he said, "Drew's want, 4 dozen stockings, 4 dozen table-cloths, 192 napkins and 3 dozen capes." He crossed to his office and then called back to them, "by the middle of next week!"

Even Edna had stayed late at her machine, Annie had delivered more cloth to May and now worked on the capes. At least the sewing was straight forward, not intricate as some of their commissioned work could be. The workshop was just comfortably warm, Saul was about his books. Edna decided she'd had enough festivity for one day and packed away her red linen and gold braid declaring herself to be that 'ungry she'd 'ave to stop at The Standard for a bag o' scratchin's. A comfortable quietness existed between Annie and Saul, each concentrated on their own task and found no reason to hinder the other's progress. There came a sound from outside, someone approached the door, it was Charles. His visits had become fewer, in fact it was the first one for which Annie had been present since the birth of the baby.

"Hello Annie," said Charles, "you look busy."

She smiled, "How is William?" Asked Annie.

"He's well, doing really well," replied Charles, "Why don't you come to see him, it would be good for Enid to have some company of her own age too, she has no young friends at all and the older women she mixes with, apart from Bertha, fill her head with notions of want."

Charles' remarks made Annie feel awkward but she thanked him and said, "I shall call on them soon, is Mrs.Duffin able to help Enid on some days?"

"Bertha is stoic, she listens to all Enid's woes with saintly patience."

Annie smiled to herself, recalling Enid's peevishness, she would visit as soon as she had chance.

Charles went to Saul in the office, their voices lowered and Annie turned her machine faster to make more sound immediately about her.

After a little while Charles bid his father goodnight and crossed the workshop to the door, he opened it, looked out into the street, then without turning his head to Annie said, "I shall tell Enid that you will call on her very soon."

Before Annie could reply he was gone, closing the door firmly behind him.

A further twenty minutes of sewing brought her to a sensible stage at which to finish for the evening. She busily packed away her work and covered her machine.

She called to Saul, "Shall I put more wood on the stove Mr.Eddowes, or will you be leaving soon too?"

She turned towards the office for his reply. Saul sat in his chair but with his head forward, gripping the arms of his chair tightly with both hands.

"What is it Mr.Eddowes, are you unwell?" Annie hurried to Saul's desk.

"No need to be troubled Annie, it is indigestion, probably ate dinner too late and too quickly, as we grow older I'm sure our stomachs have every right to protest any abuse of them. I wonder if Edna got her scratchings? You see, even at her youthful time of life the stomach complained."

Annie did feel troubled, he look strained, she hoped it might be entirely unrelated to Charles' visit but the coincidence weighted her thoughts.

"You go home Annie, Bella will be waiting, push the damper in on the stove, I won't need more warmth, we have had a busy day, I shall go home now too."

"If you are sure everything is alright," said Annie.

As she walked along Winchester Street Annie determined herself to call on Enid and William, she would make a special little yuletide stocking for the child, somehow she must do her best to reduce Enid's wants and lessen the pressure on Charles and Saul, for everyone's sake. She would visit Enid this coming Sunday and Davina the next.

The machines at the workshop hummed with perpetual motion and at No.28 May and Alfred produced the stockings between the all vital sewing of shirts. The shared activity and ready distraction worked wonders on May's household. Mabel found her joyful laughter once more, young Alfred did his errands with a will to enable his mother to stay at her machine. Alfred senior took on the role of cook, making sure his workforce was nourished to the very best of his ability. May however, was aware that in the new year, Mabel would begin lessons at the schoolhouse with her brother and she would have to return to the workshop. Whilst she could sew on into the night under the present arrangement she could not allow Annie to continue all the fetching and carrying or her late evening work at Saul's when the necessity for it had passed. May felt anxious for her husband, he had shown such improvement over the months since she had begun to work at home, she could only hope his spirits would hold when finding himself alone.

By the end of the week, Drew's order was almost finished, Annie would collect the stockings from May's on Monday whilst Edna sewed hooks and eyes onto the capes, then all could be pressed and packed ready for delivery to Castle Road. Annie had made one very small stocking for William, she wrapped it in soft paper and now had it tucked into her pocket as she set out to visit Enid. The morning was cold but dry, the chilling winds of the previous week had decided to take a rest on this Sunday morning. Annie inwardly hoped that Charles might be out, he was more pleasant of late but his presence still unsettled her. The nappies hung motionless on the line as Annie turned into the yard, two of the gowns she and Edna had made confirmed their usefulness as they lined up alongside the nappies. Annie knocked gently at the door, only a few seconds passed before it was opened by Enid dressed in a rather lavish robe, slippers on her feet, her hair tied back with a ribbon.

"Oh, I'm sorry have I come too early?" Said Annie.

Enid laughed sharply, "Depends what you consider early, my son thinks two o'clock in the morning isn't too early."

She made no attempt to stifle or hide a huge yawn. "Come in Annie, Edna, whichever one you are," said Enid rather rudely.

"I am Annie." She spoke the words as though underlining them for Enid's future reference. Charles stood in the living room looking embarrassed by Enid's lack of good manners. Annie went swiftly to a very large carriage sprung pram, easily large enough to accommodate two babies, expecting to see William lying within its grand dimensions.

"He's upstairs," said Enid, "performing his highly unusual act of sleeping. He is shortly to accompany his father on a walk to The Standard. The two men of the house can make themselves useful by fetching a basin of beef and ale pie for dinner."

Enid was in a strange mood and Annie sensed Charles' discomfort. With the boldness Annie could muster when circumstances so demanded, she looked to Enid and said.

"Why don't you and I take William for a walk, the air is cold but there is little wind, he will be quite warm enough in his pram, we could go to the arboretum, Charles may have to wait some time at The Standard. It might be a nice change for you Enid. Put on your clothes, I'll pin your hair if you like and we'll take some fresh air."

"Are you always so bossy? You are worse than Bertha." Enid almost scowled.

"For pity's sake Enid, Annie isn't being bossy, she's just trying to be friendly." Charles' voice held annoyance.

Enid took herself up the stairs giving Annie and Charles no hint of her intentions.

"Why don't you take the basin and go for the pie?" Annie said to Charles. If you come back past Arthur Sewell's he may have some bunches of chrysanthemums left in his pail. He puts flowers from his allotment outside every Sunday morning for the ladies to buy as they go down to decorate St. Andrews Church. Try to get a bunch for Enid, in fact you better go that way in case they are all gone when you return. I'll keep Enid company."

Annie cleared away the dishes that still sat on the table from breakfast and filled the coal bucket which had travelled as far as the scullery before being abandoned, forgotten, obviously not a task claimed readily by either Charles or Enid. Eventually Enid appeared, her hair was done, her outfit smart, her expression more amenable, in her arms she held William, still asleep.

"If we are going for a walk it better be now 'cause it won't be long before he demands to be fed and I won't get my tit out in the arboretum, not even to please you Annie, Edna, or whoever you are."

Annie had to lower her head to conceal her amusement, a smile had spread quite wilfully across her face, Enid was laying William in his pram so fortunately did not notice. As they walked the sun struck boldly at the cloud and for an hour held on to its dominance. The arboretum lacked the bright carpet of colour the summer flower beds displayed but the russet coloured ferns, the last yellowing leaves on the birch trees and the rich, glossy dark green foliage of the hollies combined to provide any who paused to look, a sight of mother nature's good will, her silent attendance on mankind. The two young women were so very different in their attitude, Enid constantly judging life about her, doubting sincerity, always seeking motive for any kindness shown. Annie believing in the wisdom of fate, accepting kindness for the simple act it was.

"Do you have a man Annie?" Asked Enid with no preamble to such a direct question.

"I have a very dear friend Harold," replied Annie.

"A dear friend, uhm, and what does your dear friend do?" Enid's tone was snide.

"He works at Josiah Toft's slaughter yard," said Annie.

"Dear God, he must carry the stench of blood under his fingernails."

"No, surprisingly even at his humble house they permit themselves the luxury of soap and water." If Annie sounded abrasive she didn't care. Of Enid's rudeness, she would tolerate only so much, Harold worked hard and honestly, he showed the greatest respect to Samuel and Sarah and cared for his brother and sisters. Enid would benefit greatly from any lesson taught her by Harold. Annie would not indulge her in this offensive behaviour. Enid fell quiet, seldom did anyone correct her.

"Bertha says I need to rein in my tongue 'cause it gallops ahead of my brain, is that what you think Annie?"

Annie was never less than truthful, "I think you are very fortunate to have such a loyal friend as Mrs.Duffin, only a true friend will remind us of our faults, a mere acquaintance will not concern themselves enough to bother."

"It's a bloody miracle he hasn't woken yet, I shall have to bring him to the arboretum more often," said Enid.

"Yes, you might even grow to enjoy yourself," said Annie.

The two began to laugh, an understanding now between them, they walked back to Enid's happily. Only when the pram stopped outside the back door did William stir.

"Are you coming in for a cuppa?" Asked Enid.

"I shall come in and put some coals on the fire, to save you having to scrub your hands before you feed him but then I must go. I shall see Harold after dinner. Oh, I almost forgot," Annie took the little stocking from her pocket, "this is for William to hang up at Christmas."

She tended the fire, washed her fingers in the scullery and called goodbye to Enid who sat feeding her son.

"Will you come again Annie?" Enid's words were sincere, she had learned that in Annie's company she needed no pretence, falsehood served no purpose.

"Alright, it won't be for a couple of weeks but I will come again, I promise."

Annie pulled the door closed behind her and hurried on her way. She had not walked far when Charles turned into the street carrying his dinner in a cloth, the corners knotted together as a handle and in the other hand two splendid bunches of chrysanthemums.

"The Church will be a little less colourful today Annie," he said.

"I'm sure the good Lord will be happy to see some of his glory displayed in your house Charles," said Annie, she paused briefly then with a mischievous wink told him to ask Enid if he might be allowed a look at her new stocking, the very latest design!

Annie walked on hastily leaving Charles to ponder the remark, Annie felt she had done her best with the morning. After dinner with aunt Bella she would join the usual Sunday afternoon happiness that filled Samuel and Sarah's home. That is just as our home shall be, Harold's and mine thought Annie as she daydreamed her way back to Winchester Street, somehow she would bring aunt Bella to know such joy too.

The week at the workshop went quickly. Annie had collected the stockings from May, all the items had been finished, checked carefully, pressed and packed ready for delivery. The flat iron had to take its heat from the old pot bellied stove which, on such occasions, required extra fuel. By the time all was done the warmth of the workshop gave a soothing effect and when Edward Meade knocked loudly at the door to gather the packages, Edna, who had supposedly begun to hand stitch the hem on a curtain, nearly fell off her stool. Annie smiled to herself, poor Edna, the extra work and her determination to see Billy had made her so tired she could hardly keep her eyes open. Saul had been impressed by the girls' willingness to complete the additional order alongside their routine tasks. In a gesture of gratitude he told them to enjoy a day off on Saturday.

"Rest and recover because next week we must put through all the drapes for Louisa Burton," he said.

"Wonder if the order includes a new bathin' costume for Hannibal," whispered Edna as Saul returned to his office, " 'is old one must 'ave gone in a hole where it got singed, we can't 'ave Louisa's Christmas present gettin' unwrapped at the embankment!"

"Do hush Edna" said Annie, "you really are too bad."

Both girls giggled as they worked but their minds had already started to plan their rare weekend off.

Harold had arrived at Bella's that Friday evening with his encyclopaedia, he and Bella had reached the E's and his fascination now lay with the Egyptians. Annie could happily spend hours reading her own book, listening to their debate and discussion. The time passed easily it seemed scarcely possible that the clock could be chiming ten.

Annie walked to the entry with Harold, "Do you have to work late tomorrow?" She asked, "only I promised Davina that I would call to see her and she wants so much for you to come too. I haven't to go to Saul's tomorrow, I hoped we might go together perhaps late in the afternoon."

"Can't resist me charms Annie, that's what 'tis, women fallin' at me feet, but I tell 'em all they'll just 'ave to find another 'cause I'm spoken for."

He gave her a saucy peck on the cheek, grinned widely then kissed her goodnight with the real love and tenderness with which he left her at every parting.

"Why don't you go see mam tomorrow, then when I get home I'll 'ave a quick wash and we'll go visit me latest admirer." He ran up to the corner, clutching his book, waved back, then was gone.

"Sit down for a minute," aunt Bella obviously had something important to say. Annie tried to perceive Bella's mood, it had been affable all evening and she could recall nothing happening to alter it.

"Has he spoken of marriage yet?" Asked Bella.

Annie was taken by surprise but could only respond truthfully. "Yes, Harold would like us to marry next spring."

She could feel herself trembling, her heart beat wildly, like the wayward pace of her machine at the workshop when the spool ran out of thread.

"Marry him, he's as good as you'll find." Then Bella rose from her chair. "His ambition is the right kind, he's driven to learn and know, not to want and have, don't lose him." Bella issued the statement as though she read it from a text book, her authority taken from factual account. "Bolt the door."

Annie sat motionless, unable to propel herself to the back door, listening to aunt Bella on the stairs, the bedroom door closed above her, she felt relieved yet bewildered. Perhaps she should thank the ancient Egyptians for her passage to a new world. Marry in the spring, the thought filled Annie with elation.

The following afternoon Annie and Sarah chattered contentedly. Nora and the younger girls had gone to the shops, lamp oil, dolly blue for the laundry, soda crystals for scrubbing the yard, 'Zeebo' for black leading the grate and a small bag of Tom Thumb drops to share if they all carried something home. Sarah had baked a dish of bread pudding and the spicy smell clung to every corner of the house. A piece of boiled brisket sat on a large plate alongside an apple pie, the steam from the hot fruit within making escape through a hole in the crisp golden pastry. Sarah took a bag of brown sugar from the shelf and sprinkled some over the pie crust.

"Put sugar on while it's pipin' hot and it sets to the pastry like caramel, the little 'ens love it," said Sarah, "mind you so do the big 'ens!" She laughed, as always the house held only good things, Annie felt not even Royalty dwelt amidst such delights.

Harold arrived home, "Pay day" he called out as he entered the kitchen with his beaming smile. He gave his mother a small packet then turned to Annie and handed her a small package too, "for both my girls," he said.

Sarah's voice sounded her pleasure, "How did you know I had none left?" She asked.

Harold winked at Annie, "Magic, magic Mam," he answered.

Sarah held up a sachet of chamomile, "I always rinse my hair in rainwater steeped with chamomile." She said, "It's my only indulgence."

Annie had opened her packet to reveal a tiny linen pouch containing rose petals, Harold lowered his voice, "for your underwear drawer," he said and blew her a kiss. Then he crossed to the scullery and put a bottle of stout on the shelf by the coat hooks, "that's for father when he gets home."

Harold's pleasure in giving was plain to see. Annie thought of Bella's words 'Don't lose him', she would follow aunt Bella's instruction in this as she had in all other things. Harold washed and changed hastily and by the time daylight had faded, he and Annie were turning into the gates of Davina's house. The wisteria, now bereft of its opulent blooms seemed much smaller, the leaves coating the border below, the woody, twisted stems entwining one another as they travelled up the stonework, like capillary veins which threaded randomly across skin when cold winter winds drove away the healthy complexion of summer. Ivy answered their knock at the door.

"Oh, stand inside Miss Annie out of the cold, I'll tell ma'am you are here."

Harold stuffed his cap into his pocket, from where they stood Harold and Annie heard Davina's excited response, she appeared alongside Ivy and left the young woman behind in her eagerness to reach her visitors.

"Oh my dears, I am so pleased to see you, come through to the fire, Ivy will take your coat Annie. Do sit, I had just been about to take my fourth sugared almond, bless you for coming, my boredom these long winter evenings shrinks my brain to a chestnut and spreads my hips to a fatted goose. There are so few distractions and root liquorice just doesn't comfort in the same way at all. Dear Harold, take that dish of almonds and hide it away but not until each of you has put some in your pocket."

Harold looked at Annie and grinned. He couldn't help thinking that although their backgrounds and lifestyles were very different, Davina Wright and his dear mam Sarah, given the chance, could be the best of friends, both bursting with affection and craving nothing more than to be wanted. He took a packet from his side pocket, Annie had no knowledge of it.

"I thought you might like this," he said and handed it to Davina. Although the room in which they sat contained numerous objects of decoration and ornament, Davina's face filled with wonder as her pale fingers smoothed the surface of a small festive candle, bound at its base with gold ribbon.

"I did a bit of shoppin' on me way home from work," he said, "all my ladies deserve something special." He winked at Annie.

Davina placed it carefully in a holder on the mantelpiece, she gazed at it for a good minute or more, her young company could have no way of knowing her thoughts. The pretty gifts, just small treats Nathan would bring home to her. 'You deserve something special Dee' he would say.

Annie could detect the tear in Davina's eye when she turned to Harold and said, "Thank you so much Harold, it is a very long time since I was given anything so special, I shall find more pleasure in it than you could ever imagine."

Harold very quickly brought laughter back to Davina's heart when, with a great, "phew, do you mind if I take my jacket off? 'Tis hot enough to melt feathers in 'ere!"

Ivy arrived with a tray of tea and sandwiches of baked ham.

"I expect you are getting busier at Mr.Toft's, this time of year must surely bring extra demand for meat," said Davina after insisting they try the ham.

"Yes ma'am, that's exactly the case, the big houses begin to shout orders at the butchers, the butchers start shouting their orders at Josiah, then Josiah shouts loudest of all at Billy an' me. We was havin' a break yesterday an' Billy got to thinkin', like Billy does, an' 'e reckons he's washed that many puddin' skins in this past week that if anybody stretched 'em full length an' put 'em end to end, they'd go fifty times 'round the Castle."

Davina broke into gales of laughter, Annie couldn't contain hers and Harold laughed at their abandon. The moment was truly happy, the sandwiches were indeed excellent and the group relaxed in one another's company.

"Now Annie, what has been happening at the workshop and how is May, has she picked up a little since losing her mother?" Asked Davina.

"May and all her family are doing well, even Mr.Watkinson has been involved in the latest project." Annie went on to tell Davina all about the Christmas items.

"My dear, I shall go to Drew's next week and make my purchases. I shall send a table-cloth and napkins to cousin Isobel and another set to my great friend Alice Hemsley."

Annie looked surprised as she said, "Aunt Bella has a very good friend of that name, could it be the same person? They correspond often. The Hemsleys aunt Bella writes to live in Sheffield."

"That's right dear," said Davina, "Alice lives in Sheffield with Walter, they used to live here in The Park, that is how we came to know each other and become so close. It is good to know that your aunt and I share a very dear mutual friend, it makes me feel that fate has bound us all together. Do have another sandwich Harold."

Davina and Harold chatted away happily but Annie's thoughts had begun to stray from Davina's hearth. That look Bella and Davina had given her, what accounted for it?

"That's right isn't it Annie?" She heard her name spoken, "I'm sorry, what did you say Harold?" She was confused.

"I was telling Mrs.Wright how you went to see Mr.Eddowes' new grandson," replied Harold.

Now it was Davina's mind which wandered from the group, so, Nathan had a grandchild, another boy.

"I think William has mellowed his father, Charles seems more at ease since the baby arrived."

Annie's words reached the distant Davina and brought her back to the present. "That is good news Annie dear, I'm sure they must be so pleased."

Her response was vague but the two young people seemed not to notice. Harold's easy chatter, the wholesome supper and comfortable warmth all combined to pass the hour very quickly. It was time to make their way back to Winchester Street or Harold would be very late reaching home after seeing Annie safely to her aunt Bella's.

"At least I don't need to be at the yard by five in the mornin', " he said as he stood outside the door with Annie, bidding Davina goodnight. He pulled on his cap, took Annie's hand and with the other waved back to the light of the open doorway where Davina stood watching them, until they turned the corner, out of sight. Ivy collected the tray and busied herself in the kitchen.

Davina prodded the fire to send a myriad of sparks to the back of the grate where they clung like magic, twinkling, animated, moving across the sooty blackness, brought to life as if the dull, ordinary poker had turned into the wand of a sorcerer. Davina had delighted in the sight since her days of childhood, she sat back in her chair, her eyes fell on the little festive candle, it lured her memories .... 'You deserve something special Dee', she mouthed the words silently to herself.

Nathan had arrived home from Birchdale, the weather had been chill and Davina had made sure a well tended fire kept welcoming heat in the house. He rubbed his hands by the blaze in the grate, he was quiet, pensive. Davina had been about to ask if he felt a cold coming on when Nathan turned from the fire to face her, his eyes were filled with tears.

"There is something I have to tell you Dee, it is a bad thing and my shame and regret are more than a man could measure." Davina felt alarm, she moved close to him.

"Why, whatever is it my dear?" She asked.

In his desperation to bleed his soul free of guilt he had poured out the whole sorry story, almost choking on the sobs and tightness of breath his misery induced. He had withheld nothing, the Braithwaite's anguish, Hilda's innocence, the baby, the financial agreement, the planned wedding of Saul Eddowes to the pregnant Hilda, Davina had near drowned in his flood of confession. She fell on to a chair, clutching at the edge of the table for something, anything that would keep her from sinking. Suddenly all her world had collapsed about her. They had been married for ten years, Davina had always been aware of Nathan's flirtations but his love was ever hers, she had not once doubted him. That night brought a weight of pain and ache which near crushed her very being. She had listened for sounds of Nathan coming upstairs but there were none. At first light Davina had thrown cold water over her face, pulled on a heavy coat and let herself quietly out of the side door. She stumbled her way to her closest friend, Alice Hemsley, giving no thought to time of day or circumstance. The surprised maid opened the door, still not entirely clad in her maid's uniform, she could do no other than lead Davina through to the drawing room, whilst she urgently sought help. Alice had covered her night clothes with her robe, Walter had not stirred, she had gone downstairs immediately to her friend. Eventually Davina calmed sufficiently to tell poor Alice all that had transpired. Alice felt overwhelmed, two very dear friends, both suffering hurt and desolation in the extreme.

"Davina what I am about to tell you I entrust you to keep to yourself alone for all time, were it not for your misery I would never speak these words to you, however I am doing so in the hope that they might alleviate your intense pain by making you aware that another suffers by this terrible affair and their loss and tragedy, I do sincerely believe, to be greater than your own." Alice sat alongside Davina, holding her hand tightly, relating the events as they had happened to Ruby, Clarice, little Annie and Bella.

"How will your friend Bella ever find hope and spirit enough to continue living?" Asked Davina, "For I would end it all I'm sure if my situation mirrored hers."

Davina had been truly moved by Bella's plight, her tears fell again, not for herself alone but for this desperately unhappy young woman whose life had been starved of all compassion and rendered to be without hope.

"Bella has little Annie to think about, she allows herself no pity, no maudlin, all her time is spent in working to support them both and in the care of her dear sister's child. When you go home Davina, if you find Nathan truly full of remorse and with his love for you still, then think of Bella, that thought may just enable you to gather the strength to continue. We shall always be true friends, somehow we must move forward." Alice held Davina tightly, fortified by her friend's solid support and wisdom, Davina returned to Nathan. Their union would never be as before but she bore all with dignity and he lived from day to day in the shadow of his own failing.

A light knock came to the door, Ivy appeared, "I expect the scuttle needs more coal ma'am and someone has just pushed this through the door."

Ivy handed Davina a folded piece of paper, she opened it to reveal a small poster bearing an image of Hannibal Burton with an invitation to support the charity swim across The Trent on Christmas morning. She sighed, rose from her chair and set about finding the dish of sugared almonds which Harold had hidden.

"Ah, so there you are, lurking behind the plant holder." Davina spoke at the sweets as if they had full intelligence. Resigned, she returned to her chair by the fire, put the dish in her lap, popped an almond in her mouth and said aloud, "Fatted goose it is then." The dish would be empty by bedtime.

CHAPTER TWELVE

"You shouldn't have eaten pickled onions, it's filled him with colic, I told you not to have things that make the child windy." Bertha held little William against her shoulder, rubbing his back gently with her hand, seeking the all vital 'burp' which might restore calm to the troubled household.

"I've been up all night," snapped Enid, "pity he doesn't take after his father, if they learned to snore and fart in harmony they could draw crowds."

Bertha resisted the desire to lay the baby back in his pram and to put Enid across her knee instead. There were times when Bertha could have happily administered a good hiding, she had maintained her tolerance only by reminding herself of Enid's unfortunate mother. Enid would almost certainly have been a wilful child, her invalid mother, too frail to control the young Enid's tantrums, must have relied on her husband to check her difficult behaviour. Bertha was aware that Enid did not get on with her father, doubtless as a result of his need to be strict with his daughter, he could hardly allow her to grow up with less gentleness and decorum than her two elder brothers. Bertha felt quite convinced that Enid had grown in naughtiness and rebelled against discipline. There was another side to Enid however, she could at times be innocent, vulnerable. Naturally beautiful, some were drawn to her, like a jackdaw is drawn to a jewel, others stepped back unsure, just a little afraid that what sparkles ahead might be a lure to perils unknown.

"Now that's more like it young man," came the cry of satisfaction from Bertha. A healthy 'burp' had erupted from William.

"There's rumbling of activity in his nappy," she further declared, but Enid appeared more interested in the welfare of her own fingernails. She sat by the window, under the light, a small manicure case on her lap, she had obviously completed the session of self pampering as she now held the backs of both hands before her, she inspected each finger as a General would inspect his line of men. Bertha changed the baby and lay him in the pram, exhausted from his spell of colic, his eyes closed and his rhythmic breathing confirmed sound sleep.

"When is your friend Annie coming again?" Asked Bertha.

"So you think she is a friend then, she could be just a snooper sent by grandfather to find out what his son's wife is up to." Enid's tongue could drip pure acid when her mind was set in obnoxious mode.

"Annie is your best hope of a true friend, I don't see anyone else from your circle of 'so called' ladies coming to visit with a will to help. Anyway I have to go now, I've promised to sit with Maud Hodge for an hour, while her daughter runs errands." Bertha's tone was stern, "I'll see you tomorrow, don't forget, no onions or cabbage." She donned her hat and coat and let herself out of the back door.

"Do this, do that, no onions or cabbage, go torment Maud Hodge then." Enid muttered to herself, vexed and lonely she had not yet found the company in her son which came automatically to most mothers. She crossed the room to look at him and pulled the covers up around his chest, now Bertha had gone she could smile into the pram, her contrariness troubled even herself. There were moments when the desire to pick him up, smother him with kisses and sing happy songs to him pushed so hard at her emotions she nearly gave in but always that gremlin inside her head cautioned her. 'No, don't soften, they'll make you ache, they'll scratch at your heart 'til it weeps from its sores.' Enid left William to his sleep and began to make a meal for Charles, he would be home from the bank before five. When she put her mind to it Enid could cook very well, Bertha had given her basic instruction when they lived together. Her ability in most things was good, her dedication to the more mundane tasks however, fell well below average. Charles arrived home a little earlier than usual, he had very quickly learned it did not do to show their son his first attentions so Charles kissed Enid warmly before gazing into the pram at the slumbering William. The tiny fingers flexed over the edge of the blanket, the dimples on the child's cheeks pulsed steadily. Charles felt a dream, an infant fantasy was being lived out behind those tight closed eyes.

"As we finished a bit earlier at the bank today I called in at the workshop, father sends his love and Annie said if it would be alright, she will come to see you on Sunday morning."

Enid stood in the scullery doorway holding half a Savoy cabbage. "Mrs. Beeton says that I must cook just enough bloody cabbage for you, so how many leaves would you like?" She asked sarcastically.

"You don't have to do anything specially for me, whatever you're having will be alright," replied Charles.

He watched her as she worked, her fine features and pretty hair, the full bosom from nursing William only added to the deep attraction he felt for her, that evidence of motherhood mellowing Enid's normally very erect, sharp lines. A murmur came from within the pram, Charles gently pushed to and fro and all fell silent again. After a little while Enid announced that their meal was ready.

"For what you are about to receive you aught to be bloody thankful." She put a plate in front of Charles bearing a lamb shank, potatoes, carrots and a portion of cabbage that could have fed at least four. He did not comment but waited politely for her to return to the table with her own meal.

"Why haven't you any meat?" He said.

Her plate held potato, some carrot and a little gravy. Charles cut half the lamb from the bone and transferred it to Enid's plate. "I will eat your cabbage but not your meat, you must have that to ......"

"Make milk," interrupted Enid in a voice which mimicked Bertha. "You and Mrs.Beeton should have married each other."

Enid had been so dismissive of Bertha's advice that 'the book' accepted by almost everybody as being the complete reference had travelled in Bertha's bag from her house to Enid and had been positioned on the living room table like a monument to success. Enid's first perusal had caught her interest between the pages which instructed the reader on the preparation of a poultice to draw out puss from an abscess or boil. She still reeled from her fear and anguish of the night William was born and in her turmoil wished Charles might develop either abscess or boil. The whole passage struck her as just the right remedy for her festering resentment, that would balance the scales nicely she thought, a magnificent fiery poultice prepared by her own fair hands.

Later that evening Charles sat looking at his wife feeding their son, the child's fingers exploring the soft skin of Enid's breast, the dancing light of the fire dappling her dark wavy hair. It had been more than three months since they had made love, Charles felt no jealousy of William but he wanted to feel again that special warmth. He longed for the tempest to return, that storm which blew all routine and safeness to the street outside leaving him and Enid swirling within, airborne, rising in uncontrolled flight 'til in its wake they fell to earth exhausted and lay still.

William slept in his cot by the bed, Enid took the combs from her hair and brushed in slow downward strokes 'til the liberated tresses covered the pretty ribbon trim at the neck of her nightgown. She climbed into bed beside Charles, his fingers ventured to follow William's. She caught hold his hand and dug her fingernails into his palm, he cried out.

"You're not normal you punish a man for living." His raised voice woke William, the child pushed at his covers and began to cry.

"Damn, see what you've done, how is 'man' going to help now. You expect me to roll over for your delight then let your son pull on my tit while you snore your wife into oblivion, well you do it, you feed him, see just how useful 'man' is."

Enid snarled the words like a warning, she flounced out the bed and over to the cot muttering inaudible curses. She lifted the child to her arms, carried him to the chair in the corner by the nightlight and changed him, making the process last much longer than necessary, willing their son to cry much louder lest his father should fall asleep. She fed him, then with sheer contrariness began to sing, not a gentle calming lullaby but a raucous music hall rendition. William paid it no attention, his comforts now met, his eyes closed to the subdued nightlight. Enid returned to bed, Charles lay facing the wall.

"Do you think I never get tired? Don't you ever consider how sore I might be?" She prodded his back, he gave no answer. "Don't ignore me, I know you're not asleep." She prodded him again more robustly, this time he turned to face her.

"Why can't you be like other women? They don't create all this fuss, they just get on with it."

She grabbed a lock of his hair and tugged it 'til he grasped her hand to stem the pain.

"If you pull my hair again I'm warning you, I shall do the same to you." Charles' tone was purposeful.

Enid's eyes set with devilment, she clutched at the hair above his brow and twisted her wrist to intensify the pain. His hand travelled up through one side of her hair, tangling it between his fingers, he clenched his fist 'til every strand drew taut, wrenching at her scalp, driving brutal hurt right through her being. She kissed him so hard on the lips his jawbone ached from the pressure, he kissed back, equally determined to bruise any tenderness. The storm had struck, it raged wildly, surging, tearing asunder all sanctuary. At the mercy of the elements they soared to heights which denied them breath, their flight so fast it carried them to the ends of the earth and back again. When the tempest finally passed over, every sense had been challenged, the calm which followed used the small hours to soothe and mend.

Annie's mind drifted towards Christmas as she walked to Enid's, how different it would be this year, all Christmases past had been spent so quietly, were it not for the beautiful card which always arrived from the Hemsleys and the calendar that confirmed the pending new year, given to all customers by Mr.Cheetham, the butcher, Annie would have not detected anything special about the time of year. Aunt Bella had shown no pleasure in carols or decorations, their meal was never extravagant and in all the years Annie could remember, no one had ever visited the house at Christmas. This year,

Harold's presence at aunt Bella's would bring more brightness than the solitary red candle Annie was permitted to light on the mantelpiece each Christmas Eve. Annie had sat with Bella in comparative silence so many times watching the molten wax creep down to the holder below, where it surrendered life, paled of colour, lost of spirit, gone from sight. Davina had made Annie promise to call on her over Christmas. 'Bring dear Harold with you' she had said.

A baby in the house at such time of year must be magical thought Annie as she approached Enid's house. Her visits to Davina and Enid had rescued her from the repeated prophecies of doom and destruction dispensed by Minister Shawcross. Her Sunday afternoons were a time of great happiness, they inspired the early part of each week and drew the later part, eagerly towards that promised reward for all labours. The time spent with Harold and his family at Mitchell Street every Sunday provided Annie with a source of strength which enabled her to smile at the stubborn coal shed door, to dismiss aunt Bella's stern rebuke, 'Just you remember what you are my girl', whenever these words assailed her. Sunday mornings she genuinely believed, might be better spent in heartening Davina and helping Enid, the Mission would doubtless function perfectly well without her.

Charles opened the door, "Come in Annie," he said in a light voice which suggested his spirits were good. Enid was dressed and occupied in taking a multitude of clothing from the clothes horse.

"You've been very busy with laundry," observed Annie cheerily. Enid looked at her as if she could not believe Annie's naivety.

"This is an example of Bertha's expertise," said Enid, "Duffin with the dolly tub is something to behold."

"I'm off to fetch kindlers, it's no place for a bloke when two women get together," said Charles. He pulled on a thick jacket and warm cap, "See if you can convince her that housework doesn't prove fatal Annie," he said with a chuckle. He waved through the window to them both before disappearing across the yard.

"Charles seems very happy," said Annie.

"Uhm men are usually happy when they get what they want," replied Enid.

Annie did not pursue the subject, if Enid was in a prickly mood then it was much the best to let her decide the nature of the conversation. William had awoken, he lay in his pram quite contentedly. Annie crossed the room to speak to him.

"Can I lift him out?" She asked.

"Carry on," replied Enid. "He'll likely pee on you or worse, he hasn't grasped what good manners are yet."

Annie was sorely tempted to suggest that it might be because he seldom witnessed any but instead she carried William to the window to show him a cat, sitting on top of the wall outside.

"Look, that's a lucky black cat, it probably means you will have some presents from Santa Claus and it won't be long 'til he comes will it mum?" Annie turned to Enid.

"He's happy in your arms, I can tell, I don't think he likes his mother very much, he thinks I'm not like other mothers."

Enid spoke the words so seriously that Annie felt she could not give the light hearted reply that first came to her lips. Instead she said, "You are everything to William, he knows and loves his father of course but you Enid are his lifeline, his anchor. When he opens his eyes from sleep it is your face he seeks first and when he closes his eyes, he will dream of you before anyone else."

"Do you really think that?" Asked Enid.

"I promise you it is the truth."

Annie passed the little boy to his mother, then turned away quickly and picked up the kettle. "I shall make us some tea," inwardly just a little afraid that William might cry, Enid did seem so detached at times, the child could feel insecure. The water over the fire to heat and the teapot and cups ready, Annie watched as Enid changed him.

"Play with him for a few minutes before he feeds," she said encouragingly.

"How are you supposed to play with a baby? He's too young," declared Enid.

Annie tickled him and lifted an antimacassar in front of her face, playing peek-a-boo, he gurgled with delight, his arms and legs so animated they very nearly propelled him from Enid's lap.

"You live with an aunt don't you," said Enid, "didn't you get on with your father?"

"I never knew my father" replied Annie, "he died when I was too young to remember him."

"What about your mother?" Said Enid curiously.

"She died giving birth to me."

Enid fell silent.

"And you, do you have parents still?" Asked Annie.

"We are not close," replied Enid and in her desperation to change the conversation she grabbed the antimacassar and hid her face behind it. The game afforded her a few precious seconds in which to regain her composure but now she must follow through and play peek-a-boo with her son. He lifted his hands to her face and displayed such pleasure that Enid found herself repeating this game of innocent childhood fun and laughed back to William, even tickling his chin to promote more gurgles of delight. Enid had at last found passage across the barrier which until this moment had confined her motherhood. Annie poured the tea, drank her own cup quickly and making the excuse of needing to get a bunch of flowers for Harold's mam, left Enid and William to their new found harmony.

As Annie walked along Sherwood Road clutching a small spray of chrysanthemums, she found herself wondering if aunt Bella had ever played with her when she was a baby. The answer seemed all too certain, Annie imagined she could hear the words 'You just remember what you are, now go to sleep'. Then aunt Bella would have put out the lamp and gone to bed.

CHAPTER THIRTEEN

The past few weeks had melted away like snow in the sun. The workshop had been busy, Drew's had required more of the Christmas stock but all the material left was some course red linen. Edna managed to squeeze from it, four table-cloths and a dozen napkins. Saul had been pleased and declared, 'Next Christmas we shall begin earlier and place the items at a number of shops'.

There were just a few finishing off jobs, then the workshop would be closed for two and a half days. Saul had promised that on the following day, Christmas Eve, they would all be able to leave at midday. The slaughter yard had put through so much work, both Harold and Billy were looking forward greatly to a few days away from it all. Edna had designs on a Christmas dance to be held in the Masonic Hall at Clumber Street on Christmas Eve, she could be very persuasive when she needed to be.

"I know you're feelin' buggered Billy but you can sleep all next day, or at least all that's left o' the day when we've watched the swim at the embankment."

"I'll go if Harold will," said Billy, "I don't want to be the only bloke there wi' a pair of boots. Some go wi' proper shoes, they don't make a bloody row but when you're pullin' a lass round in work boots the wooden plankin' shudders and echos like a deep blast down soddin' pit."

Billy had duly consulted Harold, who in turn spoke with Annie and Bella, the outcome being that a local dance on Christmas Eve, held at such a respectable venue as the Masonic Hall couldn't cause any untoward event. Annie's excitement grew daily, just as the fair had been, attending a dance was yet another new experience. The two young women chatted as they worked, Annie was hand stitching the scalloped edge of a satin petticoat and Edna was sewing buttons on liberty bodices.

"What will you wear Annie?" She asked.

"I have one pretty skirt and blouse which I think will be alright, aunt

Bella's friend, Alice Hemsley sent them for me a couple of years ago. Her daughter didn't wear them any more so she thought I might like them, I put them away just after they came and I haven't taken them out of the drawer since, until I tried them on last night."

The previous evening Annie had laid the scented rose petals which Harold had given her around the cream satin blouse. The buttons were very small and covered with the same material, the collar had a tiny pink rosebud embroidered at the tip on either side. The cuffs were quite long and fastened with the same neat buttons and the bodice was shaped so as to narrow at the waist. The skirt was dark chocolate brown and entirely plain apart from the waistband which deepened at the front.

"I shall wear the frock I had for our Ada's weddin', it's not too fussy and it's Billy's favourite colour, a dark red, same colour as the cherries on aunt Win's 'at. What a box 'o ferrets that wer," said Edna with a peal of laughter. "Ada met Morley when she wer' out carol singin' must be five year' ago now. Well this group o' men an' women used to go street to street singin' an' collectin' money for that 'ome for orphaned kids at Snenton, did it every year. Ada wer' friendly wi' Violet Dallymore and it wer' 'er father ran the place. Now Morely Craddock lived on 'is own down by The Meadows, bit of a recluse I s'pose yer could say, 'is mam and dad were both dead. Some reckoned 'e wer' only 'arf baked, still a bit doughy in the middle like. Others thought 'e wer' just bone idle, 'e never come out the 'ouse 'ardly. But when folk passed by they could 'ear 'im in there singin', 'e wer' allus singin' old hymns and Churchy stuff. Well, it seems 'e 'ad some sort 'o breakdown, come over all depressed and bloody miserable. Somebody sent for the doctor, 'fraid for Morely's safety. Apparently the doctor examined 'im, told 'im to get off 'is arse 'an do summat useful. That wer' when 'e started singin' wi' this group of people for charity. What our Ada seen in 'im God knows, but she took a shine to summat, hidden talents I reckon, but that doctor, well 'e wer' bloody good 'cause just from that one visit, 'e lifted Morely out of 'is depression and by following April our Ada wer' up the duff! Our mam wer' mortified, she didn't eat for a week. Aunt Win said she should 'ave guessed when 'e started singin' 'Rise up o men of God', dad wer' ready to throttle 'im but Ada declared 'er undying love so that wer' that. They 'ad to get wed quick. Mornin' of the weddin' Morely took out a suit of 'is father's, goin' to wear that to get married in, when 'e put 'is leg down the trouser, the bloody thing fell apart down the crease, it 'ad been in the cupboard that long the cloth 'ad rotted. Poor Ada, 'e turned up in the same old trousers and jacket 'e'd been wearing for weeks, she looked lovely an' smelled o' gardenias, 'e looked like a sack of mangolds an' stank o' lamp oil. Course 'e's twelve year older than Ada but the old tadpoles keep comin', they've got three kids now. Morely got work at the candle factory, dad says the job wer' meant for 'im. Morely dips the wicks".

Edna burst into laughter then cried out 'bugger' when she caught her finger with the needle. Annie found Edna shocking and yet pure delight at the same time. To be without her company as she worked would have been like losing the sun, Edna brought brightness to the workshop on the cold dark days.

It was now late afternoon, Annie had collected the shirts from May's and promised young Mabel and Alfred that after work the following day she would go to see them. Mabel was just the right age to enjoy the magic of Christmas time, Annie couldn't miss seeing that happy little face as Santa's visit grew imminent. Edna had just left and Annie was about to start some hemming when Saul called to her, she crossed to his office, he smiled.

"No need to work on later tonight Annie, what has still to be done you and Edna can work on together in the morning." He paused for a few seconds. "Thank you for all your interest and help, I know you have taken the trouble to visit Enid."

"Oh that's no trouble really, William is lovely and Enid just needs to find some confidence, I think at times she feels a bit lost, I'm sure we all would. The responsibility of a baby, especially the first one, must be daunting. Will you go to Charles and Enid for your Christmas dinner?" Said Annie.

"I am going to have tea with them," replied Saul, "I think it will be less stressful for Enid if she doesn't have me to think about on Christmas morning and I believe Mrs.Duffin is joining them for dinner."

Annie would have liked to ask him to have dinner with aunt Bella and herself but she knew that would not do. Aunt Bella never strayed from their traditional Christmas, the exchange of a simple gift, an adequate meal with no frivolous extras but if the weather permitted, before any festivity reached the streets, a walk on Christmas morning. The afternoon was to be spent quietly with a book. That was it, Bella would not stand any attempt at merriment, even the card from the Hemsleys got taken down immediately after Boxing Day. Sarah and Samuel had sent the invitation through Harold, 'ask Miss Pownall if she and Annie will come for dinner', Harold had tried his best but even his entreaty had served no purpose.

'Annie can go but I shall have dinner here as always,' Bella had replied firmly.

'I will come to your house after dinner', Annie had told Harold, 'I won't leave her on her own until the afternoon, she will take a nap then. All these years we have spent the time together, were it not for aunt Bella, I might have been in that home at Snenton for all my childhood Christmases'.

Harold had kissed her, 'I understand', he'd said, 'so will mam and father but I will bring a sprig of mistletoe when I call for you Christmas Eve. Harold Boucher will make history, I shall give your aunt Bella a Christmas kiss this year and every year, from now on'.

He'd produced that big broad grin that could soften stone. Annie could think of no other soul who might hold mistletoe above Bella and steal a kiss but she felt no doubt that somehow Harold would do just that.

"Will you be spending Christmas day with Harold?" Asked Saul.

"Not until after dinner, I shall go to Harold's after aunt Bella and I have spent the morning together and shared the meal."

"How is your aunt Bella?"

"I think she is well, it's difficult to tell, she seldom says how she is feeling but she seems as always," replied Annie.

"Well, I mustn't keep you, I'm sure there are many things you need to do, run along home now, I'll see you in the morning."

Saul appeared a lonely figure, Annie turned at the front door of the workshop to call goodnight to him. Surely as William grew, he and his grandfather would spend more time together. With that thought to cheer her Annie set off for home, tonight she must wrap the few small gifts she had purchased. Bella sat reading a letter, a large card with scenes of the 'twelve days of Christmas' sat on the mantelpiece.

"That is a lovely card," said Annie, "are the Hemsleys well?"

"You can read it for yourself in a minute," replied Bella, "Along with that."

She pointed to an envelope on the table. It was addressed to Miss Annie Bundy. Annie looked at the writing intently, "I can't imagine who it is from, I've not had a Christmas card before."

"Well open it then you'll know," said Bella impatiently.

Annie's fingers lifted the flap on the envelope very carefully, it was such an unusual occurrence she felt strangely tense.

"It's from Mrs.Wright and Ivy, isn't that nice to have put Ivy's name on the card too, look Aunt Bella."

Annie held out the card eagerly but Bella's response was slight.

"Put it up with the other one then," she said giving it only the briefest glance.

Annie put the two cards at either side of the clock, leaving Harold's wooden horse at one end of the mantelpiece and making a space alongside the box of sulphurs for the Christmas candle at the other. After they had eaten their meal and cleared away the dishes Annie tended the fire, she left aunt Bella sitting silently by the hearth with just the light from the small flames which had begun to creep through the coals to perform their routine of dance and mime. Upstairs, Annie took a box from beneath her bed and lay the contents, one by one across her counterpane. Two lengths of red velvet ribbon for Mabel's hair, a small bag of glass marbles for young Alfred. A pretty embroidered lavender bag for Sarah and a tray of treacle toffee for the rest of the family. A lace trimmed handkerchief for Edna and for Harold, a cap made from warm tweed. For aunt Bella she had bought a bottle of lavender water and a bar of scented soap in a pretty box lined with padded silk. Annie wrapped each one in red paper and tied them with red and white plaited twine. Tomorrow she would go to Peverell Street in the afternoon, then come back to get ready for the dance. On Boxing Day she and Harold were to call on Davina and Ivy. This Christmas felt good and in the new year they would make wedding plans, her happiness was complete.

Christmas Eve had begun with a clear moonlit sky. Annie crossed the yard to tip the ashes in the garden, the air felt chill, the ledge on the gate nipped at her fingers and the coating of frost sparkled as though it were bedecked in diamonds especially for the season. The moon was full, dawn seemed to be resisting day, stealing just a few more glorious minutes of stillness under its silvery blanket, counting the rows of chimney pots, all different sizes and shapes, silhouetted against the advancing light of morning. This particular morning's cloak had been cut from silk of the finest quality, it had been dyed with Vermilion, patterned by immortal hand with strokes of jet, sapphire and pure gold. Away in the distance Annie could hear the clock of St. Andrews Church, it was half past six, she must hurry, just this morning to spend at the workshop then so much to look forward to. Her excitement 'cocked a snook' at the irritable coal shed door, her fingers paid no heed to the icy water in the jug by the wash bowl and the coarse cloth floated across her hands like lambs wool.

She called "Good morning," to Winnie Bacon who had just opened her back door to tip the tea leaves from the previous evening's brew. The entry seemed elongated, so dark under its time blackened ceiling, the once bright red bricks no longer showing any colour, hidden by layers of sooty residue, sucked in from the smoky fog which so often swirled about either end, the winds siphoning air through the entry whichever direction they blew.

Today however was different, Annie's feet were drawn to the brilliant sunshine which now filled Winchester Street with Christmas spirit. In her bag she had the gifts for Mabel and Alfred and wrapped in newspaper a knuckle bone from aunt Bella's pea and ham soup, a present for Shawcross.

The pot bellied stove had now established a good bed of fire and the heat reached all corners of the workshop. Edna had taken off her coat to reveal a large gold bauble hanging from sheering elastic around her neck and a small 'robin red breast' made from clay, pinned into her hair by its wire feet. Every movement at her table was so comical even Saul chuckled at the sight. The bauble danced under her chin with the beat of the machine and the bird appeared to pick among the waves of her hair as it bobbed up and down with the motion of Edna's head. The work was completed and everything was tidied away, the morning had been light-hearted and as the girls prepared to leave Saul joined them at the door, he gave Edna a small packet and passed two more to Annie.

"They are all the same," he said "if you would give one to May please Annie and tell her I wish them all a Happy Christmas."

They looked up to wave as they latched the gates, Saul watched them walk out of sight, the sky still bright and clear, not even the smoke from the chimneys dallied today, everything busied itself in preparation for tomorrow's events. He closed the door and lingered for a moment by the stove, warming his hands. It felt comforting, the office was solitary, he drew Annie's stool closer to the heat and sat by the old stove. It offered a source of companionship, the wood inside crackled to confirm life, every now and then a wisp of smoke would seep through a crack in the frame of the aging cast iron door, as if to let Saul know it breathed. He remembered the evening he had sat with only the stove to share in his cogitation.

He had been about to lock up and go home to Hilda and young Charles, his son was almost ten years old, Saul's efforts to be close to the boy occupied much of his evenings but however hard he had tried, from behind the boundary fence where Hilda had positioned him, his reach fell just short, often within a fingertip of contact but cruelly, never quite able to touch. A knock had come at the door of the workshop, Saul had opened the door expecting to see one of the women, back to collect some item they had forgotten to take a few minutes earlier. A smartly dressed lady stood very erect, very composed, smiling politely. He recognised her, though not from any work the business had undertaken on her behalf, he could not recall ever having had dealings with the family but he was in no doubt over her identity, it was Alice Hemsley.

"May I come in?" She said.

Saul could remember that feeling of apprehension, he ran a business favoured by a number of clients from The Park and yet he instinctively knew that this visit was not of that nature. He asked her to go through to the office where she might take a seat.

"We know of each other Mr.Eddowes which is entirely different to knowing one another as acquaintances. I am a practical woman and have no time for foolish dithering in the guise of etiquette. As a family we are obliged to move from Nottingham to Sheffield where I must take some care of my mother, as you know, my husband Walter has managed the accounts of numerous businesses and trades people in the city for many years, helped considerably by the honest and diligent efforts of Miss Bella Pownall."

Saul flinched from the memories that name provoked, Alice continued.

"Annie is ten years old, one of the brightest young things I have ever known, Bella has taught her well. When we leave, the work which Bella has relied on for the past decade will be no more. You are in a position to help me secure that child's future at no expense to yourself as believe me, Annie would learn so quickly and be a great asset to your industry here. You must go to see Bella, persuade her of this. I have discovered a small house in Winchester Street which is available to rent from the end of this month, the rent is modest as indeed is the property, but Bella and Annie have never *known luxury. You have to convince Bella that to move from Lenton to enable Annie to learn a valuable skill here at your workshop, would be an opportunity for the child to prosper."*

Saul did not speak at first, he felt inert, unable to respond, numbed in mind and body.

"If I can overcome the barriers that would defy us then so can you. Be a man, as much for your own sake as for anyone else." Her tone was stern.

"I will speak with Bella if indeed she will tolerate such a thing, I fear she would rather have me dead than standing at her door. To let me in, to allow me any utterance, I cannot imagine she would countenance that for even a moment," Saul answered sincerely.

"Don't fail Mr.Eddowes, this time you must not fail." Alice looked directly into his eyes, "very seldom does life offer any chance to redeem a spent opportunity, this may well be your only one." With that she bid him goodbye and walked away from the workshop gates, after closing them carefully behind her.

He had watched Alice Hemsley disappear from view that evening, just as he had watched Annie this afternoon. Saul opened the door of the pot bellied stove and laid two more logs on the fire within. He sat forward, holding his brow in his cupped hands, blanking the room in which he sat from his view, replacing it with the image of the back door of Bella's house at Lenton.

He had knocked very gently at the door, willing her not to hear so that he might truthfully say he had tried but no one answered. It was not the case, footsteps crossing the scullery floor became more defined until they stopped at the other side of the door and the latch lifted. Saul felt someone should have shielded his eyes, offered him one final comfort before he fell at the feet of his executioner. The door opened, Bella might have been cast from bronze, her features pronounced, but set, a certain light fell from her eyes but it seemed soulless, nothing more than a reflection, if she felt shock or alarm, she showed none.

"Why Mr.Eddowes, have you lost your way?"

Even in this situation Bella's quick mind delivered words of the deepest irony. Saul recognised their true meaning, all his elaborate plans, his business empire that would stretch across counties, here he stood, proprietor of one small workshop and an outsider still, to his family of ten years.

"How are you Bella?" He asked. He cautioned his eyes to look directly into her face, Saul knew that if they should lower for even an instant, he would not be granted an audience.

"Come in," said Bella coldly.

She led him in to the living room where a young girl sat at the table, paper, pen and a number of books in front of her. It was spontaneous, immediate, her mouth broke into a wide smile and the young voice spoke confidently.

"Hello sir."

Annie's life with her aunt Bella might be austere but it was constant, she felt no threat, the days varied only with the seasons and through her lessons but aunt Bella was ever present and Annie had no reason to fear this man if he had been invited to enter by her aunt. Saul would have picked that smile from its stem and pressed it between the pages of his ledger, to keep for all time, if such were possible. If only Charles, so similar in age, would greet him as warmly.

"I don't believe you have met Annie. Bella said to him, "this is my pupil, Annie Bundy."

"I think I saw you very briefly when you were a tiny baby and I was a young man too intent on foolish dreams to notice, I am pleased to meet you properly at last." Saul offered his hand to Annie and she shook it firmly.

Bella knew exactly what she was doing when she asked Saul into the house, the child was a delight, but she was not his and never would be, he had made his choice.

"There is a reason for your visit no doubt," said Bella.

Whatever he had to say it must be said in front of Annie, she would grant him no easement. Saul had told Bella of Alice Hemsley's visit to the workshop and the ensuing conversation, only truth could abide between him and Bella now.

"I would genuinely welcome a bright young woman to take instruction from my best seamstress."

Bella interrupted him, "Young woman," she snapped, "she's but a child."

"Do you suppose I would treat her with anything other than concern," he did not raise his voice but kept his tone calm, gentle, aware that young Annie, while studying her books, would not fail to note any harsh exchange. "It has been ten years Bella, let the past be, this is a way forward for the child, perhaps for us all. Alice Hemsley is right, she is a practical woman, go with her to see the house in Winchester Street, if you prefer you could send your decision on paper, you don't have to see me again. You have my solemn word that Annie would receive the finest instruction and only kindness. Her financial reward would be more than fair." He waved back to Annie and called out, "goodbye for now."

Bella closed the back door, the same door she had closed so firmly all those years ago. It sickened her but the reality was plain enough, she would take Annie and they would call on Alice Hemsley the next day.

Saul pushed in the damper on the stove, and placed Annie's stool beside her table. In the office he tidied away his books and locked the drawer of his desk. His eyes cast around the workshop, checking all was in order, he pulled up his collar against the cold air and let himself out of the door locking it securely behind him. He paused outside the gates, he felt a compulsion to walk up Winchester Street, the opposite direction to home, Bella would be on her own, Annie had gone to May's. In the eleven years which had passed since that day he had gone to Lenton, he and Bella had barely spoken yet she lived only ten minutes away, he needed to make peace between them. His feet moved of their own volition, the closer he came to the house the faster his heart raced, he stopped just short of the entry, those pains beat at his chest like pistons, his breathing grew short, laboured. He leaned back against the wall, it would pass, soon the pain would pass, it always did. Two elderly women walked by on the other side of the street, he heard one say 'It's disgusting, and he a family man, with a business and reputation to think about, drunk and it's not yet 3 o'clock, disgusting it is'. The words stung him like a whip, he didn't want to be there, he wanted to be behind his own door, away from the world. He calmed, the pains retreated, his breathing returned to normal, whatever assailed him had gone. Saul looked up at the roof above, just yards from him, Bella sat alone but it was too late. It was not those few yards which separated them, it was all those years of time. He could not travel such a distance, he stood very still for a few seconds then turned and began to walk back along the way he had come.

Annie found Peverell Street in turmoil, she could hear raised voices, women shouting, a dog barking as she approached the corner. In spite of the cold most doors were opened and one or more occupants stood at the thresholds, Annie wondered what all the furore was about. A man possibly in his mid thirties, walked slowly up the middle of the cobbles, every few yards he raised his arms above his head and cried out.

"Hallelujah, God is good!" People cheered, older women blew kisses while younger children stood behind their mothers' skirts looking puzzled. Shawcross barked so loudly the sound reverberated back and forth across the street, growing louder and louder in its efforts to escape the confines of the narrow gap between the terraced houses. It reminded Annie of the hornet's drone, becoming ever more threatening as it bounced side to side the privy walls, suggesting fury when the poor creature sought only release.

Annie must keep walking, she would save the bone for Shawcross until later. As she drew level with the man he raised his arms and looking straight up to the sky above, called out.

"Jesus saves, joy to the world."

At that moment an older woman walked slowly from her door, Annie could see she was crying, tears rolling silently down her cheeks. The woman stood before the young man and they embraced, then together, they walked to the house, entered and closed the door. All other doors now closed too and for a moment Annie was the only person in the street. She was so relieved to reach May's, not from fear but from a strange feeling of unease which made her want to see Mabel's smile, to rub her hand over young Alfred's hair and see his grin.

"Come sit down for a minute Annie," said Alfred senior, "the kettle is hot we'll have a cuppa."

May patted Annie on the shoulder. "It was enough to frighten you to death," she said, "it was unfortunate it happened just as you reached the street. That is Luke Bastion, he was released from jail first thing this morning, they locked him up twenty years ago."

"What did he do that was so bad?" Asked Annie.

"He killed his father," said May.

Annie gasped, "That's awful."

"But not before his father had killed Lillian," said May quickly, "Their father was a brute of a man, dominated the household, they were all afraid of him. Lillian was just fourteen and Luke fifteen. A younger sibling was already dead no one knew what had happened, only that a child was taken away and buried. They say he struck Lillian so hard she never got up from the floor. Luke waited for his father to fall asleep then broke his neck with a single blow from a slate fender. A plea for leniency saved him from hanging but he was taken away from his poor mother for all those years. While he was in prison, he found religion, God spoke to him his mother says. I don't know Annie, I'm just glad she has got him back and on Christmas Eve too."

Annie found the story so sad, the old woman's face as she walked towards her son, but there could surely be no finer gift at Christmas.

Alfred put a cup of steaming hot tea in Annie's hand and kissed her on the forehead. "Happy Christmas Annie," he said.

Mabel tugged at Annie's sleeve, "Look, come and look Aunty Annie," the excited child took her to the corner of the room where a holly bough, its base resting in a pail of stones to prevent it tipping stood partially decorated. "My Alfred did it, he's not finished yet, he's gone to find more shiny paper." Mabel's little legs jumped up and down in anticipation.

"Alfred has been scouring the streets for weeks, picking up any scraps of lead foil from inside discarded tobacco packets," said May. "He's determined to find one or two more to decorate the lower stems of holly."

Mabel's face now looked worried, "Aunty Annie, that man in the street, is that Santa Claus?" Annie and May looked at each other and smiled, no wonder the poor child looked concerned.

"No Mabel, Santa Claus doesn't come until you are fast asleep tonight. He is a jolly man and brings happiness to all the children, he wears a warm red jacket with a fleecy collar and he sings happy songs," said Annie.

"Who was that man then?" Mabel persisted.

"He is someone who had to go away from home a long time ago but he has come back today to have a special Christmas with his mam."

The little head took in all that was said, sorted the explanation to her satisfaction and then, as if to confirm the process complete, gave a great big beaming smile and danced around the table singing her very own version of 'While Shepherds Watched'.

Annie beckoned to May and the two women went to the scullery, "Quickly before she sees." Annie took the little packages from her bag, "One for Mabel and this one for Alfred, oh, and this is for you from Saul, he gave one to Edna and to me as well, he sends his very best wishes to you all."

"I shall keep it until tomorrow and open it with the children," said May.

Young Alfred arrived back, "Couldn't find very much, but that little man in the hardware shop gave me this," he said. He produced some deep red raffia. "He uses it to tie up spills, but he said I could have this bit, we can make it into bows around the holly leaves."

Annie felt happy for them all. They had lived through a hard year with little to lift their spirits, but today they were able to laugh again.

"I must be going now May, I want to spend a little while with aunt Bella before Harold comes to take me to the dance."

It had been arranged for Josiah to collect the sewing machine and take it back to the workshop after Boxing Day. May would resume her work at Saul's in the new year. Peverell Street had returned to normal and Shawcross sat watching the every day movements he had observed over the year.

"Happy Christmas dear friend." Annie stroked his head and looked down into his deep, dark eyes, she took the paper wrapped bone from her bag, undid one end for him to smell, laughed at his eagerness, his big paws rising from the ground one at a time, trying to take it from her with good grace. "Here you are," she put the knuckle into his mouth and he held it there as he looked back at her. As she walked away Annie heard the thud as he let it fall to the ground followed immediately by the sound of determined grinding of his teeth against the bone. Shawcross was happy too. Annie looked across to the house where Luke and his mother had found refuge from the eyes of the world. It was a small, plain dwelling, of no significance in the overall scheme of things, yet it had seen and endured the most dire events, she hoped it might now find peace and keep those two tragic beings safe within. Annie hurried home, that felt like a good place to be.

Stepping into the scullery she could see that Nobby had delivered the greengrocery and that Mr.Cheetham had been with aunt Bella's meat order. An ox tongue sat in a bowl of water, aunt Bella always soaked tongue, 'no good straight from the brine' she would say. The array of vegetables looked particularly attractive, dark green savoy cabbage, pink eyed potatoes, deep cream fleshed parsnips, blanched white leeks sleek and shiny, tightly closed brussels sprouts, golden skinned sweet onions, long slender carrots vivid in colour but most special of all, three large oranges and three fat pears, it was truly Christmas. Whatever meat was to be their dinner tomorrow would be on a large oval plate which was kept solely for use in the meat safe.

Mr.Cheetham's calendar lay face down on the shelf, 'bad luck to see it before January 1st. Aunt Bella said the same thing every year as though Annie had never been given this vital information until that moment.

Aunt Bella had washed her hair and now sat close to the fire to dry it before pinning it up. Annie took off her hat and coat and began to relate the day's events, Edna's bauble and Robin, the beautiful dawn sky which must have greeted the unfortunate Luke Bastion too as he stepped out from his imprisonment. Annie told Bella the story of the tragic family.

"If they put the boy behind bars and kept him there for twenty years then it was not a man they released this morning but a tortured soul, a mind disabled from madness. That poor wretched woman will never find her son, only the dark distorted shadow that occupies his being."

Bella's words were so sombre, Annie wanted to believe that Luke and his mother now sat before a warm fire talking happily together, looking forward to a Christmas morning which began a new chapter of their lives. But the reality Annie could not help thinking, was probably just as aunt Bella had so miserably described. Annie pictured again his face as he looked up and cried out, those arms reaching out for a heavenly Father, he could never have reached for his earthly father. 'May God bless them' thought Annie to herself. Today though, she would not dwell on gloom.

"I'll start tea," she said and laid the table. Aunt Bella had a pan of soup on the hearth.

"If you look in the bread bin you will find two crusty 'cobs', we will have those today, I bought a bloomer loaf for Boxing Day, Harold will enjoy that with some pressed tongue," said Bella.

Annie smiled, so Harold is invited to eat with us on Boxing Day, she felt pleased, she had so wanted aunt Bella to suggest it and not to have to ask herself. They had promised to call on Davina but the day should present plenty of time for that. Annie cleared away the dishes and brought in coal.

"I shall put the Christmas candle on the mantelpiece," said Annie, "and before we go to the dance I shall light it for you Aunt Bella."

Annie took the candle from the drawer in the cupboard where Bella had put it the week before, took the holder down from the scullery shelf, trimmed the bottom of the candle just slightly so it fitted snugly into the small cup on the base of the china holder. Moving the sulphurs closer to the end of the mantelpiece, she placed the candle where its flame would illuminate the scenes on Alice Hemsley's card.

"You'd better get yourself ready," said Bella, "no need to be fussing about with that candle, Harold will be here soon."

Annie went upstairs with a jug of hot water, she would wash and change, then pin up her hair afresh. She took the skirt and blouse from the drawer, Harold's rose petals had imparted a soft scent to the satin, her tidy shoes she kept in a box beneath the wash stand, she bent down to retrieve them and as she straightened, Alfred's verse on the little picture caught her eye. Her fingers traced the words, 'so that you may as the seasons run, look out upon a world of happy days'. Strangely, a lump came to her throat and tears welled in her eyes, yet her happiness was so great.

"Shake yourself Annie Bundy, remember what you are." She spoke the words faintly to herself. She remembered the water, it would be going cold, she must make haste. In aunt Bella's room there was a full length mirror in the wardrobe door, Annie had only a hand mirror on her shelf.

She called down the stairs to Bella, "Please may I go in your room to use the big mirror?"

"Yes" came the reply.

Annie stood before her reflection and felt pleased, the clothes fitted well, by the time she had done her hair she would look quite presentable, even for a dance in the Masonic Hall. She could hear steps on the stairs, Bella appeared in the doorway.

"Uhm, just a minute," she said and crossed to the chest of drawers by the bed. She lifted the lid from a small box and took out a brooch, it was oval in shape, a silver rim around Mother of Pearl.

"Come here."

Annie stood by her, Bella pinned the brooch at the neck of the cream satin blouse so that it sat between the two embroidered rose buds on the collar. "That's better," she said and turned Annie around to look again in the mirror. "It's time for you to have that, it was your grandmother's, she used to wear it on a blouse very similar to the one Alice has sent to you."

"But Aunt Bella, you should wear it," protested Annie.

"Nonsense, what call do I have for jewellery? Anyway I have another, just look after it."

Bella put the lid back on the little box and paused for a second in front of the mirror. "Live Annie, take your Harold and live or one day it will all be too late." She went downstairs, sighed at the creaking tread and poked the fire from its apathy. Annie followed her down.

"I shall cook the tongue tonight," said Bella, she went to the scullery , drained the water from the ox tongue and put the meat in the large pan which had sat over the fire all the years Annie could remember, spitting back at the flames that tormented its peace, surviving every assault but bearing the scars, so that now it was a true veteran. Annie wondered at what point it would be retired like the old pan Mrs.Bacon kept outside her back door in which to tip the spent tea leaves.

Harold had arrived looking very wholesome, a crisp white collar on his shirt, a flecked jacket and dark brown trousers but most importantly, wearing his happy smile which Annie was convinced had fitted him perfectly as an infant and had simply been 'let out' by Mother Nature each growing year, refusing to wear out, proving more than adequate to adorn Harold in adulthood as endearingly as it did in infancy. He winked at Annie as he turned into the living room where Bella had just checked under the lid of the pan to see if the water had come to the boil.

"How are you Miss Pownall?" He asked.

"Steamy," she replied, wiping her face on the hem of her pinafore.

"All the family send their best especially father, he says you've put sense in my head where before only bats roosted. It's true you've taught me so much, none of the teachers at school could explain things like you do. Anyway father says ……"

Bella interrupted him, "Your father says a lot doesn't he?"

"Yes he does," replied Harold, "but he always says what's right and proper. 'When thanks are due son, make sure you pay 'em', that's what he told me, so thank you very much Miss Pownall."

Quick as a flash Harold pulled a sprig of mistletoe from the inside of his jacket where he had been holding it out of sight, suspended it above Bella's head and kissed her firmly on the cheek. Annie stood rooted to the spot, she could scarcely believe her eyes. Bella put one hand to her cheek as if to hold the kiss there for a moment before it faded. Annie knew from her aunt's expression that Bella was touched by it but the defences were dropped only briefly.

"If you can't find anything better to do on Christmas Eve than kiss old women young man, then there are still too many bats roosting up there." Bella clipped his head with her hand and sat down in her chair. "Look after Annie tonight, bring her home by eleven."

"You know I will," he replied and cast his big smile over Bella, she smiled back and shooed him away with her hand.

Annie didn't speak afraid if she did it might break the spell. Harold had worked magic, for those few seconds Bella's eyes had lost their empty gaze and come alive, Annie remembered the words 'Live Annie, take your Harold and live'. It was time to put on her hat and coat and leave with Harold for the dance, they had agreed to meet Edna and Billy outside the Masonic Hall at half past seven.

Annie reached up for the sulphurs, "I'm lighting the candle for you Aunt Bella, we always light a candle on Christmas Eve." She cupped her fingers around the flame until it was established.

"Get along to your dancing and stop fussing about," said Bella.

The two young people called 'goodbye' and the back door rattled into its frame. Bella prodded at the fire to keep the pan simmering.

"Father says indeed," she muttered to herself.

She took Alice Hemsley's card down from the mantelpiece and studied the words written inside, her thoughts travelled back eight years to the time that chilling letter had arrived with the annual card. Now Bella placed Alice's

Christmas greetings back on the shelf, watched the light from the candle flicker across the card, hesitated for just a moment, then snuffed out the flame with her fingers. She leaned back in her chair, the wisp of smoke from the extinguished candle slowly rising, swirling, taunting, a dark sinister spirit that eventually vanished to somewhere in the house, out of sight but not gone.

The Hemsleys had been living in Sheffield for almost three years, Walter's work had increased steadily and the family had adapted well. Alice saw her mother every day, although the old lady's health was poor, mentally she remained bright and mother and daughter spent many hours together in conversation. One evening Alice had become so involved in the topic she and her mother had been discussing that it was later than usual when she left for home, it was not too far and Alice walked on most days. This particular evening in November she hurried, Walter would be home before her if she didn't make haste. As she approached Plowright Street she could hear a commotion, it was just possible in the dim light to make out a gathering of people stirred by some event. The sound of their collective voices rose and fell like a wave advancing and retreating over shingle. When Alice reached the rear of the crowd she heard a man's voice shout the words.

"You've killed 'im, you've bloody well killed 'im."

Women, of which there were a surprising number now clawed at the mass of people, desperately seeking a way through. They sped off into the darkness, the men remaining, black figures, menacing in the gloom, all stared at a body on the ground. One figure stood over the dead man, Alice recoiled, her stomach heaved as she saw the man kick the body and spit on it, casting abuse over the wretch before turning and shuffling away from the scene. No one had noticed Alice standing in the shadows, she raised her heels from the ground and walked back the way she had come using only the soles of her shoes, she made no sound and found herself clinging to the gate of her mother's house without any awareness of distance. Alice composed herself and went inside to her mother, she would wait for Walter, he would surely come looking for her.

The incident troubled Alice, it had seemed so barbaric, the crowd of spectators, no respect for the human being, almost a contempt like a Christian thrown to the lions, watched by the baying throng. A few days had passed when Walter came home from work with news which shook Alice but also answered years of doubt.

Through his work, Walter had been to the printers to collect a packet of business cards, the proprietor had been discussing the demise of someone who had once worked for him. Walter, always polite, waited patiently.

"I told 'im, I must 'ave told 'im scores o' times, you'll end up like a dead dog in the gutter Sefton."

The other man had replied, "I 'eard 'e left wicked troubles behind 'issen, come from Nottingham 'e did, drink, couldn't turn away from drink, would pick a fight wi' any man."

The proprietor then spoke the name that Walter recognised instantly.

"Sefton Pownall wer' a damn good printer, but a damnable bad man." Then he turned his attention to Walter, "I'm sorry to keep you waiting Sir, now what name is it again, Hemsley, yes, just one moment."

Walter stood quietly whilst the proprietor moved his hand along a shelf of packages, eventually finding the name he sought. "There you are Mr. Hemsley."

The business completed, Walter thanked the man and left the premises.

So, the brawl in Plowright Street had taken Bella's father from this earth. May God rest his soul.

Alice felt she could not keep this information from Bella, all the years that had passed since those bitter trials at Lenton must have haunted Bella's thoughts, not ever knowing whether Sefton lived or whether he was dead, if he might return of if he would not. Bella must be told the truth so she might lay this torment finally to rest and so with that Christmas card had come the fateful letter.

Suddenly, realising how much time had passed while she sat with her memories, Bella rose from her chair, took the thick towel from the table to hold the lid of the pan as she checked it had not boiled dry. Just in time. She crossed to the scullery to fetch the carving fork, speared the ox tongue to test for readiness and declared.

"It's done." The memory of eight years ago now lodged once more in the annals of Bella's mind, the tongue must be freed of bones, skinned, cut in half lengthways and pressed back to back. This was for Harold. She completed the task and put on the kettle for some tea. Soon the young ones would be back.

The dance had been a great success. Any concerns Annie might have had about her ability to move about the dance floor without causing Harold any embarrassment were soon dispelled. The atmosphere held no formality and the mix of age added tremendously to the fun of the evening. One quite elderly lady in defiance of years, sported a headdress made from a stiffened hat band, removed from its original situation and now adorned with mistletoe, she had a large curtain ring over her middle finger to which was attached a small silver bell, this she cupped in the palm of her hand but each time her festive spirit earned her a kiss, she raised her hand and rang the bell triumphantly.

As Billy roguishly declared, "That old gal 'as rung more bells tonight than 'Quasi-Bleedin'-Modo', rang all 'is soddin' days."

Billy had applied Dubbin to his work boots and buffered them until they shone like clean ice. Edna's eyes had been drawn to them as soon as the light in the hall caught their sheen.

"Before you say anything Edna, 'tis not to impress the toffs, 'tis so you'll slide off 'em when you trample on me bloody feet."

"Funny that," said Harold, "I call 'em nobs and you call 'em toffs Billy."

"Well they're both right aren't they, toffs is short for toffee-nosed and nobs is short for nobility," said Edna with authority.

While this debate took place, Annie viewed the scene with delight, the colours of the frocks, the decorations on the window ledges, the group of musicians playing seasonal tunes and some old favourites for people who ventured to make requests. Just to the side of this small band, a trestle table had been set up and on it, several large plates of mince pies and jugs of lemonade awaited the interval. Harold had gently lead Annie among all the other couples, she was surprised, it didn't seem too difficult, her feet moved with the music and lost as they were among so many other people, it felt entirely natural. Edna and Billy insisted that for at least one dance they swap partners.

" 'E's a smashin' bloke your Harold," said Billy as he squeezed Annie's waist to waltz past the mince pies. "Sorry," he said, "did I 'old you too tight? 'Tis cause I'm gettin' 'ungry, Harold says 'e allus knows when it's time to knock off for dinner cause I start gettin' 'eavy 'anded. Pulled that 'ard on the rope one time, nearly demolished Josiah's wall wi' bloody Black Angus bull."

By the end of the waltz Annie wondered how purple from bruising her waist might be tomorrow but she liked Billy a lot, he was a good friend and genuinely cared for Edna. Thankfully the interval was announced, Billy steered Edna to the food table like a wasp homing in on jam.

Harold laughed, "Just look at 'im, reckon 'e might 'ave worms. Grandad used to make 'is whippet chew on a bit 'o baccy, swore it did the trick, the old dog'll shed 'em in a nice neat ball 'e'd say and sure enough it did, actually seen it once. Come on Annie lets get some lemonade." Harold took her hand, "Two please," he said to the woman behind the table, "would you like a mince pie Annie?" He asked.

"No really, I'm alright with just a drink thank you."

Harold handed her a tumbler of lemonade, it tasted sharp and refreshing, he held out his mince pie saying, "Go on, 'ave a bite and make a wish if it's your first mince pie of the season. Mam says you 'ave to make a wish but tell no one what 'tis if it's your very first one."

Annie laughed and took a bite, mainly to please Harold but also to follow Sarah's belief in good things, she did not wish anything for herself but that Alfred Watkinson should stay well, May's new year would depend so much on that. The band started up again, everyone now inspired by their food and drink. The wooden floor once more joined the musicians in making music, the old planking, perforated where over the years the knots had fallen from the grain, leaving holes just big enough to create sound. It added a drumming effect which really came into its own for the Gay Gordons. When the band leader spoke to the gathering wishing everybody a happy Christmas and declared.

"We shall all sing, God Save The King, but not until after you have taken your partners for the last waltz." Annie felt she could have danced on longer, the atmosphere, the music, the closeness of Harold had all be wonderful.

"Well that's that Annie, a man 'as to dance the last waltz wi' the girl 'e's walkin' 'ome."

They could see Edna and Billy on the other side of the hall, Billy was looking towards the old lady with the bell and winking back at Harold. She had clearly claimed her partner for this crucial finale, a rather dapper looking man with a huge handlebar moustache.

"Looks like she's 'ad a good time, God bless 'er," said Harold.

The band began to play and the couples moved off, Harold put his face closer to Annie's and began to sing the words.

"When I grow too old to dream I'll have you to remember," he sang as he whirled her around the floor and at the last "Your love will stay in my heart." The music stopped and he kissed her "Happy Christmas Annie," he said.

Annie gazed back at that all comforting smile and whispered, "In my heart too."

The band played the anthem and all sang heartily. It had been an evening of glorious happiness and as everyone gathered coats and streamed out through the heavy double doors, the biting chill of the night air seemed to go unnoticed. Billy and Edna were waiting outside by the railings, Billy had wasted no time in rolling a cigarette and was just about to light it but paused to watch the old lady and her 'gent' pass by , arm in arm.

"What do you reckon Harold, more hair more tickle and more tickle more fun." He laughed, his roguish humour was infectious and all four walked along in the best of spirits.

"Still can't get used to singin' God Save our King," said Harold, "poor old 'Vicky'."

They reached the corner where the two couples had to go their separate ways.

"I have something for you Edna," said Annie and took the little red package from her pocket.

"Snap," cried Edna and produced an odd shaped item wrapped in newspaper. "Sorry about the wrappin' but it's fragile so a sheet of newspaper seemed the best thing. Are you goin' to the embankment tomorrow mornin'," she asked eagerly.

"I can't really," replied Annie, "I'm going to Harold's after dinner so I shall stay home with aunt Bella until then, I couldn't leave her on her own all day."

"Do you think she'd notice?" Said Edna.

"Now that's not fair Edna, leave Annie alone, she knows what's best, you and me can go for a while but not for very long, I'd rather spend some time with our mam than be waitin' about for the likes of Hannibal Burton to get 'is long johns back on." Said Billy.

They waved back to each other before disappearing into the darkness.

"Lets make haste Annie, 'tis a bit nippy out 'ere."

The temperature was low but the ground was as yet free of frost, they walked quickly.

"Race you to the entry," he said laughing. He slowed down purposefully to allow Annie to catch up, he took her hand and led her through to the yard, the moon was high, "Old Jack Frost will be 'ere soon, I reckon 'e's just turnin' the corner by The Standard, if you run in quick Miss Bundy you might escape him."

Harold took her into his arms and kissed her with such warmth, "I'll see you tomorrow afternoon then," he said, "give my love to your aunt Bella." He turned and was gone but just seconds later, Annie heard singing, echoing down the entry. "Your love will stay in my heart." Then silence.

She opened the back door, in the light that filtered through from the living room she could see on the scullery table, a basin covered by a saucer, in the middle of which was the big 2lb weight from the balance scales and on top of that, the flat iron. So aunt Bella has pressed the ox tongue, she said to herself. Bella was still up, sitting by the fire, the tea pot warming in the hearth, three cups were laid on the table by a jug of milk.

"Where's Harold?" She asked.

"He brought me to the yard but has gone home now, it is getting very cold, there will be ice forming soon I'm sure, he said to give you his love."

Annie recognised disappointment in Bella's eyes, she quickly added, "but you will see him tomorrow when he walks me home and he is looking forward to coming for tea on Boxing Day."

Annie began to tell her about the dance then suddenly noticed the candle, "Why Aunt Bella the candle has hardly burned at all," she said.

"No, it went out quite early on and I didn't feel the need to re-light it," said Bella, she rose from her chair.

"Shall we have a cup of tea now then?" Suggested Annie.

"It's late, I shall go up to bed, you have one if you want, make the fire safe before you come to bed and put out the lamp."

Annie listened to Bella as she climbed the stairs, waiting for her to close the bedroom door. The three cups still sat on the table, it was at that moment that Annie realised how lonely her aunt was.

Annie lay in bed, a mix of feelings moving around her mind as if they were still dancing to the music in the Masonic Hall. It had been a happy day and even now Annie felt she could not contain any more joy or she would burst, but just across the landing aunt Bella lay in the dark, so alone and that thought saddened Annie, she resolved to make this Christmas a special time for Bella. 'Jesus saves, joy to the world', that poor young man had cried out at seeing his mother. Aunt Bella was the only mother Annie had ever known, she would bring her joy and save her from such loneliness, Harold's kiss was just a beginning.

Next morning Annie awoke and for a few seconds could not bring her mind to what day it was, then she saw her blouse and skirt on the chair in the corner, Christmas, it's Christmas Day. She dressed quickly in her everyday things, she would go downstairs and do her chores, light had already come, she drew back the curtains, she had slept later than usual.

The fire looked quite dead, her first job must be to create some warmth before aunt Bella stirred. Annie pulled on her coat and slid back the bolts on the back door. On mornings like this the wooden seat on the privy sent shivers through her entire body. The small gap at the bottom of the door was a godsend summertime when the heat on the tin roof melted any poor soul needing to occupy 'the little house' for an extended visit but in the depths of winter it felt as though it led directly to the arctic, to linger might allow the ice to seal the door until spring. Annie knew such notions were a nonsense but it still achieved to impose urgency. The water in the jug on the scullery table made her fingers tingle, she thought of the charity swim and had to admire the stoic nature of those who participated. Raking the ashes and laying in the fire was a well practised routine, Annie soon had a good blaze in the grate, that measure of rancid dripping always came to her rescue if the wood was damp or paper was in short supply. She heard movement above, aunt Bella was awake. The kettle would soon be boiling then she could put on some porridge.

A knock came at the back door "Happy Christmas Annie", Winnie Bacon stood outside holding a plate covered by a tea cloth. "I made a few extra for you and Bella, give her my best."

"Won't you come in?" Said Annie.

"No dear, I must get on, our Elsie is coming for dinner with all her brood, the youngest is just at that climbing stage, you know what it's like, I shall have to put me bit of Crown Derby on top the wardrobe 'til they're gone.

Last week 'e climbed on top of Elsie's sideboard and got 'is 'and stuck inside 'is mam's wedding present from aunt Martha, lovely little vase it wer', painted all over with birds an' flowers. They 'ad to break it to get it off, tried to stick it back together again they did but it were no use. Like Elsie said, aunt Martha'll be right upset, she paid for that wi' money she got for sellin' Ike's bike when they took 'is leg off. You can let me have the plate back when you've eaten 'em," she whipped off the cloth to reveal four mince pies and four pieces of shortbread.

"Thank you ever so much Winnie," said Annie but the dear woman was already half way to her back door. She always seemed to be bustling about but had a generous heart and over the years had been a good neighbour.

Bella was in the living room when Annie carried the plate of baking indoors, "Look what Winnie has done for us." Annie held out the plate for aunt Bella to see.

"She's a good woman," said Bella, "put them in the front room with a cloth over them."

Annie hadn't been in the front room for weeks, she pulled to one side the heavy curtain which hung across the door to keep out draughts. It was always dim in this room, the front door opened straight on to the street, the nets at the windows were heavy and let in very little light. It had a 'musty' lifeless smell, the air was stirred by humankind so infrequently that it felt stale, no sunshine ever found a way in to cheer the drab walls. It was sparsely furnished, a number of books in a bookcase, two very plain chairs, a clock on the wall which no longer worked, its pendulum motionless it appeared to have lost all heart, with no one to call on its purpose it had simply lain still and died. The table in the centre had always been covered in a rust coloured cloth which had a fringe of tassels all round. The oranges and pears were on the table with a cake tin, a bottle of dandelion and burdock, a cheese dish and a plate bearing a deep pork pie. Annie added Mrs.Bacon's mincepies and biscuits to the assembly and returned to aunt Bella.

"I haven't had a chance to put the porridge on yet because of Winnie calling," she said.

"I've done it, there's tea made, sit down and have your breakfast." Aunt Bella was already spooning the porridge into bowls, the dish of brown sugar sat on the table in readiness, that was the way they always ate porridge, sprinkled with brown sugar and a dash of cream from the top of the milk.

"What vegetables would you like me to prepare?" Asked Annie.

"I've got a pie fowl to steam," said Bella, "we'll have some sprouts, carrots, parsnips and potatoes"

If Bella asked Mr.Cheetham in good time he would always manage to get a fowl, the older bird needed slower cooking but the flavour was excellent and the juices made very good gravy.

"Would you like to go for a short walk presently Aunt Bella?"

Annie had noticed how much slower her aunt had become over the past year but it seemed almost a ritual on Christmas morning, when the vegetables were prepared and the meat over the fire, Bella would put on her hat and coat, Annie had always done the same as a child, whatever aunt Bella declared they would do, so it was.

"We'll walk along Sherwood Road and back," she replied.

The two women set about their tasks and by mid morning the meal had been organized, it would simmer quietly whilst they were out. They had reached the corner and turned into Sherwood Road without meeting anyone. In the distance a man walked a dog but other than that the road was deserted. Annie had come to believe that this was the reason aunt Bella chose Christmas morning for their walk, men still lay abed nursing sore heads from too much ale the previous night, women toiled in their sculleries, feeding large families with a Christmas dinner most could ill afford and the children, allowed into the front room for that one day of the year, now fought with brothers and sisters over who should have what. The afternoon would be entirely different, men would gather in various locations to smoke and bemoan the lack of peace at home, women would battle their way through stacks of pots, pans and dishes, made ever more ill tempered by squabbling offspring 'til the young offenders were booted out through the door, with the seasonal message, 'go find your father and torment 'im'. By mid afternoon the women exchanged their very own Christmas stories over the dividing walls of the back yards, their voices becoming louder as they vied for the title of 'Most Taken for Granted'. Aunt Bella would be well ensconced in her chair with a book before the local populace pursued this long held tradition.

The air had brought a red flush to Bella's cheeks but her fingers looked pallid with cold.

"You should put on proper gloves when it is so cold," said Annie.

"These will do," replied Bella. The fingerless gloves which she wore almost constantly offered no comfort to her arthritic joints. Annie wished at that moment that she had bought her aunt a pair of warm woollen gloves instead of lavender water. They had reached the corner to turn back into Winchester Street, they would soon be by the fire.

Their meal was plain but wholesome, the meat from the fowl, tender and delicious. Bella had put aside a basin of juice for soup later in the week and thickened the remainder for the gravy which coated the vegetables in a rich savoury sauce. She considered Christmas pudding to be an extravagance which served no purpose other than to 'bind the belly' well into the new year. Instead they had dried fruit which she had stewed with a little sugar and one of Mrs. Bacon's shortbread biscuits. Their meal over, Annie cleared away and tended the fire, soon she would be on her way to Mitchell Street to give Harold his present, but first she would bring down from her bedroom the gift for Bella and the packages she had not yet opened from Edna and Saul.

"Happy Christmas Aunt Bella," said Annie, she kissed her cheek and handed her the box wrapped in festive red.

"Go up to my bedroom," said Bella, "you'll see a parcel on the end of my bed, that's for you."

Annie found a soft package wrapped in brown paper, she untied the string very carefully, aunt Bella never cut the string from a parcel, the knot had to be undone even if it took ages and wore away all fingernails in the process. The only exception was the presence of sealing wax, in that instance the string must be cut as close to the seal as possible. The contents were beautiful, a set of dressing table cloths, one larger oval shaped and two smaller rounds, each embroidered in the most delicate silks, pansies and forget-me-nots around the edges. Annie held them up to the window to see them better, she wrapped them again in the paper and carried them to her own bedroom where she put them on her bed. Downstairs Bella had opened the pretty silk lined box and sat with it in her lap.

When Annie came to the foot of the stairs Bella said, "It's time you started a bottom drawer, they are old but I've kept them well, the cloth is sound. Your grandmother embroidered them not long before she died, I've never used them, they were always for you."

"I shall treasure them all my days."

Bella looked into Annie's eyes, "If I seem cold it's because I think too much, being a teacher makes you think too much, don't pay it any consequence. I've given you all the lessons I can, what more you must learn will come from your life with Harold." She looked down at the lavender water, "I shall put some on later." She picked up the bottle undid the stopper and smelled the scent, "Lavender induces sleep, I shall have a nap while you are at Harold's."

Annie took the little higgledy-piggeldy newspaper clad item which Edna had given her after the dance and peeled back the layers.

"Oh, look Aunt Bella," she held out a small figurine of a terrier dog, sitting on its haunches, all white apart from a brown patch over the left eye and ear. It was just as she imagined their dog would be if she and Harold ever had one, a cross between Eli and Shawcross. Now she opened the package from Saul, a pair of stockings with the label, 'Drew's Hosiery'.

"We all have the same, Edna, May and myself," said Annie, "he is on his own for dinner today but he will be with Charles and Enid, and young William of course, for his tea."

Bella made no answer, she poked the fire and placed the kettle on the coals.

"You'd better be off, they'll all be waiting for you, I shall have a cup of tea and have an hour with a book."

As Annie walked along clutching her little bag of presents, she thought of Billy and Edna and the swim across the Trent. It would be such a diverse gathering, some of the wealthiest and most noted members of the community in the company of some of the poorest paid and housed, but each would drop something into the collection tins. Guineas and farthings would briefly abide together like the rich and poor on the embankment.

She could hear the children's laughter as she crossed the yard and the door opened before she had time to knock.

"We saw you comin'," said Frank, he stood in the scullery with one of Gertie's hats on his head, he had draped the two braids meant to be tied under the chin over his ears with a suspender hanging from each like earrings. He wore one of his mam's pinafores over his shirt and trousers, around his neck hung a string of beads made from empty cotton bobbins and an old pair of Nora's shoes almost clad his feet. "I've changed places with mam today Annie" he said, "I've nearly finished me dishes."

Inside the house Eli scanned the floor with his nose, searching through crumpled paper, nut shells and orange peel for any little morsel which might have been lost in passage between hand and mouth. Nora helped Frank in the scullery, Mavis and Maggie played with a rag doll made by Sarah and a dear little cot created by Samuel and Harold in which to put the doll. Jean sat at the table with paints and paper and Gertie had a sewing set. Samuel and Sarah, from their chairs by the fireplace surveyed the scene, their faces displayed total contentment. The chatter, laughter, barking and scattered debris surrounded them in concentrated essence of family. They knew how valuable this was, some never achieved to hold it even for a few minutes in a lifetime, they held it in good measure day on day.

Annie couldn't see Harold, recognising her puzzlement Samuel said, "It's alright Annie lass, 'e's gone upstairs, I think 'e asked Santa to leave your present up there," he winked at her. Father and son were so alike in their ways, Annie could well understand the bond between them, it came from the complete understanding they had of each other and the respect which that bred.

Harold appeared, his grin seemed to have stretched even wider in honour of the day. He gave Annie a kiss then handed her a box.

"Happy Christmas, my Annie," he said, "go on then open it."

She lifted the lid, inside cushioned by a pad of kapok, lay a hat pin, the shank long and silvery, the decorative head was of deep amber colour.

"It's not real," he said, " 'tis nickel and glass but one day I shall buy you proper silver and a jewel from the Amber Coast."

"Then you would be sadly misguided," she said, "because I shall never swap this for any other, it is beautiful Harold, thank-you. Now you must open this." Annie gave him the parcel containing the warm tweed cap and passed the wrapped lavender bag to Sarah, the tray of toffee for all to share she gave to Samuel saying. "You shall be keeper of the sweets."

He laughed, "I shall administer them according to my peoples' good deeds," he replied.

"This is a real bobby dazzler look Father," declared Harold as he paraded past Sarah and Samuel wearing his new cap, it did indeed look smart.

Annie had noticed how worn and faded his old cap had become, worn from the number of times it had been rolled up to fit into a pocket and faded from the years it had been weathered by the elements. He caught Annie's hand, put his arm about her waist, then cap still in place he whirled her through the litter strewn across the floor just as he had led her at the dance. Eli couldn't contain his enthusiasm and rushed between the chair and table legs, barking and yapping. Mavis and Maggie clapped their hands and Frank, still attired in his mam's pinafore stood in the scullery doorway blowing into an empty lemonade bottle.

Sarah now sat forward in her chair saying over and over, "Oh my sides ache." Rubbing her hands down her middle to ease the 'stitch' she had from so much laughter.

The afternoon passed so quickly, Gertie had been industrious and proudly held up a good four inches of French knitting.

"I shall do the next strip in yellow," she said excitedly.

Jean had painted a picture for her mam of Eli, it portrayed him as a rather fearsome character with big teeth and enormous eyes, but Sarah said.

"That's lovely Jean dear," and put it up on the shelf beside a framed picture of grandad Boucher. The rag doll had been dressed and undressed that many times by Mavis and Maggie that the knitted bloomers were so stretched they now reached the doll's armpits but the love with which they took it in turns to lay it in the cot was a credit to Sarah, they played out the scene just as they had witnessed it.

The time came for Annie and Harold to leave for Winchester Street. The family had eaten from an amazing array of cakes and biscuits baked by Sarah, a selection of each put into a bag for Annie to take home to aunt Bella. The little house was so cosy from the warmth generated by all its happy occupants that when Harold opened the back door, Annie felt they were about to step across to a different world entirely, as though the back yard straddled the globe to a cold dark continent.

"I do wish aunt Bella had come to see you Sarah," said Annie as they stood together saying goodbye, "it would have done her good."

"You have to understand Annie, that if a being is weakened by a long period of starvation, then a plate of dinner would likely kill them, nourishment needs to be dispensed in small doses, just a little at a time. It's the same if that being has lacked merriment and gladness, their spirits can only be lifted slowly, bit by bit. I dare say our household when it's full, would be too big a dose. Don't you fret, we'll find a way of making her happier."

Sarah gave Annie a hug and waved as Harold took her hand and the two disappeared into the darkness.

Back in Winchester Street, they walked hastily past all the chinks of light, the only evidence of life behind closed curtains. The back door was on the latch, Annie quickly let them in from the cold and called out to aunt Bella. The living room felt comfortably warm, a light scent of lavender mingled with the hot smell of recently stoked fire.

"Happy Christmas Miss Pownall," said Harold. He had deliberately avoided folding his new cap so instead of sticking out from his pocket as it would normally do, it required an appropriate parking space.

"I'll hang it on the door knob," said Annie.

Relieved of his cap Harold now took a package from his jacket pocket and handed it to Bella. "I 'aven't any mistletoe tonight but I shall give you a kiss anyway."

Bella carefully unwrapped her present, Annie thought it was incredible, Bella's gift was a pair of woollen gloves, a lovely rich plum colour. How did Harold know what she had been thinking just those few hours earlier?

"They are the very thing you needed aren't they Aunt Bella? How did you know Harold?" Said Annie.

"Ah, well it's like I tell me mam when she says, 'how did you know I needed that?' Us fellas know what a girl needs, it's magic, that's what 'tis, magic, all the magicians are blokes aren't they." Harold was delighted to discover that he had chosen well. Annie showed Bella her hat pin which led to Harold being told by aunt Bella to fetch the book atlas from the shelf in the front room, she would show him on the map where in the world was situated the Amber Coast.

Bella turned to Annie, "Light the Christmas candle, it can burn while we sit together."

Perhaps this was what Sarah had meant, small doses of happiness over a length of time which would eventually establish a contentment, a gladness in aunt Bella. Annie listened to the dialogue between Harold and her aunt, completely at ease with one another. The fire warmed Annie's toes, the scene before her, warmed her heart. Before Harold left for home they agreed to meet next day on the corner of Connaught Street at half past one and from there they would go to spend an hour with Davina as they had promised.

Bella declared she would eat another of Sarah's biscuits before going to bed.

Annie lay contemplating the day's events, her hat pin rested in its box beside Edna's little dog on the shelf by her bed. How curious that Harold should have given Aunt Bella gloves and Edna have chosen the very dog that Annie had pictured in her daydreams. It had been a very good day, the beautiful embroidered cloths Annie had put away in the bottom drawer of the chest, her thoughts, this night, were too serene to resist and sleep very quickly overcame them.

Harold was waiting at the corner, "Good job you've come, all the women were givin' me the glad eye, 'tis this smart cap," said Harold.

"Come on, lets show you to Davina she already thinks you're the cat's whiskers and she hasn't yet seen you in your new cap."

"Handsome bloke, that's me," said Harold and began to sing, "I'm Burlington Bertie ......"

They walked along for a few minutes, "I looked at mam and father last night, you saw what our house was like yesterday Annie," said Harold, "they worked so 'ard to give us all a good Christmas especially the young 'ens. If we tell 'em we're gettin' married they'll beggar thesels' to give us a 'do'. I could tell 'em that's not what we want, I could say that to 'em 'til I wer' blue in the face but it 'ould make no difference, they'd still work thesels' to the bone. There are too many mouths to feed, shoes to buy for father to be spendin' money on our weddin'."

"I would have to tell aunt Bella," said Annie, "I couldn't keep something so important from her, she is very wise in all matters, perhaps we should ask her advice, I think she would help if she could."

"We'll speak with her this evenin' after tea, if you really think she'll understand, then that's what we'll do," said Harold.

Davina was in good spirits, proudly showing off her festive tablecloth purchased at Drew's. A number of cards decorated the room including one from Davina's cousin Isobel. "I shall reply to her letter in the new year, it will require considerable fortitude, I shall bolster my constitution by taking a few measures of sherry before I embark on such a challenge," said Davina.

"She sounds like quite a character, your cousin," said Harold.

"Yes dear, she is, in fact Isobel is an experience, to know and understand her is a revelation of almost biblical proportion, she leaves me entirely in awe and utterly exhausted." They chatted happily, Davina so eager to hear about their time at the dance and the events of the previous day. By the time they all stood at the door, waving goodbye, Annie and Harold had enjoyed much laughter, a warming glass of mulled wine and several marzipan fruits.

'Do have another one my dears, I shall be too large for any of my dresses and woefully constipated if you don't relieve me of these temptations', had been Davina's plea.

Annie thanked both Davina and Ivy for their card and good wishes, she looked back for one last wave before turning the corner, they had all become so close since that first meeting in the spring. A great deal had changed in just a few months and the wedding would bring more change. Annie clutched Harold's arm tightly as a shiver passed through her.

"Are you cold?" He asked.

"No, not really, it was one of those strange shivers," she replied.

"Someone trod on your grave," said Harold, "that's what mam says."

He wrapped his arm around her and they walked briskly back to Bella's.

She had been busy, the table was laid, slices of tongue sat on a large plate alongside wedges of pork pie, cheese, the bloomer loaf and a boiled fruit cake. All graced the table with their goodness. On the sideboard, the three pears were in line as though they travelled towards the feast on the table like the three Kings of the Orient, making their way to the manger.

Bella made a pot of tea and passed a steaming hot cup to both Harold and Annie.

"Help yourself," she prompted. They ate heartily, even Bella took a slice of tongue, "I'll taste it to see that it's not salty," she said.

" 'Ave I ever told you that a cow can get its tongue right up its nostril," said Harold, "Billy an' me 'ave watched 'em do it. Now I'm only repeatin' what Billy said but 'e reckons Edna could likely do it an'all, 'er tongue 'as wagged that much it's stretched too far to fit back in proper so she 'as to roll it up behind 'er teeth like a pickled herrin'."

Harold chuckled wickedly and aunt Bella said, "Shame on Billy Dodds," but Annie could tell that the story had amused her. The meal over Annie cleared away, she whispered to Harold.

"You talk with aunt Bella while I do the dishes."

Annie had already told Bella of Harold's wish for them to marry in the spring but Bella had not spoken of it to Harold.

"I don't know what to do Miss Pownall," said Harold, "I want to marry Annie and you know I shall always look after her. Josiah is goin' to pay me more wages in the new year, Annie and me could find a little place to live, close to you, because she will want to see you every day. You think that would be alright don't you?" Said Harold

"I think it is to Annie you must direct that question," replied Bella.

"Oh but I already 'ave," he declared with absolute honesty.

"Then what troubles you Harold?" Bella's voice was calm and reassuring.

"Our house is full of family, father 'ardly ever stops workin' if 'e's not sweepin' chimneys then 'e's down the allotment, mam pushes food through that old stove day after day, just puttin' shoes on the young 'ens feet costs 'em dear. If I tell 'em about us gettin' married they'll make thesels' paupers tryin' to give us a 'do'. Neither Annie nor me want any fuss but I could tell 'em 'til I was blue in the face and they'd carry on just the same."

"Do you know what kind of wedding your mother and father had?" Asked Bella.

"I've heard mam tell how they were married half past nine in the mornin' and by eleven father was down Hood Street sweeping chimneys and mam and her best friend Ida Pickering were down The Meadows pickin' sloes for grandad Boucher's sloe gin."

"Are your mother and father happy?" Asked Bella.

"You only 'ave to look at 'em to know they are," said Harold, "father comes in from work tired and sooty, gives mam a smile and a kiss and you can tell from 'er face that's the best part of 'er day."

"Remind them of their own wedding, its simplicity. Tell them you would rather have their help with everyday things than you would have a fuss on your wedding day. Convince them you will always need them in the future as you have in the past." Bella patted his hand, "They will understand."

Harold felt more confident, what Annie had said was true, Bella Pownall did have great wisdom. Like 'The owl in the oak tree', she surveyed mankind from her hidden corner, most people not even aware of her quiet observations.

Annie came through from the scullery to join them by the fire, Harold took a bag of humbugs from his pocket.

" 'Ave a mint, it'll do yer good," he passed the bag from Bella to Annie. The three sat together sucking Harold's sweets, silently, each with their own thoughts. Christmas was almost over, tomorrow would be a working day.

Harold stood at the back door fixing his cap, Annie knew that she wanted these nights of parting to end, sending him into the darkness whilst she went to her room alone pained her.

Bella stood at the foot of the stairs. "You and Harold are both bright and strong, you could achieve a great deal together but you must be free of all encumbrance, don't burden Harold with concerns about me."

"But Aunt Bella, I shall always be concerned for you, I love you like a mother," said Annie.

Aunt Bella had already reached the first tread of the stairs, she did not look back but called out as she climbed further, "I shall reply to Alice Hemsley's letter tomorrow."

Bella needed the solitude of her room, behind the closed door she could cry unseen.

CHAPTER FOURTEEN

May had settled back into the routine of the workshop and Alfred had readily embraced his role of housekeeper, as Annie had taken pains to point out, with two children in the home his duties were paramount. Mabel had begun her lessons and walked proudly to school with 'her Alfred'.

Saul seemed preoccupied, now that May was back, Annie had not been late leaving in the evenings so had no way of knowing whether Charles' visits to his father continued or not but each time she called on Enid and young William, some new set of clothing or household item had been in evidence. The child grew quickly, soon he would be six months old. The winter faded fast, leaf buds now appeared on the trees, the days lengthened in light. Annie and Harold were to be married in three weeks time. After much agonising, Harold had told Samuel and Sarah of the wedding plans, at first his big fear threatened to become reality but Bella had encouraged him to persist in reassuring them that it was the future happiness and well-being of all the family which mattered the most to Annie and himself. Finally they agreed to his request for a quiet affair but insisted that on the day after the wedding, a Sunday, he and Annie come for dinner, it was accepted by all as a fair compromise.

Josiah had been as good as his word and from the start of the new year Harold had been paid an increase of 1/9d a week.

A very small house, in some need of repair had come available for rent not far from aunt Bella's.

Harold held Annie's hand tightly as they waited while the landlord unlocked the door to show them the interior.

"It'll need scrubbin'" the man said as he led them into a room no more than twelve feet square. The walls showed no individual shade of colour, their surface reminded Annie of the results of a terrible 'Pox', pitted, scabby. The floorboards creaked beneath their feet as they followed him to a door which led to a scullery, a pane of glass in the window had been broken and boarded up with a piece of old tea chest. The back door opened to a narrow cobbled yard with the usual privy and coal shed. At the end of the yard a very loose, ramshackled wooden gate led to a patch of brambles and stinging nettles roughly the size of the living room.

"It could be a good garden this could," the man said as he kicked his hobnailed boot at a bushy thistle, from underneath which a very pregnant rat ran to the shelter of a hole in the brickwork of the wall. The open privy door revealed an example of man's idleness and apathy.

"Our Eli takes more care than that." Said Harold.

The landlord coughed, spat at the cobbles and said sarcastically, "Well, perhaps your Eli won't be so careful when 'e's old enough to swallow half a dozen pints of ale on an empty stomach."

"Eli's a dog," declared Harold with real feeling.

The man made no answer but called them back inside the house. "Mind yourself, one or two of the treads are weak," he cautioned as he pointed to the stairs. "No point in us all goin' up there, you look at what you need to look at," he said.

The stairs were dark and quite narrow, Harold found the rotted treads, three were very weak, the others felt reasonably sound. In the two rooms above, the general disrepair and dirtiness continued but the larger room had a fireplace and Annie had noticed an old range downstairs, which in her optimism she thought might be redeemed to enable some baking. Upstairs, the windows were at least intact. Harold looked up at the ceiling, intent on finding any sign of water penetration from the roof above, thankfully there was none.

"The floorboards seem strong enough up 'ere," said Harold, "father and Frank will 'elp us, a good scrubbin', a bit of woodwork and a lick 'o paint will make all the difference. I know it looks grim now Annie but 'tis the only place close to your aunt Bella."

The rent was manageable, Annie and Harold had agreed it would be wonderful to have their own place rather than live with Bella, they could not live at Sarah's, the house already bulged at the seams.

"I must give aunt Bella money to help with food and rent for herself, at her age, she couldn't manage without some of my earnings." Annie had told Harold.

"That's alright, we'll manage, you'll see," Harold had replied.

He had paid a month's rent in advance and the last two Sundays had been devoted to No.24 Winchester Street. Samuel and Harold made safe the stairs and fitted a new pane of glass in the scullery window.   Annie and Nora had scrubbed 'til their hands became locked in position around their brushes. The next Sunday they would begin painting and Frank was quite determined to do as May had suggested, and collect on his way the heavy curtains which had come from Davina's. One each week, 'I have no more need of them now Annie' May had said, 'they will give you enough material for all your windows and you are just the person to sew them'.

Aunt Bella had taken from the cupboard a quantity of bed linen and towels which Annie had never seen before. 'I knew you would need them one day, I've kept them as well as I could, they will do for you to start', said Bella.

Sarah had presented them with pots and pans. 'I don't use these any more, they aren't pretty but they'll stand the heat'.

Edna had brought to the workshop one morning a rolled 'rag mat'. 'Mam makes these, I told 'er she's got plenty 'o time to make one for my bottom drawer, Billy's still takin' me off the 'ook an' throwin' me back in the river to catch again'.

'I think Billy will be putting you in his keep net any day', said Annie, 'he loves you to bits'.

Edna laughed and declared, 'I love 'is bits an'all'.

But it was Saul who had most surprised Annie. He had asked her to stay for a minute as he needed to speak with her about something.   The workshop was quiet, May and Edna had left for home.

'Over several months you have taken on more responsibility here, I am getting older Annie, some days that tiredness borne of age, makes me slower. If one day I felt unable to be here at the workshop I am quite confident you would be capable of 'holding the fort', for me to spend some time at home. It is because of this I am giving you a small increase in pay and entrusting you with keys to these premises'.

Annie began to express concern but he interrupted, 'Please Annie, there is no one else I can ask. You are at the threshold of marriage and starting a home, these new arrangements will help me and you and Harold also. The larger key is the one for the lock on the front door, the smaller key opens the drawer of my desk where I keep the ledger and the petty cash, keep them safely at home until you need them'.

'Are you sure there is no one else you would rather hold your keys'? Asked Annie.

Saul smiled, 'I consider them to be safest in your charge. I have to think of the business, it may be small but our clients rely on us. Look on it as a kind of insurance Annie, rather like your aunt Bella taught you lessons far beyond those given to most young women, she knew you would be just as capable of managing as she has always been. I too have tried to give you vital skills, I also know you are as capable as myself and could run the workshop very well. It is what we older people do, a natural progression'.

'I will take the greatest care of the keys and do my very best to look after things here if you should need to rest', said Annie.

More than three weeks had passed since that evening, Saul had been at the workshop each day and Annie believed it was as Saul had said, an insurance against difficulty if at any time he felt too tired to come in to work. She had found an extra 1/3d in her envelope each week. An increase of three shillings a week on their combined income made a big difference. In spite of the shabby state of No.24 their spirits had been lifted. Sunday had arrived in brilliant sunshine and with real warmth in the air. Samuel and Harold had redeemed the privy, it now smelled of lime wash and disinfectant.

The rusting door latch had been replaced and Samuel had fitted a strip of metal gauze to the bottom of the door, 'That'll keep the rats out Annie lass', he said.

Frank had thought better of riding Cyril Lovatt's bicycle through the streets on a Sunday, giving Mavis and Maggie a bit of a laugh in Mitchell Street was harmless fun, riding openly from there to Winchester Street was entirely different. He and Nora walked together, the curtain travelled in a small tin bath, Frank took one handle and Nora the other.

"We won't need the bath until tonight," said May, "but young Alfred better have a wash before school tomorrow. He was out yesterday with all the other lads, playing football with a pig's bladder from Josiah's. It's awful rough and he comes home so scruffy, but he loves it. His father says, 'he'll be alright, the lad's got to toughen up a bit'." May had given a big sigh and cautioned Nora not to strain herself.

Bella had told Annie to come across at dinner time and she would put some food together for her to take back to No.24.

"Won't you come over to see what we are doing?" Asked Annie.

"I'll see it time enough, take this as well," Bella gave Annie some lemonade, "leave the cups there save taking them again, I've more here in the cupboard I can use."

The basket held bread, cheese, apples, gingerbread and five cups.

"She isn't comin' across then?" Harold said quietly to Annie.

"No, sometimes I think she just can't face people, she has spent so much time alone."

Harold gave Annie that wink which meant everything would be alright. "When we've got a good fire goin' and the place is tidied up I'll get her 'ere, you'll see."

They worked until late afternoon, upstairs the ceilings and walls were cleaned and ready for painting. The scullery was looking much less bare, Harold had put up some shelves and the floor, now it had been scrubbed, allowed them to walk across it without becoming stuck to the flags. Samuel had discovered the old range to be sound, filthy but workable.

"I shall come here one or two evenings in the week and clean it," said Annie.

Samuel encouraged everyone by saying, "A bit of paint about the place and a few bits and pieces of furniture brought in, you'll look around and feel that proud you wouldn't call the King your Uncle."

They all laughed, it had been a happy day, the sunlight streaming in through the cleaned glass in the windows, the good humoured chatter and aunt Bella's basket of nourishment had all felt good.

"I'll go home with the others now Annie," said Harold, "I have to be at the yard early in the mornin', tell your aunt Bella I shall see her in the week and thank her for our dinner." He kissed her and held up his hand, "smell that," he said with a chuckle.

"What is that smell?" Asked Annie.

"Linseed oil from the putty, some of the panes upstairs were loose but they'll keep us warm now, don't want to be in me birthday suit feelin' draughty," he laughed as Annie blushed, he kissed her again and ran to catch up with Samuel, Frank and Nora, the latter two walking side by side with May's tin bath between them, swinging it to and fro like the swing boats at the fair. "Goodbye Annie," the united farewell echoed back up the street, she waved until they had passed the workshop then picked up the empty basket and went in to aunt Bella.

In the evenings Annie worked on the range, cleaning the oven and grate, by the time she had 'black leaded' the casting and buffered it to a shine, it had been transformed. Before they could finish painting, Samuel was to sweep the chimney. Harold had gone to the house straight from work, only agreeing to put down his tools when Bella had declared the meal ready.

"It will be spoiled if you don't come now." She had ventured across the street to inspect their progress.

"What do you think of it then Miss Pownall?" Harold asked. He took great pride in showing her a sturdy shelf he had fixed to the wall of the living room, "That's to put me books on," he said with immense satisfaction.

"It is a house like scores of others, what makes it uniquely yours is the creation of a home, where the world outside does not dominate the life within. It is not the strength of the door which keeps the world at bay but the will of those who dwell behind it." Aunt Bella said nothing more.

Harold and Annie followed her back to No. 11, there her philosophy displayed its truth, the world had ever stopped at Miss Pownall's door, what lay within was her domain uniquely.

Annie's machine sped across the linen, Samuel would be at the house with his brushes sweeping the chimney, it was Saturday afternoon, Harold would go there straight from the yard. This time next Saturday we shall be married, Annie's thoughts were racing with the shuttle. Billy and Edna were to be witnesses. The marriage was to take place at 11 o'clock at the registry office at Friar Gate, between now and then, the last of the painting must be done and a few pieces of furniture put inside the house. Josiah had generously offered the use of his waggon to transport these. Sarah had mysteriously produced a table and two chairs, Harold had purchased a secondhand fireside chair and in a gesture of affection, Davina had insisted they accept her offer of a bed which as she put it, 'has done nothing but prevent Ivy properly cleaning the floor and caused her tiresome efforts in keeping the mattress aired'.

Tomorrow Harold and Samuel would take the furniture to Winchester Street, Davina had been thrilled at the prospect of meeting Samuel. Josiah's waggon had to be washed down in readiness, a considerable task but Harold was to be entrusted with the keys to the yard, Josiah clung tightly to his Sundays of rest.

'You'll 'ave to be in early Monday Harold, to unlock the gates, sheep are comin' in from Bobbers Mill', he cautioned firmly.

When her work was finished Annie hurriedly donned her coat, anxious to join the others at No. 24.

"Do you have most of the things you need Annie?" Asked Saul.

"Oh yes, more than, everyone has been so kind," replied Annie, she waved back then ran up the street.

How satisfied Annie is with what must surely be the barest essentials, if only Enid were half as easily pleased thought Saul. Charles' need of money had not lessened, his manner was at least more gracious. There were times when he actually sat with Saul and chatted about the bank, William and events in the city, but the steady flow of funds continued. Saul had pondered the situation, it caused him great concern, for all that Charles seemed less distant of late, he still showed no interest in the business.

When Annie reached the house, Samuel's barrow stood outside, the brushes and bags of soot, evidence of the job done, she opened the door and called out.

"Up 'ere lass," came a voice from above. She found Samuel in the larger bedroom, the room with the fireplace. "The chimney's done Annie, I've nearly finished in 'ere."

Frank was in the smaller room, both men had almost completed painting the walls.

"Harold hasn't arrived yet but when he does, me and Frank must get back home."

"Of course," said Annie, "I'll just go in to make sure aunt Bella is alright then I'll come back to carry on painting while I wait for Harold"

He had come soon after and together they worked industriously until the light faded and the decorating was done. Bella had delayed their meal to enable them to make best use of the daylight but now they were hungry and tired. The stew was comforting, Bella would eat only a small amount.

"I shan't sleep if I take too much onion at this hour," she said, but Annie encouraged her to eat some bread and butter with her cup of tea.

"You won't find sleep if your stomach is barely filled either," Annie told her, knowing her aunt could hardly protest as that same reasoning had been used by Bella many times when Annie was younger and didn't particularly favour her tea.

That night Annie couldn't remember her head touching the pillow she was so tired. When dawn broke, her legs complained when she bent down to tend the fire, her arms ached from the endless brushwork but her spirits felt nothing but eagerness for the day. Fortunately the weather was dry, moving the furniture in rain would be very difficult. Aunt Bella had gathered together numerous household items declaring them to be, 'more use to you than me'. The two dwellings being so close, was a big comfort to Annie, when she stood on the step of No.24 and looked up the street she could see quite plainly, the scrubbed white step on Mrs.Bacon's house and just a few feet the nearside of that, was the rarely opened front door of No.11.

"Come across later and meet Harold's family Aunt Bella," Annie said hopefully.

"I'll see," was all the reply Annie was given.

When the waggon arrived, Annie looked out from the living room window and chuckled at the spectacle. Sarah had been so anxious to see everything that Nora had stayed with the young ones to enable their mam to go with the men. Sarah sat aloft the waggon on a fireside chair, clutching a mirror as though her life depended on it.

Harold gave Josiah's horse a bag of oats, "That'll keep 'im 'appy for a bit," he said.

"Never mind the horse Harold," cried poor Sarah, "take this mirror before I drop the dear thing, such bad luck to break a mirror, I can't stand the thought."

Harold laughed and teased her, "You've gripped it that 'ard Mam I reckon you've cracked it." She pretended to clip him round the ear.

Samuel had alighted and carried into the house the other curtain from May's which he'd held on the seat all the way from Peverell Street. Frank was lifting down the chairs and table, packed about Sarah's feet were buckets, bowls, bags of firewood and coal, a fork and spade for gardening and what Annie thought was the most comical of all, a large china 'po' with a decorative border of blue flowers, in which sat Eli.

" 'E wasn't going to miss out on all this," said Sarah.

Another trip would be necessary to collect the bed.

"I brushed the old 'orses mane and tail," said Harold jokingly, "can't 'ave 'im trottin' through The Park lookin' unkempt."

As soon as the waggon was unloaded the men left for Davina's.

"Lets have a go at lighting that range Annie," said Sarah, "then we can put a pan of water on to boil for some tea."

The two women busied themselves, putting china on shelves, rugs on floors, the precious mirror on the wall. "You'll need a chest of drawers to put your clothes in and a washstand," said Sarah.

"Aunt Bella says we can have those from my bedroom".

A sound came at the front door, it was Bella, she had watched the men leave from behind the nets, Bella could face them only a little at a time, to begin with Harold's mother seemed only proper. Sarah greeted her warmly, that smile which Harold gave so readily came just as naturally to Sarah.

"Oh Miss Pownall, I am so glad our Harold met your Annie, they go together like moon and stars, I've never seen Harold happier. I know he could do with a bit of polishin' here and there but he'll always look after her and give her a good life. He wants to show Annie all the world bless him, the things he talks about, I don't know where he gets it all from. Anyway, we've got a good fire in that old range and the water's boilin' so we'll 'ave a nice cuppa. You sit down there on that chair."

Annie was amused at the way Sarah fussed over aunt Bella, as though she were senior in years and yet given the age of Nora, it must be the reverse. Eli rushed in from the back yard where he had investigated every chink and crevice in the garden wall and sniffed every square inch of cobbles. He stood in front of Bella, not recognising this visitor he looked puzzled but made up his mind within seconds, to Annie's surprise he lay down at Bella's feet, he had decided she was a friend. The warmth from the grate, the accepted company and Sarah's familiar chatter, all soothed Eli to a contented sleep, his back leg twitching and high pitched abbreviated barks confirmed he was dreaming. Annie observed aunt Bella's reaction, she gazed down at the sleeping dog, a smile on her face and her hand went down to stroke his back, gently, lovingly. The tea was welcome, it tasted even better to Annie, knowing it had been made on their own range.

"I reckon that will be a good baker, the way that fire got up, it should cook like a little furnace in there," said Sarah happily.

Bella had sat very quietly sipping her tea, Annie knew it would not be long before she made some reason to go home, 'small doses' Sarah had said.

Bella rose from the chair, "I'll make a basket of food Annie, you come over for it at dinnertime." She walked to the door, Sarah beside her. "Your Harold needs no polish, he shines among men of much less copper, Annie is fortunate to have him."

The two women exchanged a look which spoke more than words, both dreaded the emptiness which had already begun to creep into their hearts, each acknowledged it in the other without utterance.

The house now smelled clean and fresh, in spite of the rooms' bareness it began to feel right. Annie had thoroughly scrubbed the floor of the bedroom yet again before the men returned with the bed. The air from the open windows had all but dried the boards when Annie heard the sound of the waggon outside.

Samuel beamed, "By gum Sarah, they'll sleep well on this."

The foot and headboard were of dark oak, carved at each corner in a sort of feather pattern. The sprung base secured to a brass frame, the mattress a good four inches of flock.

"What a grand lady," said Samuel, "lovely woman, kindness itself. I told her I shall be along next week to get rid of all that winter soot from her chimneys and I shan't stand for any argument, it'll be done and that's that."

Harold stood behind his father winking, "I reckon our Frank thought Ivy was a bit of alright an'all."

"Give over Harold," said Frank, looking slightly flushed.

"Never mind all that now," said Sarah, "we've got to get that bed up those stairs, we can't leave Nora on her own with the young ens all day."

Suitably chastened, Samuel redeemed himself by giving his wife a kiss and declaring, "There's not a woman in this land could hold a candle to you my love."

The bed frame was squeezed up the stairs with little more than a whisker to spare.

"There's a good bit 'o weight in that Harold," said Samuel, but the floors were sound, he had made sure of that. It was soon erected and the mattress put in place. Annie had fetched the basket of food from aunt Bella's which they all ate and enjoyed before preparing to leave for Mitchell Street. Harold must deposit them at home then take the waggon back to the yard.

Sarah sat up the front with Harold, "Miss Pownall came across for a little while," she said, "I can tell she's goin' to miss her Annie but it's a blessin' they'll be so close to one another, a real blessin'." Sarah's voice trembled, Harold took one hand off the reins and put his arm around his mother.

"Don't fret Mam, you can't get rid 'o me that easily."

Maggie and Mavis were peering through the window, watching for their return. Harold had promised them a ride but they would have to walk all the way home. Frank lifted Eli down and the excited dog promptly cocked his leg and piddled up the waggon wheel.

Samuel lifted Sarah from the seat, "There's a bit more 'o you than there used to be lass," he said roguishly.

"If you're not careful there might be a bit less 'o you," replied Sarah and moved her fingers like a pair of scissors.

Frank and Harold were enjoying the moment, Eli, now relieved, rushed around to the back yard to make sure his own familiar cobbles smelled as they should. Gertie and Jean decided they too would ride to Josiah's, so Harold set off with the four girls, waving and laughing, this was even more fun than Lovatt's bicycle.

CHAPTER FIFTEEN

Annie had made No.24 as homely as she could, aunt Bella's bed linen, the chest, washstand and rug from her bedroom, all now awaited the newlyweds. Food sat in a cupboard in the scullery, the water buckets were filled, only some clothes and the remainder of Harold's things had still to be installed.

Annie had lit the fire and sat in Bella's chair waiting for the water to boil, by midday she would be married, Edna and Billy were to meet them at Friar Gate. Josiah had closed the yard for the day, without Harold and Billy there would be no heavy work undertaken, the two young men had worked later each evening to make up their time and to keep on top of activities at the yard. Aunt Bella had been very quiet all week, Annie sensed it was not an irritable quietness and felt convinced that as the days progressed and aunt Bella realised she would see both Harold and herself often, her spirits would cheer a little. Saul had decided to give the women the day off, he knew they would meet the orders and to call in May to work alone seemed a nonsense.

'I wish you happiness Annie' he had told her as she left the evening before. 'Give my kind regards to Harold and enjoy the day tomorrow'.

The water boiled, she put tea to brew and set a pan of milk and oats over the coals, this day called for porridge. Annie felt happier than words could describe yet a nervousness played mischief with her stomach, the soft porridge and sweet brown sugar might soothe away those silly anxieties. Outside the sky was heavy with cloud.

'If it rains on me bit 'o best I shall swear' had been Edna's caution as they'd sat in the workshop eating their dinner.

'They say you should have a bit of everything on your wedding day for luck' remarked May.

Edna gave her an old fashioned look and said, 'I'd be 'appy wi' a nice bit 'o one thing', then she lowered her voice so Saul could not hear, 'I reckon that's what 'e could do with to buck 'im up a bit'.

'Eat your barm cake and do hush' Annie had replied, feeling disloyal to Saul at even hearing the words.

Her thoughts came back to the present as she heard movement above, aunt Bella was stirring. Annie laid the table, doing so made her realise she didn't have a bread knife at No.24. Bella heard Annie thinking aloud, she reached the foot of the stairs and said.

"There's another one in the drawer of the table in the front room, take it across with the cake tin. I've put a fruit cake in there for you to cut if Edna and Billy come back with you afterwards."

"We shall come and see you this evening," said Annie.

"No, not tonight," Bella spoke firmly, "I am perfectly capable of doing for myself, it is your own coal bucket you must fill now, not mine."

"Thank you for the cake Aunt Bella," Annie suddenly felt very close to tears.

"Don't you start snivelling, you've too much to be doing, I'll clear up here, take those things over the road with your bag of clothes then you can come back and wash and change ready for when Harold gets here."

This little room has been my refuge for twelve years, thought Annie as she looked about the now empty space. Come on, she told herself, no time to dwell on the past. She pinned the Mother of Pearl brooch at the neck of her blouse, slipped on her tidy shoes and took her little jacket from the only remaining item of furniture, the little chair which had always been in the corner. Her everyday clothes she put in a bag, Harold was to bring the rest of his things today so they could all be taken to No.24 before they left for Friar Gate.

Aunt Bella's voice called up the stairs, "Harold is here."

He had arrived with three pink roses, one for Annie, one to give to Edna and the other he presented to Bella saying, "Miss Pownall, in just a little while I shall be Annie's husband, when I see you after our wedding, may I call you Aunt Bella? 'Cause if you say yes that will really make my day."

Bella took the rose with the reply, "I shall not see you today after the wedding, I am too set in my ways to stand the excitement you two will be filled with. Tomorrow, when you have raked your grate, lit your fire and filled your buckets, then you will be suitable company again. You can call on 'your' aunt Bella and she will be pleased to see you."

She fetched a jug from the scullery, placing her rose in the water. "Now hurry up," she said, "it will take you a good half hour to walk to Friar Gate and you've yet to take those bags across to your house."

Harold smiled to himself, so she will be my aunt Bella from tomorrow, the thought amused him.

The sky was still threatening, Edna had begged an umbrella, just in case, from her sister Ada. Billy had borrowed a suit from his father, the two hurried towards the registry office.

"Get a move on Billy, they'll be waitin' for us"

"It's these soddin' trousers," said Billy, "the jacket fits alright but the trousers are too big around the waist, me braces are stretched anyway so me crotch is sittin' somewhere just above me bloody knees. It's a good job father's got ducks disease 'cause if 'e weren't short legged me turnups would be six soddin' inches deep."

"Just so long as it don't rain on me suede shoes," said Edna.

Harold and Annie reached Friar Gate but could see no sign of their witnesses.

"We're a bit early, another ten minutes yet," said Harold. He squeezed Annie's hand, in the other she clutched Edna's rose. The pretty pink bloom pinned to her jacket must have been indication to all those people they passed, of the young couple's destination.

The registry office was not a large building yet it seemed to declare its importance, claim some reverence, through the heavy panelled door and ornate railings, the granite lintel above the deep window, a dark brown brocade drape which swagged either side of the leaded glass.

Billy and Edna appeared, rushing, waving, "Slow down," called Harold, "plenty 'o time."

Billy's huge grin as he greeted Harold showed the depth of friendship between the two men.

" 'E's 'avin' trouble wi' 'is crotch," said Edna, "I offered to adjust it for 'im but 'e insisted that outside the Mission wi' old po faced Shawcross takin' the Women's Fellowship weren't the right place nor time," she giggled. Annie pinned the rose to Edna's lapel.

"That's too ladylike for 'er Annie," said Billy, "Edna aught to 'ave a dog daisy."

Harold laughed at their banter, "Come on, we 'ave to go in now."

The door opened to a hallway, two doors led off, one unmarked, the other with a nameplate, 'Registrar'. The clock on the wall above read one minute to eleven.

"Here goes," said Harold, he knocked gently, a brief sound of movement in the room was followed immediately by the opening of the door.

A very officious looking gentleman surveyed the group. "Mr.Boucher," he said casting his eyes to Billy.

"That's me," said Harold.

"Come in please."

They followed him into a very dark room, oak panelling covered all the walls, everything appeared a very sombre brown colour. A table, its surface very highly polished, stood in the middle of the room, in the centre of which a tall glass vase awaited its purpose. The Registrar passed his eyes over the four young people, seeing no flowers to decorate the occasion he promptly removed the vase to a window sill. Billy looked at Harold and winked. The formalities took only ten minutes, Annie had not known what to expect and as they stepped out of the echoing hallway into the street she felt bewildered. No one could deny the past few minutes had been ceremonial, but the union of two people, enduring, in love abiding, surely called for more joy. Billy's thoughts apparently coincided with her own.

"What a miserable bugger 'e is, couldn't crack 'is face to smile to save 'is life." Billy declared as they walked away from the ornate railings.

"Don't be daft," said Edna, " 'e's meant to be like that, didn't you read the notice on the wall, 'Marriages Solemnized' it said, that's what solemn is, all serious and bloody miserable. Anyway, the best bit's still to come isn't it Billy, our treat, we're goin' to The Nelson, for a plate of pie and mash. Come on if you get there late you end up wi' nearly all crust, they run out o' the jollup from underneath."

Edna quickened her pace and all four, with a new found enthusiasm, headed towards Connaught Street singing, 'down at the old bull and bush'.

"Hello Billy lad," a loud voice erupted from behind the bar and spilled out across the room, others joined in the chorus of greeting. A muscular, heavily jowled man looked at them from his position by the ale pumps.

"What's this then?" He said at the sight of Annie and Edna's pink roses.

Billy proudly announced, "This is my best mate Harold and his wife Annie and you know Edna."

"Well bless my soul, I didn't recognise you Edna, if you don't look the real lady today." Then he turned to Annie, "Congratulations my dear," and to Harold, "aren't you the lucky one."

Annie's cheeks burned, she was not used to being the centre of attention. Harold took her hand and steered her to a table in the corner. Billy and Edna spoke softly to the barman and then joined them in the sanctuary of the dimly lit area in which Harold had chosen to sit. Annie now felt less conspicuous and her curiosity at these new surroundings propelled her gaze around the room. The ceiling was so low, any tall man had need to bend his shoulders, the smell of hops, smoke and cooking hung in the air. If any managed to escape when the door was opened, it was immediately replaced as the men puffed on pipes and smoked their rollups, taking great gulps of beer as if they needed to drink it faster than the next man, and plates of piping hot beef and ale pie travelled around the room in the hands of a very buxom serving girl. In just the few minutes Annie had been observing the scene, this stoic soul had endured repeated attempts by most of the men to grasp generous handfuls of her flesh, whilst she carefully laid a plate of hot gravy on the table, only inches away from their manhood. Any woman of spare covering would have been black and blue, Annie felt amazed at the restraint shown by even such a well endowed young woman, these men live dangerously was Annie's earnest opinion. After a little while the food arrived and it certainly looked good. Harold and Billy had a pint jug of bitter each and Edna had ordered half a pint of pale ale for herself and Annie. A pot of mustard sat in the middle of the table along with four chunks of crusty bread and a dish of soft beef dripping.

" 'Ere's a toast to Harold and Annie," said Billy as he rose from his seat. "We drink to your 'ealth and 'appiness and to friendship, 'cause we love you both."

Edna clapped, "Ere ere," she cried, then her fork attacked the beef and ale pie with all the joy and eagerness the Registrar had so sorely lacked, this was the true celebration of their marriage. Annie cleared her plate and enjoyed every mouthful, she spoke aunt Bella's words silently to herself, 'Take your Harold and live', then she drank the last drop of ale, sighed and proclaimed to her husband and friends.

"I am in all things replete."

Edna and Billy were keen to see No.24, that and the prospect of fruit cake was more than enough enticement. Harold hastily shed his tidy clothes, now comfortable in his everyday attire, he set about lighting the fire.

Edna was envious, "A little palace this is Annie, when you've got those curtains made it'll look a treat."

Bella's cake was well received and the chatter warmed the house in advance of the fire. Edna and Billy were such cheerful company, the sound of laughter travelled from room to room, blessing each one with hope. As Annie waved goodbye she looked forward to seeing these two dear friends, married and happy in their own home as she and Harold were. It had begun to rain, poor Edna, if they hurried the suede shoes might be safely home before too many puddles developed. The fire had established and the room felt cosy, the one fireside chair offered ample comfort, Harold held Annie on his lap. The pink rose sat in a cup of water on the shelf above them, his eyes, only inches from her own spoke to Annie softly, reassuringly. She lay her head on his shoulder and for a while, they sat in the flicker of the flames, neither felt the need of words, the stillness, the knowledge that the world outside could not steal this moment, made them blissfully content.

The doors were bolted but the windows as yet were bare of curtains, the rain now tapped rhythmically on the glass.

Harold whispered across Annie's brow, "Come upstairs with me." He led her over the treads, his hand wrapped around her fingers, sending his strength to her timid thoughts. He knowingly stood at the window, looking across to aunt Bella's. "All looks quiet over there Annie, we shall see her in the mornin'."

Not until the sound of her undressing had ceased and the slight creak of the bed confirmed Annie lay beneath the covers, did he turn away from the window to look at his wife. The light had faded, but his smile reached Annie even in the darkness, he slipped under the sheets beside her.

"Don't be nervous Annie, it requires no art or skill, it needs no direction or plan, it just 'appens, like the first word we speak or the first step we take. One word leads to another, one step takes us to the next. What we do now carries us to the rest of our lives but it is as natural as our childhood endeavours and just as simple." He kissed her forehead, "we shall learn together."

His strong hands and arms supported his weight, he whispered her name as he lowered his face to hers, his breath teased Annie's lips, lightly, tenderly, showing no urgency, but slowly drawing her thoughts away from tense anxieties to a dream of perfect love. His legs trained her trembling thighs to stillness and only when he felt her body rise to unite more tightly with his own did a rush of intense desire for her warmest flesh finally lock them together. Now as one passion, one sublime ecstasy, they rose and fell, over and over, their movement ever quickening, paced by their racing breath. Harold called out, Annie answered, her cry louder, it told the hosts of heaven she was in their midst, she had come to them. Her soul was freed of body, her soul danced to the music of Angels' harps, it flew upon Seraphs' wings, frolicked with ageless Cherubim. This could not be of earth and yet, surrendering to exhaustion Harold lay his body onto Annie, his head curled, childlike into the softness of her neck and hair, his weight full and heavy brought her back to an awareness of her earthly being. Her hands passed slowly down either side of his spine until they reached a resting place in the small of his back. She entwined her fingers so as not to let him go. Annie now knew what she was, who she was, Annie was a wife, she was Mrs. Harold Boucher. Behind her tightly closed eyelids she could see his face, she smiled back to him, "My husband," she spoke the words out loud, then in utter contentment , 'Annie Bundy' was lost to a deep sleep.

CHAPTER SIXTEEN

Annie and Harold had been married for more than two weeks, a happy routine had developed. Aunt Bella conceded to Harold's determined plan, he would bring in coal and water each night and one evening a week she would come across to No.24 for tea and he and Annie would have tea with aunt Bella another evening. Sunday dinner was to be with Sarah and the family at Mitchell Street.

Annie was preparing to leave the workshop for home when Saul came out of his office to say.

"Have you a minute before you go Annie? I need you to open up in the morning I have an appointment to keep, I shall come to the workshop later in the day but if you would be kind enough to come just a minute or two earlier to be here before May and Edna arrive I would be very grateful."

"Of course," said Annie, "that is no problem at all."

Saul seemed troubled by something more, he hesitated but when Annie asked, "Is everything alright?" He surprised her by saying.

"Enid is going to have another child, Charles told me last Sunday."

"Oh, that is good news, the two children will be close in age and I am sure William will benefit from the company of a brother or sister," replied Annie.

"I don't think Charles has told anyone else as yet," said Saul anxiously.

"I won't breathe a word, don't worry." Annie smiled, it strangely reassured him, how Annie could ever ease the worries he harboured he could not imagine but nonetheless, her steady words, her ready smile gave him confidence.

Saul had requested Edward Meade collect him at half past ten to drive him to London Road. Saul sat quietly in the carriage, putting his thoughts in order, they turned the corner and he prepared to alight.

"Pick me up again in an hour," he said.

He waited for Meade to drive off then walked several yards, stopping outside the offices of 'Meakin and Kirk' Solicitors, Commissioner for Oaths. The large brass plate on the wall outside he did not wish to be obvious to Meade, walking those few yards removed any possible speculation Edward Meade might attach to Saul's business with a solicitor. Saul was greeted by the clerk.

"Ah yes, Mr.Eddowes is it not, just one moment sir, I will check that Mr. Meakin is ready for you."

The clerk disappeared through a door just beyond his desk, Gerald Meakin had been Saul's solicitor for many years and throughout that time, Meakin had employed the same clerk, this slightly built man who had just received Saul. His appearance Saul had always found amusing. He wore an unusually deep collar, stiffly starched and had an amazing ability to extend his slender neck and equally to retract it, rather like a goose. Saul imagined some sort of hydraulic mechanism lay hidden beneath that protective collar. His skin was heavily freckled and his hair more ginger than ginger itself. On one finger of his right hand he wore a large signet ring, engraved with the letters, T.B. unfortunate initials for any individual but the curiosity lay with the fact that Meakin's clerk was named Dermot Mahoney. Although his efforts at elocution were to be admired, he could not disguise the lyrical sound of the leprechauns dancing on his tongue.

Gerald Meakin had been moulded in the other extreme. A broad, heavy framed man, bald of hair, hands that looked more suited to wielding a shovel than shuffling paper. Not a man preoccupied with dress, at times looking almost shabby. A loud forceful voice but a surprisingly gentle character, sympathetic to another man's tribulation. Here was a man who knew a great deal of Saul's past but had not ever judged or mocked but remained a constant adviser, preferring not to cast stones. Who Mr.Kirk might be, Saul had no idea, the name had ever been on the brass plate but at no time had Saul caught sight of, or ever been introduced to this mysterious associate.

Mahoney returned to his desk and said, "You may go through now sir."

Saul found Meakin, as always, surrounded by papers and files but of pleasant demeanour.

"Good to see you Saul," he said with a firm handshake. "I trust you are well, please, take a seat."

Saul went straight to the matter requiring Meakin's good offices.

"I wish to amend my Will by one small bequest and the attachment of a condition," he said purposefully.

"I see," replied Meakin, "bear with me for just a minute, I shall fetch the relevant documents."

Saul looked around the room, so many secrets must have passed through this small office to the rooms beyond, all those surprises, some good, some bad, all waiting to be revealed. It was not long before Meakin returned.

"Now Saul, explain to me what it is that you intend."

"I wish to leave a small sum of money to Mrs.Annie Boucher, nee Bundy. She has been a most loyal employee, and has shown considerable ability and more conscientious effort than could be expected of her."

"How much?" Asked Meakin.

"Ten Guineas," replied Saul. "Further, I must amend my Will as it deals with the business and premises. Charles is to inherit as the Will states but with the condition that he shall not sell either or both until at least five years have elapsed from the date of my death."

"What of the house and capital?" Asked Meakin.

Saul gave a deep sigh, "Charles will have whatever money might remain."

Meakin gave Saul a quizzical look, Saul explained.

"Charles has been in need of funds over several months, his wife Enid, seems to covet many accessories but sadly, has not the management skills to enable Charles to afford them. They have started a family, I do not want their disputes to become so severe as to threaten the home, so I give Charles what I can, if it continues there will be nothing left, he cannot have it whilst I live and after my death also. My house shall be his, I can only hope he has sufficient sense to keep it for the security it would give him and his family. He has shown no interest in the business at any time, the women who work for me are good, honest and diligent, they rely on their income from the workshop. While Charles would have no knowledge of the every day activity of ordering etc, Mrs.Boucher is capable of running that business and ensuring the women's wages. I fear Charles would sell it immediately, giving no thought to these loyal people, the proceeds would adorn Enid and repay his gambling debts for a while, after that, they would return to their hand to mouth existence. The business would be gone with nothing of any worth to show for it. At least five years might allow Annie, May and Edna to anticipate change and to plan for it accordingly. I feel I cannot impose the condition for a longer period. Charles may learn in that time and have no wish to sell, on the other hand, he may not."

Meakin had listened intently, making no comment. Now he leaned back in his chair, rubbing his fingers across his ample chin.

"Your health Saul, is it causing you any distress?"

Saul answered as truthfully as he could, "I begin to feel the aches and pains of age and weariness. Who is to know when this tired body might resign, it is only prudent to have things in order, this is true of any man, is it not?"

Meakin smiled, "I shall attend to the matter before the end of the week, you will need to sign the amended document, I shall prepare a Codicil to attach to the original Will."

He rose from his chair and walked Saul to the door, they shook hands and parted company with the genuine caution on Meakin's part, "Take care Saul." Saul nodded agreement and made his way to the front door, acknowledging Mahoney with a polite, "Good day."

Saul walked quickly away from the premises and waited the necessary five minutes for Meade to arrive. He felt relieved, just a signature then it would be finished, he could do no more than trust his own judgement.

When he entered the workshop Saul noted everything to be in order, the sound of the busy machines confirmed a healthy level of industry.

"Is everything alright Annie?" He asked.

"Yes, we are all on time with the work, Mrs.Appleyard called, she asked for some samples and a fitting next Tuesday morning if possible. There is to be a dinner dance to mark Mr.Appleyard's retirement at the end of July. I have entered it in the diary, she is set on a shade of blue, I did offer to show her some fabric samples this morning but she had to hurry, she undertakes some voluntary work at the hospital apparently. She was so proud to tell me that her husband has been a senior doctor for more than thirty years."

"Thank you Annie, for what you have done."

He crossed to the office and sank into his chair, content to sit quietly for a few minutes. So, Mr.Appleyard is retiring thought Saul. When Dr.Baragruy had been so concerned at Hilda's continuing fever and weakness he had consulted Mr.Appleyard to obtain his opinion but their combined efforts and expertise had failed to reverse her decline. Saul read the entry Annie had made in the diary, her handwriting neat, confident, he would have expected no other, given the calibre of her teacher.

The evenings now were much lighter and even after walking home from her work and cooking a meal, daylight held long enough to encourage Annie to think of some gardening. Harold had cleared away all the weeds and forked the ground, it was not a big area but a comparatively small patch of garden could produce a surprising amount of vegetables. Annie planned to grow some potatoes, those first sweet early ones, carrots, onions and beans and if there was enough space, just a row of flowers. That evening, after they had eaten, she decided to tell Harold of her intentions, he listened whilst Annie identified the produce she thought might be most useful, smiling to himself, waiting for her to seek his opinion.

"It sounds ideal Annie, but I need you to wait until after next Saturday before you begin your plan, why will become apparent by then."

Harold would give no further explanation, telling Annie to be patient, it was already Wednesday.

She had managed to contain herself but now her urgency to return to No.24 to discover why this day was so significant, propelled her feet up Winchester Street as if they were steam powered.

Harold got home from the slaughter yard earlier on Saturdays and was usually waiting for Annie to arrive, the back door however was still bolted, she took a key from her pocket and walked back to the front door, the house was empty, surely Harold would be home soon, he hadn't said he would be late. She hurried to put some wood and coal in the range, the fire was low in the grate but it would soon recover. Samuel kept the logs and kindling dry in his shed by covering them over with old canvas and Harold had done the same in their own store. She filled a pan with water to make some tea and unbolted the back door to bring in the laundry from the line. Annie was washing by hand in a deep enamel bowl, 'One day very soon' Harold had said, 'we will be able to 'ave a boiler to stand out the back. I've asked at the secondhand yard to keep one for me if any come in. Abel said they handle 'em regular'.

Harold turned the corner from Sherwood Road, peeping first to make sure Annie wasn't walking home from Saul's. There was no sign of her, "Come on boy, lets go find yer new mam," said Harold On the other end of a length of rope which Harold had looped around his wrist, stood a Staffordshire Bull Terrier, it was all white, but for a brown and black splash over one ear. Its broad strong head held eyes which looked up to Harold, two deep brown pools of affection. It trotted alongside him as they crossed the street and turned into the back yard of No.24.

Annie was busily folding the laundry on the scullery table. Harold opened the door just an inch and called out.

"Stand in the living room with your back to the scullery door and don't turn around."

Annie's excitement was spilling over, her toes danced in her boots,

"Alright, I'm not looking," she cried out gleefully.

Harold opened wide the door and untied the rope from the dog's collar, "Go on then, find Annie." The delighted animal rushed inside, his paws sliding over the flags, knocking the wash basket asunder in his haste, he leapt up to Annie before she had chance to turn around.

"Harold he's beautiful."

She knelt on the floor to meet him rubbing his neck, he licked her hands. Harold laughed at the sight. He put a bundle down on the table calling out, "Josiah gave us some scraps for 'im, 'e's alright isn't 'e Annie?"

Annie thought he was more than alright, his big intelligent eyes, powerful chest and strong muscular legs, he was indeed a masterpiece.

"Where did you get him?" She asked.

"Well, I've been telling Josiah 'ow you would like a dog, and to be truthful, I miss Eli in a silly sort o' way. Then last Tuesday, Josiah said, 'I reckon I might 'ave found you a dog Harold'. 'E explained that in the street where 'e lives, an old lady 'ad died and there was nobody to take on 'er animals. She used to be quite 'well to do' apparently, lived in a big house at one time. Over the years she spent all 'er money on animals, rescuin' 'em, findin' 'omes for 'em. Mrs.Toft used to spend a bit 'o time wi' the old lady, felt sorry for 'er I suppose. She was very well educated, 'ad lots o' books. Mrs.Toft decided to give a home to the canary, that was called 'Keats' and Nobby the greengrocer took the cat, the old lady called that 'Shelley' and our new friend 'ere, well 'is name is 'Byron'. 'E's six years old so it wouldn't be fair to change 'is name now so we'll just 'ave to get used to it."

"I think it's a good name for him," said Annie, "almost every street has a 'Jack' or a 'Rover', he deserves to be more individual. The old lady must have enjoyed poetry."

"If I hadn't been readin' these past months with aunt Bella, I wouldn't 'ave 'eard of any of 'em," Harold said with a chuckle. "Now you know why I said wait for the garden. I'll put grass seed in that patch so 'e can run around in there, father will let us 'ave some veg' from the allotment."

"Can we take him across to see aunt Bella after tea?" Asked Annie.

"Course we can, what is for tea?" Harold suddenly felt hungry.

"Liver and onions," came the reply from the scullery where Annie had already set about the meal. Within minutes potatoes were boiling on the range. She remembered aunt Bella's reaction to little Eli, her obvious pleasure when he lay at her feet. Meanwhile Byron had found that warm place on the mat in front of the fire. Harold had taken hot water upstairs to wash and Annie sang to herself as she sliced the liver. Simple though it was, many would have envied their bliss.

Aunt Bella was drinking her tea when Annie stepped inside. "Where's Harold?"

"He's just behind me," said Annie, "we've brought a visitor to see you."

Bella looked concerned but when Harold walked into the room with Byron, her expression changed at once. The dog behaved as though he had been given strict instructions, when in fact, he sat at Bella's feet, gazing up with those knowledgeable eyes, alert, willing her to speak, entirely of his own doing. Bella's fingers smoothed his head.

"What is he called?" She asked, not taking her eyes from this new acquaintance.

"Byron," said Harold, he explained the circumstances of the old lady.

Annie stretched the pot of tea and handed a cup to Harold.

"What will you do with him while you are at work?" Asked Bella.

Annie glanced at Harold they both had the same thought.

"Well Aunt Bella, I shall give 'im a walk before I leave for the yard and 'e will just 'ave to stay indoors 'till Annie gets back from the workshop." Harold winked at Annie.

"Uhm, the dog is intelligent I can tell, if you shut him up in isolation he will lose his good sense, you'd better bring him across to me before you leave Annie, I am down early in the morning now I have to do the fire."

So it was agreed, aunt Bella had found some company.

The following day Samuel found a lead in his shed which grandad

Boucher had used for the whippet.

"I'm not sure our Eli and Byron wouldn't fight," he said.

"I thought of that Father, I reckon it might be best to keep 'em apart, save any bother," replied Harold, " 'e's alright back at the house and aunt Bella is goin' to 'ave 'im while we're workin'."

Byron settled to his new routine like he'd been born to it. His lively bouts of play, followed by deep snoring slumber brought a joyful life to No.24 and Bella had created great amusement when she had informed Harold and Annie of his rapt attention if she read poetry to him.

"That old lady definitely spent a lot of time in reading to Byron," declared Bella, "I honestly believe that if he could speak he would be able to recite every word of 'Don Juan'!"

CHAPTER SEVENTEEN

Annie and Harold had taken great delight in walking Byron to The Park one evening to visit Davina. Byron had been overjoyed at the sight of trees, Winchester Street offered little to interest a dog but The Park presented an abundance of gateposts and the laurels and laburnums which decorated the walkways, held a diversity of smells which engaged Byron's attentions as he moved between each and every one.

"Come on boy, we shall never get there," said Harold pulling on the lead as Byron completed his third circuit of a large birch tree.

Annie laughed as Harold followed the eager animal calling out, "You'll be dizzy if you go round again."

They finally made it to the side door of Davina's house. Ivy abandoned all etiquette, completely ignoring Davina's visitors but seizing upon Byron with a passion.

"Oh, he's just like grandad's dog only whiter."

She kissed the top of his head several times and Byron, enjoying such a display of affection, responded with a swift, sloppy swipe of Ivy's cheek with his tongue. Davina, hearing the commotion, came to the door and on seeing Byron, clapped her hands in glee saying.

"Bring him in my dears, do bring him in." Davina's drawing room was transformed, Ivy knelt on the floor at Davina's insistence, "Make him feel welcome Ivy, I would get down there myself if I didn't have on this infernal corset."

Harold could not contain his laughter, he thought back to the day they had collected the bed, what Frank would have given for even half the attention from Ivy. A little calm was eventually restored and Davina chatted over a tray of tea.

"Your father is charming Harold," she said. "He was quite determined to sweep all the chimneys and as if that were not enough, he then insisted on forking all the soot and ash into the azalea bed. I have made him promise to bring your dear mother Sarah to see me Harold, they are coming for tea next Saturday afternoon, my birthday, I have ordered one of Mr.Lovatt's special cakes."

The two remaining arrowroot biscuits she lovingly fed to Byron.

"He has wonderful manners Annie, so much better than cousin Isobel's, why you could comfortably take him anywhere but Isobel, oh my dear, the embarrassment, I shall never forget Daphne's wedding, I wished the ground to swallow me up."

Harold had noted the cake order and inwardly smiled at the prospect of Frank delivering this confection into the capable hands of Ivy. As they walked home, guided by the ever enthusiastic Byron, Harold began to chuckle.

"You know Annie, I reckon mam and Davina will get on like a house afire, I'd love to be a fly on the wall next Saturday, father will be 'appy for 'arf an hour, then 'e'll be fidgetin', wantin' to get down the allotment and mam will be nervous as a kitten for five minutes 'til her tongue gets up speed, then 'er and Davina will be well away. Ivy will be able to leave 'em to it and go out for an hour."

"I hope they all enjoy themselves," said Annie, "they deserve to."

She had been thinking about Enid, since Saul had told Annie about the baby there had been no further mention, but now a few weeks had passed, she thought it might be alright to call on Enid and William. Annie felt sure the child would love to see Byron and Enid might be in need of a distraction. Harold wanted to put the grass seed in the garden, his earlier finish on a Saturday gave him the best opportunity. Annie decided to take Byron out of the way and walk him to Charles' house. This route they had not taken before and all the new smells had to be investigated, it made progress somewhat slower than usual. As Annie approached The Standard, Charles appeared, he waved and called out, "Are you going my way Mrs.Boucher?"

Annie knew at once that Charles had been drinking but she could not turn away now, that would be rude.

"You have a dog, he said and stooped, very unsteadily to pat Byron's head. "Come on Annie, lets go see my beautiful, sweet tempered wife."

He took Annie's arm as he laughed mockingly. Annie wished she had stayed at home, Charles made her feel most uncomfortable. Thankfully, he fell quiet and they walked unhindered, even Byron seemed to sense the tension, he abandoned his pursuit of piddling posts preferring to keep his ears erect, one eye on this strange man.

Enid's mood was stern, William crawled about the floor dragging a cushion with him, stopping every few seconds to chew on one soggy corner, where his few teeth and sore gums had managed to release some of the Kapok within, a trail of which covered the living room, clinging to rugs and floating around the floorboards in the breeze from the open window. Then William spotted Byron, standing alongside Annie in the scullery doorway. The cushion was forgotten, sore gums dismissed in his haste to reach the dog. Byron sat back on his haunches as if waiting to receive another eager embrace and when William's chubby arms encircled Byron's neck, that long soft tongue licked the little boy's ear causing a peal of glorious infant laughter.

"My goodness William, you have been busy," said Annie on seeing his exploits.

"More than can be said for his father." Enid's remark was barbed and Annie felt desperate to relieve the dreadful atmosphere, if only for the child's sake, she sensed it was only her presence which prevented an almighty row.

"It's a nice evening, I'm sure William would like to go out in his pram, we could take Byron to the arboretum and give Charles a chance to clear up a little whilst we are out of the way."

Annie looked hard at Charles but his muddled senses denied him any perception.

"That's woman's work."

He may as well have waved a red rag to a bull, Enid charged at him with her fists, her cries of contempt frightened William, his bottom lip trembled, tears filled his eyes, Byron barked loudly.

"Take that wild animal away," shrieked Enid and kicked the cushion from its resting place, sending ever more Kapok into the room. Then she erupted into floods of tears, prompting William to cry even harder. Charles put his hands to his head and swore over and over in drunken frustration.

Annie crossed the room to Charles and with an authority which surprised even herself said, "Hold Byron's lead."

She picked William off the floor and put him in his pram, removing her hat and placing it in his lap where his little fingers immediately found the ribbon bow and thrust it into his mouth, sucking the cloth for comfort. Enid had slumped into a chair, her shoulders rounded, swaying to and fro in sullen silence. Annie began to gather up the Kapok, pulling it free of the rugs and stuffing it into her pockets, no one spoke, Byron sat watching her efforts, bemused, if this was a game then he had never observed it before.

She took the lead from Charles saying, "Make some tea, we all need a strong cup of tea." He made no protest. Enid's eyes stared at the floor.

"There's no brightness down there," said Annie, "but if you look through the window you will see sunshine. You have both, his mother and father, shown William the darkest of times, you should feel ashamed. Fetch his coat Enid and change him, when we have had our tea we are going for a walk and that means you too Charles. Before this little boy is put to bed he must see happiness and hear laughter or his sleep will be tormented by your selfish, intolerable behaviour."

Annie's words stung their conscience, both were intelligent enough to recognise their own disgrace. Subdued, they responded to Annie's direction and did as she bid them.

As they made their way to the arboretum, Annie, now pushing the pram sang a cheerful song to William. Charles led Byron and Enid walked by his side. Charles, still a little less than alert, hadn't noticed a tabby cat sitting on the front step of a house towards the end of the street. Byron however, had fixed his gaze on this adversary at least three houses back and began to quicken his pace. Suddenly his ears cocked and he took off, cats were not to be tolerated. Charles' shoes clattered over the cobbles, his jacket flew open like a pair of wings as he hurtled down the street, the lead tight over his hand, he called out.

"I can't stop the bugger and I need to pee."

Enid began to laugh, louder and louder, William took his thumb from his mouth and gurgled happily. Annie at first anxious that Charles might let go the lead, now relaxed as Byron stood on his back legs against the base of the wall, staring at the spot above him where the cat had disappeared from view. Charles still holding on to the lead, stood urinating over a clump of dandelions.

Enid turned to Annie a big grin on her face, "Serves him right, he should have gone before we left home, daft sod."

By the time they had reached the arboretum Charles and Enid walked hand in hand.

William slept and Byron, now fatigued from the chase, walked steadily beside Annie, his lead attached to the handlebar of the pram. They sat for a while, watching the multi-coloured pigeons busily searching for anything edible among the flower beds and pathways, calmed by the faint scent of the blossoms.

When Annie was satisfied that genuine peace prevailed, she rose to her feet, untied Byron's lead and put Enid's hands on the handlebar of the pram.

"I am taking my wild animal and my soggy hat home," she said.

Enid and Charles smiled, they were embarrassed but truly penitent.

"Will you come again soon?" Asked Enid anxiously, "I wanted to tell you something, didn't we Charles."

He nodded agreement but at that moment all Charles wanted to do was curl up like his son and sleep.

"There is no reason you should not come and see me," said Annie, it had obviously not occurred to Enid, she looked both pleased and surprised.

"Are you sure Harold wouldn't mind?"

Annie blew a kiss into the pram, "Harold would not mind at all," she answered. "Come on Byron, time to go."

She paused at the gates and waved back, the two still sat quietly with the slumbering William. Annie felt weary, no wonder Saul seemed so preoccupied at times, she could understand why he carried such a worn, tired look. No.24 beckoned, Annie's feet joined Byron's in the direction of Winchester Street.

"Home," she said, "oh yes please, lets go home."

The next day Samuel and Sarah had told of their time with Davina. Just as Harold had imagined, his mam and their dear friend in The Park had found delight in one another's company.

"She told me to give you her thanks for the lemon drops Annie," said Sarah.

"I reckon Mrs.Wright enjoyed her birthday this year," said Samuel, "I've to go one day and mend the door of her shed, won't take me long, only needs a new hinge."

Annie was pleased for Davina, she led a lonely existence much of the time, but for Ivy, many days would pass with no company at all. Aunt Bella didn't really seek regular company, she was very different to Davina in that way. Annie had always been there before and after work and Harold had now added to Bella's days but Davina, Annie could only hope, might see more of Sarah in the future.

The following Wednesday evening Annie had been busy ironing. They were to have a meal with aunt Bella so Harold had gone across earlier to fill the buckets and do some reading whilst he and Bella waited for Annie. They had reached 'M' in the encyclopaedia and tonight's subject was to be the 'Magna Carta'. A knock came at the back door, Annie put the flat iron back on the range and followed Byron, who already sat at the bottom of the door awaiting sight of the caller. Enid stood outside with William in his pram, she looked nervous, unsure of the situation.

"Come in," said Annie cheerily, taking William from his pram.

"We've come at the wrong time, I can see you are occupied," said Enid at the sight of the clothes on the table.

"Don't worry about that, I can do the ironing at any time, sit down, I shall make some tea."

Annie handed the child to his mother and fetched a wooden spoon for him to bite on.

"His teeth are coming quickly now aren't they?" Said Annie.

Enid's hands were trembling. "I'm having another baby." The words came out as a pitiful, agonised declaration of catastrophe.

"That is good news surely Enid, when William has a little brother or sister to play with he will be so much more amused, that will make life a little easier for you."

Annie tried to encourage her but she seemed frightened at the prospect.

"It's alright for you, what do you know about it, have you felt the pain, well have you?"

Enid's tone was scornful, "That's all he's good for, he should have the kid then he'd be different, let him be ripped apart, that's what it did, it ripped me apart, I can feel it now."

Her fingers clenched so hard they began to mark the flesh on her hand. Annie put William on the floor to crawl and held Enid's arm.

"It is the most natural thing on earth Enid, all of us come into the world the same way, you must try to think of that. Women since the beginning of mankind have lived that pain but only for a short time, afterwards the wonder of motherhood drives all stress away and fills the days with unconditional love. Look at William, he will always love you first and foremost."

"It wasn't like that for your mother was it? You told me she died having you."

It was difficult to form the right answer to give poor Enid but Annie said, "My mother had been very ill and her weakness was more than could be remedied by the doctor. I have wondered many times, how different my life might have been had she lived. You are not ill Enid, you have strength to spare, why not even Charles has your robust spirit."

Annie gave Enid a wry smile, it invoked a chuckle, the fingers relaxed and Enid looked directly at Annie as she said.

"Alright, if you say so but if I died, promise me you would love my children."

Annie laughed, "You are not going to die Enid, but if it gives you comfort then I will gladly promise to love your children."

They had talked easily about ordinary everyday things for a little while and William had crawled over every inch of the living room floor, accompanied by Byron, until the small boy's eyes became droopy with tiredness.

"I must go home and put him to bed now," said Enid. "We have a bloody 'Money Bags' Beeton stew for tea but with half the meat. Charles will be late tonight, he has to work on at the bank, that's what he says anyway but the work probably involves shuffling cards more than accounts. You are lucky to have your slaughter man."

Annie waved 'till they were out of sight then quickly made up the fire before crossing the road to Bella's. She looked at the clock, my goodness Harold and aunt Bella would be on the Napoleonic Wars by now.

The workshop had a steady flow of activity. Saul and May had been to Mrs.Appleyard's with samples and to measure her for the gown. He had again asked Annie to open the workshop for him one morning the previous week but had soon returned to arrange the order of fabrics to replace the depleted stocks and to finalise Oliver Blackmore's account.

Annie had been a little concerned when he had asked her to come into the office saying he needed to talk to her about the ledgers, she could think of nothing, which in his absence she might have done incorrectly. In the event he wanted only to explain the fabric order to her and to go through the invoices for Blackmore's School. 'My old head becomes contrary sometimes

Annie, it just won't remember all that it should and two heads are much better than one', Saul had told her by way of explanation, noticing her troubled expression.

It was Monday morning, Annie had arrived at the workshop in good time, she would need to run home for a few minutes later in the day when the tubman came, so an earlier start made up her time. Saul was always at his desk before the women reached the workshop. The stubborn, rusting gates were unwilling to open this morning, perhaps Saul had closed them a little too firmly. At last they yielded to Annie's gloved fingers, she closed them again, very lightly, so as to make it easier for May and Edna. The front door was locked, aside from the two mornings which Saul had asked Annie to open up, she had never known him not to be at the workshop early, he must have been delayed by something, he won't be long Annie thought.

Soon May arrived at the gates, Annie explained, Edna came a few minutes late.

"The Lord is good," she declared, "Saul won't know I'm late 'cause 'e is an'all."

Ten minutes passed, "I'm going to fetch my key from home," said Annie.

At least No.24 was close, she would soon have the door opened and the work underway, Saul would be relieved when he came to find everything as it should be.

Annie looked at the clock, they had stopped for dinner and been back at their machines for some time, now it was almost 3 o'clock, she felt puzzled by Saul's absence, he had mentioned nothing of appointments before she left the workshop last Saturday.

" 'E's a dark 'orse, I reckon 'e must 'ave found 'isself a woman an' she's sleepin' on 'is shirt tail, e'll come just afore we're supposed to go 'ome to make sure we didn't finish early, you'll see," was Edna's prediction.

It proved to be incorrect. Annie watched May and Edna walk to the corner, she was worried, while Saul would have relied on her to open up and organize the work, for him not to have come in at all, with no word of reason caused her concern. Annie locked the desk, checked the machines and hurriedly donned her jacket, as she turned the key in the front door she shivered, 'someone's trod on your grave'. She thought of Harold's words, then dismissed such silly nonsense and made haste, she would not go to aunt Bella's to collect Byron, he would be alright there until she got back. Annie's feet sped over the ground, her mind wrestled with troublesome thoughts, Harold would be home from the yard, Bella might wonder why she was late fetching Byron and Saul could be annoyed if she arrived at his house when all was well and he had simply chosen to spend some time quietly at home.

The house was of good size, two windows, one either side of the heavy wooden door and three windows above. Annie knocked on the door nervously, she could hear no sound from within. She clenched her hand again and beat her knuckles more loudly on the weathered oak, there was no response, she found the back door, a few items of clothing hung on the line, a white shirt looking sad with a long splash of bird droppings staining its front panel, they were bone dry. Annie tried the door, it was unbolted. She let herself into a large scullery, everything appeared tidy, she called out.

"Mr.Eddowes," she repeated the call several times.

The open door to the passageway enabled her to see through to the inside of the front door, an envelope lay on the floor. Annie knew, before she ever entered the living room she knew, the door was ajar by an inch. Aunt Bella had told Annie what it was necessary to do after a death, not in any macabre way but as in all things, to educate Annie, to provide her with every knowledge possible. 'It is important to pad the deceased, the body will excrete waste as the muscles and organs close down', aunt Bella had said. Annie had assumed this lesson was delivered in order to benefit them both should anything befall Bella. At the time Annie had very quickly put it to the back of her mind, now it had made its way to the fore. Saul sat in a chair by the fireplace, he had died alone, no one to perform that final act of kindness. His head lay forward on his chest, his hands on the arms of the chair. Strangely, Annie felt no fear as she stood beside him, his fingers were ice cold, she could not stop the tears which rolled down her cheeks. He had so little time with William and would never know his second grandchild. Annie believed he had missed his wife Hilda very much, she prayed they might now be reunited. Leaving him all alone again hurt Annie deeply, it seemed entirely wrong but she had no choice, she must get word to Charles. First she needed to return home and explain before Harold and Bella became anxious about her. As Annie turned the corner into Winchester Street the now familiar door of No.24 soothed her. Harold had been home only a few minutes, he began to tell her something about a boiler but she could not listen, not now, she poured out the sorry story.

"I must fetch Byron and tell aunt Bella, she'll wonder where I've got to."

"Well you do that and I'll go to Charles' house an' speak with 'im," said Harold.

"No, I'd better go myself," said Annie, "as Enid's pregnant she may need me to stay with her whilst Charles goes to Hood Street, it will be a big shock for them both. Perhaps you could get Byron and speak to aunt Bella."

Harold watched Annie go from view, concerned, not just for the present but for the changes it would assuredly bring to the workshop, Charles was a very different character to Saul.

Annie reached Charles' back door, she could see through the window that he and Enid were eating their evening meal. William would be in bed, she knocked gently, not wanting to disturb the child. Enid stood in the doorway, she looked surprised at Annie's arrival.

"I'm sorry to disturb your tea Enid but I need to speak with Charles."

"Something's wrong isn't it? I can tell from your face," said Enid.

Annie followed her to the living room, at that moment Bertha Duffin appeared at the foot of the stairs.

"He's gone off now, he should sleep all night he's that tired bless him.

Hello Annie, how are you?" Bertha smiled across the room.

Annie sighed, "I am so sorry Charles. Your father didn't come into the workshop today, I felt there must have been a good reason, he hadn't mentioned any need to be elsewhere, I was concerned so I went to the house." Annie paused, Bertha's expression showed she had already made the natural deduction.

"Your father is dead Charles," said Annie, "he passed away in his chair by the fireside, I'm sure it would have been in his sleep, as he rested."

She tried to help Charles' anguish, his face had turned ashen, his eyes looked terrified.

Enid was the first to speak, "Go with Annie Charles, she will know what to do." She lifted his hands from their trembling grip on the back of the chair. "It will be alright, I'll wait up for you, Bertha will keep me company for a while." She put his jacket on for him and kissed his cheek.

"I think we should go immediately to Dr.Baragruy's, he will need to certify death and attend to your father, perhaps he will go with us to Hood Street." Annie spoke calmly but Charles was too shaken to comprehend. Fortunately the doctor was at home, the three walked quickly, Annie ventured to suggest to Charles that she might go home as the doctor was now present but Charles caught hold her hand and clung to it tightly. Dr. Baragruy asked Annie to occupy Charles in finding his father's clean clothes. He needed hot water, Annie went to the shed for sticks and coal, the fire was burned through to fine ash and had been out for hours. Annie picked up the envelope from the floor of the hall and gave it to Charles, "It may be important," she said.

He put it in his pocket and sat with his head cupped in his hands at the living room table.

"I must go home Charles, Harold will be worried."

The doctor, recognising Annie's predicament came to her rescue. "I shall stay with Charles until we are able to move his father to the undertaker's but I do need you to inform Mr.Handley if you would Miss Bundy."

Annie felt disinclined to correct him, it was a matter far too trivial in this present miserable situation to warrant attention. She gave James Handley the doctor's message and made her way home.

Harold had baked potatoes and insisted she sit by the fire and eat and drink, a cup of boiled milk and sugar followed the potato. Byron lay on the floor, his soft chin across her feet, his delight at her home coming obvious, first licking her neck and hands in a show of deep affection before settling himself to sleep in a spot where he would be aware, should she move. It was dim outside, soon the last light of day would sink beyond the houses and the street would be in darkness.

"I must go across and see aunt Bella for just a few minutes," said Annie, "I feel sure she won't go to bed until I do."

"Shall I go too?" Asked Harold.

Annie smiled, "You remain here with Byron then aunt Bella won't want me to stay for long if she knows I have to return in the darkness alone."

Annie walked through the entry and into the backyard of Bella's. The curtains were drawn across but light, vivid, dancing light could be seen behind their folds. Annie opened the back door, the room was so hot, as she crossed the scullery she heard the fire crackling and spitting. Aunt Bella sat in the corner she had not lit the lamp, the flames roared up the back of the grate, the black cast iron canopy almost glowed red with the heat. The reflections leapt up and down the walls in frenzied, wild abandon. Annie could smell the hearth rug singeing, she saw the little glass salt dish on the sideboard, glistening in the fire's angry light. She quickly took the shovel spoon from the salt and threw the contents of the dish onto the fire, where it fell the flames lowered instantly. The poker was too hot to pick up, even with the old towel. She fetched the 'wash dolly' from the corner of the scullery and thrust it at the damper. Bella spoke not a word. Annie ran to the ash pile in the garden, she smelled burning soot, sparks flew into the night sky from the chimney pot. She filled the old pail with damp ash, rushed indoors, shovelled the ash, a little at a time over the grate, the heat stung her face cruelly. She had deadened the flames, now she could only hope the fire in the chimney would burn itself out. The canopy displayed a crack from top to bottom.

"Whatever did you think you were doing?" She shrieked at Bella angrily in her fear, "you could have been burned alive in this house and you just sat there watching it happen."

"It's my house, no one else lives here, they were my flames, that was my salt, it's my life," Bella screamed the words back at Annie, clenching her hands in her lap.

Harold arrived, he had not seen the chimney fire until he'd opened the heavy curtains at No.24 to look for Annie returning, he had gone across the street at once.

"Whatever is all the shouting about?" He asked looking alarmed, he had never heard upset like this between Annie and Bella.

"Annie thinks I've gone mad, take her home Harold, I shall go to bed now, the fire is out, there is nothing to fret about, a good blaze clears the chimney, you ask your father if that isn't so." Bella rose to her feet, she turned to Annie, "Put the little spoon back in the salt dish before it gets lost. That was all the salt I had, you'd better bring me some in the morning before you go to work. You must open that workshop, he would want those machines to carry on as usual, nothing must stand in the way of his business you know, compassion doesn't win orders. You keep those shuttles flying Annie."

She began to climb the stairs, Harold and Annie looked at each other in bewilderment.

"What about bolting the door?" Asked Annie.

"Go out through the front and take the key with you, bring it back in the morning when you bring Byron."

Annie lay awake for some time before tiredness eventually overcame her, it was the comfort Harold gave that calmed her frantic thoughts. What a dreadful time and what should she do tomorrow, what would Charles expect her to do? May and Edna would come to work not knowing any of this night's events.

It was just after midnight when Charles reached home, Enid sat in the armchair, she put her fingers to her lips, "Shush," she whispered, "I've only just got him to sleep again."

"Has Bertha gone home?" Asked Charles.

"She stayed until half past ten, I told her she shouldn't leave any later, not on her own so she agreed to go. What happened Charles?" Enid looked very sleepy.

"The doctor thinks he died while resting in his chair by the fire, I asked if he could tell how long father had been there like that, he said he couldn't be accurate but possibly since Saturday evening. You go up to bed now, I won't be long, Mr.Handley has taken his body to the Chapel of Rest, I've locked father's house. I shall go to the bank in the morning and explain what has happened, I don't know what to do about the workshop, I'll speak to Annie tomorrow."

Charles sat for a while on his own, his emotions pulled his thoughts in all directions, regret induced tears, insecurity brought alarm and not knowing what he should do created torment. He took off his jacket and hung it on the back of the living room door, his eye caught the tip of the envelope, still unopened in his pocket. He held it under the lamp. Saul Eddowes Esq., 14 Hood Street, Sherwood. It was written in a bold, flowing hand. He broke the seal and took out the folded parchment, it was the receipt for a sum of cash paid to 'Meakin & Kirk' Solicitors, Commissioner for Oaths, London Road. It would appear his father had recently consulted with one Gerald Meakin. Charles carefully put the receipt back in the envelope and placed it in the more secure, less conspicuous, inside pocket of his jacket. Reading the note had propelled his thoughts ahead of this night's troubles to matters of even greater importance. He would need to speak with Meakin & Kirk in the coming days, his father's assets must surely amount to a considerable sum. Charles turned out the lamp and went to his wife, his steps now much steadier on the stairs, his mind firmly focused on 'Charles Eddowes Esq'.

Annie took Byron and a cup of salt to aunt Bella's, she was dressed and raking the grate.

"Shall I do that before I go to work?" Asked Annie.

"You don't need to worry yourself, I shan't incinerate the place."

Annie thought aunt Bella's eyes looked glazed from lack of sleep, she hadn't yet pinned her hair, the tangled tresses were still unbrushed, they had tossed and turned for hours on the pillow. Annie began to question in her mind whether aunt Bella had actually undressed to go to bed last night, the creases in her frock were severe, in fact her whole appearance was dishevelled and dejected.

"I shall come back later to see that you are alright," said Annie.

"Just leave us be, we shall soon have some hot tea and a piece of bread and butter, won't we?" Said Bella, directing her last words at Byron. The dog's eyes looked back at her, those soft, fond eyes which watched her swollen fingers turn the pages as she read, waiting for her hand to reach down to stroke his head when she paused to ponder the script. Annie must leave them, aunt Bella seemed happier in Byron's company than in the company of humankind, for now, Annie was content to leave it like that, she needed to be at the workshop before May and Edna arrived.

Opening the desk in Saul's office pained her, she felt it almost irreverent, as though he was already dismissed, replaced, given no credit. May and Edna arrived together, Edna was about to make some unfortunate remark when May caught hold her arm.

"No Edna." May, older and wiser recognised the despair and exhaustion in Annie's face.

"I think we must work as well as we can, Mr.Eddowes was always fair with us, much of his life was spent in these small premises, until Charles gives us any other instruction we shall endeavour to run the business just as Saul taught us, he died at the weekend." Annie could not speak another word.

May turned to her machine, "Come on Edna, Annie is quite right, we shall stitch for Mr.Eddowes, without this place I know my family would have endured hunger."

Edna sat on her stool, threading more cotton onto her bobbin, tears streamed down her face, "I really wish it 'ad been a woman."

Charles received sympathy at the bank and was told, 'Attend to your family and the funeral, take a few days'.

His visit to the workshop left Annie more concerned than before, he barely spoke to May and Edna, asked nothing of the orders on which they worked, spent several minutes with the ledgers and carefully counted the sum of cash in the metal cash box, his only enquiry being.

"Do we have good orders in hand at present Annie?"

She noted the 'we', if only there could have been more of the 'we' when his father sat at the desk.

Enid had already planned their move to the big house in Hood Street, she had pestered Charles as he sat with his tea early that morning.

"You must be entitled to live there, no one else could have any right over you, find out, ask a lawyer."

By dinner time Enid had packed their few items of best china and all the clothes William had outgrown. The activity put her in ebullient mood and by late afternoon, when Charles came home she was all ears. He had been to the undertakers and established that the funeral would take place on Friday at 2.30pm at St. Saviours Church, interment would follow at Rock Cemetery where his mother had been buried five years before. From Handleys, Charles had gone to London Road to the offices of Meakin & Kirk.

Dermot Mahoney extended his neck and looked intently at Charles, he did not recognise him, a new client possibly. "Can I be of help sir?" He asked.

"I need to speak with either Mr.Meakin or Mr.Kirk, whichever of the two dealt with my father's affairs," answered Charles impatiently.

"I see sir, may I ask firstly your name and then the name of your father."

Charles obliged Mahoney immediately with both names adding, "I am Mr.Eddowes' only son, in fact only close relative."

"Just one moment," said Mahoney and disappeared through the door behind his desk.

Gerald Meakin listened to Dermot's account of Charles Eddowes. His clerk throughout the years had always delivered the pertinent details of a client's visit but in addition, conveyed his own reference as to their character. With that echo from Ireland which could often emphasise Dermot's words he declared.

"Holy Mother, 'dis ones goin to be an awkward bastard," Mahoney's guide to the machinations of Charles Eddowes.

Meakin offered his hand to Charles saying, "Please, do take a seat."

The handshake lacked any substance. Charles informed Meakin of Saul's death like he described a discovery of gold and was now wishing to stake his claim through official channels.

"If you are able to confirm your identity and relationship to Saul Eddowes, then I can reveal to you the content of his Will. You will appreciate that without sight of such credentials I am not empowered to do so."

"How do I go about that?" Asked Charles coldly, he felt annoyed at not yet knowing the details of his inheritance. Enid would allow him no peace until he could enlighten her with figures of pounds, shillings and pence and elevate her with deeds of ownership.

"I suggest you find your Birth Certificate and bring it to this office, that document will suffice."

Charles left, offering no courtesy to Mahoney, walking straight past him and into the street.

"BeJesus, what a Shite." Mahoney muttered to himself.

Charles kept his birth certificate in a box with a picture of his mother, it had been there since his marriage to Enid. Unbeknown to anyone, he had carried the small photograph in his jacket pocket the day of the wedding, he had wanted his mother to be with him. Following the ceremony, when he had found a moment of quietness alone, he had put the two together, her photograph and his birth certificate in the small box which he kept in the drawer of his chest beneath his best shirt.

All had been revealed in Meakin's office the next day. He had been advised that moving into his father's house was permissible but that he would dwell there rather as a caretaker, keeping the property secure. It would not pass to his ownership until Meakin proved Probate. Charles drew a short breath when Meakin read the recent Codicil. Five years! He was unable to sell the business or premises for five years. Saul's depleted capital, if he'd had any sense, should not have come as any surprise to him but the bequest of ten guineas to Annie galled.

"Why did he leave money to one of his employees," exclaimed Charles, not so much a question as a cry of consternation.

Meakin answered anyway, "I can recall your father's words almost exactly, 'Mrs.Boucher has worked for me through many years, showing more effort, indeed more conscientious effort' said Meakin, 'than could be expected of her'. That was your father's sentiment."

As Charles walked home he cogitated, deliberated and ultimately decided, his earnings from the bank would not meet his needs and certainly not those of his wife, he could not manage without money from the business. If he could not sell to convert the proceeds for his own purpose, then he must leave the bank and take over the workshop. Annie would show him what to do, he would work the women hard, increase the profits. Five years would pass quickly, then he would be free to do as he pleased. Perhaps the ten guineas might serve a useful purpose in the event, a little 'soft soap' as Enid would say. He would get the funeral out of the way then he could hand in his notice, everything should be in place and progressing before the baby arrived. His pace quickened towards home, Enid would be impressed. Perhaps first, he would call in for a pint at The Standard, it would only delay him for a few minutes, a man was entitled to drink to the future after all.

CHAPTER EIGHTEEN

Three weeks had passed since Saul's funeral, Annie had seen little of Charles in the days which immediately followed his father's death and in the absence of any direction from him, she had closed the workshop at midday on the Friday to enable May, Edna and herself to attend the funeral. Charles had made no reference to her decision, he needed Annie's knowledge, her ability, and if the business was to prosper, he must keep her goodwill. It was aunt Bella who gave Annie most cause for concern, her depressed state of mind persisted, she was not eating enough, her appearance had become out of character, Bella had never been a slave to fashion but she would normally appear tidy, correct, never unkempt. Annie had persuaded aunt Bella to let her wash her hair just the day before, it was so tangled from lack of brushing it took Annie ages to free the knots. Some days her buttons had been fastened in the wrong sequence and she had made no attempt to correct them. The least thing could barb her tongue with hurtful words, even Harold had borne the brunt of her annoyance and resentment when, on the previous Sunday, he and Annie had helped Charles and Enid move to Hood Street. As Annie had explained, Enid was now six months pregnant and couldn't lift anything heavy and for whatever reason, there seemed to be no one else able or willing to offer assistance.

Annie began to despair, aunt Bella's reaction to Saul's death defied her understanding. Annie decided to walk Byron to Davina's after work, Harold was going straight from the yard to Samuel's to help his father repair the roof. Half a dozen slates had slipped, just below the ridge, Harold had insisted his father wait for him to help.

'You can stand at the bottom o' the ladder Father while I'm up top'.

Frank couldn't stand heights and Harold preferred to have the weightier figure of his father to secure the ladder than 'a throw back from grandad's whippet' as Harold teasingly described his younger brother.

Ivy was pleased to see Annie and Byron and he, equally delighted to find himself at that big house where ladies plied him with biscuits and endless attention. Annie poured out her concerns about aunt Bella, Davina listened in silence, almost an impossibility for Davina. If Annie had not been so distracted by the complexities of Bella's moods, she might have pondered the intense concentration which Davina gave to Annie's account.

She patted Annie's hand. "You must understand my dear, that you were taken on at the workshop by Mr.Eddowes twelve years ago, your aunt Bella would have been anxious at the time, you were so young. However, he taught you a skill, a trade and your earnings enabled Bella to keep a home around you both. With his death would have come worry for Bella, would your work continue? I am quite sure she would feel a little regret that she had not made her gratitude known to him, we are all guilty at times of leaving it too late to speak our feelings, express our thoughts and emotions. Treat her as normally as you can, encourage Harold to read with her. Give it a little time Annie and I am convinced she will find her old self."

Davina's words reassured her, as did the sweet candy they both sucked as they sat watching Byron fast asleep on the hearth rug, the breath from his broad nostrils gently lifting the hem of Davina's frock.

"I wish I could sleep so soundly," said Davina, "the older I become Annie dear, the less interest the sleep fairy has in putting 'Moon Dust' over my eyes" she began to giggle, "I think possibly the wand gets stuck among all the wrinkles underneath."

They both laughed at the notion and when the time came for Annie to leave, her spirits felt much lighter. They had been despatched with a bag of scones, 'too stale for me now dear, but ideal for Byron' and a ham bone still bearing enough meat for Harold's sandwiches. 'It will do the dog's teeth good to chew on that bone when you've picked it clean' had been Davina's way of covering up her need to spoil Byron, as a grandparent might spoil a small child. When Annie reached home Harold was already there.

"Dad just won't give in, you try to 'elp 'im but no, 'e 'as to do it all 'imself. When I got there, Frank wer' standing five rungs up the ladder, as far as 'e'd go, and dad wer' just fixing the last slate. Mam called me indoors and made me sit to eat a plate o' boiled beef, she's sent a basin full home for you too. That was all I 'ad to do, sit and feed me face."

Annie chuckled, Sarah and Samuel loved all their family so much, Harold might be peeved at their antics but Annie knew them well enough to appreciate the delight they would have derived from having Harold sit at the table in Mitchell Street for his tea, Sunday dinner alone just wasn't sufficient for his mam and dad, sometimes they needed to see his smiling face, hear his familiar happy voice in a 'larger dose' as Sarah would describe her measures of contentment.

Davina stood by the window, Ivy had brought her jacket in readiness, she watched for the driver to approach the side door. Davina had ordered a carriage to collect her at half past one. The day was warm and fine, she wished her legs were young enough to stand the walk from The Park to Sherwood, her spirit was more than willing but the aging bones refused to be swayed by the sunshine, the scent of lavender and geraniums. Such temptations could be fickle, ice cold winds and stinging rain might creep up at any time and then where would the old bones be. That was their logic, Davina was quite convinced, why else would they resist, she had never treated them any differently when she was a young woman. Spirit was constant, loyal, but bones, well they were contrary, they let you down. Davina's thoughts rambled on 'til the sound of someone clearing their throat heralded the arrival of the carriage. The driver turned the corner of the house and walked towards the side door where his figure became lost among the fading garlands of wisteria blooms. Davina put on her jacket, by the time Ivy had opened the door to the man, Davina stood close behind her.

"I shall be back by half past three Ivy."

The driver helped Davina into her seat, she thanked him, "Would you take me to Winchester Street."

Davina stood at the front door of Bella's house, she took a deep breath and knocked firmly, she was patient, Bella would almost certainly be at the back of the house, from the corner of her eye she caught the slight movement of a net curtain. The door opened slowly, stubbornly, not used often it creaked on its hinges, Bella didn't speak but looked intently at her caller.

"My name is Davina Wright," she was about to add we have a mutual friend but Bella interrupted.

"I know who you are," she said, her voice was steady, she showed no particular reaction.

"May I come in for just a little while?" Asked Davina.

Bella opened the door wider and stood to one side, she led Davina through to the living room, holding back the heavy curtain to enable her visitor to walk through unhindered.

"Oh, I was about to say that we share a mutual friend, now I see we share two friends."

Byron was pleased to see his lady with the 'treats' and greeted her with enthusiasm, this marked all the more Bella's cool reception.

"Sit," said Bella.

Poor Davina was not at all sure whether the command had been directed at her or dear Byron, but as if able to read each others mind, both sat down simultaneously, leaving Bella standing over them like the school mistress, which indeed she was.

"Would you like tea?" She asked.

"Thank you Bella but I had a cup not long before leaving home. I hope you don't mind my calling you Bella, please do call me Davina, I feel we know each other through our good friend Alice Hemsley. I know that she has told you much about me, and you, I know, are wise enough to believe that she would have in turn spoken to me of those events which strangely bind us." Davina sighed. "It is time we sat together Bella, we both grow older." She looked into Bella's eyes and smiled. "There is another chapter of my past without which the story is not entirely told. When Nathan died I had a visit from Jack Braithwaite, he took no account of my grief, understandably he wanted to be sure that I was aware of his own misery and the torment of his wife Constance. She never got over it you know, that is why, just five years after Charles was born, Jack Braithwaite sold all his interest in the bank and he and Constance moved to Skegness, she hoped that if they lived by the sea Hilda would visit them for periods with the child. I really don't know if that happened, I sincerely hope for the poor woman's sake that it did. Jack had come to the house to tell me of the agreement between himself, Nathan and Saul. Presumably he was afraid I may not honour it or even be aware of it. Nathan had told me everything, more, so much more than I wished to know."

Davina's voice trembled but she continued. "I assured Jack that he need not worry, the payments would continue. My cousin's husband was in mining, not in Nottingham but in Derby, Owen would help me with the sale of Birchdale, I was sure of that. He left the house satisfied I think at the obvious distress I felt. What I had ever done that was in any way bad I could not comprehend but his own wife had been made so desperately miserable, I suppose he needed to see that Nathan's wife too was filled with despair. The very next day, Jack came to the house again, I don't think it took him more than a minute to inform me that Saul Eddowes had come to him at the bank that morning insisting that he wished all payments to cease immediately. 'I shall attend to the paperwork and furnish you with the annulment personally', those were his words, cold as charity. Alice Hemsley would have made you aware I'm sure, that after less than two years, Saul refused the payments, perhaps his principles changed as he matured, who is to know."

Bella sat listening, one hand on Byron's head, staring at the hearth, making no sound.

Davina drew a deeper breath, "I didn't tell Alice Hemsley everything. What I am about to confide in you no other living soul has knowledge of. When Nathan told me about Hilda and the baby I near drowned in my own tears. He flirted with most young women, he always had, but he loved me, I knew it was me he really loved. Then my mind began to torment me. We were childless after ten years of marriage, this young woman Hilda

Braithwaite, had conceived Nathan's baby. I had failed to give him that, I began to feel inadequate. You will think me weak, pathetic, but truly I never kept him from our bed, not even when he told me, we would lay side by side. I felt I could not have been a proper wife or this would not have happened. I should have spoken my thoughts and feelings to him but I did not. The nights were spent in the same bed but in silence, because I was so quiet, so remote from him, Nathan believed I could not forgive him, that I let him in my bed just to save face. He missed me, he missed 'us', but he didn't speak his feelings and thoughts either. Then, it was all too late. I had been writing a letter, I heard the front door bell, Mr.Gilbert, the undertaker asked to speak with me. I can remember his expression as he entered the room. The doctor had gone to the pit too but there was nothing he could do other than confirm death. Nathan was found on the ground by the winch cage, he appeared to have been checking the mechanism. No one could understand why he was there but on his desk they found a note, a sort of memo, it said, 'Shudder on winch, check pulley belts and chains'. It could have been written by anyone, the hand was untidy and the spelling inaccurate, but it was legible. Why Nathan had gone himself and not sent maintenance the men could not understand. He had fallen from the top of the steel housing to the ground striking his head on the edge of the cage, it was that impact which broke his neck. The men were asked who put the memo on Nathan's desk but no one declared they had. At the time I supposed they were afraid it would lead to some trouble for them. Mr.Gilbert handed me Nathan's watch and chain and his wallet, he asked if I would like to see him. I went to the Chapel, the day before the funeral. 'Would you like me to remove his ring?' That's what he asked me you know."

Davina was struggling to retain her composure. "I told him that I gave it to Nathan to keep for always, it must stay on his finger. The funeral was a blur, I can't remember the faces of the people who attended, I don't even remember what the vicar said about Nathan. I just could not bring myself to open his wallet, it lay in the top drawer of my dressing table for a month until one day, I saw it there, I took it in my hands and held it tightly, picturing him as he would be each morning when he left for his work. It was then that I opened it, between two five pound notes I found an envelope, sealed, my name, just the one word 'Davina', was written on the front. I have recited the words so many times over the past twenty years.

'My dearest Dee,
How could I, even for one moment, have believed you might forgive me. I am
so sorry and ashamed. I cannot continue without that dearest thing in all the
world, that which I destroyed, your love Davina. Your were always my own
dearest Dee.
May I still, sometimes, however briefly, be your Nathan.
My Love

Davina's fingers shook, she felt Bella's hands envelope her own and when she turned her gaze from the cracked canopy above the grate to Bella, she saw the tears which imprisoned Bella's grief, at last find release, they both wept. In their emotion they had forgotten Byron, he lay on the floor between them, as if trying to comfort them both equally, whimpering softly as Bella's tears fell on his back and Davina's tears just brushed his nose as they slipped from her cheeks. The two women had shared a heartache for so long.

Davina steadied her voice as she said, "Nathan took his own life, wrote the memo himself, aimed his fall. He thought I didn't forgive him, but Bella, I did, I truly did. Sometimes we leave it too late, we just don't talk to one another but you have something special, I envy you very much. All these years you have had Annie's love, you should be proud Bella, it is you, her teacher, her mother in every true sense of the word, who has made her the fine young woman she is. Don't let anything else become too late, enjoy Annie and Harold, grasp the life they bring you. They will have children and you will be so wanted and needed."

"Have you told Annie anything of the past?" Asked Bella anxiously.

"No, I have not, if Annie is to learn of the past, then it must be you who tells her, no one else. You will keep my memories safely locked away won't you?" Said Davina.

"They are your memories, no concern of any other," replied Bella.

The carriage had returned and the two women parted with a deep understanding between them. Bella watched from behind the nets as the carriage disappeared into Sherwood Road, before returning to the living room she took a book from the shelves. Bella sat in her chair, then leaned forward and slowly drew her finger down the crack in the canopy.

"Beyond mending, but still serves its purpose," she said softly to herself. Byron gave a small bark, "Alright," she looked down at her friend, "we shall read 'Childe Harold's Pilgrimage'." His ears were alert, his attention all Bella's. "No more tears," her words were strong, her fingers turned the book cover, Bella and Byron looked forward to what came next.

The workshop had functioned as always, the books were all up to date and the machines sped over the fabrics producing the quality of which Saul had always been proud. Annie had travelled with Meade to Mrs.Appleyard's the week after the funeral, to do the final fitting. It had been fortunate that the design she had chosen had been simple, classic lines with few adornments, just some small bows of the same material attached to the bodice and a scalloped hemline. Mrs.Appleyard had been delighted.

'My dear Mrs.Boucher, I had prepared myself for a garment, possibly a little less accomplished than Eddowes' usual standard. This dreadfully sad business of Mr.Eddowes' sudden demise I felt sure would affect matters adversely. However, I declare the gown to be faultless'.

As Annie had left the good lady she'd felt encouraged. Charles had told Annie of his intention to hand in his notice at the bank and to take on the running of his father's business. It troubled Annie, if Charles proved capable of actually listening and observing, then all should be well, but if his past lack of interest undermined his concentration, then his presence would be nothing more than a hindrance and his earnings, a severe drain on finances. A development, just a few days after Annie's appointment with Mrs.Appleyard, had helped bring a positive attitude to Charles. He had recognised the value of Annie's skills, not simply at her machine but in her approach to clients and in her relationship with May and Edna, they obviously cared for Annie greatly and responded to her suggestions and subtle prompting.

Mrs.Appleyard had called at the workshop on the way to her voluntary work, Annie showed her to the office where the excited lady could not wait to tell Annie proudly of her husband's donation.

'Do you know my dear, the hospital has not had new uniforms for the nurses in ages. I told Mr.Appleyard, it is long past time those drab, dowdy, dark green uniforms his nurses have to wear were abandoned. How can they be expected to take a pride in the hospital when they look like wilted Savoys. He has agreed my idea for a fitting gift from him to the hospital to mark his retirement after so many years of devoted service. We would like you to make, here at the workshop, new uniforms, blue, I would like a crisp, mid blue, a colour far more appropriate for busy young women than dreary, cabbage green'.

Annie had explained they were not a large production line, it would take a little longer than if she ordered from a bigger concern. Mrs.Appleyard was adamant, she had been so impressed by the gown, created amidst such difficult times, that she had quite made up her mind, the new uniforms donated to the hospital by Mr.Appleyard must be made at Eddowes'. It was a good order for them and Annie had felt happy and relieved to impart the news to Charles. He was now at Winchester Street in the office, sitting at Saul's desk most of the time. There had been one or two late arrivals and a similar number of early departures but his spirit seemed good. His work at the bank had at least equipped him with a grasp of figures, converting orders to quantities of material however, remained a mystery to him. The suitability of certain fabrics to particular garments and the individual purpose of various threads and elastics escaped him entirely. Annie had assured him that in time he would come to know, quite naturally, all these calculations. Whilst in the company of the women he seemed quite relaxed, amenable, he had lost his desire to impose his 'rule', preferring to laugh at Edna's earthy yarns and show appreciation of the rare conversations May offered, which almost always gave Charles advice on how to keep young William occupied. At home in Hood Street however, Charles' demeanour needed to be very different. Enid had rejoiced in their new status, her husband a respected businessman, master over his own affairs. Charles must live up to her expectations or at least appear to do so. It was a lesson neither Charles nor Enid had yet learned, a business, the premises and employees did not automatically bring respect. It was something Annie knew she must teach them, tactfully but thoroughly, she would do her best.

It had been a long day and Annie was glad to have walked Byron and reached home, she hung her jacket behind the door and set about making their meal, Harold would be home at any time. Several minutes passed before Annie noticed an envelope on the floor inside the front door, she looked at the writing, it seemed strangely familiar, a flowing hand had addressed the envelope:-

Mrs. Annie Boucher

24 Winchester Street

Sherwood

It puzzled her, whilst she waited for the water to boil she opened the seal, it looked official. The letter revealed the sender to be, Meakin & Kirk Solicitors. It advised Annie that a matter to her advantage required her to call at their offices as soon as might be convenient, it gave no indication as to what the matter might be.

"Sorry Byron," she said, "you're hungry aren't you?"

Bryon had sat patiently waiting for the dish of food which Annie gave him each evening at about this time, she pondered on what this letter might lead to, Harold would know what to do.

"Here you are, now don't gobble it down too quickly or you'll have hiccups again."

Annie put the letter on the table and busied herself with the pork chops. Harold came across the yard whistling happily, "I have gifts for you both, sent with love from Josiah."

He put a parcel on the scullery table, kissed his wife, as always and said, "Lamb's kidneys for the lady and tripe for Lord Byron."

After their meal Annie showed Harold the letter, "What can it be?" She said.

"Only one way to find out my love, you must go and see these people."

A couple of days went by whilst Annie thought about the letter, she decided Harold was right, nervous though she felt, it was time to face Meakin & Kirk. It was a good thirty minutes walk from the workshop to London Road, she would leave her machine a little earlier than usual and make up her time the next day. Annie explained to Charles, he guessed her destination although she had said only that she needed to attend to a certain matter. To bolster her confidence, she wore the pretty pin in her hat and the pearl brooch on her jacket but neither prevented her stomach from filling with 'Colly Wobbles' as dear Sarah described nervousness. Annie gripped the large brass door knob and turned it with trepidation. Her first sight on entry was Mahoney, his odd appearance not striking Annie in the least, but his softly rounded vowels wrapped his words in velvet.

"Good afternoon ma'am, can I be of help?".

At once Annie felt less anxious, she took the letter from her bag and handed it to Mahoney.

"Ah yes, if you will just wait one moment, please take a seat ma'am."

Annie sat quietly on a small upholstered settle, looking across the room to a picture on the opposite wall. It was a peaceful scene of hills and lakes and tiny cottages, remote, only grazing sheep dotted the pastures.

Mahoney returned, "If you would come with me I will take you to Mr.Meakin."

He led her into the office where Gerald Meakin sat amidst reams of paper, he rose from his chair and crossed the room to meet her. Mahoney turned to leave.

Annie spoke quickly, "Thank you sir," she said to the surprised clerk, her smile a rarity in Mahoney's domain.

Meakin offered his hand, Annie shook it firmly. The two men were completely different, yet her nervousness had faded, neither caused her to feel uneasy. He revealed the details of Saul's bequest and the high regard of which he had spoken. Annie sat silently, unable to respond with anything beyond tears which welled in her eyes.

"Mr.Eddowes was always kind, not at any time did I dread my work, I never heard his voice raised, not ever. Mr.Eddowes gave me such care and friendship in life, he had no need to present me with money after his death."

Meakin smiled, "It was his wish and we must abide by it, I have prepared a receipt which I need ask you to sign."

He watched as her slim fingers propelled the pen across the paper, the writing neat and accurate. He handed her a thick brown envelope, tightly sealed.

"You may count it if you wish but I assure you the content is correct."

Annie thanked him, her sadness at Saul's death so obviously the stronger emotion, she had shown no jubilation at the unexpected windfall. Meakin thought of Charles and the difference between the two young people, he showed her to the door.

"It has been a pleasure meeting you Mrs.Boucher. I knew Mr.Eddowes over a period of very many years, I am truly sorry he has died, I found him to be a gentle man, or perhaps it might be better put, a man of gentle nature."

Annie paused by Mahoney's desk, he immediately crossed to the front door, opening it for Annie to pass through.

"Oh, I didn't mean you to leave your work, I only stopped to thank you and say goodbye, I'm sorry I don't know your name?" Said Annie.

"Mahoney ma'am, Dermot Mahoney."

Annie smiled and offered her hand, "Goodbye Mr.Mahoney."

He shut the door and bolted it, Annie was the last client today, the office was now closed to the outside world. Meakin awaited his clerk's deliberations, it took only a minute for Mahoney to enter the office declaring in words which rolled from the hills of Eire.

"A real Lady, a real honest to God Lady."

Meakin watched as Mahoney unlocked the cabinet, his thoughts drifted, poor Saul, so misunderstood. The world could be such a cruel place, unforgiving, unwilling to tolerate any perceived weakness. He waited for the beginning of Mahoney's evening ritual.

"Well, would ye ever know Gerald, there's only Whiskey again!"

He took two glasses and a bottle from the cabinet and put them on Meakin's desk, he poured a measure into each glass, handing one to Meakin. Then he put one arm on Meakin's shoulder, gently kissed the top of his bald head, kissed the face of the signet ring on his own right hand, picked up his glass and raised his arm in a toast.

"To Buggery." Mahoney's daily act of defiance at a world which showed him no grace.

Gerald Meakin gave a deep sigh, "Nothing changes Dermot, nothing ever changes."

When Annie told Harold of the afternoon's events, he wiped her tears and said, "Put the money away in a safe place, you must keep that for the future. We are managing on the earnings we have, Saul would want you to use that for something special. Wait to see what the future brings."

"I don't know what to do, normally I would tell aunt Bella everything and this is so significant but she has only just begun to recover her spirit. You know how dejected and lifeless she has been since Saul died, I'm afraid if I tell her about this it will bring back all her depression again," said Annie.

They agreed that for the time, it would be kinder not to risk upsetting Bella, she had seemed so much brighter over recent days. The ten guineas were put in a tin box and hidden inside a larger box filled with washing soda.

Annie put it on the top shelf of the scullery, beside a box of candles, a packet of 'Dolly Blue' and a tin of Zeebo. There it would remain until circumstances demanded its reappearance. Annie found another box in which to store her soda but the gift and the giver were remembered every day as she cast her eyes to the shelf. Annie would not forget the man who had dispelled her nervousness as a child in that first week at the workshop. They had journeyed twelve years together since then. Annie would miss Saul Eddowes, that anchor in her life which held fast, when aunt Bella's harsh words left her adrift.

CHAPTER NINETEEN

The summer melted into autumn, the workshop prospered under Annie's guidance and Bella had found a simple contentment, spending much time with Byron and thriving on her great discussions with Harold. His easy chatter in the evenings, as he filled the buckets and drank tea with her, brought Bella out of her seclusion to be a part of day to day events. Sarah and Davina had managed to spend a little time together, easing Davina's loneliness and giving Sarah a break from her activities in the kitchen. As Nora had told her, 'Mam, if you don't let me do the baking from time to time, how shall I ever learn'.

William had continued to grow at an impressive rate, now a little over twelve months, he was walking as strong and steady as a dray horse. The second child was due at any time and Charles had confided in Annie the depth of fear Enid now displayed at the slightest twinge, be it cramp, stitch, headache or any other minor discomfort. Bertha was staying at Hood Street by day and night until after the birth. Charles too was nervous, his concentration at work fleeting.

Annie felt it might be easier if he stayed at home with Enid and Bertha but she sensed he needed to be away from the house until the actual event, otherwise he might never recover from the lashings which Enid's tongue brought down on his weary frame, ever more frequently the closer to the birth they became.

It was the beginning of November, Annie, May and Edna were combining routine sewing with the stitching of Christmas items. Annie had sent Charles to Drew's outfitters a couple of weeks earlier, to secure an order for the festive season. His approach needed a degree of modification and in order to equip him with the necessary tact and diplomacy, she had directed him in acting out the scene. Now satisfied that he was suitably confident but not arrogant, pleasant but not sugary, and capable of listening to the highly experienced Mr.Drew and not ignoring the gentleman in supposing he, Charles, knew best, Annie had despatched him to Castle Road with fingers crossed.

He had returned with his chest plumped with pride, Edna said he looked like Morley's game cockerel when it had served the last hen. The order was even better than Annie had hoped and would keep the machines fully occupied until the end of the year.

Charles was late, Annie felt unsettled, whilst he could be late for any number of reasons Enid's condition seemed the most likely. Her thoughts proved correct. At Hood Street, Bertha had endured stress beyond comprehension. The hours which led up to William's birth had been a strain to tax even Bertha's stoic character but Freddy Eddowes had made his entrance before an audience so stretched of nerves, that only his blesséd, easy delivery into the world had saved Bertha and Charles from emotional collapse.

Enid's labour had been short, she required no stitches and the baby was a glorious mop haired, chubby little boy who found his thumb almost at once. Freddy was born at six a.m., but the night hours which preceded the event held more trauma and desperation than any mortal was designed to bear. Enid's disparaging verbal assault of her husband grew to such volume, Bertha had no option but to send Charles downstairs with William.

"Go down to the living room, shut the door tightly on yourselves, distract the child, cover his ears if you have to but take the frightened mite away from his tortured, hell bent mother."

Bertha shook with feeling. It was worse than the last time, there would be no labour until Enid turned from this possessed hysteria to the reality of giving birth.

Enid screamed for Charles with every curse known to man, her eyes wild with fear, pursued Bertha to every corner of the room, allowing the poor woman no release. Sheer exhaustion finally took the ground and Enid's tormentors were cut down, beaten back, scattered about the scene behind the torn bedcovers, the chewed pillows, the ripped pages of a book. She slept deeply, peacefully until just before five o'clock.

The familiar early morning sounds from the street provided Bertha with fresh strength. Charles and William slept fitfully by the fire in the living room. As Enid stirred, Bertha removed the coat from around her own shoulders and stood up to speak purposefully to the waking Enid.

"Now we shall have a baby," she said calmly.

Freddy caused no alarm and less than one hour of discomfort. Enid held him across her chest and gazing up to Charles and her first born son she said in a faint voice.

"The Devil wasn't ready for me, he doesn't want Enid Cole yet."

Charles put her ramblings down to tiredness, her maiden name had not been spoken since their wedding, he smoothed her brow and lay a kiss on each closed eyelid. Enid would sleep 'til Freddy's next feed. Bertha would attend the necessary tasks then hand over the charge to Charles whilst she attempted some recovery from the ordeal.

It was late afternoon before circumstances permitted Charles to call at the workshop, his rest starved eyes and subdued announcement of the birth, revealed to Annie all the strain of the previous night, she would go to see Enid as soon as she could.

The following Saturday afternoon Annie closed the workshop a little earlier than usual. Edna grinned her delight at the unexpected bonus and May quietly gathered her coat, only then mentioning the fact that it was Alfred senior's birthday.

"He has been so good about the house, he will be surprised to see me home early on his birthday."

The simplest of pleasures satisfied May. Annie had been so pleased to find Alfred in reasonable health and good spirits on the occasions she had visited the family through the summer. Young Alfred had grown by a good two inches and showed signs of making a man of much greater height and girth than his father. Mabel continued to convey every joy to anyone who might pause to acknowledge the child. Shawcross had produced a token growl as Annie had walked past with Byron but his tail had not managed to contain itself and that old familiar 'wag' of pleasure and friendliness was unabated. Today however, Annie's destination was Hood Street. She locked the workshop and made her way directly to Charles and Enid, a parcel containing two flannelette cot sheets tucked under her arm. Harold would expect her to be later home, he and aunt Bella would no doubt read together. Their excursions through the encyclopaedia had taken them to the letter 'V' in the index. Harold expected to reach the final pages by Christmas so had already nominated the atlas as their next great study.

'I shall show you the best places in the world Annie', he had said as they sat together in No.24, 'but I shall need to learn which ones are the best'.

Harold's dreams carried Annie and himself beyond Sherwood, beyond Nottingham and England to exotic climes where factory chimneys were replaced by towering palm trees, where uneven cobbles lay hidden beneath vast deposits of smooth golden sand and deep blue ocean not dense grimy smog, swept across the land with each cleansing tide. Annie smiled at her thoughts as she turned into Hood Street. Bertha was staying at the house for a week or so until Enid established a routine. Poor Bertha had sounded far from convinced.

William held Annie's hand as they crossed the room to look at the infant, he walked so confidently now and his first few words were followed always by a smile of satisfaction at his achievement. Annie lifted him so he could see into the Moses basket, his plump fingers tried earnestly to reach the mouth of his slumbering brother.

"Ello, Ello." He propelled his fingers even closer to the blissfully quiet baby, he looked around to Annie, "s'eepy," said William.

She just caught the finger before it reached those tiny pursed lips, "Shush," she said "mustn't wake him he will only grow whilst he is asleep and we want him to grow big so he can play with you don't we?" Annie lowered the stocky young William to the floor.

The feeling Annie experienced as his warm sticky fingers searched for her own and held on to her hand, sent a wave of maternal longing through her entire being. Each month she had hoped 'this might be the one' but still she bled. It was early days, they had been married only a short while but the desire, the anticipation were so strong every time.

"Freddy is beautiful Enid, you are so lucky to have two sons, William, already so handsome," said Annie blowing a kiss to him as he stood by her side, "and his new brother is a little dear, you must be so proud."

"If you think they are impressive then you should look at the wash basket, now that really is a sight you won't forget." Said Enid ungraciously.

Bertha frowned and poked the fire, "Charles should be back soon, he's gone for bread and meat," she said, "have a cuppa Annie, we could all do with one."

When Charles appeared in the doorway, William ran across to him, arms outstretched. Now sitting on his father's arm, the child sang a nursery rhyme, taught him by Bertha, the words tumbling out in no particular order and the tune following the words rather than the other way about.

"Sings like his dad," said Enid.

Charles handed her a package. "It will suit your colouring," he said hopefully.

Enid held up a silk scarf in a pretty shade of lilac, although her gratitude was grudging, Annie by now knew Enid well enough to recognise the real pleasure the gift had brought. Annie caught Charles' eye and mouthed the words silently, 'she likes it'. He looked relieved. There were times when Annie thought Charles to be hard and lacking sensitivity but today she thought him to be as vulnerable as the two small boys he had fathered.

The weeks ahead would make demands on each of this family, but that time would strengthen them also, of that Annie felt quite convinced.

November passed with a series of foggy, cold days, the old pot bellied stove once more provided the workshop's warmth. Charles was back at his desk but at Annie's suggestion left earlier, leaving her to lock up.

"It will enable you to help Enid prepare the boys for bed," she had told him, hoping the gesture might bring a little peace and stability to the often fraught household at Hood Street.

The books confirmed a healthy advance of orders and a good net profit which together put the business on a sound footing. Charles unwisely boasted to Enid of his skills in management and the resultant figures. He had agreed her want of smart new clothes.

'In the world of commerce as we are, surely you want your wife to look elegant. It is not my fault that my waist size has increased by two inches, having babies does that you know. A woman requires fine clothes to restore her confidence'. Enid's wants seemed never to be met.

Annie and Harold felt the need of nothing more than each other, the cosy evenings spent with Byron by the fire at home, the love which occupied the house along with them, created the purest sweetest rhythms, both by day and by night. The end of January teased Annie's longings, this month she had not bled. The differences between the two young couples could not have been greater. Annie, for months, had washed clothing and bedding by hand with no complaint, or even thought of complaint and when the boiler arrived she felt as proud of this appliance as many would feel of a grand piano.

Enid now held designs on another status symbol. Charles was endeavouring to eat his tea, not an easy task when the meal was made from an oxtail. The small irregular shaped bones threatened his teeth with every mouthful taken. Enid made the most of her captive audience.

"This house is far too big for me to keep clean without daily help."

"For heavens sake Enid," said Charles, "you've got Bertha doing everything for you now while you sit preening yourself."

"That's nonsense, why some days she only stays for an hour, we need a daily cleaning woman."

Charles spat a bone out onto his plate and rounded on Enid harshly. "Just where do you think the money comes from, if you didn't fritter it away on silk stockings and cologne, a man might get a decent piece of meat instead of this miserable offering of gristle and bone."

Enid's eyes flared with temper, "That business is making good money, you told me so yourself, it's our business, so that makes the money ours, what else is it for if not for us?"

"Fabrics have be to paid for, the costs of the office, what if a machine goes down, how do you suppose we would get a new one. A business must carry capital"

Charles was agitated, the argument continued until Freddy woke for his feed, forcing hostilities to cease. Charles sat with the child in his arms whilst Enid fetched the cream and nappies. His son looked up and raised one plump little hand to his father's face, Charles tickled the tiny palm with his tongue. Even at this age, Freddy responded with a smile of delight and returned the affection by trying to grasp Charles' nose. Enid returned, she lay the infant across her lap and changed him, her fingers now adept at the task, it was soon done. Freddy cuddled into his mother for milk, the scene touched Charles' soft spot. This woman had given him two beautiful sons and she, their mother, looked on him every day with that striking beauty after which so many men would hanker. Her features tauntingly fine, her skin soft and clear as though perfectly painted by some great artist, and that hair, which at night could wrap his shoulder in sweet smelling Enid as she slept in the warmth of his back. That night brought acquiescence, Enid would have her cleaner and Charles had the devotions of his wife, it was their way and the dawn found both satisfied.

Annie had been on tenterhooks, she told herself if nothing happened in March then she would tell Harold and aunt Bella. Her body felt different, her tastes were not as usual, sometimes the smell of their food as she cooked and baked made her feel nauseous. Now Annie was sure, the warm blossom scented days of April had arrived and she had not bled since Christmas. She felt happier than words could adequately describe, after tea she would tell Harold.

The needle seemed to direct itself across the cloth, Annie dreamed as she worked, of pretty little girls' frocks, or boys' sailor suits. Imagined walks in the arboretum and the feeling of tiny fingers seeking her own.

The men's shirts on which she worked passed over her machine, each one perfectly sewn, Annie's expertise gained from all those years of eager learning.

"A penny for 'em," said Edna. Annie smiled. "It's your weddin' anniversary in a few days isn't, I wonder what Harold's plannin' on givin' yer?" Edna was ever curious.

"When our Ada and Morely 'ad been married their first year, 'e gave 'er an Aylesbury duck an' drake, 'e told Ada that birds mated for life an' 'e an' she would allus be just like them two birds. Next day the duck got run over by the coal waggon an' the bloody drake flew over the wall to next door an' jumped their Karki Campbell." Edna burst into laughter, "Followin' day, Morely 'ad duck for 'is tea, our Ada 'anged its feet above the fireplace an' told Morely, 'if you're goin' to be just like 'im, it won't be yer feet as gets hanged up there to toast.'

Annie had collected Byron from aunt Bella's and put a pan of broth on the coals. Soup and cold meat with bubble and squeek made up their meal, Harold would be home very soon. The grass was well established in the small patch of garden and Byron now lay full length on his belly in the evening sunshine, chewing on the marrow bone. The laundry had dried well and Annie picked it down from the line, folding it as she lay the clothes in the basket. 'Good folding is better than bad ironing', aunt Bella had often told her. She hadn't noticed Harold standing at the back of the yard.

"You made me jump," said Annie, "Why didn't you speak?"

Harold laughed, "I was enjoyin' watchin' you, a man can look at 'is wife can't 'e?"

Annie gathered up the basket and they walked inside. Byron acknowledged Harold's arrival with a welcoming bark but the bone won his immediate attention.

Annie took Harold's dinner bag and as she lay it on the scullery table, she said, "I have something to tell you." She turned to look at him. He stood with his arms overlapped, rocking, as one would rock a baby, a big grin straddling his face, "How did you know?" Cried Annie.

"I couldn't be sure but I hoped, I knew you'd missed so when you said you 'ad somethin' to tell me, I guessed."

Their togetherness was complete, they kissed, oblivious to the presence of Byron who was looking on with a knowing expression. Only when their embrace ended and the smell of broth alerted Annie to the fire, did the affectionate animal thrust a cold wet nose into Harold's hand.

"I reckon you guessed too," he rubbed the dog's head lovingly. "Happy days comin' Byron, a world of happy days."

They decided to tell Bella, Sarah and Samuel at the weekend, Annie would tell May and Edna the following week. Their news was greeted joyously by everyone except Bella, who asked only when and told Annie firmly, 'Eat properly, keep yourself strong and save your pennies'.

The evenings now gave enough light to enable Annie to walk to Hood Street after work. She had not seen Enid, William and Freddy for a month. She walked Byron the long way round, to tire him so he would sleep whilst she chatted to Enid. William usually curled up on a rug with the dog, finding comfort in Byron's warmth, their breathing quickly united in harmonious sound, a soft, humming contentedness.

Freddy displayed 'roly-poly' knees and double chins, waves and curls just like his brother's, a delightful temperament that responded to Annie's playful actions with gurgles of real pleasure. Enid was putting away clean clothes, neatly pressed, in the chest of drawers by the bed. Charles was downstairs, reading the newspaper, watching over William.

"You will be an old hand at all this Enid," said Annie. "When I have my baby you'll be able to show me what to do."

Enid stared at Annie for several seconds without speaking.

"Surely it cannot be such a surprise," said Annie, "Harold and I have been married for twelve months."

"Congratulations, but don't rely on me to tell you anything, I will send Bertha to you."

Enid's reaction was no more heartening than aunt Bella's had been, Annie stayed for only a little while, conversation with Enid seemed awkward. Perhaps Charles and his wife had disagreed again, whatever the reason, Annie felt her presence there served no purpose. She kissed Freddy and downstairs said goodbye to Charles and William, giving the little boy a 'Jelly jube' as she left. It would surely pass, all Enid's moods passed eventually, by her next visit she would find Enid entirely different.

"We shall not allow our spirits to be dulled Byron, come on, we've some treacle toffee at home."

Enid lay the last vest in the drawer, her hands shook as she closed the chest. Sitting on the edge of the bed, her back to Freddy, she heard him softly murmur in his crib, close to sleep his fleshy arms fell still at his sides. Enid loved her sons dearly but she could not face again that agony of fear and torment. Bertha brought life into the world, she didn't take it away, Annie now carried life inside her, neither would understand. Enid had missed her last two periods, three mornings she had been sick, she knew her own body and shuddered at the reality, pregnant again. It could not go on, if it was done early then it would be no sin, nothing more than a tiny blob of shapeless tissue. A simple procedure, no one need know. Estelle Downing would be able to arrange it, Enid had not seen her since before William was born but tomorrow she would call on her. There could be no delay, Estelle would know where to go for such services.

Enid lifted William into the foot end of the pram. "Now keep your legs still, don't wake Freddy." She called out to Evelyn, her long suffering 'Daily', "I won't be long, underneath the sideboard needs doing and you forgot to polish the brass toasting fork when you did the fender yesterday."

Estelle Downing lived not far from The Standard in Forest Road, Enid had been there before, the group of women with whom she socialised prior to her confinement with William, met in each other's houses in turn. The gossip and general tittle-tattle Enid took part in then seemed a lifetime ago and far removed from her present world of baby talk and Bertha's lectures.

They reached the house, even from the outside it felt strangely different from the others on the road. Enid knocked at the door with the heavy brass stirrup, green and roughened from many years of weathering. It clattered against the brass plate beneath, that too, tarnished and pitted but for the point at which the stirrup struck, that shone, perfectly smooth, evidence of regular use. The door opened, Estelle stood before Enid, a look of surprise and puzzlement on her heavily made-up face. She was a woman older than Enid by some years but nevertheless, clung to a youthful style of fashion, it achieved only to show more mutton. As Bertha Duffin was proficient in all things wholesome and desirable, Estelle Downing excelled in the radical and nonconformist, at only their first meeting she had insisted on showing Enid her tattoo.

"Why my goodness, if it isn't Enid Eddowes and with company, now what does one call them, 'fruits of love', I believe."

"I need to talk to you for just a few minutes," said Enid timidly.

"Take the pram up the side to the back door, it will be easier there," replied Estelle.

The two women went through to a sitting room, Freddy still asleep, remained in his pram, William gripped his mother's hand like a vice and walked close beside her, not making a sound. Enid could smell tobacco, although the house was well furnished and the windows finely draped, it gave not the slightest sense of a 'home'. She was uncomfortable, tense, it was no place for a child. Enid told Estelle of her plight. Even this hardened character recognised the intense dread in Enid's trembling voice, the shaking in her hands as she related the nature of her request, choosing the words with care, aware that William was present. A chiming clock on the shelf alongside where they stood struck the half hour and near' made the child jump out of his skin. He began to whimper, before this progressed to a full cry Estelle said.

"I will attend to the matter right away, when I have the necessary details I will come to you at Hood Street. Fret not, it will be done very soon."

Estelle watched from the doorway as Enid pushed the pram back onto the road.

"She used to be a spirited young thing, possessed of such beauty and rebellion, I really thought she would go far but it seems Charles Eddowes has achieved to cage her after all."

Estelle closed the door and turned to face a tall, middle aged man who stood behind her, she smiled as she walked slowly up the stairs.

"Some things are all the better for waiting on, my dear."

The dark undertone to her words had coated them in rich, sticky molasses, enticing, entrapping, the man could do nothing but follow, 'home' was the last thing on his mind.

Four days passed, Enid had just put Freddy down for a nap in his crib upstairs and returned to William, playing on the living room floor with his wooden building blocks, Evelyn was polishing the landing.

The front door bell rang, "It's alright Evelyn, I'll answer it."

Enid had been jumpy all week, her waiting was over. Estelle Downing stood at the door, a brightly adorned hat proclaiming her arrival in a fanfare of feathers and ribbons.

"I can't stay so listen carefully," she spoke softly, "next Tuesday as darkness falls, it has to be a Tuesday, they won't do it any other time. Have with you five guineas, wait at the corner of Peverell Street, someone will meet you there and take you to the place. Not until dark, don't forget that."

She turned to go but hesitated for an instant, "Good luck." Then she was gone.

It was Friday, Enid needed to plan. She would tell Charles and Bertha that she had been invited to a get together of some old girl friends, she had not been out to any social event for so long she deserved a break. It would only be for an hour or two. If Bertha stayed the night then she wouldn't need to walk home after dark, William and Freddy both slept well, but should either wake before she got home, Bertha might save Charles from being disturbed. Both boys had been given gifts of money at their birth, Enid felt sure she could raise the five guineas by borrowing from their money boxes. Each week she would save some of her housekeeping and pay it back. By this time next week, the whole affair would be over and done with and by the end of the summer, the boys' money boxes would be restored and with more besides, she would put an extra guinea into each. A wave of relief washed over Enid, for the next hour she played with William building towers, hide and seek, singing with him, she even made some tea and gave a cup to Evelyn, ironing in the scullery.

It would be alright, two children were enough, some people had none, motherhood suddenly seemed attractive. She would be a better wife too and Annie must bring her child to visit them, the children would play together happily, the business would grow and their prospects with it.

She would make Charles a beef and ale pie for Sunday, just as Mrs.Beeton wrote and show him how capable and considerate she could be. It was only one evening anyway, he would surely permit that.

"Would you like another cup Evelyn?" Asked Enid, "don't worry about finishing the ironing, I shall do some this afternoon."

Evelyn raised her eyebrows, she had no idea who the caller had been, only hearing it was a woman's voice and catching a few words, 'wait at the corner of Peverell Street', but if this was the effect the woman produced then Evelyn hoped she might call frequently.

Enid's persuasive charms had achieved the vital result. The weekend had been blissfully pleasant at 14.Hood Street. Bertha had come close to a seizure when Enid had made her sit whilst she brushed and styled her hair.

"It will relax you Bertha, it will calm your mind from the taxing my boys have dealt it."

Charles had been left in peace with the Gazette and a bottle of stout.

"I shall take them to the arboretum for an hour, give you the chance to read the trade pages."

When her desire to go out for a while on Tuesday evening finally became voiced, both Charles and Bertha at once realised why they had been so cherished. Neither however, had any notion of Enid's real intentions and finding it all amusingly childlike, they agreed to her request.

The five guineas concealed in the inside pocket of her jacket, Enid carried a small handbag with only a handkerchief, some cashews and her door key. It was too early to attend the rendezvous at the corner of Peverell Street. However, Bertha and Charles would have been curious if she had not left the house at an appropriate time. It would not be dark for another hour. Enid made her way slowly to St.Andrews Church, from there it should take no more than fifteen minutes to reach her destination, she would sit out of sight in the porch at the Church until it was time.

A tiny shapeless blob of tissue, she kept saying the words over and over to herself as she sucked a violet cashew. At one point, she thought voices close by were approaching but they passed through the headstones and out of the lich-gate. She had eaten virtually nothing all day and limited her drinks, she didn't want to have to use the tub when she got there.

The Church clock struck a quarter past eight, she would make her way now. The light was already fading as she walked down the path to the gate and the street beyond, alone, she swallowed hard, her thoughts intense, how easily seen she must be by the Almighty as he looked down on his creation but he must surely know her torment, all William's Bible stories told of his love and forgiveness, even of the weak, especially the weak.

As she neared the corner a tall man appeared, he had turned out of Peverell Street. He limped heavily, even in the twilight Enid could define his rolling gait. She paused a yard from him, in a low voice but with no menacing tone he asked.

"Have yer brought the five guineas?"

"Yes," replied Enid.

"Come with me, it isn't far."

He did not ask her name, she could hear the uneven sound his boot made on the cobbles as one leg laboured harder than the other. Not until they had walked past a dozen houses or so did he stop and speak again, not to Enid but to a creature in the darkness. She heard the metallic sound of the gate, dragging across the ground, the man sniffed.

"Get out o' the way damn yer," a boot had obviously been directed at a dog, the poor animal yelped, then barked in protest, so loud and deep in volume it made Enid jump.

"No need to worry about 'im, 'e won't 'urt yer," he sniffed again.

In the gloom Enid could just make out the outline of a large dog, she felt soft fur brush her hand, she had no fear of it, but of the man, she trembled with foreboding. Please God let it be a kindly woman inside.

Enid was led through a back yard to a door which opened as they reached it, the bark from the dog must have alerted the woman, already standing there.

"Come in my dear, what a lovely day of sunshine we've 'ad, does the soul good, quite rallies the spirit don't you think dear?"

The house was dimly lit and a strong smell of disinfectant and carbolic bombarded Enid's nose and caused it to fidget, she was used to baby powder and the smell of lavender oil which she put about the bedroom to encourage Freddy to sleep, she could stifle a sneeze no longer.

"You need to be careful dear, a summer cold can be stubborn to move," said the woman.

All Enid's senses were troubled, she could not see enough to be confident, so far, no one had extended a hand of kindness and a clock ticking somewhere in another room, boards which creaked beneath her feet and the sound of the woman's skirts as they rustled ahead of her did nothing to reassure Enid's anxious mind.

"Through here my dear," Enid followed the woman into a small room, a single bed occupied the centre, a small table and cupboard to one side. The woman lit another lamp, the better light revealed the area to be clean but sparse. No picture or mirror hung on the walls, no rug softened the floor. The bed was covered in a white sheet, towels lay at the foot.

"Now dear, I need first to dispense with the financial requirement."

Enid took the five guineas from her jacket and handed them to the woman.

"That's right dear, now let me take your jacket and 'ang it on the 'ook and your bag. Don't you worry, everyone is 'onest 'ere, your bag will be perfectly safe. You just sit down on the bed while I put the money away and scrub me 'ands."

Enid forced her mind to be still, staring at the boards by her feet, counting the knots in the grain was as much challenge as she could stand. The woman returned after just a minute or two.

"Here you are my dear, take this small measure, drink it down, it will make you feel completely relaxed and sleepy. I tell all my clients the same thing, let your thoughts drift to 'appy times, to your youth when these adult problems were far off, when play and free spirit filled each day and sleep 'eld you safely in its arms."

She spoke very slowly, putting Enid to lay back on the bed, smoothing her brow, the carbolic smelled stronger than ever but drowsiness had reached all Enid's senses and now carried them to a place where the present went unrecorded, she felt only a vague awareness of her lower clothes being removed, Enid slept.

"Bring my tray and bucket, then watch her face, listen to her breathing, mind you concentrate."

The woman spoke sharply to the man, he grunted a miserable agreement. She set about her God forsaken task with speed, it had to be swift, the rate at which she performed the procedure, her only skill, the plight of the muscle and tissue she could not be expected to resolve, that must be down to nature.

Enid murmured, "What's she sayin'?"

"It's alright she's only ramblin' in 'er sleep," said the man, "she's callin' for 'er father." He lay his face close to Enid's, "she's breathin' regular." He raised his head back upright, sniffed and drew the back of his hand across his nose. The woman scowled at him, "It only runs when I put me head down," he said, making one last sweep of his upper lip with his sleeve.

Enid relived her childhood under a veil of Laudanum.

Her mother sat before her, so frail, her features delicate, her colouring pallid.

"You must be a good girl Enid and not cross your dear father, he tries so hard to look after us all and he loves us so very much."

Enid now lay in her small bed, her older brothers still sat with their mother. She could hear his tread on the stairs, the door opened.

"My own beautiful 'Eni', your mother asks me to kiss you goodnight."

Enid waited for his hands to leave the door, always he would close it without making a sound, using both hands to turn the doorknob so tightly it seemed to impel her heart, the motion as he turned, driving her heartbeat ever faster as if he somehow controlled her with that inanimate china object.

"Dear little 'Eni'."

His fingers brushed the ringlets of her hair, his knuckles skimmed her cheeks as they travelled slowly down the tresses. They threaded through the ribbon bow on her nightgown, loosening, opening the cotton bodice.

"Eni, Meni, Mini" he almost sang the words like a lullaby but they held no soothing inducement of sleep, Enid wanted to scream out but she could not.

"Father, no Father," her pleadings faint from fear. She was afraid of him, afraid to be heard, afraid of being the shameful creature she became each night. Her voice barely audible, she stifled even her breathing as his fingers moved about her breasts, circling, time after time, his smile so sickening Enid's stomach rose up in her torment. She could taste in her mouth fear and disgust, they choked her, he drew back.

"Why my dear 'Eni', lay on your side you will breathe more easily."

He turned her shoulders 'til she faced the door, knowing her eyes would not close until she saw him leave. Then, only then, did her eyelids come down on deep wells of tears.

Enid's vision was blurred but she could vaguely see a man standing over her.

"No Father, no." Enid began to scream louder and louder, her arms thrashed the air wildly.

"For God's sake she'll alert the whole neighbourhood. Pass me that bag, make haste." The woman shouted urgently at the man, she padded Enid and pulled on her drawers, quickly restoring Enid's other clothing.

"That'll 'ave to do." she pushed the bucket beneath the bed, take them towels away to the dolly tub, 'urry."

The man sped awkwardly from the room, the bundle of blooded towels in his arms.

"Shush, my dear, you've been dreamin'." She took Enid's hand, "Now, now, it's all over, it's done, 'twas just the medicine makin' you dream. Lie there for a few minutes, then we'll get your jacket and bag and you can be on your way 'ome. Now I've padded you, there will be some bleeding for a while but that will pass. Try not to exert yourself, you need to be sensible."

The man walked with her to the street, the dog no longer there must have been put in a shed for the night.

"I shall be alright to walk alone," said Enid.

"I 'ave to walk yer to the corner, from there you're on yer own."

He said nothing more and when they parted he uttered no goodbye.

She moved anxiously, the surroundings and her soreness threatened her far more than the darkness. She could not hurry, her pace limited, it took twice the time to cover the distance.

When she reached Hood Street, the sight of her home drew her, all she now wanted was to be in bed where she could feel Charles' warmth beside her and hear little Freddy making familiar sucking sounds as his lips pursed around his thumb.

Charles was still up, he noticed her unsteady progress through the hallway, "Have you been drinking?"

The hour was late, normally he would have been in bed, but concern to see her safely home had kept him up, the thought of her sitting all this time with alcohol close by annoyed him.

"Only a small measure," replied Enid, "but foolishly, in my excitement at going out to meet old friends, I ate very little today and I fear it has gone straight to my head."

"Well now you're in, I'm going to bed."

"How long has Bertha been upstairs?" She asked.

"Bertha went up about an hour ago, you should get to bed yourself," said Charles gruffly.

"I'll be up very soon but to help me settle, I think I shall boil some milk and just peep at William."

Charles muttered as he climbed the stairs.

Enid unbolted the back door, slowly, desperate not to make any noise, she wanted Charles to be asleep before she reached their bed. Outside in the privy she lit the candle, she felt wet, the padding was soaked, she must pad herself afresh. The sore aching feeling seemed to creep along her groin, her fingers worked at the bloody cloth, even as she put the clean pad to herself, the hot sensation of more bleeding and a dull pain in the small of her back turned the familiar privy into a very lonely place. Hopefully, now she had no need of walking any distance, it would ease.

She heated some milk, she felt the need of nourishment, it comforted. No wonder Freddy called for milk when tiredness threatened him, now she could understand why. Charles was asleep, 'thank God' thought Enid, William had looked cherub like when she had peeped round his door, his hair so thick with curls it adorned his sleeping features like a royal crown.

Freddy gently sucked on his beloved thumb, she slipped into bed beside Charles and lay totally still, she held the notion that to move not a muscle may cause all her tribulation to surrender to sleep but sleep would not come to Enid. All she wanted was to lose this wakefulness, to be unaware of feeling, to find instead daybreak when all would be well as she opened her eyes to Wednesday.

Charles disturbed, he was barely waking but a strange shuddering had broken his sleep.

"Enid, what's the matter?" He touched her shoulder, Enid's entire body shook and shivered violently.

"No, no father," her voice pained and frightened, she repeated the words over and over. Charles was now fully awake, the bed clothes felt wet. He got out of bed and lit the lamp, Freddy murmured but did not stir. Enid's face was as white as her nightgown, her uncontrolled shaking alarmed Charles. He threw back the covers, she lay in heavy staining. He covered her again, pulled on his dressing gown and went to Bertha. His frantic words made little sense but Bertha knew real fear and Charles was terrified, she took one look at Enid. "Dress quickly Charles, fetch the doctor, tell him not to delay."

"What is it Bertha?"

"I think she has miscarried but there is no time to speculate, go, hurry Charles."

The streets were deserted but for amorous cats, Charles ran as far as he could but his breath became short, he paused for a minute, a clock in the distance struck three. Dr.Baragruy answered Charles' frenzied knocking, it took just a minute or two for the doctor to dress and gather his bag. The two men sped through the streets unhindered but for their own complaining lungs.

Bertha held Freddy in her arms, the only way she could pacify him, the child seemed to sense the tension within the room. William mercifully remained asleep.

"Take the infant downstairs Mrs.Duffin, feed him some milk then perhaps you could lay him down to sleep in his pram."

The doctor took Enid's pulse and put his hand to her brow, he lowered the skin below her eyes and looked intently at her colour. As he lifted the bedcovers to one side he spoke calmly to Charles.

"I need to wash my hands before I examine your wife."

Charles went at once to the wash stand and poured fresh water into a bowl.

"I shall fetch some hot water doctor."

"Yes, that would be helpful Charles."

He was glad to send Charles from the room whilst he satisfied himself that his diagnosis was correct. In his many years in practice, sadly, he had seen this far too often, each and every time it sickened him to his soul. It was a 'butchery' which showed no compassion, no regard or respect for the lives, which two at a time, it culled for no other purpose than monetary gain. Charles returned with a jug of hot water.

"Some clean towels Charles and another nightdress for Enid if you will."

With all the tenderness and care her previous appointment had denied her, the doctor washed her weakened body and placed clean, soft padding between her legs, laid the towels beneath her and with fresh warm water he washed her face and hands and slipped a clean nightgown over her feeble frame. The medication he administered stopped the shaking but her mouth quivered in spasms.

"Has she lost a baby doctor? Bertha could only think that she has miscarried, she's said nothing of being pregnant, surely Enid would have told us if she had been expecting again." Charles' face pleaded for explanation.

"Charles, it pains me to tell you but Enid has lost a baby, however, she has not suffered a miscarriage, indeed her suffering is much worse, she has ....." Doctor Baragruy was filled with such anger, he felt so hateful of the situation, he could scarcely form the words.

"Enid has had an abortion Charles and I fear it may threaten her life, the next few hours will be critical. I have given her something to fight infection but she is very weak, the blood loss is severe, if infection should take hold her body will be unable to replace the loss."

The early hours seemed unending. Charles and the doctor sat by the bed, no change but for brief periods of delirium. The words Enid uttered made little sense.

"No father, out o' the way, big dog, No no father."

"She has been given Laudanum Charles, her words may result from last night or may be echoing from a distant memory, we can pay them but scant heed. All we can do is hope and pray for the bleeding to stop and calm to reach her mind."

Bertha came to the room but her distress was so great the doctor gently persuaded her that to listen for the children was the very best thing she could do to help her young friends. Enid's condition remained the same, as light broke the doctor gave more medication and instructed Charles to stay watchful.

"I must go home for a little while, there are matters regarding other patients to which I must attend, I shall return by no later than ten o'clock. Call me before then if anything should change."

Bertha and Charles took turns at sitting by Enid, sharing the time with the two bewildered children.

"I wish I could get word to Annie," said Charles.

"Now isn't the time to be worrying about the workshop," Bertha reprimanded him.

"No, I didn't mean it in that way, Annie seems able to soothe Enid, she's the only one of similar age who has ever befriended her."

"When the doctor gets back I'll put the boys in the pram and take them to Winchester Street, I'll fetch Annie then."

Bertha patted his hand and returned to William and Freddy.

It reached nine o'clock, Bertha occupied the children in the living room and Charles kept vigil over his wife, her ramblings had become more frequent, he pulled the covers about her to help keep her warm, the temperature outside was spring like but Enid's extremities felt cold. Suddenly downstairs he heard a voice calling.

"Mornin', it's threatenin' showers so I'll scrub the yard an' steps first."

Evelyn, he had forgotten all about Evelyn. Bertha appeared at the bedroom door.

"Do you want me to send her home Charles?"

"No, send her to Winchester Street, tell her to ask Mrs.Boucher to leave the workshop for a while and to come back here with her. It will be another hour before the doctor comes and I would rather you stay here with us if you don't mind Bertha."

She smiled, touched by his need of her. "I'll ask Evelyn to go right away."

Evelyn was perplexed, "I've just walked all the way from the bottom of Sherwood Road, if it rains afore I get back then I'm not scrubbin' the yard in the wet, not wi' my rheumatism, it won't get done today if it rains."

Annie, May and Edna were busy at their machines. Edna had made remark, " 'E's late again, 'e couldn't run a tombola, this place 'ould never survive wi' out us."

Neither Annie nor May made comment, it was after all Charles' business but defending his lateness was difficult when Edna was aware of Charles' liking for time spent with a pint or two at The Standard. The latch on the gates rattled.

"Ah, 'ere comes 'is Lordship," said Edna, but a knock came at the door. Annie left her machine.

"Good morning, can we help you?" Said Annie to the caller.

Evelyn stood at the threshold, the two women had not met before, Annie was amused by the agility of the woman's neck as she turned her head from left to right, her eyes searching beyond Annie's shoulders for a better sight of what lay within the workshop.

"Whichever one of you is Mrs.Boucher 'as to come wi' me to Mr.Eddowes' 'ouse, that's what they told me to say."

"Do I have to come right away?" Asked Annie, puzzled by the request.

"Yes right away, you don't need to tell me 'ow funny they are and that's funny peculiar, not funny ha ha, I never know where I am with 'em, especially 'er."

Annie spoke to May and Edna, "I don't suppose I shall be long."

May looked at her and smiled, "We know what to be getting on with, don't worry about things here."

Annie took her jacket and left with the woman.

"I hope nothing is wrong Edna, Annie shouldn't be troubled now she's carrying a baby."

Edna looked up from her machine, "Well I don't know who that messenger is but she sounded like she knew the boss and 'is missus, 'funny peculiar', that's puttin' it mildly."

Annie and Evelyn turned out of Winchester Street, "Slow down a bit, I've got to do Mrs.Merryweather after dinner, I shan't 'ave enough breath left in me to beat 'er Persian rug, 'eavy thing that is, I reckon it weighs more 'an me, the struggle I 'ave to get it over the back wall, I can feel me innards rupturin' every time, 'tis little wonder I 'ave to cross me legs when I cough."

Annie ventured to ask the name of her companion.

"Evelyn Easter, that's me name, they wouldn't find better than me you know, but I've told 'em, I can't kneel on wet ground, not wi' me rheumatism, I allus scrub the steps on a Wednesday but no, when I said I'd do the yard first 'cause rain wer' comin', they sent me to Winchester Street if you please, my corns can't stand all this walkin'."

"Do you clean for Mrs.Eddowes?"

Annie had no idea Enid now had a cleaning lady, Charles had not mentioned it.

"That's right but for 'ow much longer I wouldn't like to say. One day you get barked at, then the next she's all sweetness and light. Why last Friday, after that woman called, she made me a cup o' tea, I could 'ave fell through the floor and when she said she'd finish the ironin', well, you could 'ave knocked me down wi' a feather."

Evelyn Easter talked and talked. Annie thought the name unusual, she had never known of anyone called by the name Easter.

They reached Hood Street, Annie followed Evelyn into the scullery, Bertha had heard the door and stood in the hall, Annie knew at once that something was very wrong. Bertha spoke first to Evelyn.

"Mr.Eddowes says to thank you Mrs.Easter and to tell you that it is alright for you to take the rest of the morning off, you will be paid as usual of course."

"Well now, that's all very fine but before I walk again, all the way back to the bottom end of Sherwood Road, I need to sit down for 'arf an hour wi' a cup o' tea."

"Yes Mrs.Easter I do understand." Bertha sighed and turned to Annie, "Come and see the boys dear, they are in here, close the door Annie," said Bertha, as they reached the sanctuary of the living room. William beamed and held up his gollywog,

"That's lovely William," said Annie, she knelt down and the little hands pushed the doll to her mouth for her to kiss it. Freddy lay on the rug, arms and legs in the air, chuckling happily.

"Where's doggy?" Asked William.

"He's at home with aunt Bella but I shall bring him to see you very soon."

The answer satisfied him and he returned to his play.

"The doctor is upstairs Annie." Bertha's words were weakened by emotion, "I hardly know how to tell you it is so awful."

She looked towards the children, William was intent on his game and paid no heed to their conversation.

"Has there been an accident?" Annie became very anxious.

"Enid is in a very poor way, her condition has worsened, she has been somewhere, oh dear Annie", Bertha struggled to continue, drawing deep breaths, "She's had an abortion." With that the tears flowed freely.

"The children, don't let them see you so distressed, please Bertha, try to be calm."

Bertha held her handkerchief to her cheeks and blew her nose.

"Silly me, must have caught a cold," she said looking over the top of the hanky at the two little boys.

"Tishoo, tishoo, all fall down," sang William.

"I shall stay here with them," said Bertha, "you go up to Charles and the doctor."

Enid's face looked waxen, Charles' despair engulfed him, his eyes found Annie and she felt his anguish in their bleak stare.

The doctor spoke softly, "It is a dire circumstance Miss Bundy."

Charles corrected him, "Annie is married now this twelve months or more."

"I am sorry, I wasn't aware."

"There is no reason you would be Dr.Baragruy" said Annie, "I have been in good health fortunately, I was going to register my married name when I next called on you," she smiled.

He nodded, his gaze stayed with her for several seconds before he looked back at the bed. Annie crossed the room to where Enid lay, she sat down at her side, the confused ramblings came again.

"Out 'o the way, big dog, No, no father, big dog."

"She makes no sense Annie," said Charles, "she repeats the words over and over." He told Annie of Enid's meeting with old friends the evening before, her return home and the dreadful night hours which had brought them to this morning. "She didn't say anything to me, I didn't know she was expecting."

Annie looked across to the doctor, "Mrs.Easter mentioned a caller at the house." Annie wondered if the caller might be significant, Evelyn's account of Enid's behaviour following the event would suggest this person might have had an effect on Enid's mood.

"Would you go downstairs Annie and speak with Evelyn, ask her if Enid has been anywhere unusual, ask who the caller was but don't reveal the nature of Enid's condition," said Charles, his torment grew with every passing hour.

"Of course," said Annie.

Evelyn Easter sat by the scullery table with a jug of tea, her shoes lay on the floor beside the chair her stockinged feet rested on an old newspaper, she flexed her toes and winced as she said.

"The flags are cold but I 'ad to ease 'em before I set off again."

"Yes, I can imagine," replied Annie.

"What's up, summat's up, I been 'round too many gooseberry seasons, you can't fool me," declared Evelyn, taking another mouthful of tea.

"Mrs.Eddowes is unwell and we are trying to establish where she may have picked up the malady, can you recall if she went anywhere out of the ordinary?"

"My dear she don't tell me where she's goin' but she wer' never gone long, just time enough to walk the children to the arboretum and back or to the shops."

Annie smiled at Evelyn to encourage co-operation.

"You mentioned a caller, a woman I believe you said."

"Yes that's right, it wer' last Friday, I know it wer' Friday 'cause I wer' polishing the landin', I allus do the landin' on a Friday. I 'eard the bell, she called up, said she'd answer it. Now I'm not one fer eavesdroppin' you understand but I could tell it wer' a woman's voice, no one came in, I didn't see 'er and in just two minutes she wer' gone."

"Did you hear anything that was said?" Asked Annie.

"Now look 'ere, I don't make 'abbit o' listenin' to other folks' conversations, I'm a good cleaner wi' good references."

"This is true indeed Mrs.Easter but if you could think really hard, might you have heard just a few words drifting upstairs on the wind, from the open door of course."

Annie's tactful appeal produced a result.

"I 'eard one sentence, only one, the woman said, 'Wait at the corner of Peverell Street'. That wer' it, them wer' the words exactly."

Annie swallowed hard, a knot of tension near' closed her throat.

"Thank you Mrs.Easter, you have been really helpful."

Annie's quick mind put together poor Enid's words and that moment when Evelyn spoke of 'Peverell Street'. 'Big Dog', Annie remembered Alfred's remark that day when she had first spoken to him of Shawcross, 'You can see what it's like round here, if someone can afford to feed a dog such as you describe, then they must pursue a trade which goes unseen'. Annie remembered the lame man who came from the house where Shawcross sat behind the gate, the exchange he and the tubman had made, Wednesday was Peverell Street's turn for the tubman, today is Wednesday. Annie felt sick but she could not show it in front of Mrs.Easter. She went back upstairs, she would tell Charles what Evelyn had heard but she could not speak of her own dread, not now, it was too awful, Charles endured suffering enough.

Annie held Enid's hand, the room felt abandoned of solace. Those same words of delirium came from Enid but fainter, now barely audible, her mouth too weak to form the sounds. Annie stifled her tears for Charles' sake, he sat at Enid's other side, both held one of her hands. For what must have been half an hour, that is how the scene remained, Dr.Baragruy sat in the corner, now present more for Charles' need than for Enid's.

Then slowly, agonizingly slowly, Enid's eyes opened, she looked at her husband, with grey searching lips she formed a kiss, then her eyes passed to Annie, a feeble smile came to her mouth, Annie could feel a real intensity in her soft gaze and through Enid's fingers which tightened around her own, fleeting, engaging only a trice. The eyes fell shut, her grip loosened. Annie looked to the doctor, her own sureness conveyed but unspoken. He passed his hand across Enid's face, seeking breath, he felt for a pulse. Annie could hear his own deep intake of breath before finding strength to tell Charles.

"Enid has gone, I am so very sorry Charles."

Annie could not stay in the room, she ran down the stairs and out into the yard. Mercifully, Evelyn Easter had taken her weary feet home. Annie leaned against the wall, the sky now shed a dampness, it cooled her face, eased the pounding inside her. She thought of Harold and Billy at the slaughter yard, Harold had once told her that he never killed any beast without saying 'God Bless'. Enid had died little better than an animal at Josiah's yard, indeed she doubted anyone had asked God to bless poor Enid wherever she had lain when they performed their gruesome deed.

Dr.Baragruy appeared at the back door, he crossed to Annie.

"Are you alright Mrs.Boucher?" Her face was so pale, her lips colourless with sickness. "Are you pregnant Annie?" He asked.

"I told Enid just a few days ago, I do so wish I had not, she might have confided in me but how could she when she knew I was expecting too. How did you know doctor?"

"Over the years Annie a doctor comes to recognise signs, sometimes only small indications, it was your expression as you told me you would register your married name when you came to see me and your reaction to this tragedy. It was intuition rather than knowledge. Enid was a complex young woman, I feel her exterior belied what lay within, she leaves a desolate husband, two vulnerable infants and a friend and guide, dear Bertha is heartbroken. Inside this house Annie is utter despair, it is human nature to want to surround them with sympathy, to weep with them, as much to release our own heartache as to relieve theirs. You must go to them Annie but you must carry strength with you, that is what they will most need. Don't stay too long, in your condition you should go home, take comfort from things familiar."

"Aunt Bella says soft words don't feed the belly nor stay the soul, practical help is what sustains." Annie looked troubled.

"Your aunt Bella is right, it is not a harsh philosophy but a reality which comes from the wisdom of years."

"I have to attend to matters at the workshop," said Annie.

The doctor lay his hand on Annie's shoulder. "Lock up the workshop, Charles will have no thought for it today, the women could have no concentration once they are told and no one would expect otherwise."

Annie held Bertha, Charles and the boys in turn.

"Charles, amuse William and Freddy, Bertha and I need to go upstairs, come with me, we shall work together."

Dr.Baragruy had left and would inform Mr.Handley.

"Find a bolster case, the oldest you can," said Annie

Bertha returned from the cupboard with a cotton bolster which had lost its once pretty tatting border and now displayed signs of wear. Annie stuffed inside the pile of bloody linen.

"I will not leave this here for Charles to deal with, I shall drag it if I have to and burn it when I reach home."

Annie had found Enid's lavender oil and put droplets around the room, she searched through the drawers of the chest until she found the silk scarf Charles had bought for Enid when Freddy was born, she gently lifted Enid's head and put the scarf around her neck, the soft lilac cloth fell across the white nightgown in which the doctor had laid her. Even now she was beautiful, like a porcelain doll designed for the nursery of a gracious and wealthy family. Annie kissed her forehead and whispered.

"I shall always love your children, I promise."

Bertha stood in the doorway silent tears washing her cheeks.

"I must go now Bertha, but I shall come tomorrow, busy yourself, make Charles a meal, however small. Prepare a list of anything the larder is in need of, tomorrow we shall take the children to the shops and I shall send Charles to his desk whilst I am away from the workshop with you. I will tell him that he is needed there, he must not sit and dwell on misery, such a way would fail him and the boys."

Annie embraced Bertha tightly, "Your guidance is needed all the more, Enid held you very close, be her strength today just as you were yesterday."

Annie said goodbye to Charles and the children as she would at any other time.

The street was quiet, the men at their work, the women occupied with domestic duties. Annie pulled the heavy bolster behind her, the curious look people gave her as she walked back to Winchester Street of no consequence. She opened the gate of the workshop, leaving the linen outside the door. Annie saw through the window Edna's head lift from her machine in anticipation of her return.

"Let Annie catch her breath Edna, be patient," said May in response to Edna's immediate quizzing.

"Enid lost a baby last night, the bleeding was too severe, she didn't recover."

"You mean she's dead," cried Edna.

Annie could only nod confirmation. May sat at her machine, both were motionless, unable to create a sound.

Edna took Annie's arm, "You ought to 'ave a nip o' spirits, shall I fetch some brandy?"

"No thank you Edna, I couldn't drink it anyway because of the baby. We are to go home, I am locking up the workshop for the rest of the day but tomorrow we shall work again. Charles has two sons to feed and Mrs.Duffin to think about, weeping will help him with neither."

Annie watched May and Edna out of sight, pulled the bolster to the street and made her way to No.24, not pausing for a warming drink of tea or a moment of rest, she took the sulphurs from the mantelpiece, gathered an old gazette from the shelf and her pot of rancid fat. In the corner of the yard she lit the fire and as the bolster and its contents yielded to the flames she cried 'til her heart could bear no more tears.

Bella and Byron were in the living room, the dog watched intently as she carved some belly pork. Bella was about to make herself a plate of dinner when Annie stepped into the scullery, surprised to see her at that time of day she asked.

"What are you doing here?"

Annie sat at the table and told Bella the truth, she could only ever tell aunt Bella the truth.

"I have explained it to May and Edna as a miscarriage and I shall not say otherwise except to you and Harold."

"Don't you go upsetting yourself, I can see you've been crying, you have to think about Harold and your baby, don't you go weak with misery, eat and keep strong."

Bella was alarmed by Annie's pale complexion, her tired eyes from weeping. All Bella could think about was Ruby's desperate weakness and anguish which took life from her all those years ago.

"Eat some of this," said Bella, putting bread and meat in front of Annie.

"I know I must keep strong, not just for Harold and our baby but for Enid's children too and for Charles, he has lost his father and his wife in less than a year."

"Yes, yes, that's right you must keep strong for Charles as well, they will need you I am sure."

Normally any reference to Charles and his family caused aunt Bella to be irritable but her overwhelming desire for Annie to be of good health and stout heart completely overruled any other consideration. Annie sat in the familiar safety of aunt Bella's home for an hour then, with Byron at her side, she crossed the street to No.24.

Byron ran about the small patch of grass, stopping frequently, his nose raised to scent the air. The fire had burned to almost nothing, Annie with pan and brush picked up the ashes and buried them into the compost heap. Byron sniffed at the corner of the yard, his senses acute.

"Come on," Annie called to him and with the promise of a biscuit he followed her indoors.

That evening Annie told Harold of the tragedy, she still pondered Enid's ramblings and the connection with Peverell Street, Harold listened patiently.

"If Enid had survived then she could have told you but without Enid's word there is no proof. Charles might torment himself pursuing the probability but almost certainly, to no avail. Let it be Annie, let Enid rest in peace and Charles grieve naturally.

Their bed was Annie's comfort and solace, she lay in Harold's arms, his warmth reached her very soul. He kissed her hair, "I shall tell you a bedtime story," he said, "and you must go to sleep like a good child." He stroked the underside of her chin with his weathered fingers, rough though they were it felt glorious.

"Once upon a time a young man met a young woman and they fell instantly in love, together, they and their children travelled the world. They saw snow capped mountains, rich dense forests where trees grew so tall they touched the clouds. Their children played in fields filled with wild flowers, poppies, daisies, campions ....."

Harold's story went on into time but Annie heard only the beginning, for now she slept soundly under the blanket of her husband's dreams.

CHAPTER TWENTY

"Just look at those two Annie," said Bertha.

William ran around the yard in just his pants, his cockatoo under one arm. Byron lay on his back under the clothesline, cooling himself in a puddle of water which had dripped into a hollow in the cobbles from a pair of Freddy's rompers hanging above.

"He's getting better Annie, that's the first pair he's wet today so far," said Bertha, kissing the child she held in her arms. "I shall have to put you down young man, you're getting too heavy."

Annie found the scene amusing. Since Charles had relented and bought the old cockatoo for William, the child was never to be seen without it. He had espied it in a shop window and could not be dissuaded, William longed to have it for his own, this strange plaything, a slightly worse for wear stuffed cockatoo.

On seeing it for the first time Byron had sniffed it, barked at it and ultimately decided that young William was welcome to it.

Freddy grew beautifully, his eyes and colouring held so much of his mother. Bertha had been stoic, following Enid's death she had moved into the house in Hood Street, renting her own property to a family who had moved to Nottingham from Leicester, the father worked for the Judiciary and expected to be assigned to the Courts in the city for a period of two years, it seemed a satisfactory arrangement.

Charles had dire need of someone to care for the children and Bertha, already so fond of them, suggested it would be much less upsetting for the boys to continue to grow under her care and guidance than to be left with a stranger.

In spite of Charles' concerns at the workload she was undertaking, Bertha nevertheless insisted Charles diplomatically inform Evelyn Easter that her services would no longer be required.

'I may not scrub the yard every Wednesday, I might sometimes decide to scrub it on a Monday and some weeks the landing might not get polished at all, but I would rather manage on my own than be subjected to the endless monologue, delivered in monotone, by madam Easter'.

It was now August, Annie's baby was due around the end of September, seven weeks time. It was the short distance from the workshop which enabled her to carry on, but Harold had been firm when he declared 'this must be the last week'.

Annie's determined streak, no doubt inherited from aunt Bella, had achieved to persuade him that it could only benefit her to have at least some activity. 'I cannot sit endlessly reading Harold, my fingers must be occupied'.

It had been agreed that Annie, like May, whilst she could not attend the workshop, could stitch at home on a machine which Charles and Harold would carry to No.24.

'It will help if I can earn a little money, I shall rest when I feel the need'.

On this basis the plan had been accepted by all parties and next weekend, the sewing machine would be installed at home.

This Sunday was Bertha Duffin's birthday. Annie held a great regard for Bertha, she had kept house and cared for William and Freddy with skill for the former and devotion to the latter. Annie had asked Harold if he thought Sarah would mind very much if she spent some time with Bertha and missed their usual Sunday dinner. Harold had laughed, 'Mam'll be disappointed at first, then she'll think 'ow good it 'ould be for you to mark Mrs.Duffin's birthday, given all that good woman does for those babies. I can 'ear 'er sayin' those exact same words to 'erself. Anyway, it gives me the excuse to stay at 'ome, I want to get on wi' me woodwork, the weeks are racing by an' I need to finish the crib'.

Anne had taken flowers and a cake, which she had baked herself.

"There are times Bertha when Charles should return the blessing and care for you."

Annie was annoyed and dismayed at Charles' absence, Bertha made light of it but today of all days, he should not be sitting in The Standard.

The two women had tried so hard to encourage him, whenever they met Bertha would enquire of Annie how Charles had been at his work and Annie would feel the need to ask Bertha if he was coping at home.

At the workshop, while he conversed with May, Edna and herself, Annie felt his responses were given rather like William's new plaything, parrot fashion, no real feeling or interest lay behind his words.

Bertha revealed her concerns at his brooding quietness and his absence from the home in the evenings and on Sundays, when the pub seemed to attract his attentions more than his sons ever could.

Annie glanced at the clock.

"I must be getting back to Harold, he's busy making the crib, he enjoys his woodwork, it is so different from his labours at the yard. He explained it to me, with wood I create Annie, at Josiah's I destroy."

"I can understand that," said Bertha, "and you should be at home with him, we've had some lovely cake and my flowers are beautiful, you be on your way, don't worry about Charles, he'll be back soon and he can have a piece of cake then."

Annie was showing her impending motherhood, she dressed loosely and walked erect but the tell tale swelling made it quite apparent. When she reached the corner she paused, it was entirely wrong that Charles should neglect to show his appreciation of Bertha. Annie felt compelled to find him and point him firmly in the direction of Hood Street. Harold would be engrossed in his planing and dovetailing, just a few more minutes would make little difference, she would look in at The Standard, if he was not there she would go straight home.

Annie sighed and stepped inside the pub, the room was so filled with smoke she could hardly see but sitting on his own, in the far corner, was Charles. The place was busy, mostly men, Annie imagined the women to be at home, tending their offspring with Sunday dinner. She moved slowly through the throng, some faces she knew, most she did not.

A voice somewhere close by called out, "Tell me who done it to yer lass, I'll remind 'im of 'is duty." There was a sickening laugh.

Annie ignored all around her, eventually reaching Charles. He lifted his eyes, "I'm not drunk Annie, you needn't worry, I know exactly who I am and where I live." His words were steady enough but downcast, she could tell he'd drunk several beers.

"Come on Charles, time to go home."

Another voice called out, "That's right missus, you take 'im 'ome an' give 'im a piece o' your mind, looks like e's already give yer 'is piece."

Charles' eyes flashed anger, he rose from his stool sending it crashing to the floor with a thud.

"Who said that? Come on show yourself."

Annie could see the aggression in his face and felt his arm shaking with temper.

"No Charles, we are leaving."

A broad shouldered, heavily jowled man, now stood just a couple of yards away. Such words held no importance to Annie, they were the pathetic utterings of men starved of sense through their over indulgence of drink. Growling and snapping, pulling at their traces, like a build up to a dog fight was something very different and totally unbearable.

Annie tried desperately to propel Charles to the door but the man was ignorant and made the clucking sounds of a hen, taunting Charles, goading him.

Another came to Annie's aid, taking Charles' arm and guiding him to the street. Annie turned and went back to where their tormentor now sat laughing with a group of similar individuals, a look of surprise came to their faces.

She directed her words to the man, looking intently at his eyes, "How old are you sir?" She asked.

Completely taken aback by her boldness, he replied, "Don't rightly know, fifty somethin' I reckon."

The others sat in silence, overcome by her presence.

"I am not Mr.Eddowes' wife but I am his friend, it grieves me sir, that in fifty and some years you have not come to know and understand friendship or to recognise its worth. If there is a man among you who does," Annie paused and cast her gaze to each of the group, "then I sincerely hope that he might teach you of its great value, for no man, not even you sir, should have to live his days without the saving grace of a true friend. Good day to you."

A subdued hush descended upon the room as Annie walked to the door where Charles waited somewhat unwillingly under the persuasive hold of one Edwin Garbett, a previous colleague of Charles' at the bank.

"You have spirit young lady," he said, smiling amusedly as he introduced himself.

"I wish, Mr.Garbett, that my aunt Bella could have been here in my stead, believe me, if she had, then that man would now be standing face to the corner with a dunces hat placed firmly on his head and there he would remain until aunt Bella considered his disgrace had been sufficient to instil in him a desire to be of better character."

He laughed, "I like the sound of your aunt Bella."

He looked at Charles, the fire that had flared in Charles a few moments before had now died to an ember, beer, tiredness and depression all weighted his being.

Annie thanked Edwin Garbett and taking Charles' arm, she walked him towards home. When they reached the corner at which Annie must turn and send Charles in the other direction, she took his hands in her own and said.

"In that place we have just left no one longs to creep inside your heart but at Hood Street two little boys wait, wanting nothing more than that. I know how much you miss Enid but in your sons she still lives. Look at Freddy's eyes and colouring, they are Enid. Listen to William's persuasive charm, his words which draw you, just as Enid could win your agreement with her appeal and Bertha, she is not a young woman Charles but her efforts given so freely, surely deserve more of your gratitude and respect. You know it is her birthday, go home, make things right, be a man Charles, be a man."

Annie watched him as he walked away, his gait was steady, she felt no concern for his physical progress but his mental state troubled her. 'Soft words won't stay the soul', Annie knew aunt Bella was right but inwardly she felt pity for his pain.

Harold stood beaming with satisfaction, "Look at this Annie."

He had fixed the crib to rockers and when he tapped gently, the baby's bed rocked from side to side. Byron lay on his belly, fascinated by this new contraption, his eyes following the motion of the crib. How wonderfully different this place of contentment was to the loveless ale house she had just left.

Bella had watched over Annie these past months, ever concerned about her eating and sleeping, cautioning Harold to be mindful of her condition. Between the two Annie felt no pregnant woman could possibly be more cared for.

"Harold, that really is clever," she knelt down to rock it herself. "It's beautifully made Harold."

"Well if you really love the carpenter you'll make him a nice cup o' tea," he said and gave her a kiss.

"Those sheets and covers you've sewn should be just the right size I reckon and mam 'as a pile o' stuff for us. You know what she's like, won't tempt fate by bringin' it too soon but there'll be spare even if you 'ave twins."

The weeks went by, Annie stitched at home, Harold hurrying back from work each evening to be close . Charles making an effort to be brighter with May and Edna and to be more help to Bertha and more company for his sons.

Aunt Bella was Annie's only worry, the closer it drew to the end of September, the more agitated and restless Bella became. Her nerves seemed raw, she had worked herself into such a state of tension that even Byron seemed unwilling to spend time at No. 11. Bella could speak to no one of her torment, on her own, in the solitude of that house as the time for Annie's baby drew near, her anguished mind could only dwell on Sefton Pownall's damnations. Although twenty three years had passed and Sefton himself was now dead, Bella could not drive from her mind his bitter words. She had lost her mother and sister, Annie was all she had. Her father's curses, his promise to bring down on them the wrath of the Almighty, kept her eyes from sleep and her mind from rest.

It was the 28th of September, Annie had assembled the layette and at aunt Bella's insistence, given her word that if she felt any pain then she or Harold would fetch her at once. Annie felt no anxiety for giving birth, she longed to hold their baby, any pain would be transient. Secretly she hoped their first born might be a boy. For Harold to have a son, Annie believed would create again that magical bond which Harold's own birth had created between him and Samuel. To see Harold and his father together was sheer joy, their delight in each other, the absolute understanding, warmed the heart of the onlooker.

Through the afternoon Annie had felt spasms of pain, cramp at the base of her spine. It was now so close to the time Harold would be home from work at the yard, she waited quietly in the chair for his arrival.

She smiled as he bent to kiss her, "Are you alright?" He asked, it was a rare thing indeed to find Annie sitting still.

"I am very well Harold but I think our baby might soon be joining us, there is no need of haste but when you have eaten your meal, then I think you could fetch aunt Bella."

The light had faded, Harold lit the lamps and made up the fire to keep warmth through the night hours.

"Shall I go now Annie?"

"I think so but don't panic aunt Bella she is so nervous, we must be calm for her sake." Annie spoke with no trace of alarm, her manner serene.

Harold sat downstairs by the fire, listening to Bella's feet as they chafed the boards above so restless was her mood. The kettle sat full on the coals gently simmering, a pan of boiled water in the hearth. Annie had laid papers and old sheets over the bed in readiness. The crib was lined with the softest flannelette and sitting on a stool by the side, a knitted bear, a present made by Nora.

Annie's pain was now intense, she smiled at aunt Bella, not making a sound, new life was very close, she fixed her eyes on the little brown bear and gripped the edge of the sheet beneath her. She was about to become a mother, her effort produced a weighty sigh but nothing more dramatic than this one release of determination.

Bella's hands shook as she lifted the baby a few inches from Annie, "Push again," her voice trembled, she could barely contain the emotion which racked her weary frame, fear tore at Bella cruelly. Now she worked with intent, Bella had done all that was required, wrapping the infant, a boy and gathering the old sheet and paper which hid the afterbirth, placing it in the corner.

Downstairs, Harold heard the cry of his baby, "I'm a dad Byron," he patted the dog's head with such enthusiasm, Byron rushed to the foot of the stairs, as eager as Harold to follow the sound of this new voice.

After a few minutes Bella called down to him. Annie held their son, a miniature version of his dad. Bella stood at the window, looking through a gap in the curtains to the darkness of the street, tears streamed down her face as she left Harold and Annie to their happiness. He went to her side and with tenderness turned Bella towards him, twenty three years of lonely dread finally surfaced, Harold held her in his arms while it poured from her shaking shoulders, exhaustion finally stemmed its flow.

He whispered in her ear, "You will never be a 'Great' aunt, only ever a 'Grand' mother. Annie has your strength, given by you, look on your grandson and show Annie a smile."

Her hands nervously smoothed the baby's face, he appeared a healthy, good sized infant who called loudly for his first feed.

Bella had found her authority, "You must suckle him now Annie, then I will wash him and lay him down to sleep, you must rest for a while."

Harold had taken the bundle from the corner to the back yard for burning.

"Aunt Bella, what do you think of George as a name?" Asked Annie.

Bella thought for a moment, "George Boucher," she spoke the name slowly, "yes, a good solid name but George Harold Boucher I think sounds exactly right."

A look passed between Annie and Bella which said more than any words, no matter how carefully chosen.

Bella sat by the fire downstairs, her companion Byron, lay at her feet, she sipped some tea pensively, she dared to ponder that Sefton had at last found some peace and wished no more heartache on his family. The tea warmed her, grandmother, Harold had called her grandmother. Byron's deep breathing confirmed his slumber, its rhythm leadened her eyelids, they closed her mind to rest. Bella slept more soundly than she had in months.

Upstairs Harold held his son, he kissed the little fingers.

"He's perfect Annie, I wonder what these hands will do, I hope they achieve good things," said Harold.

"They will no doubt do all manner of naughty, mischievous things before they achieve something more," said Annie with a chuckle, "especially if grandad Samuel has anything to do with it."

Harold set off for work next day, first calling at the doctor's to ask him if he would look in on Annie and make sure all was well. When he reached the yard, the anticipation on Billy's face was a picture. Harold was never late for work it had to be the baby.

"It's a boy," Harold called across the yard so Josiah would hear in his office.

Billy hugged his best friend, "You're a clever bugger Harold, what's 'is name, you'd better tell me all yer can, Edna'll want to know the lot, weight, hair, size of its feet, black or white," he gave a wicked grin.

"You cheeky sod, Billy Dodds."

Harold tugged on the string of Billy's heavy apron and their laughter still rang through the air when poor old Josiah, struggling his way lamely across the yard, reached their side.

"Well done Harold, is Annie alright?" He asked kindly.

"Annie is well thank you Josiah, well and happy. Will I be able to finish a bit earlier today only mam and dad don't know yet."

Josiah patted him on the back, "I reckon you should be on your way to tell them right now, me and Billy will manage today, just be here good time tomorrow to help us catch up."

The smell of baking already wafted from the open window as Harold approached the back door at Mitchell Street, his big grin greeted his mam as Sarah looked up from her mixing bowl, "It's a boy Mam, it's a lovely little boy."

"Oh Harold, what a time to tell me when me hands are drippin' in pastry, you just stand there and wait for me to wash 'em so I can give you a proper hug."

Harold laughed at his mother's dilemma, "You can hug me just as you are Mam, I wouldn't worry."

"That might suit you but I'm not sendin' you 'ome to Annie and Miss Pownall with fat and flour over your clothes, what would they think o' me."

Sarah dried her hands on her apron, "Come 'ere Harold," she squeezed him so tightly that he cried out, "Mam if you don't let go the clip on the back o' me braces'll pop out me belly button."

"Is Annie alright, her aunt Bella is with her isn't she?"

"Annie is fine Mam, I think Bella'll take longer to get over it than Annie will, she wer' so nervous, worried that somethin' would go wrong."

Sarah put one hand to her chest, "God bless 'er, 'tis little wonder, what wi' Annie's mother dyin' like she did, I'll put some buns in a bag for you to take 'ome to them. You see that they both eat well, Annie needs to make milk and poor Miss Pownall needs to stay her strength. We shall all come to see the baby on Sunday and I shall bring a bit o' food to help out."

Harold smiled, his mam's so called bit o' food would more than likely turn out to be enough to feed a regiment.

"My silly head Harold, I 'aven't asked the baby's name."

"His name is George Harold Boucher, what do you reckon to that Mam?"

The tears began to well in her eyes, "That's just right, Samuel'll be beside 'imself wi' pride, you'll 'ave to go an' tell 'im, 'e's doin' Phyllis Oates on Valley Road."

Harold gave his mother a kiss and wiped her tears with the corner of her apron. Sarah stood at the back door waving, looking emotional, just before he turned from the yard she called out.

"Tell Phyllis, she'll let everybody know, that woman can spread news faster than a notice in the Gazette."

Samuel's barrow stood outside No.57 Valley Road. Harold went round to the back, the door was wide open, he could hear splashing sounds and a young lad's voice.

"It's bloody draughty in 'ere Mam, I'm catchin' me death o' cold, when are yer goin' to shut the doors?"

A woman's voice became louder as it drew closer, "Yer should 'ave thought o' that afore yer decided to go down the canal instead o' goin' to school. I've got to watch for Mr.Boucher's brush comin' out o' the pot, you scrub them socks an' don't you swear, yer little bugger."

Harold tapped on the back door frame to attract attention, Phyllis turned to see him standing on the back step.

"Bless us, there's somebody 'ere already," she muttered to herself. "I'm sorry sir, 'is father an' me 'ave told 'im time an' time again, to go straight to 'is lessons but that canal draws 'im like a magnet. You needn't concern yourself any more on the matter, Mr.Inspector sir, I'll see that 'e don't play truant again."

"Mrs.Oates, it's Harold, Samuel's son, I just need to speak to father for a minute."

"You aren't the School Inspector then?" She said.

"No I'm nothin' to do wi' the school," replied Harold.

Phyllis immediately turned her attention back to the lad in the bath, "You scrub them socks clean yer little bugger, if I don't get yer dried up an' yer clothes clean 'afore yer dad finds out 'e'll leather yer backside 'til yer can't sit on the lavy." She clipped him across the ear. "Ow long 'e'd 'ave bin splashin' about in the canal if Nobby 'adn't seen 'im I really don't know. Me father leathered our Norman once when 'e tied Vicar's cat to the spokes of a waggon wheel. Norman's arse ended up worse than the cat's, it wer' just lucky grandad's haemorrhoids were goin' through a good patch, 'cause wi'out the borro' o' grandad's ring our Norman would 'ave 'ad to shit standin' up for a fortnight. Mr. Boucher," she shouted so loudly even Harold jumped, "your Harold is 'ere," then she ran through the open doorway to the yard, "It's clear o' the pot, the brush 'as come through."

Samuel appeared in the scullery and winked at the young lad, "Your mam'll be able to shut the door now Tom."

Harold couldn't wait any longer to tell Samuel the news. "You're a grandad, he's a proper little man Father, a real Boucher, George, that's what we've called 'im, George Harold Boucher."

Samuel laughed as only Samuel could, lifting Harold off the ground and dancing around the room with him, "Well done Son, is the lass alright?"

"Everythin's alright Father," said Harold

Suddenly Phyllis Oates reminded them of her presence, "Well bless me, 'ere I was thinkin' 'e wer' school man an' tis' news 'o your grandchild Mr.Boucher. Congratulations young Harold, now you're a family man, when somebody fishes your George out o' the canal you'll remember this little bugger."

She swiped poor Tom about the neck with a towel, the unfortunate lad shivered in the now cold water, his socks were draped over the side of the bath, the toe ends dripped water onto the flags.

"Get out afore yer turn to a jellied eel."

Phyllis took no account of his bashfulness but Samuel took pity on the youngster, "We'll go outside Harold and check on the brush," he gave Harold a knowing wink. In the calm of the yard father and son embraced again.

"You've responsibilities now Harold, look after 'em but don't ever forget, if you need help, come to your old dad."

With the bag of buns clutched in one hand, Harold whistled and sang his way back to Winchester Street. He would call at the workshop and tell them about George before going home to his wife and son. It was a good feeling, he found a sticky humbug in his jacket pocket, 'I wouldn't call the King me uncle', he said to himself with a great surge of satisfaction. He sucked on the mint as he walked and his mind turned to fatherly things. A man could have no better example, he loved Samuel dearly, I must make George as proud of me as I am of father he thought. He quickened his pace, he would begin right away.

Aunt Bella was busy making a meal for them all when he reached home, her mood was much lighter, she carried a bowl of peelings across the yard to the compost heap with a real lift in her step.

Annie sat up in bed looking perplexed, "Aunt Bella says I am to stay in bed today, she won't let me walk further than to the 'po' but I can get up tomorrow, provided I just feed and change George and leave the work to her."

Annie looked at Harold appealingly, to be unoccupied taxed Annie more than a hard day's work.

That big grin came to his face and he lowered his voice so Bella couldn't hear. "You should see her down there Annie, it's as if she went to 'er bed last night a weary, worried woman and woke up this mornin' with a new lease o' life. You might feel bored up 'ere but you've got our son to feed an' tend."

Harold crossed to the crib, he stood looking at the sleeping child. "'E's just perfect, I reckon our George'll be a proper lad, wonder who'll fish 'im out o' the canal."

"What did you say?" Annie's voice was concerned.

"Nothin' to worry about my love," said Harold, "I shall tell you all about it when I've walked Byron and filled the buckets. Oh, and I nearly forgot, Edna and May are comin' just for five minutes after work, they promised not to stop and tire you."

"Tire me," said Annie with a 'huff' of sarcasm., " I feel like an ornament up here. I shall be downstairs tomorrow new lease of life or not."

With a hearty peal of laughter Harold ran down the stairs.

Annie 'tip-toed' across the floor so as not to alert aunt Bella and took paper, pen and ink from the top of the chest. Back in bed she rested the paper on her book and began to write a note to Davina, she had almost completed the letter when Bella came up with a tray of tea and some bread and dripping. Now I shall be told off, thought Annie but Bella simply put the tray down at Annie's side and said.

"I shall write to Alice Hemsley and tell her the news, she will be pleased. Eat your meal, Harold has taken Byron out, after I've cleared away I'll write my letter then Harold can post them both. I have prepared boiled beef for this evening and we'll have a rice pudding, Mr.Cheetham found me a nice piece of brisket." With that, she made her way downstairs.

Harold was right, she had lost that dour mantle, perhaps after all this time Bella was shedding her veil. Two letters now sat in their envelopes ready for posting, the savoury smell of beef and root vegetables filled the living room with homeliness and a bowl of rice rested in the oven, a soft buttery skin sealing the creamy pudding beneath.

A knock came to the back door, "Hello Miss Pownall, we've come to see Annie and the baby," said Edna, "only for a minute or two, we won't stop."

Bella would have preferred Annie and George to be left in peace, until the next evening at least, the doctor however had been satisfied that all was well, so just a little while should be alright.

Bella processed the thought quickly and led them up to the bedroom with the caution, "Don't be too long."

She left the good friends to their happy chatter. Annie was relieved that no further remarks were delivered that might cause poor timid May to feel unwelcome. Both women eagerly sought George.

"He's such a beautiful baby Annie," said May, gazing at the contented face in the crib.

"All babies are beautiful," replied Annie, "I've never seen one that wasn't lovely."

"I have," piped up Edna. "Our Ada and Morely's second one, it made our mam cry so much she couldn't eat 'er tea the day she first saw it. Still it's a bit better these days, the squint seemed to naturally right itself and as mam says, bein' a girl now 'er hair 'as grown thick 'an frizzy, Ada can pull it around the ears, it works a treat, you 'ardly notice 'em stickin' out now except for when 'er hair's wet. The nose, well, not a lot anybody can do about that, I've never seen a nose so broad, first time Billy saw 'er 'e said 'e reckoned she could smell onions fryin' in Nottingham wi' the right nostril an' liver cookin' in Derby wi' the left."

"Really Edna you shouldn't be so unkind," said May, genuinely feeling for poor Ada's distress.

"If you think that's unkind then you should 'ave 'eard what Phyllis Oates said about it. First time she saw 'er in the pram, she told the world an' 'is wife that Morely Craddock's baby looked like the monkey on top o' Silas Bendink's barrel organ. Our Ada went round to 'er 'ouse an' give 'er a right mouthful, all Valley Road could 'ear the 'to do'. Didn't do any good though, 'cause by the end o' the week, Phyllis 'ad told all the neighbourhood our Ada were that depressed at birthin' such an ugly kid she'd gone off 'er 'ead."

Annie chuckled, dear Edna, without any effort on her part could bring amusement and good humour to any situation.

In latter weeks Edna had proved a Godsend, with Annie being absent from the workshop, the spirited tales and lively chatter which flowed so readily from Edna, lifted Charles from his lowest ebb and carried him to safer ground.

Harold had made up aunt Bella's fire and their own little home was warm and cosy. He had promised Bella to lift the baby to Annie when it woke and to fetch her if anything was needed in the night hours, but for now, she had gone home to No.11 and on the orders of Harold, taken herself to bed for a good night of sleep, she would be across in the morning before he left for work.

The family settled to a comfortable routine. Sunday brought Samuel, Sarah and all the Boucher clan to visit. Bella and Sarah watched over the proceedings, ushering the young ones to the garden to play with Byron the moment things became too boisterous. Just as Harold had imagined, Sarah's 'bit o' food' would keep them happily munching away for days. Flowers from Samuel's allotment and a picture painted by Jean sat proudly on the sideboard, while a well used baby's rattle was thrust into George's crib by an adoring Maggie.

"I shall tell Eli all about you when I get 'ome" the little girl said to her sleeping nephew, blowing a big wet kiss over him.

The men sat around the scullery table discussing the recent news of more workers being taken on at the chain makers.

"A man needs the power of an ox to drive 'is arms 'an the hide on 'is 'ands to go wi' it," said Samuel.

"They say it's down to the shipyards that the demand for big chain is growin' fast," observed Frank.

Harold's thoughts were deep and beyond his age, "The world is opening up, I reckon the next ten years'll bring change." He propelled the salt and mustard pots around the table as if to demonstrate his belief. "Such powerful changes folks'll stand an' marvel at construction, at new ways o' drivin' machines. We'll see big industry an' great brain power behind it." Harold spoke with real conviction.

Just then, Nora's voice called out from the yard where she had been watching the young ones play. "Mam, Mam." It sounded urgent. Sarah came bustling through to the scullery, her first thought being the children.

"What is it? Who fell down?" She cried.

Nora stood by the back door looking concerned. "Did you lift that pork out of the range before we came away? 'Cause I didn't."

"Oh my godfathers!" Said Sarah, "it'll be burned to a cinder."

Samuel rose from his chair, "No use gettin' all lathered up now, 'tis time we wer' goin' home anyway, Annie needs a bit o' peace."

He rubbed Harold's hair with his strong hand. "If brainpower can come up wi' a way of gettin' folk's chimneys clean o' soot then I'll stand and marvel alright, but I reckon old Samuel Boucher's barrow will be a sight in this city for a few years yet."

The men chuckled, Sarah could not be pacified, Harold teased her all the more.

"When you get home Mam and open that range door I reckon the steam and smoke'll be like an eruption o' Vesuvius."

Sarah raised her hands in dismay, "You bugger Harold," said Frank, a big grin over his face as he mimicked his mother's actions.

All gathered up and heads counted, the family set off for Mitchell Street, waved out of sight by Annie and Harold. Even Bella watched the group, walking, skipping, singing, laughing 'til they turned the corner.

"You wouldn't want that bedlam every day would you Aunt Bella?" Said Harold, she just smiled, a deep wistful smile, but spoke not a word.

The early October days brought a nip to the air, Annie felt well and George obliged her by sleeping between feeds. Aunt Bella had been quite firm when she told Annie to play with the child.

"He has ears, eyes and fingers, give his senses something to do, he isn't a doll."

Before putting him down to sleep, Annie would enjoy simple baby play with George, Bella was usually right and it did indeed make sense to stimulate his learning even at this early stage of development.

Annie sat at the machine sewing nightshirts. The nurses' uniforms for the hospital had proved a useful advertisement, the workshop had since been given an order by the authorities for nightwear at the children's home. Very basic and made to meet a limited budget, Annie was able to complete them very quickly and without the need of too much concentration, it was an ideal task for her present circumstances.

She heard the sound of a horse close by, looking through the window to satisfy her curiosity revealed Davina, alighting from a carriage. Annie felt so pleased to see her friend and opened the front door to greet her.

"Annie my dear, I don't want to send this good man away until I know it is alright for me to stay for a little while."

"Of course you must stay," replied Annie, "there is a young man here who has yet to make your acquaintance."

Davina instructed the driver to return in one hour and sailed in through the door on a wave of anticipation.

"Annie my dear, where is the child?"

"Come," said Annie. Upstairs in his crib, looking angelic in sleep, lay George. "He will wake anytime now, his tummy tells him the hour of the day."

Almost as if he had heard the remark and understood, the little mouth began to search for vital comfort. Annie changed and fed him, Davina looked on with a pleasure which induced oohs and aahs and envious gaze.

"Would you like to hold him?" Asked Annie. She passed the sweet smelling bundle of young life to her aging friend.

"You know Annie, this makes me realise how seldom I have known such moments, in fact I begin to think that all my life has been spent waiting for someone to lay in my arms, the purpose of my existence. Now I feel that at last I have found it, every day from now on, I shall have a reason for this silly fat old woman to pull on her corsets and greet the world. I can be a sort of aunt to George can't I Annie?"

Her desperate appeal touched Annie, she smiled, "You have been promoted, we have given great aunt Bella the new role of grandmother and you are no longer simply a friend but now officially, aunt Davina."

They put George back in his crib and went downstairs to chat over a cup of tea.

"How is Bella?" Asked Davina between munching happily on a sizeable piece of Sarah's fruit cake.

"She is so much better, before the baby was born she had become that agitated I was afraid she would make herself ill, now her spirit is wonderful. Harold and I have both noticed her inclination to smile quite readily and even at times to actually laugh. She is still very authoritative and we all know our place." Annie paused and chuckled with amusement. "In all these years I have never before felt her heart was happy, now I dare to believe that it is."

Davina patted Annie's hand, she felt in her purse and produced an envelope. "I have just a little something for his money box."

"Oh no, really you shouldn't," said Annie with genuine concern.

"If I should not do this, then tell me what it is that I should do, for I fear I shall die before anyone allows me any sense of belonging."

Davina began to cry, Annie took her hand, "Very well, George will come to know that his money box was begun by his aunt Davina but she must make sure that he grows to be a good boy with no spoiling."

Their friendship and understanding of one another had grown over the past two years to a deep bond and easy trust. The hour sped by and when the carriage returned both women were anxious to agree a meeting again soon.

"I shall bring George in the pram which Samuel is so determined to restore, 'It'll do another batch o' Bouchers for sure' is what he said."

Annie and Davina laughed at Samuel's hopes for the future.

The carriage drove off and as they passed No.11 Davina thought of Bella, happiness was overdue them both, little George had brought change to their lives and it felt glorious.

The arrangement of tea with aunt Bella once a week and Sunday dinner at Mitchell Street had been abandoned for a more flexible plan. It was agreed that they would let the days produce the opportunity or not, whichever the case may be and so it was, on the following Sunday afternoon, that Annie and Harold were at home, quite content to be occupied with their respective tasks, Harold chopping logs and Annie baking sweet sponge cakes. A knock came at the door, Annie was surprised, aunt Bella came to the back since George had been born so she could let herself in without having to knock and disturb the baby. Sarah and the family had said they would not come again until at least the end of the month, 'You can't 'ave all of us too often lass', Samuel had said, 'we'd wear out your floorboards'.

She quickly checked the oven, thought about taking off her apron but decided it would be a vanity so opened the door as she was.

Charles, William and Freddy waited at the step, the two boys looking excited, Charles showing nervousness. Freddy was still not walking and sat aloft Charles' shoulders, his fat little hands reaching down to Annie to be transferred to her arms. William clutching the old cockatoo had espied his best friend Byron and rushed to shower the surprised dog with greatest love. Poor Byron seemed to disappear beneath the mop of William's curly hair and the grubby mass of feathers on the bedraggled bird, it was a display of delighted reunion.

"They wanted so much to see you and the new baby, I hope you and Harold don't mind Annie," said Charles.

"Don't be silly, we are pleased you have come, Harold is in the yard, I'll call him just let me rescue my cakes."

"Baby," said Freddy looking about the room for a pram.

"The baby is upstairs but next week he will have a pram and then he will be in this room when you come to see him. His grandad Samuel is making the pram all nice and smart for him. Come on, we'll go to find George."

Annie picked Freddy from the rug and with the eager child in her arms and with William walking in front of her they went to the bedroom. William was almost two years old, Annie had spent as much time as she could with Bertha and the boys since Enid's death. Neither child was old enough to understand what had happened, they knew only that their mother was no longer there and like their father, content was not the word to describe their feelings, an acceptance at most and even that unsure.

William had adopted Byron as his closest friend, the dog, almost as if aware of the child's longings returned the adoration, licking, cuddling, showing deep fondness.

Freddy offered his love to everyone, just in case from beneath the hat and coat, Enid might appear from a long walk, or a lengthy visit to the shops. It pulled at Annie's heart strings every time.

Now they looked on George, their faces for that moment were completely set on the baby, their thoughts entirely absorbed by the tiny fingers, the dark hair and the soft murmurs which seeped gently from the little mouth.

"Baby," said Freddy again.

William seemed deep in thought then, turning to Annie, his confused and troubled young mind prompted him to say, "Mummy had a baby."

He looked at Annie so intently she knew she must reply.

"Yes, that's right William, isn't it fortunate that you know all about babies because you will be able to help me look after George, shall we get his clean nappy ready, then in a minute, when he wakes up, if daddy isn't in a hurry you can help me to bathe him."

The response achieved to move forward his little mind at a pace only a child's thoughts seemed capable of.

Charles and Harold chatted in the yard over the woodpile. When George had been washed and powdered and fed he was sent back to sleep with an abundance of kisses.

Annie made tea and gave the boys milk and sweet cake.

"I've just been sayin' to Charles that 'im an' me should get together and make a swing for the lads, they're sure to play together as time goes on, Charles says there's room for a swing at Hood Street so that's our project for the winter. I've got the tools and Charles will get some wood an' two lengths o' chain. I shall 'ave to tell our Frank that it's not only the shipyards that are uppin' the demand."

It was time for them to go home, Annie felt sure that they had enjoyed themselves. Charles looked back as she waved, little Freddy pivoted round automatically on his dad's shoulders, the little hand waved back.

William shouted, "Bye, bye Byron," and held up the weary old bird in farewell.

Charles' expression seemed to plead 'don't abandon us'.

Annie watched until they were nearly at the corner, she called out, "I'll bring George to see you soon, tell Bertha."

They were a lonely group, Enid's moods may have been difficult at times but it was impossible to replace such a vibrant character in their lives, the sadness of it all invaded Annie's thoughts often.

"Poor Charles," said Harold, "strikes me, other than Mrs.Duffin 'e 'asn't any real friends. We'll get 'im through somehow Annie, a bit o' woodwork is good therapy to start with, I might even persuade Billy to take 'im fishin' one Sunday."

Annie loved Harold more than words could adequately express. He had even found aunt Bella's deepest emotions and dispelled her morose nature with his enthusiasm for life. If he could achieve that then surely Charles could be helped in the company of Harold. 'Go on it'll do yer good' was his abiding philosophy. She kissed her husband tenderly, her own Mr.Boucher and now a Master Boucher too, inwardly Annie's entire being glowed.

CHAPTER TWENTY ONE

Annie and Bertha sat on the garden seat which Harold and Charles had made as their second project, George had just begun to walk, a little unsteady but encouraged by William and Freddy, his progress was determined. The cries to be pushed, 'again, again', on the swing had for the time being, been denied.

"It's no use," said Bertha, "we shall both be round shouldered if we don't straighten our backs for a bit."

Annie laughed, they had taken it in turns to push the three boys for the last half hour. Bertha was quite right, Annie's back ached from the activity. The men had made the swing safe for even a child the age of George and it had proved the most popular of pastimes. A small piece of chocolate had been dispensed to each of the boys and they now played happily a game created of their own imagination. Byron chased around the garden with them, a slight altercation between Freddy and George had been dealt with when Byron seized the object of the argument, an old orange box, and ran off with it the three boys in pursuit, trying to retrieve the cockatoo which bounced its way around the circuit like a gladiator in a chariot.

"That old bird is nearly bald," said Bertha, "goodness knows what William will do when the stuffing starts to come out, he won't go to bed without it you know, it makes me shudder when I have to kiss it goodnight."

Dear Bertha, she would do anything to make Enid's sons happy, given her age she was remarkable but the strain of the past eighteen months was evident in the lines on her face and the prominent veins over the back of her hands.

Annie had continued to sew on the machine at home but over recent weeks had left George with aunt Bella in the afternoons so she could spend some time at the workshop, stitching the trimming and fastening to some of the more elaborate commissions.

George would sleep for a while after his dinner, as would Bella, so the two were quite content whilst Annie worked. Bella took delight in playing with the child, although the chosen activity always held a measure of learning.

Since George came into the world, Bella had taken on a very different temperament. Through the summer months she had pushed her grandson in his pram to the arboretum, with the result that her own cheeks held a little natural colour, never one for idle chit-chat, she nevertheless exchanged courteous conversation with others who chose to sit on the seats and observe the birds and flowers. George, protected from the colourful language borne of poverty and frustration which assailed the ears of so many working class children, grew in goodness. If Harold forgot himself for an instant, then bugger became urgently extended to 'Buggersham Castle'. It amused Annie but Bella had instructed Harold on the subject, 'If you want the boy to achieve and make well of himself, then you'll have to keep him on firm ground, away from the mire'.

Harold and Bella had a very special relationship, Annie had watched it develop and establish since that very first meeting when, almost at once, they had engaged in deep debate, always sincere, ever respectful of each other's opinions but by her long held method of teaching, Bella had always brought Harold to the most accurate interpretation of facts.

Annie had come to realise that Bella had allowed herself an attachment to Harold, something which she had seemed stubbornly opposed to doing with anyone else. When younger, Annie had often wondered if Bella had held any feelings for her at all, now Annie knew that she did. Her fear at the possibility of losing Annie when George was born had been so intense, Bella's previously hidden need of her had suddenly become apparent. Voicing such things however, was still beyond Bella's strict composure, it remained unsaid but Annie knew and that was all that mattered.

Business at the workshop was good, in fact Charles had taken on another seamstress, purchasing a new machine accordingly. At Annie's suggestion he had put May to work on the more advanced piece of equipment.

'I think it might be more diplomatic to start this young lady on one of the older machines, May would be unlikely to voice any resentment regardless but Edna almost certainly would, if May is put to work on the new acquisition however, Edna would accept that as being altogether correct', Annie had told Charles.

The new employee was a pleasant enough young woman, unmarried and pretty. Edna had been convinced that Charles would seize upon any chance to woo Violet Raithby but to her disappointment he had shown no desire. Unknown to Edna, Charles had become friendly with a young lady working at Burton's, Annie was only aware because Bertha had told her. The friendship had lasted a few weeks but for whatever reason had come to nought. He concentrated on his work and did at least in that area of his life find satisfaction.

His knowledge of the trade had increased so much he even held ambitions of moving to larger premises in the future. His private life however, remained drawn to the memory of Enid.

Billy had finally popped the question and he and Edna were now engaged. Annie felt so pleased for Edna but on hearing her account of the proposal, had begun to feel just a little sorry for poor Billy.

'I told 'im we won't be wed 'til 'e finds a proper place to live, just a room at our mam's house 'ould do 'im but if 'e thinks I'm goin' to lie in bed singin', 'Gentle Jesus meek 'an mild' at the top o' me voice every night, so me mam won't 'ear when 'e fancies a leg over, then 'e can think again'.

Samuel, Sarah and the rest of the family perpetuated happiness for all. Frank had at last taken courage to ask Ivy if she would like to walk by the embankment, they had spent several Sunday afternoons in one another's company, much to the delight of Davina.

Sarah had insisted that George's first birthday be marked by a gathering at Mitchell Street. It would be slightly belated as the family could only get together on a Sunday. 'George won't mind havin' a fuss made of 'im twice', she had said with a chuckle. Annie wondered just how everyone would fit into that small house, Bella, Davina and Ivy were invited too.

"What's happening on George's birthday?" Asked Bertha.

"Would you like to bring the boys for an hour?" Replied Annie. "I shall leave the workshop no later than four o'clock to collect him from aunt Bella's so if you come then, after we've had some tea and the children have played for a while, you can all walk home together. Charles can come to us from the workshop when he locks up. Harold won't be late this time of year, the light governs finishing time at Josiah's."

It was agreed and so on the occasion of his first birthday, George was to have two celebrations.

The first had been a very lively event, William and Freddy had arrived with Bertha, each carrying a wrapped present. Still very young themselves, neither could wait for George's little fingers to untie the ribbons so the packages became hastily undone at the hands of William and Freddy and just as quickly commandeered. George had protested noisily, wetting his rompers in the process and plucking a small fistful of feathers from the cockatoo in his frustration. William had rushed to the aid of his partially feathered friend, tripping over Freddy's foot in his urgency, banging his chin as he fell on the arm of the chair. Byron, upset by all the commotion raced across the floor to comfort his dear friend William, treading on the building blocks young Freddy had been assembling, sending them in all directions causing Freddy to howl in temper. All three boys competed to cry the loudest. Annie and Bertha were trying to bring the situation back to calm when Harold arrived.

"Buggersham bloody Castle." He cried, "what ever's 'appenin'?"

Annie began to laugh, soon Bertha began to giggle, George by now was interested only in his dad.

Charles' appearance within a few minutes of Harold, immediately diverted William and Freddy's attention and the presents, which had triggered the whole affair, now lay on the rug completely ignored by all three boys.

"Well if that isn't typical of young men," said Bertha, "fight over something they want then when they've got it they lose all interest." She sighed with exasperation.

Peace had at last been restored to No.24, Charles had taken his brood home and George, totally exhausted, lay fast asleep upstairs.

"I sometimes wonder what'll 'appen at the yard Annie," said Harold. "Now the weather is changin' and the days are gettin' colder, the demand for meat'll rise like it allus does. It's gettin' too much for Josiah, I reckon if we scrape through this winter 'e's goin' to 'ave to take a back seat 'imself an' take on another man. I can understand 'ow 'e must feel, no man wants to admit 'e's past it."

Annie sat on Harold's lap, she cuddled her head into his neck and gently smoothed his fingers. The calluses from his work ribbed the top of his palm as hard as bone. She lifted his hand to her lips and kissed each gnarl in turn, he wrapped his fingers around hers, neither spoke. Annie and Harold could sit together in absolute silence, feeling no need of words, the sounds from the fire, Byron in sleep, their own contentment softly humming them to a perfect rest. Their one year old son filled their hearts with pride and joy, their household knew only harmony.

Annie felt just a little concerned at the prospect of Bella travelling with Davina. When Sarah had invited both Davina and Ivy to Mitchell Street on Sunday, Ivy had been overjoyed, not at the thought of the carriage ride but at meeting all Frank's family and at walking with her dear Frank both to and from the gathering. Riding with Davina would have denied her that precious time of holding hands.

Davina felt amused at the eagerness of young love but had insisted her carriage would collect Bella on the way to The Park and they would then ride together declaring them both too advanced in years to walk such a distance.

Annie had anticipated opposition to the plan but when she had told Bella of Davina's intention, it had been accepted without question. It was now Sunday afternoon, Annie and Harold with George in his pram, were setting off to walk and Bella would follow on. Annie had no knowledge of Davina's visit just after Saul had died and had a dread of Bella being less than friendly, in the past she had always seemed stern at the mention of Davina's name.

"You worry too much," said Harold, "they'll be alright, by the time they get to mam's they'll know each others lineage, women are like that, always want to know who married who, an' when an' where, what their fathers did an' which side o' the bed they slept on."

"That's not fair," said Annie, "not all women gossip."

"I'm only pullin' your leg, Bella an' Davina are both intelligent women, neither one 'ould 'ave any wish to upset the other, they'll get on you'll see."

When they reached Mitchell Street, the bright faces, the warm greeting, drove all anxieties from Annie's mind. Sarah lifted George from the pram and led him by the hand into the living room. The house was cosy, the smells confirmed Sarah's usual preparation of good food. The young ones ran around George excitedly, joined by Eli. Nora and Samuel were busily bringing down chairs from the bedrooms to accommodate their number around the table.

"It's alright my love," said Samuel to his wife, "everything is organised." He placed a degree of emphasis on his last word and gave Sarah a big roguish wink.

Frank and Ivy turned into the yard, hand in hand, wearing radiant smiles.

Harold had observed Samuel's obvious satisfaction and asked, "What are you up to Dad?" Giving him a 'bear hug'.

"When Bella and Davina arrive, then you'll find out," said Samuel and laughed loudly.

The sound of the carriage approaching increased the mood of excitement and anticipation. Little George had been, 'Ring a Ring a Rosied' so many times he was dizzy and now sat with Eli in the middle of the floor looking bemused at the whole thing.

"My dears, do come in," said Sarah, bustling to the door to welcome her guests. Bella looked nervous, Annie knew how difficult it was for her to leave that familiar corner in No.11. She would not have countenanced any of this but for George and Harold, they had found her heart and she let them abide there.

Samuel and Sarah thrived on their children's happiness and their grandson's first birthday was more special to them than the King's coronation.

Nora had slipped out the back door and now re-appeared, casting a very 'knowing' look to her father. From outside, music, the sound of a barrel organ grew louder. The children were across the yard and into the street, 'whooping' with delight, Annie picked George from the rug and followed.

"Come on ladies," said Samuel, ushering Bella and Davina to the merriment.

Silas had agreed to play for the family, Samuel's offer of payment had achieved to bring Silas, monkey and organ to the house for an hour. Mavis and Maggie were already dancing to the lively tunes, soon to be joined by Gertie and Jean.

The monkey sat on top of the organ, his tightly curled tail teasing Eli, who from the cobbles could not quite reach its tip. All he could do was watch and wait for any opportunity to catch this strange smelling furry creature.

Sarah stood alongside Annie, "Samuel is a silly old bugger, he was quite determined to get Silas to come you know, 'give the young 'ens somethin' they'll always remember' he said. Look, just look Annie, bless us, whatever next."

Samuel was dancing with Davina and Harold with Bella. Frank and Ivy missed no chance to be in one another's arms and twirled about the street in a world of their own. In no time at all, other folk from the street, drawn by the laughter and music, joined in the abandon.

"Can't stop yet Aunt Bella," said Harold, "we 'ave to work up an appetite for all that food mam's made." He held Bella tightly and turned her about enthusiastically laughing each time they danced by his father and Davina. Annie looked on in amazement, she would not forget this scene as long as she lived. Davina protested she was far too old but if Samuel began to slow down she would call for 'just a few more minutes'.

Such a gathering inspired Silas to play on and the original hour was over run considerably. The monkey had accepted a large apple from someone on the street, its juicy flesh pleased the little animal and in relishing the treat, concentration weakened. Intent on the tasty fruit, the curled tail began slowly to unwind and the tip lowered just enough for the ever patient Eli to reach it. An almighty shriek erupted from the monkey and the terrified creature leapt from the organ to a drain pipe and shinned up to the roof where it sat screaming its annoyance and spitting apple skin down on the people below.

"Put that dog in the shed Samuel," cried Sarah in panic.

"Don't fret missus," said Silas, "it 'appens regular, he'll come down when the dog's gone."

Harold and Frank had been aware of Eli's interest in the monkey and unnoticed by anyone had egged him on, now the two conspirators roared with laughter at the mayhem. By the time all the children had waved Silas goodbye and everyone was assembled at the table in Sarah's kitchen, feet were weary, stomach muscles ached from laughing and the thought of food and warm tea now dominated the minds of them all, except young George in whose honour the event had been planned. He now lay in Samuel's chair fast asleep and a disappointed Eli sat by the dolly tub, gnawing on a knuckle bone for consolation, he would have much preferred a nice chunk of monkey's rump.

"Your pastry is so light Sarah," said Davina, enjoying every crumb of a piece of treacle tart.

Bella sat quietly sipping tea, observing the faces of the children, deep in thought.

"Try one of my Sarah's scones," said Samuel, he sat next to Bella and held up the plate of delicious looking buttered scones for her to take one. "I reckon my Sarah could give Lovatt a run for 'is money when it comes to scones."

Bella accepted politely but Annie sensed it was all too much for her, in spite of the doses of happiness being increased gradually over the past months, the emotions of this day had near' swept Bella away.

Salvation came as if to order, George awoke from his nap, finding himself alone in a place unfamiliar he began to whimper.

"I will sit with him, you finish your tea Annie I have eaten plenty, it was all delicious Sarah, thank you."

Annie made no protest and glanced quickly at Sarah recognising in her eyes too, a ready understanding of Bella's need to retreat.

In due course the carriage returned to take Davina and Bella home. Annie was concerned at getting back to let Byron out, so she and Harold with George in his pram, set off to walk to Winchester Street.

Ivy had looked appealingly at Davina and suggested it would be only proper for her to stay a while and help to clear away.

Davina felt amused but showed only wholehearted agreement, after all there were no pressing tasks for Ivy at The Park, it really didn't matter at what time Frank walked her back.

Davina had known the ways of first love, it may have been a long time ago but she could still remember. Ivy was not so much a maid as a companion in that big house, a young woman representing life and hope, without her Davina would lose heart.

In the carriage the understanding reached between Davina and Bella created an easy atmosphere, both women had greatly enjoyed the afternoon, to be a part of Samuel and Sarah's joyful celebration of family was to Bella and Davina like the wonderful safety of a sincere embrace.

Their conversation natural and comfortable quickly carried them to The Park where Davina, helped by the driver returned to her serene, monkey-less world. She tactfully asked him to walk her to the door.

"I am quite unsteady from all that dancing." Out of sight of Bella, she paid him for the carriage and instructed him to see Bella safely to her door.

The grate was low, a few pieces of kindling would redeem the fire. Bella sat on the edge of her chair, reflecting on the afternoon's events. She,

Bella had family now, Annie, George and Harold, it was more family than many people were blessed with but she had acquired them without that intimacy between man and woman. The flames began to lick at the sticks and send warmth to her toes.

She closed her eyes, imagination could only bloom if reality was shut out. Bella danced with a young Saul, his ambitious chatter poured over her as they circled the floor, he wanted her, she could feel it in his arms, his strength as he turned her about to the music filled her with hope and confidence for the future. They would have children, laugh together, be proud together, grow old together. A loud crackle in the fire forced her eyes to open, she put coals over the grate and winced as the ache of age caught her back when she straightened.

The dream was Annie's, not her own but Harold's arms had held her this day and they were real, she had a family and she could borrow the dream from time to time. It was enough, Bella was content.

CHAPTER TWENTY TWO

"E's a big bugger," said Billy. He and Harold looked at the bullock in the pen, it had come in from Radford early that morning.

"Fine animal, best get on wi' the cuttin', 'e's been agitated ever since we penned 'im, if we clear the work in the cuttin' shed we can see to 'im," said Harold.

Josiah was working on accounts, he ever lamented his failure to secure premises on the High Street where he could have sold meat direct.

'Cheetham makes a damn sight more out of it than I do'. Poor Josiah had observed on countless occasions when doing the books.

"Have you found anywhere to rent yet Billy?" Asked Harold.

A wry smile came to Billy's face, "No rush is there, Edna isn't like your Annie, you can still do what a man does but when I wed Edna, that'll be the end o' Billy Dodds as we know 'im. Talk about 'en pecked, I reckon I'd be bloody lucky if I ever got to 'cock-a-doodle-do' again."

"Get along wi' yer Billy, yer love Edna to bits, afraid, that's what you are, yer don't know what you're missin'. I can just picture the scene, Mr.Dodds wi' 'is boys down Trentside fishin' while Mrs.Dodds makes buns wi' 'er girls."

They laughed as they worked together, they had almost finished cutting the pigs when an almighty crashing sound came from the yard, both rushed to the door to look. The bullock, in its agitation, had somehow managed to get a section of the pen off the hangings, trampling over the rails in its bid for freedom.

Josiah had left his office and was lumbering across the yard.

"Wait Josiah," shouted Harold.

He and Billy ran out, the animal stood by the wood pile, fear drove the beast. "Let it be for a minute, 'tis all worked up," cried Harold

Josiah, very slowly, began to move, trying to get closer to the back wall of the yard, he called across to Billy and Harold, "Pick up the rails and you Harold, keep 'em steady, Billy stand over by the sheds, stop it goin' that way. I'll drive him on, when he goes in the pen you come forward quick Billy to help Harold bring the rails around."

Josiah was a patient man, all the years he had worked with animals had taught him to be so, very gently he edged around the back of the bullock, speaking to it slowly, one step at a time. The animal moved a few feet, it thrust its head from side to side, calling noisily. Josiah crept forward again, bit by bit the animal made its way to the open pen, where Harold waited behind the rails to lift them into place as soon as the creature was inside.

Billy stood like a coiled spring, ready to rush the instant those strong hind quarters were far enough forward. Josiah's patience seemed to have won the day, then, just as he took his last step, his knee joint gave way and he stumbled. It spooked the bullock, that powerful head went up, the eyes flashed wildly, it charged at the rails where Harold stood, sending him to the ground, the rails over the top of him. It rose up on its haunches, the two front feet flailing the air, as it came down, one foot came through the rails and onto Harold's chest. Billy travelled across the ground like a charging buffalo, cursing and swearing, arms lashing out at the bullock, his fury unleashed and trained on the creature before him knew no limit. The beast's fear and confusion drove it straight into the pen.

Billy grabbed at the rails, screaming at Josiah to help him lift them onto the hangings, Josiah had been rendered inert by the shock.

"God Almighty Josiah, I can't 'old the bugger on me own."

Josiah heaved on the corner of the rails, Billy's forehead near ruptured, his sheer effort had brought the veins to the point of almost bursting through the skin. The animal was contained.

Both men knelt by Harold, Billy shaking uncontrollably with anger and dread, Josiah trembling with the pain in his old joints and the sight of Harold motionless on the ground.

"Say somethin' Harold, God make 'im say somethin'." Billy's tears fell as a great flood.

Harold was still, one dirty hoof mark on the bib of his apron.

"Run Billy lad, run as fast as you can, fetch the doctor, tell 'im to leave what he's doin' and come right away. Then you go to Annie, tell her to come quick. God help us Billy, run!"

As if knowing the terror was now theirs the bullock stood quietly, making no sound or movement, observing the scene like a captive spectator at some awesome event.

Josiah held Harold's hand, he could feel no life, he would have gladly given up his own to feel Harold's fingers move, to see his eyes flicker. It was more than Josiah could bear, the pain deep inside him greater than any his tired old joints had ever created. He cried out to God, he cried for the doctor and he called out for his wife, Josiah wept of the despair which engulfed him.

Billy tore through the streets, his heart pounded in his chest, his emotions vent only by his endless tears.

Dr.Baragruy was attending to a poisoned thumb, having just lanced it, he had begun a dressing. Billy's distress was so urgent the doctor directed his wife to continue the task for him, he was gone within seconds.

By the time Billy reached Winchester Street he could barely speak, he had run 'til breath almost left him entirely. Annie appeared at the door, little George squatted by the scullery table, one arm wrapped around Byron's neck. Annie stood with a length of calico in her hand.

"Annie, you've to go to the yard quick, Harold's 'ad an accident."

Billy was distraught, his anguished tone and gasping breath alarmed George.

Annie took Billy outside, "Listen to me Billy, I need to go but George is only a baby, you're frightening him, please stop Billy." She held him tightly, comforting his sobs to calm him. "You must stay with George, I haven't time to take him to aunt Bella. Play with him, read to him, please Billy I need you to be calm."

His tears subsided, he became still, his eyes looked raw from the times he had rubbed his arm across them in order to see through the tears as he'd raced from the yard.

Annie led him inside, "uncle Billy is going to stay here with you."

George's lips began to pucker. "Now you find your book for uncle Billy and show him your building blocks. Mummy won't be long, don't cry, you'll frighten Byron if you cry."

Annie smiled to reassure him and gave him a kiss, she threw the calico onto the machine, grabbed her jacket from behind the door and looking back pleadingly at Billy, ran through the yard to the street.

As Annie sped down Sherwood Road Evelyn Easter appeared from a doorway, Annie could not stop.

"What's 'appenin'?" called out Evelyn, "I'll come an'all if 'tis worth lookin' at."

Annie kept her pace and uttered not a word. Evelyn disgruntled at being ignored and perplexed at not knowing what lay behind Annie's urgency, set off up the road, muttering her displeasure.

Annie turned into the yard, her hair had lost some pins in her haste. Dr. Baragruy looked up, his expression spoke to her even as she moved towards him, that same desperate expression he had given the morning Enid died.

Josiah sat on the bench by the woodpile, his head in his hands, his knees trembled causing the toe caps on his boots to strike the cobbles, tapping out a tortured message of disaster.

Annie's eyes searched the doctor's face for confirmation.

He took her arm. "The bullock trod exactly over the heart Annie, such weight would have stopped the beat instantly. I have tried everything I can but the internal damage is too great. Mercifully Harold would have known nothing, it would have been that quick."

Annie dropped to the ground beside Harold, the unpinned lock of her hair fell across his brow as she kissed him. She held so gently his fingers, feeling for the calluses across his palm, so many times she had smoothed those scars of his labours. She did not wail or scream and all her tears remained within. She stayed with him, kissing him over and over for many minutes. The doctor, wise from many years of caring, made no attempt to interrupt Annie's outpouring of love.

Then Annie's soft voice asked, "Have you attended Josiah doctor? I feel he will need more help than Billy alone can give him. His lameness is severe, Harold has long been concerned by Josiah's health. Someone will need to clear the yard, neither Billy nor Josiah or the two together could do this without some practical help."

Annie looked intently at the doctor, they understood each other perfectly.

"I have already sent word to Radford for them to remove the animal and I have given Josiah something to calm him. Annie what can I do for you?"

"Sarah and Samuel, 69.Mitchell Street, Harold's mam and dad, tell them for me please but help them all you can. Billy is with George, I can't leave them for long, Billy is in such a way I'm afraid he might alarm George if I don't return to them soon. Mr.Handley will need to come to the yard."

Doctor Baragruy spoke softly but with that authority which inspired trust. "I shall see to all these matters Annie and when I have done so, I will come to see you and George, you have your aunt Bella close by I believe?"

Annie sighed, "Yes doctor, aunt Bella lives just across the street."

As she walked through the yard gates, leaving her soul with Harold, she thought of Bella but not of an aunt close by, but of the Bella in that dark corner, behind the bonnet and the fingerless gloves, the sallow complexion and the stern eyes which stared at a feeble fire in a hearth starved of mirth. Harold, that beaming light which had drawn Bella from the shadows into the sun, had gone forever. Annie knew that she and George would not be permitted to occupy that part of Bella's heart which Harold had held so completely.

The walk back to Winchester Street brought a loneliness unlike any Annie had ever known. The grief inside her, beat with its fists, every inch of her being 'til the pain almost rent her in half, but she did not cry.

George, Bella, Billy, Sarah and Samuel all needed her to be strong, practical help stays the soul, her own was beyond help, it had already gone with Harold. She turned into the small back yard of No.24, passing by the privy door, so carefully restored by Samuel. She would not fail them, she would care for them all.

Billy sat with George on his knee, both reached out for her, George with his arms, Billy with his eyes. She held them tightly, her strength would be theirs, and so it was.

Telling aunt Bella had been heartrending. In spite of Annie's appeal to consider her grandson, 'he is too young to understand open grief and despair', Bella had faded before their eyes. Like the last strip of evening light, sinking suddenly behind the rooftops, driven away by advancing gloom.

Billy had gone from Annie's to the workshop, shedding the contents of his heart over Edna, his grief so intense the tears had flowed before all present. Violet, unsure of the situation continued at her machine. May sat very still, apart from her hands, they pulled and twisted the buttons on her frock. Edna tried earnestly to console Billy but his shoulders shook violently under the weight of his sobbing. Charles sat at his desk, clinging to the corner of the ledger as though by hanging on it might save him from falling into that deep abyss, where he had become lost and crying out to be recovered for so long after Enid's death. Finally Charles rose from his chair and crossed the back room to the scene of heartache, he spoke very clearly.

"We shall do no more today. Edna, go with Billy, stay with him. Violet you may go home. May, I know you will want to see Annie but not today. Tomorrow we shall work again. If Billy needs you for longer Edna, then of course we shall understand."

As May left Charles took her arm for a moment, "Tomorrow May, Annie will know you are coming tomorrow."

May understood, she had no words, the tightness in her throat had stifled all speech. It would be a long and wretched walk home this day to the house at the bottom of Peverell Street.

Charles covered the machines and closed the damper on the old stove, locked his desk and taking his coat from the hook, fought back tears, of which he'd thought there could be none remaining.

Annie opened the door to Charles, he possibly recognised more than any other, the circumstances now threatening George and Annie.

Straight away he went to the child, his tone normal, "Hello young George, how are you and your friend Byron today?"

The little hand picked up a picture book and held it up for Charles to see.

"Freddy has some nice books and William had a game of skittles for his birthday, would you like to come to see them?" Charles looked to Annie for approval.

"Mr.Handley will be calling shortly and the doctor, it would probably be for the best if George spent the afternoon with young friends," said Annie. "I will get his warm coat."

"Bertha is sure to want the three boys to have tea together," said Charles, "I shall bring George home straight after, will that be alright Annie?"

She nodded, moved by his kindness and simple understanding.

As he left with George's hand firmly in the clasp of his own he told Annie of May's urgent wish to see her.

"She will come tomorrow," said Charles, "as will Edna, I'm quite sure. Billy was very distraught."

"Harold and Billy were the best of friends," said Annie, "Billy's torment at witnessing the whole thing is cruel, it near' crushes him, we must help him all we can and Edna too for it will affect them both."

Annie thanked Charles, he brushed her thanks aside.

"You saved me but you are much stronger and resolute than the feeble Charles Eddowes. He learned from you however, just a little, but enough hopefully to tell what is important from what is not."

Annie waved as they turned to look back, George had been in the company of Charles sufficiently for him to be content and ever enjoyed play with William and Freddy. The months ahead would require some tender explanation of his dad's absence, his infant mind needed to be brought to an acceptance of the changes at his bedtime and at the weekends. A child so very young could not comprehend death, he could only learn, through careful words, that his dad, whilst not there, nevertheless loved him still.

Josiah had watched the cart take the bullock from the yard, his legs ached, no part of him seemed to work properly any more. He loaded the meat, clearing everything from the cutting shed and set off for Cheetham's. He could not bear to look on the spot where Harold fell, he had no heart left for any of it. He had made up his mind to offer the yard and business to Cheetham. Let him have all the profit, he had taken most of it over the years. Let him have the lot, bones for glue, tallow for candles, hides for the tannery, the smell, the flies, vats filled with blood and guts. Let it all be Cheetham's, one big empire of slaughter.

Josiah wanted to go home, this day had broken his back and his will.

He would take as much as could be prised from the butcher's fat purse and sit by the fire with his wife. By the grace of God he could still do that and do it he would.

A knock came to the door at Davina's house. Ivy was expecting a delivery from the ironmongers of lamp oil and soft soap.

"Just one moment, I'll fetch the empty jars."

She returned to the door where the young man waited.

"Bad news at the slaughter yard," he shook his head, "terrible bad news."

Ivy was afraid but felt compelled to ask what had happened.

"One bloke dead they're sayin', I've 'eard that 'e never 'ad a mark on 'im, not a drop o' blood shed, but some great beast of a creature charged 'im to the ground, killed 'im stone dead."

Ivy could not listen to any more, "Thank you," she mumbled the courtesy and closed the door, trying in vain to shut the dread out of the house.

Ivy did not want to think alone, "Please ma'am, I have to tell you," she began to weep into her apron.

"Whatever is the matter Ivy?" Asked Davina, putting down her book and standing to console the young woman. "There, there it can't be so bad surely."

Ivy related the young man's words.

"Did he not say who?"

"No ma'am, I don't think he knew who it was," Ivy trembled.

"Now we must not presume the worst, it is a tragedy whoever has suffered, if in fact it is true. Harold and Billy are fit young men, Josiah Toft is much older and I believe to be troubled greatly by arthritis, to the point of being lame. We must await a more factual account, it could well be an exaggerated version of events, people do always seem to spread dire news more hastily than good. Now make some nice hot tea and bring a cup for yourself Ivy and two small glasses of brandy, we shall grant ourselves a little measure of fortitude. Dry your eyes dear, we shall be strong and positive. I'm sure before long we shall discover it is all because someone has presumed the worst."

Davina despatched Ivy to the kitchen and now pondered what she should do. Her thoughts travelled in all directions but which ever way they went, the outcome was the same, she could not sensibly do anything until she learned more.

Dr.Baragruy had found Sarah making soup.

"Where is Samuel?" He asked.

"Oh, well now, I'm not sure doctor, he could be on Valley Road or Forest Road. I can tell 'im if you need your chimney sweepin'," Sarah stirred her large pan, "a soup boiled is a soup spoiled doctor," she chuckled, "not that my lot ever worry, I sometimes wonder if it even touches the sides they eat so fast."

To tell her when she was without the support of Samuel was more than Dr.Baragruy could bring himself to do.

"I have to go to Valley Road," he said, "I'll find Samuel I'm sure."

He needed to tell them before idle tongues delivered the brutal truth. Samuel's barrow stood just around the corner and as the doctor approached, Samuel appeared carrying his brushes, that huge smile which Samuel had with him at all times greeted the doctor warmly.

Samuel almost fell into his barrow, his great frame slumped forward. The doctor caught his arm to steady him but Samuel choked on his pain, he retched into the gutter, the sound of his despair carried on the air, that mournful, solemn sound like the tolling of a solitary bell. Were it not for the barrow to hold on to, Samuel could not have walked back with the doctor to Mitchell Street.

"Samuel, you must be strong for your wife, I know that your heart is broken but Sarah needs you to hold her, to save her from collapse. She is not a young woman, unless you show her the greatest strength I fear she may never recover from the depths of despair.

Dr.Baragruy left 69.Mitchell Street with a sadness that weighted his steps but he needed to walk hastily. He needed to advise the Coroner of Harold's death, submitting the statement of facts he had taken from Josiah. He must reach Annie, to check her mental state, she was a young woman with undeniable strength of character but this cruellest of accidents would test her spirit to its limits.

George so young, thankfully too young to be weakened by grief but not old enough to share his mother's or to take her arm to keep her from falling.

James Handley had just left. Annie sat at the table, Harold's jacket lay across her lap. Josiah had taken it down from where it hung in the cutting shed and sent it with the undertaker when he collected Harold's body.

'Josiah asks me to tell you that tomorrow he will come to see you', Mr.Handley had said.

Poor Josiah, Annie felt compassion for him, he was a gentle man, kindly as his quietly given help to May and Alfred had shown.

'Harold was not wearing the jacket, it needs not to be kept at the mortuary until the Coroner's release, I have brought it to you Mrs.Boucher as I believe there is a small amount of money in one pocket'.

James Handley had gently laid it in her arms genuinely hoping it might bring her some small comfort. Annie held it to her face, it was Harold, his unique charm, that glorious honesty, his tenderness clung to every fibre, his nature bathed her senses as she stroked the cloth, smelled the collar. On her lap she fastened each button, touching where earlier that day his own fingers had touched. The pocket, deep in one corner, as if reluctant to relinquish its charge, loyal only to the hand of the master, held three halfpennies, two pennies, two nails, a piece of twine and three mints. In the other pocket, Harold's cap, Annie's gift to him that first Christmas.

A knock came to the door, Annie took the jacket and hung it on the hook over her own.

"I'm sorry it has taken so long to reach you Annie, there are always so many things to attend to."

The doctor smiled and patted Byron as he entered the living room. He had not been to the house since that day when Harold had told him that he was a father and asked him to make sure all was well with Annie and the baby.

"Where is George?" He asked.

"Charles kindly took him to play and have some tea with William and Freddy. With Mr.Handley due to call and yourself, it seemed best that George be occupied with happy activities."

"Children are remarkably tough, they seem to overcome even the harshest times with stoicism. Your aunt Bella is not here with you?" He spoke as an enquiry.

"Aunt Bella is a very private person, she sits with her own thoughts." Annie said nothing more and the doctor did not pursue it.

"If you need me to come any time day or night, then you know you have only to send word."

"Please tell me doctor, how are Samuel and Sarah?"

"They grieve for their son Annie, but they are surrounded by family and hold such concern for you and George. Sarah's need to tend to Harold's brother and sisters, Samuel's determination to support his wife, all this will help them."

"I shall take George there tomorrow. On Sunday it will be four weeks from the day we all gathered to celebrate George's first birthday."

Annie drew a deep breath but still no tears fell, grief ever beat with its fists but found no escape.

In The Park, darkness had fallen with no further word. Davina sat counting the ever changing pattern of red sparks at the base of the chimney. She could not concentrate on her book, she had tried to do her embroidery, a challenge for Davina at the best of times but this night her needle and thread would not co-operate, three times she had unpicked the outline of a flag lily, it now lay on the table, along with the book and an uneaten sandwich of potted beef. She had sent Ivy to bed with some sweet boiled milk, now she too must go to bed and lie wakeful in the dark.

No one who had ever known Harold in their life slept that night. The hours passed slowly, tormenting them all and daylight brought only a more defined reality.

May had left home early, she must see Annie before her day at the workshop began. Her thoughts had taken her back to Grace's funeral, when Annie had stood alongside her, willing her to survive the ordeal. Now she must strengthen Annie, tell her how much Alfred and the children care for her.

May had been with Annie but ten minutes when Edna arrived. George slept upstairs, oblivious to events around him. Byron padded about the scullery, searching for Harold.

"How is Billy Edna?" Asked Annie concerned for his state of mind, yesterday had taken Billy to the edge.

Edna had tears in her eyes as she described Billy's misery.

"His mam wer' goin' to speak to Josiah, there's no way Billy can face that yard yet, if ever again," declared Edna.

Annie made them both drink hot tea.

"Josiah sent word with Mr.Handley, he is coming to see me today. I feel sorry for him, he must be feeling wretched too," said Annie.

Her machine on the table in the corner was almost hidden by the length of calico she had discarded in her haste.

"Charles came here yesterday, he kindly took George to see Bertha and play with the boys. I have told him the workshop must operate as normal, Harold would want you May, to continue to sew for your family and you Edna, to work towards your wedding. I shall walk George to Mitchell Street after Josiah has been to see me, I need to help Sarah and Samuel, they will be hurting so much. To see George, Harold's child, could only relieve their pain a little, I don't know what else I can do for them."

George was washed and dressed and had eaten his porridge when Josiah crossed the back yard. Byron barked, Josiah's uneven gait over the cobbles made a sound very different to Harold but the 'clop' of the work boots, for an instant aroused Byron's hopes. Filled with disappointment, he sank back onto his old blanket by the fireside chair and buried his face in its rucks.

Annie held Josiah in her arms as he wept, speaking softly but urgently in his ear, begging him to be calm for the child's sake.

At last he became still, "I'm selling the yard to Cheetham Annie," he said twisting his cap which he held between his hands like some old wet rag he was wringing out. "I'm too old for this I should be goin' in the ground, not your Harold, Mrs.Toft cries when I say it but 'tis the truth."

Annie took the cap from his fingers and put it on the table, she held his hands tightly and kissed his cheek.

"Harold would scold you Josiah if he heard you say such things."

She crossed to the door and put her hand in the pocket of Harold's jacket. Returning to Josiah she said, "Go home to your wife and give her a hug, take this simple thing, look upon it whenever you feel despairing, hear Harold's voice as he speaks to you, 'Go on Josiah, it'll do yer good'."

She put the mint in Josiah's old wrinkled palm and closed his fingers over it. An understanding passed between them, unspoken but certain. Before he left, he gave Annie an envelope.

"That's Harold's wages," he said, "there's something from Mrs.Toft an' me as well, if you ever need anything for your boy you just let me know."

The sky was clear, unusually so for the time of year. Smoke rose from the chimney pots but was hastily carried away by the wind. Annie had left the pram at home and set off to walk to Sarah's. She would carry George for part of the way when his little legs grew tired but she needed to hold his hand, not so much to contain him but to inspire her. The pram would have denied her that vital contact and today she doubted herself, she might not cope without it.

Davina had endured the night but could not bear even one more hour. She had sent Ivy to buy a newspaper, knowing that if there had been a dreadful accident at the slaughter yard the previous day, all tongues would be engaged in discussing it and Ivy would return with news which would end this terrible assault on their nerves. Davina heard the door, Ivy was back. Something was wrong, Ivy would have told her immediately if all was well but she had not appeared.

Davina found the young woman weeping into a pile of laundry, trying desperately to stifle her cries. She held Ivy to her, feeling the advancing tears soak through the bodice of her own dress and into her underclothes beneath.

Davina had heard only one word 'Harold' but that single sound had pierced her heart, she felt faint and sick, drained of life, desolate.

She must go to Annie, "Come on now Ivy, we shall hail the first carriage we see. Fetch my coat and purse."

Annie's plight had now overtaken all else, she could not leave Ivy alone in turmoil, the young woman would need to see Frank. They would go to Mitchell Street from Annie's house. Staying at The Park doing nothing could not be right but calling on a family so bereaved, was she entitled?

Davina's mind was in a storm of such magnitude, her head ached from the intensity.

Annie tried to shed the image of Bella from her mind, they had gone to see her and tell her of their walk to Mitchell Street. Bella sat in the cold, the fire unlit, no evidence of breakfast or even a hot drink could be seen, with George at her side Annie could not speak forcibly.

"Well George, grandma hasn't lit her fire yet, we shall have to come back later and have some warm milk and biscuits when grandma has the coals nice and red in the grate and the table laid."

Annie had looked sternly at Bella, her eyes had imparted her dismay at Bella's self indulgence. How often in the past that harsh tone had delivered Bella's doctrine to Annie, no pitying words, no snivelling, just practical help. Why had this belief forsaken her now?

At the bottom of Sherwood Road, where they passed close by The Standard, George asked to be picked up, he had done well to walk that far. Annie took him on her arm and had gone just a few paces when a voice called from a carriage which had stopped in the road.

"Annie wait, Annie, it's us."

Davina asked the driver to help her down. Ivy remained inside, sucking on the end of her gloved finger.

"We heard this morning, my dear Annie, what can we do? Surely we can take you in the carriage, George is weary."

"We are going to see poor Samuel, Sarah and the family. I have to go there, they need to be distracted and I can think of no other way than to put George in their arms. They will bear up for his sake, I know they will."

Annie agreed to ride and with George anchored firmly in Ivy's lap they travelled on.

Nora answered the door, her eyes swollen and red.

"George has come to see you all Nora," Annie said, "he has his new picture book in his pocket." She transferred his hand from her own to Nora's and looked for Sarah and Samuel.

"They are upstairs," said Nora, "Frank has taken the girls to Cyril Lovatt's to explain why he didn't go into work this morning and to buy some buns, mam says she cannot bake today."

Nora was close to breaking down but Annie quickly directed her gaze down to George and the silent appeal was acknowledged. Davina and Ivy had insisted on staying in the carriage until Annie came back to advise them what to do. Not wishing to be an intrusion but desperate to show their love, they sat out of sight, anxiously awaiting her return.

Sarah and Samuel lay on their bed, it was apparent from Samuel's pleading eyes that he searched for some way to comfort his wife.

"Annie lass, talk to Sarah."

The plump homely shape of Harold's mam, curled into a ball like a hedgehog defending itself but Sarah had no prickly spines, no actual aid against harm, the hurt and pain had found their way to her centre.

Samuel, himself distraught, hid all his own suffering in his desire to ease his wife's utter despair.

"I will sit with Sarah for a while, you go to Nora and George. Outside in a carriage Davina and Ivy wait patiently, if you would like me to tell them to leave I will go down and do that right away, they will feel only understanding, no thought of offence."

"You stay here Annie lass, I'll speak to them."

Samuel managed to smile, weakened in its radiance but it was a smile and Annie returned his bravery.

Nora and George studied the picture book. Samuel, in his wisdom, did not interrupt their concentration. Ever polite he went to the carriage.

"Why don't you come in for just a little while, Ivy can make us all a cup o' tea while she waits for Frank, 'e'll be back in a bit. Tell the driver to return in an hour, Sarah is not 'erself as I'm sure you'll appreciate." He swallowed hard, "But she'll want to see you for a few minutes, I know she will."

His voice faltered and he lowered his face as he walked Davina to the door, gathering his composure before George could detect his sadness.

Ivy was grateful to be given a task and busied herself making tea, she remembered from that Sunday when she had helped clear away, where to find the cups and saucers. Voices, low and subdued could be heard in the yard, the four girls entered the scullery first with Eli at their heels. They were pleased to find Ivy there, when Frank saw her he embraced her so tightly Ivy could feel every button on his jacket as they pressed against her frock.

Davina and Samuel, aware of George, talked calmly so not to alarm him. He greeted his four aunts enthusiastically, his early words spoken confidently due to the many hours he had spent with Bella's encouragement.

Annie lifted Sarah's shoulders from the bed and wiped her tears, squeezing her hand as she said, "George would like to see his grandma 'Sarah', I'm afraid his grandma 'Bella' is too morose to be fit company but I know you won't let him down."

It seemed a calculated ploy but Annie needed to coax Sarah from her retreat, little Maggie especially, would not understand, Harold would be bitterly disappointed in Annie if she had not done her best to protect the young ones from heartache.

Held by the strength of both Annie and Samuel all those within the small house sat together, conversed and played with George. The deep bond of love sustained them and when the carriage returned, Annie promised to bring George again in a day or two. Samuel helped Davina into her seat, Ivy handed George up to Annie who sat in the middle, then climbed into the carriage herself. Frank and Nora had been discreetly instructed by Samuel to occupy Sarah and the young sisters while the carriage drew away.

The front door was closed to keep in the warmth and to deter Sarah from watching as her grandson, Harold's only child travelled away from her, inducing once more her agonies of loss.

Samuel seldom stood by the front of his house, his own comings and goings were always through the back yard. Only when he turned from waving back to Davina's frantic goodbyes did his eyes fall directly on the smiley face, scratched into the brick by the front door. Nothing then could stem the tide, his grief engulfed him, he had to get away from No.69, away from this place where he could only be strong, to a sanctuary where he could cry for his first born son, his friend, his Harold.

Samuel sat on the old bench by the compost heap, the allotment offered him freedom to spill the tears. They fell to the ground and were lost in the earth, that same earth his father had trod before him. When Frank reached him he had found calm.

"Come 'ome Dad, mam says to tell you she's bakin' a pie an' if you don't set an example an' eat, then neither will the young 'ens."

Samuel slowly got to his feet, put his arm about Frank's shoulders and said, "Aye, I know Son, I know."

The two walked together, aware of each other's love and concern, both searching for solace, father and son.

The motion of the carriage lulled George to sleep.

"How is Bella?" Asked Davina.

Annie gave a deep sigh, her eyes gave Davina the answer even before she spoke.

"Very depressed, I shall go in to her as soon as I have tended the fire and collected Byron. He may just be the one to lift her from her gloom, he has done so in the past, we seem unable to draw her from her misery."

Annie's hand smoothed George's hair and she kissed his head.

"Tell Bella I shall see her very soon," said Davina, "we understand one another more than you could imagine Annie."

The driver pulled the horse to a halt outside No.24. The emotion that passed between the three women bound them together, reinforcing their friendship. The waving hands, the calls of encouragement, a stark difference to the bleak, cold stare that had caused Annie to shiver at No.11 just a short while ago.

She quickly made up the fire and with Bryon as her cautioned hope she took George to Bella's.

"Make her smile Byron, make her care again." Annie spoke to the dog as they approached the back door, trusting his proven capacity to comprehend and achieve.

Inside the fire was now lit and some food sat on the table. Bella looked more herself and George ran to her eagerly, holding out his favourite story book. Byron dutifully sat by Bella's feet, his patient eyes waiting to see the pages opened, alert as always, in readiness for the sound of Bella's voice as she began to read, sending a procession of words past his ears, soothing, restful, filling him with contentment. George had ensconced himself on his grandma's knee, the time he had spent with Bella whilst Annie worked had brought a great closeness, he leaned back on her chest, his small innocent hands rested on Bella's arms.

Sarah loved George dearly and he always showed happiness at seeing his grandma in Mitchell Street but so many more hours had been spent with Bella, playing, reading and just resting together, as they often did of an afternoon, she had been a constant, as much a part of his day as his mam and dad.

"I'll make the tea," said Annie, "we saw Davina, she said to tell you that very soon she will come to visit and Ivy sends her love too."

Bella paused in the story, "Do Sarah and Samuel have enough help?"

Annie was so relieved to hear Bella speak those words, "I think they will be alright, tending the young ones and concern for each other is their stay now. We cannot plan the funeral and that is hard, Samuel I believe bears up for Sarah but not knowing when the Coroner will grant the release must pain him so much. We cannot think of Harold as at rest, it hurts ……" Annie's voice trembled, her eyes watered.

"The kettle's boiling," declared Bella, "cut the bread very thin it's getting stale, I'll fetch some fresh in the morning. You and George can have your tea in here of an evening, you'll need to stitch more now than you ever did."

The words, to anyone else would have seemed cruel and heartless but to Annie, they were perfect. Aunt Bella was still there, giving the lessons, testing her progress. Failure was not allowed in Bella's classroom, it had given Annie security all her life. There had been times when Annie had misunderstood but at this moment, she grasped the lesson fully.

It was Saturday, Annie sat George to play on the rug beside her and she began to work at her machine. Until she felt aunt Bella was ready to have George as before, Annie had told Charles she would sew at home, returning to the workshop as soon as she could. He had been kind and placed no pressure on her but Annie needed to work. Aunt Bella was quite right, the activity was her salvation. She could stitch a little in the evenings when George was in bed but not wanting to disturb neighbours and create the situation they had encountered in Peverell Street, she would sew only handwork after nine o'clock. Charles had promised to send some smocking for her to do.

'I'll either drop it in myself or send it with Edna', he had said.

It was just after half past five when a voice called through from the back door, "It's only me, can I come in?"

Edna having announced her arrival walked straight to Annie and George in the living room.

"Charles says Mrs.Harbottle chose the silks 'erself an' don't mind in which order you use the colours."

Annie was to smock the bodice of an evening gown. Edna put the package down on the table and burst into tears.

"My dear Edna, what is it?"

Annie moved quickly to comfort her friend. George sat on his chair atop two cushions, to bring him up to the level of the table. He was occupied in sucking the butter off the crust of a fresh loaf, his concern at Edna's distress caused him to suck all the harder and by the time Edna had stopped crying and the two women remembered his presence the crust had been reduced to the shape of a finger.

Reassured by their smiles, he donated the soggy stick of bread to Byron and asked politely, "Nother one please."

It amused Annie and Edna and the mood was immediately lightened.

Over a cup of warming tea Edna poured out her anguish.

"It's Billy, I'm afeared 'e'll keel over dead wi' Harold. 'E's took work at the chain makers, begged 'em to let 'im start there an' then. I met one o' the other men this mornin' on me way to work, 'e said Billy took off 'is shirt and picked up the hammer and pounded that hot iron, poundin' poundin' non stop all day. The man said Billy sweat that 'ard and cried that much, the tears an' sweat made a pool o' water about 'is boots that deep, it crept up the legs of 'is trousers, 'e wer' wet through. The muscles across 'is back knotted like the chains 'e wer' makin' and 'is 'ands bled where the blisters turned 'is flesh raw. If 'e killed that bloody buggerin' beast once 'e killed it a thousand bloody times. I know I'm swearin' Annie, God forgive me the child's 'ere but I can't 'elp meself. Billy'll kill 'isself Annie 'e'll bloody well kill 'isself."

Annie took Edna's hands, "Tell Billy I need to see him, tell him it's important, for Harold's sake I must speak with him."

George now slept in his little bed and Byron lay by the hearth, the poor dog had searched the yard and garden each day, even now Annie sensed he watched, hoping the latch would lift and Harold's voice would call out. He waited on the familiar sound of Harold's dinner bag as it fell to the scullery table when he took the strap from his shoulder, the fond pat of Byron's head which always followed the kisses Harold had first given his wife and son.

The dog's eyes focused on the doorway, it was half past nine, Annie had made herself a warm drink. Before beginning the preparation for the smocked bodice she needed to gather exactly, the material to the desired width. She sat on the chair where Harold would rest, so often she would join him and they would share accounts of their day. Annie longed for her Harold but at that first threat of tears she steeled herself. Inside the pain grew day on day but outside, that strength she showed the world, refused to yield, it allowed no easement, the hurt intense.

A quiet tapping came to the back door. Byron sprung to his feet and stood in anticipation by the dolly tub. It was a late hour for a visitor, Annie opened the door just a crack and was about to ask the caller's identity when Billy's voice said.

"I've come as quick as I could Annie."

She opened the door to a sight more forlorn than words could describe.

"Edna said you needed somethin' for Harold."

"Come in Billy, it's warm by the fire."

His face looked cadaverous, since Wednesday he seemed to have lost all the flesh from his cheeks and neck. His eyes retreated from the life they should reflect, his hands, Annie shuddered at the sight of his hands, they appeared beaten, thrashed, near' through to the bone. Her stomach turned but she must not weaken.

"Sit down Billy."

His movements were restricted by strained muscles, he winced as he lowered himself to the seat. Annie drew up a chair opposite him, she stirred the coals and the blaze, for that instant, spoke to her. It was roused, angry, Harold would be angry.

"I shall need to sew many hours to keep us going Billy but no matter how many hours I sit at that machine, I cannot possibly pay two lots of rent. Aunt Bella is reliant on me as well as George, I cannot continue to live in this house. The rent is paid up to the end of November but before it becomes due again, I shall move back in with aunt Bella. There is more space there and as George grows we shall need that extra room. You are Harold's best friend, he may not be here now Billy but that changes nothing, you will always be Harold's best friend."

He began to weep.

"Look at me Billy and listen, Harold speaks to us both, I can hear his words just as if he were here in this room. Marry Edna, get wed as soon as you can, move into this little house, the rent is modest and it is a home already."

Billy spoke slowly. "We wer' workin' in the cuttin' shed, me an' Harold that mornin', I can remember every word 'e said. We was 'avin' a laugh like allus 'don't know what you're missin' Billy Dodds, I can picture you down Trentside wi' 'arf a dozen young 'ens, teachin' 'em 'ow to fish' that's what 'e said Annie, them was 'is words."

"Do it for Harold." Annie dare not squeeze his hands, they were so raw, she lay her fingers on his knee. "Marry Edna, he's telling you, for him, please Billy."

Then Annie found herself saying those words so familiar. "Live Billy, take your Edna and live."

Two weeks passed before James Handley delivered the news that the Coroner's release had been granted. The funeral could now take place. Samuel would not relent, Annie had tried desperately to persuade him to let her pay the undertaker, she still had the ten guineas from Saul.

'He's my lad, my son, I'll pay. God forbid you should ever feel it lass but with every breath in me I know that it must be so'.

Samuel was so passionate on the subject, Annie could do no other than abide by his wishes. She thought back to the time when Harold worried so much over his father's efforts for their wedding.

'E'd be pushin' that barro' an' sweepin' chimneys beyond the city boundaries and into the next to earn money enough, 'e'd pauper 'isself'.

That had been Harold's firm belief. It had troubled her greatly, Sarah's house so full of children, all to be fed and clothed.

The funeral beat at Annie's chest from within and without. Bertha had come to collect George, taking all three boys back to Hood Street until after their tea. Aunt Bella had been so quiet and withdrawn Annie dare not leave George with her today, she had been adamant in her refusal to attend the funeral.

'I'll stay here with the dog', she declared.

Annie had not pressed her, Bella would prefer to be out of sight at any time and this day would drive her even further into the shadows. At least her friend Byron would comfort her in her mourning.

Nora kept the girls busy at home. Samuel carried Sarah through the ordeal by his ever unfailing devotion. Frank took Annie's arm and never once let it go. Davina held on to Ivy and physically shook the entire time. Timid May found comfort in Charles, who with the maturity the loss of Enid had brought him, recognised her need of a steadying arm. Poor Josiah was guided by Mrs.Toft, he seemed too numbed to function. But it was Billy, who despite Edna's constant loving support, could not contain his utter desolation. It was the sight of Billy, a man reduced to a shell, barely able to be restrained from falling into the grave with his friend that tore at Annie the most.

She had not flinched at the coffin, nor as it had been lowered into the earth. Every bedtime she said goodnight to her husband, every morning she kissed his jacket as she would kiss him as he left for work. Harold was not in that box, she must observe with everyone else but her Harold was not there.

Billy's despair wrenched Annie's thoughts, she could think of nothing else. Harold was willing her to take Billy away from this, to cease his torment.

At last they could leave the cemetery.

"Frank, I need to go with Billy and Edna." Annie could only hope that Samuel and Sarah would understand. "Tell the family I shall come to see them with George tomorrow but look at Billy Frank, Harold is pleading with me to help his friend."

Frank kissed Annie's cheek, "I can hear him too, go on Annie, I'll tell mam and dad, they'll understand."

The three walked back to Winchester Street. The day had been mercifully dry but the sky was heavy and the air cold. Billy walked between Annie and Edna, both held an arm, keeping him safe from collapse. Finally his tears subsided, their pace was purposeful, not one of the three had any desire to stop for conversation and politely but firmly they acknowledged well meant sympathies but kept on walking.

No.24 welcomed them with its warmth. Annie had banked up the fire before leaving the house, soon they wrapped their chilled fingers around warming cups of tea and Annie allowed no delay in finalising the plan.

Edna and Billy were to be married very quietly, as was their wish, the following Saturday week. Morely and Ada would be witnesses. Annie would move George and herself into aunt Bella's by the day before. Annie had spoken with the landlord, his charm and manners still as becoming as that day he had met with Harold and herself to show them over the property for rent. However, he held no objection to the new tenants, Charles had given them an excellent character reference at Annie's request and the man, unpleasant though he was, satisfied that his money was safe, promised to deliver the new rent book to Mr.and Mrs.William Dodds at No.24 Winchester Street on Saturday week, when he would receive a month's rent in advance.

Edna loved Annie even more than her own sisters.

"When we 'ave our first kid you shall be its best ever aunty."

She kissed Annie with such affection it made her laugh, the first time she had felt actual joy since Harold died.

The following afternoon, Nora and Sarah greeted Annie with open arms. George was seized upon with delight and they chatted together freely, inside them still an extreme ache but their determination to do as Harold would wish dominated their days from now on.

"Samuel is workin' Annie dear, usually 'tis real quiet this time o' year, folks have got their fires lit day and night, don't want their chimneys sweepin' 'til the weather gets warmer. As luck would 'ave it, Davina is needin' a lot o' work doin' on that big house of 'ers in The Park. There's paintin' to do, she says all 'er windows need doin'. That wisteria plant 'as grown into the eaves, Samuel 'as got to cut it all back an' Davina wants them fancy gates at the front rubbin' down and seen to. 'E reckons it will be a good two week's work by the time 'e's trimmed all the hedges and shrubs Davina wants tidied up."

Annie smiled but said nothing. Dear Davina, a thoughtful friend with a heart as big as Samuel's laughter. If anyone could bring back that great loud laugh it would be Davina. Samuel would be ever grateful for the answer to his dilemma, he would work hard and honestly and Davina would relish every moment his company allowed her to feel part of the wonderful Boucher family.

The week had been busy, Annie stitched all the hours she could. She'd packed clothes and bedding into bundles, taking a little across the street each day. Davina had been content to know Edna and Billy would be grateful for the bed and Sarah had dismissed instantly, any suggestion of the items in No.24 which had come from her house being brought back.

'Goodness me, let them two dear young people 'ave anythin' that'll make 'em 'appy, bless their 'earts'.

Annie needed George's little bed to go alongside her own in her old room at Bella's, it would be one of the last things to go and Annie herself could dismantle it to carry over. Billy and Edna had come one evening earlier in the week to help take to aunt Bella's, the sewing machine, chest of drawers and the washstand. It would be difficult to manage without these but almost everything else could stay to help make a home for the newlyweds. Bella had not expressed any opinion on the matter, she seemed not to be concerned one way or the other. Annie was on her way to aunt Bella's with a box of items, when a carriage turned into the street. George and Byron were already there, Bella and the happy little boy were working on a jigsaw puzzle.

The carriage revealed Davina.

"Is it convenient to call on Bella for just a little while? I really won't stay long."

Annie was pleased, Bella should have company beyond George and herself.

"Of course, but you might well be called upon to help with the puzzle, it is one they have not done before and has quite a lot of blue sky. A few moments ago when I took some books in there, I sensed George was being a bit too eager to place anything blue together, whether the pieces fitted or not."

Annie chuckled, Davina admired so much her pleasant manner, her incredible fortitude throughout these dreadful weeks.

"How much more do you have to bring?" Asked Davina.

"Not very much now, by this evening we shall be installed."

Davina gave instruction to the driver and as they walked through the entry she whispered, "I have brought some brandy, it would do Bella well to drink a little each bedtime, she has no strong held views on the evils of alcohol I hope."

"Aunt Bella has no other type of view but strong," said Annie with a smile. "However, I think in a medicinal measure she would find brandy quite acceptable. I have begun to worry at how small her appetite seems to be, I shall see that each night she drinks some sweetened boiled milk with brandy. Thank you Davina." Annie paused outside the back door and planted a kiss on her cheek.

Inside old and young worked industriously at the jigsaw. Annie detected a look of disgruntled surprise in Bella's expression but she was gracious enough to offer Davina a seat but immediately issued the caution.

"Don't knock the tray, we've done nearly half, we can't find the end of the cat's tail and George wants to see if it's white like the paws."

The picture on the puzzle was obviously a black cat sitting on a wall with the blue sky in the background. The tiny fingers chose a piece and amazingly it fitted, the tip of the cat's tail was indeed white. George was truly proud of his achievement and in his excitement and delight cried out in his wholesome infant voice, "Buggersham Castle."

There was a moment of total silence. Annie had never before heard George repeat those words of Harold's. Bella had been completely taken aback but Davina erupted into gales of laughter.

"Bless the child Annie." Then turning to Bella with tears of joy in her eyes said, "You have not been George's only teacher Bella, he has taken lessons from a master, the finest we know."

Davina kissed the child's head and cried out jubilantly, "Buggersham Castle."

Even Bella managed a smile, it was a precious moment, one they would all cherish.

While the opportunity presented itself Annie decided to fetch the little bed, the three around the jigsaw were content at their activity and if she could put George's bed in her room and prepare it for his bedtime, then the few little ornaments still on the shelf she could gather after tea and lock up No.24 until Billy and Edna collected the key the next day.

Annie wished she could ask them to come to aunt Bella's for a meal following their wedding but that would not do. Bella's moods made it ever difficult to predict the nature of the days, Annie knew their wedding ceremony would not be that blissfully happy occasion it should. Harold's absence from their lives at such a time, left them both but especially Billy, with an emptiness which not even the first elation of marriage could rectify. Bringing them into the company of Bella, should her spirits be dour, might be disastrous for the newlyweds already struggling with painful emotions.

George having found the long searched for cat's tail now felt fulfilled and his concentration on the jigsaw waned.

Davina produced a small bag of dolly mixtures and his dextrous little fingers pursued the contents for his favourite, the orange jelly one. Triumphant, he sat alongside Byron on the rug, sucking his prize completely at peace with his surroundings.

Bella made some tea, chatting with Davina as she did so, the topic of their conversation being Samuel.

"That man works like a Trojan," remarked Davina. "It requires the sternest ultimatum to bring him to rest for even a few minutes. Yesterday I told him that if he did not come down from the ladder at once, then I would climb up myself and drag him down by his braces."

Slightly curious at the notion Bella said, "And what was his reply?"

"He said if I added my weight to the ladder, it would surely break in half and Ivy would be mortally embarrassed at having to disentangle her likely future father-in-law and her mistress from a most compromising situation. I have to admit, I secretly quite relished the prospect," Davina giggled roguishly.

Bella put a plate in her lap with little gentility saying, "Have some bloater paste," and with a heavily weighted, "tut-tut", poked at the fire, then continued to, "tut-tut", as she walked to the scullery to get her own cup of tea.

Annie appeared carrying the sections of bed, she propped them up just inside the back door calling out, "Only his mattress now," and disappeared again.

"Poor Annie, how it must hurt to leave that house where her happiest memories must abide," said Davina.

Bella did not speak but put a piece of bread and butter in George's hand and sat looking at her cup.

"Aren't you having anything to eat Bella?" Asked Davina.

"I've had enough," came back the reply. The words were vaguely expressed and Davina felt they did not refer to her appetite at all. George brought the subject to an abrupt end when he declared he needed a wee.

Davina took him to the privy where his elevated position standing on the bench called for considerable attention to aim. On completing the process successfully and remembering the reaction he had earlier won with his new words, he clapped his hands and said, "Buggersham Castle."

"Can you hear this Harold Boucher? He is his father's son." Davina whispered the words to herself and fought back the tears as she hoisted George's rompers back into place.

Annie had returned with the mattress and Davina, looking at the clock, gathered her coat and bag.

"I shall be off now, I can hear a carriage in the street. I shall come again to visit you all, whether you like it or not Bella. I do hope it will be very soon that I see you and George at The Park Annie."

Later that evening George slept upstairs and Bella, having had no chance of a nap in the afternoon sat nodding before the warmth of the hearth.

"I shall go for those few bits and pieces now, I won't be long," said Annie.

Opening the door on her little house for the last time was hard but it would soon be the home of her two good friends and to have them so near was a happy thought. She would put the things in the basket but first make sure all upstairs was as clean as it could be and leave a note of congratulation on the table with a small cake she had baked for them. A last brush over the scullery floor and some 'Zeebo' on the range finished the cleaning tasks, she could do nothing about the tub but it would soon be Monday. Carefully she lifted down from the shelf her little china dog, the gift from Edna, a small earthenware pot in which she kept the spills, two candlesticks and the picture with the verse which Alfred had given her the day they put up the curtains at May's, she read the words again;

May every window open to the sun

and life for you be full of pleasant ways,

so that you may, as the seasons run,

look out upon a world of happy days.

'We shall travel the world with our children, see mountains, forests and great lakes'. In the stillness Harold's voice spoke to her so clearly, it was then at the moment Annie heard him dream of the future, that grief's fists broke through and the pain which had pounded her heart found release. It poured in such measure, the skin across her cheeks stung from the saltiness of her tears, her throat tightened from the intensity of her sobbing. Her hands shook so severely she could not hold the basket, she lay it on the floor and she knelt beside it, her head buried in the seat of the chair, where so many times Harold had taken her on his knee and swept away with his gentleness, all the cares of the day.

Annie was startled by the hand on her shoulder, Bella stood over her. "Time to come home, there is no one here for you, he will be where you and the child are. Let Billy and Edna fill this place with their ways, Harold will follow you wherever you go, come now, George might wake."

Annie picked up the basket and returned the picture to the shelf, Bella made no question, they crossed the street in silence.

The fire was low in the grate, Bella did not sit.

"I am tired, I shall go up to bed now."

Annie remembered the brandy but it would wait until tomorrow, she was anxious to go to George, to find comfort in his gentle breathing.

"I'll make up the fire and put Byron out for a minute then I'll come up too" she said.

Bella had reached the fourth tread when she quietly called down, "Bolt the door and put out the lamp."

Annie had come home.

CHAPTER TWENTY THREE

"Cooo-ee", Mrs.Bacon's voice called after Annie, she was just leaving for the workshop and stopped short of the entry on hearing Winnie's obvious desire for her to wait a moment.

"Annie I know you're up to your eyes, it bothers me, I said to Ted only last night, that lass'll meet 'erself comin' back one o' these days. Now tomorrow I'm havin' our Jack while Elsie 'as 'er feet done, she'll collect the others from school on 'er way 'ome. My poor Elsie 'as allus suffered wi' 'er feet, for a young woman they do seem awful troublesome. You should see 'em when she takes off 'er stockin's, you'd think somebody 'ad tried to knit one purl one wi' 'er toes. I told 'er when she wer' younger, feet was never meant to be crammed up in fashion, they should be free to spread. 'Spread mother', she said, 'how much further do you want 'em to spread, they're nearly in Mapperley now'. 'Tis 'er father's fault, he wer' wearing size 11 when 'e wer' only fourteen and all our married life he's been in 13s. I remember we took the kids to the swimmin' baths one time and when Derry Murphy seen Ted's feet, 'e said to me, 'missus, I reckon 'e could walk on water wi' them, we're lookin' for a bloke as can perform miracles, accordin' to our Rosie, she's 'ad an immaculate conception, told 'er mam she's not been closer to a man than th'other side o' treadle'. Anyroad, by the time Elsie 'ad finished growin' she wer' wearin' 8s. So that'll be alright then, you just bring your George round after dinner and 'e can play wi' Jack. You don't need to worry, I shall keep me eye on 'em, they can 'ave a bit o' pastry to roll out an' some currants, it'll give Bella a rest, she does look slight these days Annie. Now you best run along dear or you're goin' to be late, by-eee."

Winnie was kindness itself, however busy and she seemed always to be busy. Annie felt anxious on the occasions that George went to play with Winnie's youngest grandson, Jack would start school in the autumn and George was still very young. Nor had Jack lost his penchant for climbing, only the previous weekend he had caused a commotion in the yard when he decided to scramble onto the lid of the water butt and from there to climb onto the roof of the coal shed, where he could cross to the tin roof of the privy. Ted Bacon, sitting with pipe and baccy over the tub below, was serenaded by young Jack who dragged a stick across the rough tin sheets for musical accompaniment as he sang 'I'm the King of the Castle, you're the dirty old rascal'. Ted irate at being disturbed in the midst of a man's God given time for reflection, cut short his period of repose, retrieved his grandson from the roof and proceeded to wallop his bared backside with such a growing fury that the smoke form his pipe now rose in volume to match. The 'King of the Castle', protested the indignity with loud screams and Winnie, able only to see the smoke rising from above the shed and hearing Jack's tortured cries, ran out with a bucket of water which came very close to being emptied over both of them.

"The sooner that lad starts school the better, let the headmaster put a withy over his arse a few times, little sod," had been Ted's verdict.

It was a fine afternoon and Alfred Brooks sat in his doorway. Since Harold died Annie had noticed how much more readily Alfred made eye contact and spoke when she stopped briefly to say hello, she sensed a deep sympathy. Then one day Alfred told her how he had lost his legs, crushed in an accident at the pit, he had come very close to death.

'Now Annie I watch life go by from this legless chair and Mrs.Brooks carries me around like some grotesque infant. Your Harold wouldn't have wanted this, sometimes I wish they'd have let me go back then, in the black depths o' the pit'. Alfred had heard only that Harold had been crushed and Annie had not found the words to explain other. Today he had managed a brief smile and Annie, aware of his despondency, valued his efforts.

Since Christmas the days had offered little respite, it was just before New Year that Bertha took a tumble in the yard at Hood Street, ice between the cobbles had caused her to slip, the outcome might have been much worse had she not been able to reach out and ease her fall by clutching at the clothes line. Fortunately, no bones had been broken but Bertha had been badly bruised and very stiff and sore for weeks afterwards. Annie had tried to help her as much as she could. Bertha stubbornly refused to give in to her aches but it was evident to anyone watching that the incident had slowed down her movements and the demands of caring for two young boys had begun to take their toll.

Annie was now at the workshop each afternoon but aunt Bella's health weighed heavily on her mind. George and his grandmother enjoyed each other's company very much, Bella continued to teach him through their reading and constructive play but her meals had become smaller and smaller. Her clothes fell loosely from her figure and despite the efforts of Annie, Davina and Sarah, Bella's interest in life around her seemed to ebb slowly away.

The one truly rewarding thing was the obvious happiness of Edna and Billy. The little home at No.24 had received new occupants with an easy transition, Edna's pride at crossing their own threshold and keeping house for her husband pleased Annie tremendously. Billy had settled to work at the chainmakers, it was gruelling but at least Billy now paced himself alongside the other men and his loyal nature and warm character had endeared him to the workforce. Few of them had not heard of the accident at Josiah's, Billy's anguish at the loss of his friend had touched them all and they had rallied round him, determined to get him through this loneliest of times.

Violet Raithby was proving to be an able addition to the workshop, although very much younger than May, she had quickly developed a friendship with the timid, older seamstress. May had taught her a number of new skills which enabled Violet to work more confidently on the more elaborate garments. A part of their walk home was along the same route, the comfortable conversation seemed to lighten the prospect of such a walk in the cold, dark evenings of winter. As Violet had pointed out, one late afternoon in January when blizzard like conditions held Nottingham in an icy grip, 'You two are lucky livin' in the same street as your work'.

Annie was relieved to have reached almost the end of March, as she opened the creaking old gates and her eyes caught sight of a snowdrop, bravely growing out from a small patch of earth at the front of the workshop, she felt able to hope that the coming months of kinder weather would inspire Bella to thrive too.

Charles called Annie through to the office.

"Mrs.Appleyard has requested that you go to her house to measure her for another gown, she is most insistent, she wants only Mrs.Boucher to oversee the matter, next Wednesday afternoon at two thirty. I shall arrange for Meade to take you and bring you back."

Annie sighed, "I really don't know why it can only be me, May is more experienced."

Charles laughed, then lowering his voice said, "May would be struck dumb by Mrs.Appleyard's authority, she has a certain air of importance don't you think?"

"Well if it is to be me, I can walk there and back, you won't need to arrange a carriage. It will be the beginning of April, I shall be perfectly alright on foot, there could be no more than a shower. The sample bag is hardly a heavy item to carry and you could not accurately know at what time to instruct Meade to return for me. I shall be quick about it and be back here to get on with the order for Blackmore's."

Annie didn't relish the notion of being far away from home at present, she would prefer to be in a position to leave as soon as the measurements were taken and the material chosen, than to have to wait patiently for Meade over tea and fondants at Mrs.Appleyard's.

"We need to be turning out more bread and butter stuff Annie," said Charles. "More shirts, underwear, work clothes but the facility here is too small. I'm thinking of renting a place where we could produce 'stock in trade' and keep the workshop here for fancy clothes and heavy drapes, what do you think?"

Annie's own affairs were so fraught already, Bella's health, the difficulty of working enough hours to support them, she had concerns for Bertha too, surely Charles must be aware that the situation at Hood Street could not continue for much longer.

"Where are these premises?" She asked.

"Basford, I haven't seen them yet but they should be about the right size. I'd have to borrow from the bank for the equipment but if I buy secondhand it would be manageable."

"You need to be cautious, without substantial orders it could be difficult to persuade the bank. There is for me the problem of aunt Bella's failing health, if she doesn't improve with the warmer weather, then I shall no longer be able to work anywhere other than at home. You too must recognise the tiredness in Bertha, if you expand the business then you will almost certainly extend the hours you work. I really don't know what to say Charles." Annie looked anxious.

"Well until after I've looked at the place we'll reserve judgement, best not to say anything to the others just in case." Charles winked and resumed his paperwork.

Annie was reluctant to appear negative, Charles had turned himself around from an arrogant, selfish, unreliable character, to a man with a capacity for caring, a desire to progress and achieve with the skill of listening, which he previously had no measure of but now displayed regularly.

The following days passed without incident, George survived his session of play with Jack and brought home to Annie and Bella, two hand crafted currant pastries which had been pronounced 'far too good to eat' and would be saved to show to grandma Sarah.

Annie, in what few quiet moments she had, thought about Charles' plans. He had said nothing more on the subject and given the complicated circumstances surrounding them both, Annie was disinclined to prompt him.

The day of Annie's visit to Mrs.Appleyard had arrived, all necessary requirements gathered into the bag, Annie set off at a brisk pace. Aunt Bella had seemed quiet all morning, George was placid in temperament and generally well behaved but at eighteen months, he needed activity, his afternoon nap had become shorter. Annie knew the time was fast approaching when she would be forced to tell Charles that it was no longer possible for her to be at the workshop. She would stitch by day as much as she could and likewise through the night but the need to be at home with her son and Bella must now take priority.

"Ah, Mrs.Boucher, in fact I shall call you Annie, I feel we are sufficiently acquainted. Before we proceed I must tell you how very saddened both Mr.Appleyard and myself were to hear of your husband's death. Dear Mr.Appleyard has devoted his entire life to matters of health and welfare. Indeed, his involvement on Boards and Committees continues still. A terrible tragedy my dear, we extend our condolences to you and your family."

"Thank you, it is kind of you both to feel concern," said Annie, she smiled and quickly opened the bag to reveal the samples. Mrs.Appleyard was very decisive, it required only ten minutes for the pale blue satin to be chosen and as with the gown Annie had made just after Saul died, it was to be very simple in style. At Annie's suggestion, a panel of fine pin tucks down the middle of the bodice, just enough to relieve the plainness, allowing the elegance of the skirt to catch the eye. The good lady was fortunate in having a slim figure for her age, as Annie observed, satin, falling gracefully over slender hips gave a classic look to a simple design. Measurements were accurately recorded, Annie was ready to leave.

"Would you like some tea before you go?" Asked Mrs.Appleyard kindly.

"I won't if you don't mind, I need to return to Winchester Street as soon as possible." Annie did not want to appear unfriendly but she was anxious at being away from George, the few yards to the workshop were far enough, this situation gave her no peace of mind.

"Take care my dear, I shall look forward to my fitting when we shall talk again."

Annie walked back hurriedly, thinking about the conversation they had exchanged. Mrs.Appleyard was a curious mix of many things, obviously moving in wealthy and important social circles, a lifestyle which would seem to deny her very little, yet her concerns lay with the poor, inadequate housing, sanitation, education and all the social issues commonly ignored by the majority of professional people, she was stoic in her voluntary work, Annie liked her.

The workshop was occupied with another order for the boys school, having given Charles the details of Mrs.Appleyard's gown she resumed her sewing of uniform jackets. Settled back into the afternoon routine, Annie had lost herself in the sound of the machines and Edna's happy rendition of the latest Marie Lloyd, to which she did great justice as she produced the sleeve linings to be eventually united with Annie's jackets.

The front door opened, just enough to enable Mrs.Bacon's head to look around it and call across the room to Annie.

"Don't panic, I've made 'er a cup o' tea and she says she's feelin' better but I told 'er, I was comin' 'ere to fetch you. George is alright, 'e's sharin' arrowroot biscuits wi' the dog. Bella called to me over the wall when I wer' pickin' in the washin', she 'ad a bit of a funny turn."

Annie ran through the back room to Charles.

"I have to go, aunt Bella's had a turn," she grabbed her coat from the hook and glancing quickly at May and Edna dashed outside to Winnie.

"Bella looked as grey as the flags when I first went in there Annie, but she's got a bit more colour now. I remember it wer' this time o' year when me grandmother took bad. Me mam said, 'she's got May hill to climb', I thought it wer' a funny thing to say but blow me come the 14th o' May she died in 'er chair wi' millet for the canary still in 'er 'and. Barely made it half way up the hill. Very next day they found the canary on its back wi' its toes turned up, she thought the world o' that bird and the bird loved 'er, they reckoned it died of a broken 'eart. Grandfather lived another ten years after that, most of 'em wi' Ida Toms, she had a linnet, me father reckoned grandad only went in wi' 'er 'cause he wer' too soddin' mean to waste the millet."

They reached the entry, Winnie's tongue not idle once in spite of their haste.

Bella sat back in the chair, her face did indeed look a shade of sickly grey, she protested the need for Annie to have been called from her work.

"I'm alright now, I told Winnie the tea had revived me."

Mrs.Bacon was having none of it. "Now what would you 'ave thought o' me Bella Pownall, if I'd left you 'ere wi' the child an' you'd dropped dead, you'd 'ave told me I wer' brainless."

If the situation hadn't been so fraught, Winnie's contradiction in terms might have been amusing but Annie felt life was closing in on her and George, the pressure from all sides ever advancing.

At least stitching at her machine in Bella's front room was no longer the miserable, perishing cold activity it had been throughout the winter. Even with her coat on Annie had felt frozen, her toes could not feel sensation and so her feet on the treadle had been guided more by instinct than by touch.

The fact that Edna lived just over the street and that Charles could easily call, enabled the completed work to be collected and cloth to be brought with no difficulty, sometimes when one or the other came, Bella would be already in bed.

Annie had noticed her displeasure at Charles' visits and yet there seemed to be no reason for her attitude. He was always polite, he took time to play with George for a few minutes and on one occasion, brought a lovely bunch of daffodils for them. Yet her mood would always become severe following any collection or delivery made by Charles. Edna however, appeared to be acceptable, arousing no ill temper. So it was and Annie could not afford to spend time pondering it. She worked through most of the night hours, she had only Mrs.Bacon's household to worry about. The other wall joined the lower entry and Winnie had declared quite forcibly, 'better to hear your machine Annie dear than to be deaf'.

Mrs.Bacon's own front room and the bedroom above it were seldom occupied, Annie's by night stitching, thankfully created no problem. It was through the day she found little time for her work, George needed her company as he played for at least some of the time and Bella's retreating presence made it almost impossible to concentrate, ever watchful in case she had another turn or should stumble when she stirred from her chair, only when she slept safely in her bed could Annie feel able to fix her mind on sewing.

May had accompanied Charles to Mrs.Appleyard's for her first fitting. On being told of Annie's need to attend her aunt and to work from home accordingly she voiced dismay, 'Oh dear, deary, deary me, I do hope the situation might be resolved soon'.

Annie for the first time had used money from Saul's gift to her, in order to pay rent for the month. Bella's condition had shown no improvement, Annie sent word to Dr.Baragruy, in the hope he may find some way of reversing the decline. Annie had made nourishing beef tea, even tried to persuade Bella to take a little stout to strengthen her but Davina's brandy, Winnie's plates of freshly baked cakes and all Annie's efforts had not resulted in any change.

When a knock came at the door, it was with relief that Annie led the doctor upstairs to see Bella. George played contentedly but the child's expression at the doctor's arrival bore a certain awareness of serious events and he stayed close to Byron.

"Hello Miss Pownall, everyone is concerned, they miss your company, let's see if we can make you feel better shall we?"

Annie smiled at Bella, "I'll go downstairs to George."

Leaving the doctor to speak with Bella alone, she hoped might allow them to talk more freely.

"What do you keep in that bag of yours to prescribe for damnation doctor, is there really an elixir to defy the Almighty?" She spoke slowly, deliberately.

"Your family need you Bella, they love you."

He saw in her eyes a vagueness he had experienced before, in circumstances where the individual had no one left in the world with whom they could share their thoughts, their existence as it had become. Bella had people who cared for her, who genuinely wanted her to be in their lives, she had no reason to retreat.

"Some things doctor cannot be cured, they can only end. It is not a failing on your part, you have no influence over this, no more have I. All my life I have been of good health, even now you will find no ailment. Believe me doctor when I tell you, Annie and the child will be better placed, all we need is an end."

In spite of her own strange prognosis, he examined her. She was pitifully thin but her chest held no congestion, her pulse was steady, her blood pressure within acceptable levels. As he picked up his bag to leave, Bella cautioned him, still her authority prevailed.

"Tell her you can find nothing of significance, she doesn't need to hear soft words, she needs help, tell her to stop worrying and get on with her stitching. And you doctor, administer to the sick and leave 'the damned' to 'Himself'."

Annie waited downstairs.

"I am of the opinion there is no disease, nor has she any fever, her weakened physical state troubles me so I am leaving a tonic which you can hopefully persuade her to take, it is quite palatable. Has there been in the past, a dramatic event, something which might have affected her strongly at the time?"

"Aunt Bella is one of the most private people I believe you could ever meet. I have known only one person to reach her spirit, to share her soul."

"Then perhaps they would help, could we send for them?" Said Dr. Baragruy hopefully.

Annie drew a deep breath, "If only we could but Harold cannot come, can he doctor?" She faltered.

He quickly distracted her, "Let me have a look at those lovely teeth young man," he stooped to give George his attention, "my word they would soon work through a nice piece of chocolate."

He produced a small bar from his pocket and gave it to George. "Don't worry mum, he will still eat his tea."

He rubbed his hand over the wavy hair on top the child's head.

"Occupy your mind with your sewing Annie, I don't believe there is anything more we can do but hope the tonic may find her spirit."

"How much do I owe you doctor?" Asked Annie.

"Let's see if it works first," he smiled encouragement and waved cheerily but he feared for Annie. So soon after Harold was cruel but he found Bella Pownall's words were not easily dismissed. His small bottle of tonic was ill equipped to divert any spirit which Bella had set on its course.

The days passed swiftly, one running into the other with no interlude. Surprisingly, Bella took the tonic without fuss. A letter had come from Davina, she would visit as soon as she could but both Ivy and herself had cough and cold, not until they were free from germs would they come. Dear Davina, ever thoughtful but Annie would have liked to see her friend.

Edna called in regularly and always asked if Annie needed any errands run, but Davina being so much older, brought with her a reassurance and some days Annie felt very unsure indeed.

George had given in to tiredness, Annie tiptoed from their bedroom to return to her sewing. Bella's voice called softly.

"Come here for a minute."

Bella slowly patted the bed with her thin white fingers. Annie sat by her on the edge of the bed, tucking the hand under the covers to keep it warm, Bella seemed completely calm. Often when Annie brought her drink or washed her she would show agitation but today was different. The hand came from under the covers once more and searched for Annie's fingers. Her words fell on Annie's ears like an echo as though they had first been uttered in another place.

"Always remember what you are."

Annie held Bella's hand tightly as she asked, "What am I?"

Bella's eyes were focused so intently on Annie that it made her feel afraid. Then Bella's lips formed a soft smile, "You are my pupil, Bella Pownall's pupil," she spoke so slowly, every word carefully emphasised. "You are my Annie, mine," and then the words Annie had waited all her life to hear. "I love you, go down and do your sewing, I'm tired."

Annie could not stitch, instead she sat in Bella's chair by the hearth and lifted Byron on to her lap, his weight over her legs and the warmth he generated comforted her, she stroked his head and neck. Harold's little wooden horse stood on the mantelpiece, a light film of dust from the fire coated its smooth back. Just the ticking of the clock, a random movement of the coals in the fire penetrated the silence. She closed her eyes, no sound of her machine, nothing but peace, Annie would have bottled its goodness, preserved it for another day if she could. For several minutes she smoothed the fur over Byron's neck, suspended between sadness of the past and trepidation for the future, she held the moment for as long as possible. A murmur from upstairs alerted Byron, he jumped from Annie's knees to the floor and looked at her in anticipation. All was quiet in Bella's room.

George drank some milk and ate a biscuit. Annie banked up the fire and whilst she could, took George and Byron for a walk. The arboretum was putting on a splendid show of colour and the pigeons picked around George's feet where he had scattered a handful of oats. His happy chatter and the sweet smell of blossom, lifted Annie from a deep feeling of anxiety. For the hour they spent there, her heart was lighter, so many things troubled her, not least their financial situation but for these precious few moments, Annie allowed the sun's warmth, the eagerness of her lovely little boy and Byron's deep loving eyes, to drive all worries away. They walked home, Annie and George singing nursery rhymes. Mrs.Bacon's front step gleamed ahead like a lighthouse, scrubbed this morning just as tirelessly as it had been scrubbed each Tuesday morning since Annie and Bella had come to live next door.

The house was warm and whilst Annie made tea, George built with his wooden blocks. She prepared a tray with a small bowl of clear soup and very thin bread and butter, she carried it upstairs to Bella.

"Try just a little," said Annie, she helped her up the pillows and put the tray across her lap, "I'll see to George and then I'll bring your tonic."

When she returned Bella had drunk the soup but the bread and butter remained untouched.

"That was all I wanted," said Bella looking at Annie, her manner still calm and serene.

George had gone to bed and Annie set about her work, she had shirts to sew, her fingers had completed more collarless working man's shirts than she would care to count, her actions almost automated, so familiar the process. After a few hours her back ached, she would allow herself five minutes by the fire, it was just after 11o'clock. Her worst tiredness seemed always to occur between three and four, that cool early hour when the night was far spent but morning forbid darkness to leave before the given time. Her eyes would fight to stay watchful of the thread, for twenty minutes or more Annie would be pressured by weariness to give in. Then having failed to break her will, tiredness would be gone, she would have conquered and work would move forward apace.

Before returning to her machine she would check that George had kept his covers over him and that Bella had no need of the po'. George slept soundly, his legs were underneath his blanket, the night was not too cold she didn't disturb him.

Bella lay asleep, one arm on top of the counterpane. She had so little flesh to keep her warm, Annie quietly stepped across to the side of the bed to tuck it back under the cover. It felt so cold, she touched Bella's cheek, her forehead, they held no life, aunt Bella was gone. Annie sat on the edge of the bed for several minutes before she was able to find strength in her legs to go downstairs. Now she must do what Bella had instructed her to do, that final act of kindness which had been denied Charles' father. Almost three years had passed since then, Annie thought of Saul often, now both were gone, the only mother she ever had and the only father figure she had ever known.

George slept, thankfully her movements on the stairs and her care of

Bella in the bedroom just across from where he lay, did not wake him.

Annie washed Bella, brushed her hair, placed padding beneath her and put on a clean night gown. She kissed her twice, one kiss from George and the other from herself.

Down in the scullery she tipped the bowl of water and bundled the linen into the dolly tub. Byron whimpered, he had observed her every movement, his eyes looked nervous.

"Come on, you need company too."

Annie encouraged him onto the first tread of the stairs, never before had he been allowed beyond the bottom, where he would stand watching them out of sight, then lay by the hearth knowing they could not go anywhere else without him seeing. He followed Annie, slowly, softly 'til they reached her bed, she patted the rug for him to settle there, between George's little bed and her own.

Fully clothed Annie lay with just the counterpane over her, Winnie was always about early, as soon as she heard movement next door she would ask if Ted would inform Mr.Handley on his way to work and tell Dr.Baragruy.

She slept only a little and the first light as it crept through the curtain was both welcome and daunting.

Annie whispered, "Harold, please make it alright."

Before her strength failed her she tip-toed downstairs with Byron, stirred the fire, put the kettle over the coals and unbolted the back door for Byron to go out for a minute. It was still too early to call on Winnie, somewhere in the distance she could hear the sound of a waggon over the cobbles, the first birdsong from the tree and from the eaves where a family of sparrows had taken up residence a couple of years before. Byron, having relieved himself, padded back inside, drank briefly from his bowl in the scullery then disappeared beneath the living room table, he knew this day would be different, he seemed unwilling to greet its beginning with any enthusiasm. The kettle boiled, Annie wrapped her fingers around the cup, sipping her tea as the light rose in the window. The sound of the latch on next door's privy confirmed Winnie Bacon's day had commenced. Annie would wait another ten minutes, then she must go across the yard to ask Ted's help before George awoke.

"Now don't you fret Annie, Ted will be on 'is way as soon as 'e's 'ad 'is breakfast, I'll do 'is dinner bag and when I've seen 'im off, I'll come round."

George had stirred and Annie quickly washed and dressed him. Now in the living room he sat on his cushions at the table, eating his porridge, the spoonful left over in the pan Annie put in Byron's dish, she could face nothing more than another cup of tea.

She took pen, ink and note paper from the sideboard, whilst George finished his breakfast she would write to Alice Hemsley, the only person with whom Bella had corresponded. It was not an easy letter to write, Annie felt sure aunt Bella would have enclosed a note with the Christmas card to tell Alice of Harold's accident, to send her the news of Bella's death so soon after the last letter of bad news was not something Annie found any pleasure in doing but Alice would want to know.

To Davina and Sarah she must also send notes, the words, repeated in each, grew no less painful to write.

Annie had just put the last one in the envelope when the back door opened and Winnie's voice called, "Cooo-ee."

George looked up from his bread and jam.

"I'm sorry Annie dear, I meant to be 'ere quicker but the range wer' nearly out and Ted, silly old fool, couldn't find 'is braces. I told 'im they must be wherever 'e dropped 'em when 'e took 'em off his dirty trousers yesterday. We've been searchin' high an' low. It wasn't 'til the old cat stood up to stretch itself in the chair, we seen 'em there, underneath that daft ha'peth."

She laughed at the sight of jam, clinging to the crease between George's lower lip and chin. "Bless 'is heart, 'e'll miss Bella."

Quickly Annie told Winnie that she had said nothing to him yet, "I shall explain as much as I can when things are more settled, the day will be difficult enough."

"You know what's best Annie, if you want to bring 'im round to me a bit later on, I reckon I could find an old puzzle in the cupboard, whether it 'ould 'ave all the pieces God knows, I found a marble, two acorns, a jigsaw piece and 'arf an Eccles cake down the back o' Ted's chair when I wer' cleanin' last week. Can I go up and see 'er Annie, bless 'er, we've been neighbours all these years."

"Of course you can Winnie, I'll stay down here with George."

Annie could hear Winnie talking upstairs as though Bella were still alive and listening to her every word. The bedroom door closed quietly and she came down.

"She looks grand Annie love, I told 'er, 'tis 27th May today so she got a lot further up the hill than me grandmother did. I reckon it'll please Bella to know that, she wer' allus that little bit anxious to win, in her own quiet way. I remember the time 'er jelly set and mine didn't, she 'anded me a jar of 'ers over the wall, all she said wer', 'I'll have the jar back when you've finished it, as you've already got plenty of empty jars'." Winnie chuckled, "Now what can I do to help?"

"Would you go to the workshop for me and tell Charles, Edna and May. If you have time I've written some letters which need to be posted. I would go myself but I have to stay here until Mr.Handley has been."

"You just leave it to me," said Winnie, busily scrutinising the names and addresses on the envelopes. "Oh, Sheffield, fancy that, me cousin lives in Sheffield, it gets right brass monkeys up there, she's 'ad chilblains for the last twenty years. I'll pop in later on, when I've got me washin' out." She patted Annie's hand and blew a kiss to George. The back door latch clattered into place, now Annie must await James Handley and plan a distraction for George. The latter was soon decided for her when Edna arrived.

"Charles told me to take George over to No.24 and play with 'im until things 'ere are attended to and that 'e will come to see you when I get back to the workshop." Edna sat with Annie, unwilling to leave her friend alone.

"I know it's not the best o' times to tell yer Annie but I think I'm expectin'." Edna's face contorted between joy and gravity.

Annie smiled and took Edna's hand, "That is the finest thing I could hear today, I am so glad you have told me. My head has been so full of gloom, I shall cling to such wonderful news. Does Billy know?"

"I 'aven't told 'im yet so don't say anythin'. I want to be sure an' by this time next week I should be."

Edna could not contain her happiness and Annie welcomed something to give her hope, she needed it far more than warmth or nourishment. When Edna took George's hand and walked with him to the entry, as she waved to them Annie recalled Bella's words . 'For every birth there's a death'.

Saul, Enid, Harold, aunt Bella, all had left this world. Just beginning life were George, William, Freddy and soon Billy and Edna's baby.

She closed the door and went upstairs, while it was usual for the deceased to lie in darkness, Annie could not bear the curtains to be closed, she drew them back and looked on Bella's face in the morning light. She thought of them both, Harold and Bella, somewhere out of sight engrossed in a book, studying every line, debating the subject within the pages, so occupied by each others thoughts and beliefs they had no need to fill the buckets, to pay the rent, to suffer the stench created by the tub man. Nor would Saul and Enid be permitted to escape those lively discussions. Enid's preference for more light-hearted pastimes and Saul's retiring nature would be dismissed by Bella as feeble excuse. She would preside over their gathering and Annie felt entirely sure that Bella Pownall would not allow any one of them to fail.

A knock came to the back door, it would be Mr.Handley. Annie kissed Bella's forehead and satisfied that everything was as Bella instructed, went downstairs, trying to swallow the lump in her throat before she opened the door. James Handley had great regard for Annie Boucher, less than seven months ago he had carried out the necessary acts and duties for her husband, such a young woman, now she faced again that stress and heartache. As he imagined, her strength and composure made his own tasks less difficult.

Alice Hemsley had replied by return, she would come to Nottingham and stay with her dear friend Davina Wright for a few days, over the funeral and to allow her a little time with Annie and of course George, whom she had not yet seen. It transpired that Bella had not told Alice of Harold's death, that she had learned of it only recently in a letter she had received from Davina, it had caused her a quandary, not knowing how best to write to Annie.

Sarah and Samuel had come together to see Annie and their grandson. Sarah very tearful and Samuel holding Annie so tightly she believed the strength of his arms was meant to sustain her through the coming days.

Davina had arrived smelling so strongly of Camphorated oil that Byron had sniffed at her the entire time she sat with Annie, to the point it became embarrassing.

"Lie down Byron," Annie had tactfully tried to dissuade him but Davina had simply said.

"It's not the dear dog's fault Annie, I'm here sitting down like an eleven stone mothball, no wonder Byron finds me a curiosity, I do hope I don't give you my cold but I had to come."

Annie assured Davina that she did not succumb to other people's ailments easily. "I believe Alice Hemsley is to stay with you whilst in Nottingham," said Annie.

"Yes dear, but Alice says she can stay only a day or two, of course she no longer has her mother to consider, she died a long time ago but Alice could never bear to be parted from Walter for any length of time. It will be nice to see her again, it's such a shame it could not have been under happier circumstances."

Davina began to sniffle and were it not for the eruption of an almighty sneeze, then tears would certainly have fallen. Her desperation to confine to her hanky, any germs which might otherwise reach Annie, engaged her immediate thoughts and the moment passed.

The morning of the funeral, Alice and Davina sat at breakfast, having a conversation which Davina would rather not have had. Alice had spent some time the day before with Annie and George, she had delighted in the little boy and found Annie's maturity and strength of character a credit to Bella.

Now over toast and preserve, Alice pursued the subject of Annie's beginnings.

"She hasn't told her has she, how can Annie ever be truly aware of her aunt Bella's sacrifice if she doesn't know?"

Davina was not a dominant character but this morning she was determined to protect and uphold Bella's wishes.

"I promised Bella some time ago that I would not tell Annie of the past. I gave her my word that if Annie was to know, then the knowledge would come only from Bella herself. If she wanted Annie to be aware, then she would have told her. Bella was strong and eminently wise, what purpose would it have served for Annie to have been told she was the result of her mother being raped, for her to discover that the man she trusted and looked up to had abandoned Bella, because of her."

Alice listened and with a sigh said, "It grieves me to believe that Bella's utter devotion might never be fully valued. All those years ago when Ruby and Clarice died, anyone else would have folded under the weight of responsibility and despair but Bella not once weakened. Her struggle to survive, to keep Annie warm and fed, touched Walter and me so much. After a few months had passed, I asked Bella if she would accept our help in paying for gravestones, I can remember her reply as if it were given just yesterday.

'They will be marked by a simple wooden cross. If I place a headstone on Ruby with her name and dates of birth and death, if I do this for my mother also, what would I say to Annie if one day in adulthood, she should see their memorial and ask where is my father buried? Where is my grandfather buried?'

All her life Bella protected, instructed and truly loved Annie, to the very end, not once did she weaken. You are quite right Davina, Bella's wisdom is far beyond my own."

Alice sipped her tea and Davina squeezing her friend's arm said softly, "Beyond us all."

Annie stood in Witford Hill Cemetery trying to stop her eyes leaving the grave in front of her to travel the few yards to her left, where Harold's body lay. Those who wept around her could not have begun to imagine her inner desolation. Then she saw Edna, standing with May, new life. It held her fast and as she climbed into the carriage with Davina and Alice, her strength returned.

As they travelled, mostly in an easy silence, Alice and Davina looked at each other as if to agree their next words.

"Annie my dear," said Davina, "we are both old women, our needs become less, we eat smaller amounts, we cannot wear out our clothes and we have no desire to travel or to be anywhere other than home."

"Yes, these things are all true," said Alice, "that is why we would like you to allow us to settle Mr.Handley's fees for our dear friend Bella. You are young, you have George, so many things you will need unlike ourselves who are past it," declared Alice with real feeling.

Annie had listened, making no attempt to interrupt. When they fell quiet, she smiled at them both.

"When Harold died, Samuel would hear of no one other than himself paying for the funeral. I wanted to help, all those children to feed and clothe. He became upset when I persisted so I let him be. Now I understand his emotion, his overwhelming need to do for his son this last deed of love. I saw aunt Bella with Harold when they read together, talked together, the way her spirit soared toward the light and away from that dim corner where she so often sat, each time Harold's company became hers. Harold made her vibrant, alive. All her life she gave to me, she didn't marry, or take happiness for herself. I shall pay James Handley, I have enough money." Annie paused then with a sigh continued. "After Saul's death, some time after, I received a letter requesting I call at a firm of Solicitors on London Road. Saul had bequeathed to me ten guineas. Harold said I should put it away safely and use it for something special, aunt Bella was something very special. I don't believe Saul Eddowes would consider my use of his gift improper, do you?" Annie looked at the two women for endorsement.

"No Annie, we are entirely sure that he would not." Alice spoke softly, moved by the irony.

Davina nodded agreement of Alice's words but made no sound except to herself. Within she proclaimed satisfaction with her favourite expletive, 'Buggersham Castle', it had reached an end and Davina sincerely hoped that Bella, from wherever she now was had heard every word of the conversation within the carriage.

Alice Hemsley returned to Sheffield, Edna had confirmed her pregnancy and Annie aware of the need to be industrious at her machine, was giving George his tea so that when she had washed and settled him to sleep, she could begin her night shift in the front room. She had just taken the dishes through to the scullery when the back door was opened and Charles' voice called through.

"May I come in Annie?"

She was surprised to see him, Edna had brought cloth just half an hour earlier.

"I need to talk to you Annie," said Charles.

She handed him a cup of tea and they sat with George as he drank his bedtime milk.

"Bertha cannot carry on for much longer, she loves the boys dearly and is reluctant to surrender their care to a stranger. I'm afraid she will soon start to suffer in health under the strain. Her own house is now vacant. Annie I would like you to consider taking the job of my housekeeper, you cannot continue to struggle on here alone, stitching all night in that small front room. William and Freddy love you and George, they even love Byron. Bertha would agree if her charge was to be handed to you. It would give you a home and security, you would have your own space, it is a big enough house as you well know. Think about it Annie, let me know soon, for Bertha's sake if for no other reason, please."

George was asleep in his bed, Byron lay by the hearth in the living room. As Annie guided the linen through the machine, Charles' words went round and round in her head. 'I will always love your children', she had promised Enid. Her own situation was vulnerable, she struggled to keep on top of the bills no matter how many hours she spent at the machine. Bertha was tired and needed to take some ease. Annie had no option but to accept Charles' job offer. George would be safe and William and Freddy would delight in having their friend Byron to live with them. Knowing his children were happy and in the care of someone they knew well, would free Charles' mind to pursue his ambitions.

Annie tied off the end of the cotton and placed the shirt on the pile, by morning she would have sewn many more but the pattern was changing, it would bring new challenges and demand even more of Annie Boucher.

CHAPTER TWENTY FOUR

Annie had moved finally to Hood Street on the sixteenth of June. Packing their belongings had been a trial, for in so doing she had been forced to go through Bella's clothes and the drawers in the front room which had revealed a curious array of Bella's keepsakes. A lock of hair wrapped in a tiny lace edged handkerchief, the words written on the paper which held them both safe, identified them as Annie's hair and Ruby's hanky. A pair of the daintiest gloves Annie had ever seen, very old and obviously meant for slender, genteel fingers. A hairbrush, the bristles worn but the handle of delicate filigree, in all the years Annie could remember it had not made an appearance. A baby's feeding bottle and a tiny bonnet. Right at the back of one drawer an old hymnbook, it smelled musty, pressed between its pages, the sad remains of a flower. Annie wondered if the hymn above and below it held any significance, the bloom had lost all life between;

'Fierce raged the tempest o'er the deep,

Watch did thine anxious servant keep

And

'O let him whose sorrow no relief can find

Trust in God and borrow, ease for heart and mind.'

Bella never sang hymns and very few songs for that matter but Annie sensed it kept some memory, important to Bella.

The clothes Annie parcelled carefully to take to the Mission, keeping the blouse with the overlaid Broderie Anglaise collar which Bella had worn that first meeting with Harold and the pair of plum coloured woollen gloves, Harold's gift that Christmas.

Most of the china and cookpots Annie offered to Edna, who had accepted them eagerly. The salt dish and the little shovel spoon travelled with Annie and George, everyday it had sat on the table, a silent witness to a life but never divulging the past, faithful to Bella, stinging the tongue of anyone who would take too much from its store of secrets. The linens and books Annie moved a few at a time, in George's pram.

Bertha's relief was quite plain to see, she had made Annie promise to bring the children to see her at least once a week.

"I shall shrivel and die, like a leaf ripped from its stem if I don't cuddle those boys," she had said, with genuine concern for her own spirits. "I cannot go from playing hide and seek and chuff, chuff trains one day to old age and cataracts the next, without some allowance of Eddowes mischief."

Bertha had occupied a small room at the back of the house, the boys in a double room alongside their father's bedroom. After Enid's death Charles could not face the bedroom he had shared with his wife and moved to another.

"Will you be alright in here Annie?" Asked Bertha, "What with all that happened."

Annie answered truthfully when she replied, "Yes, it really doesn't trouble me Bertha."

George's bed would fit alongside her own for the time. The window overlooked the street enabling George to peep over the sill to watch the horses moving the vehicles below.

Winnie Bacon had cried and cried, her apron showing a dark wet patch as she waved to Annie that last day. 'It is only a comparatively short walk to Hood Street Winnie'. Annie had been surprised at how upset she had become. 'We will come back and see you often, I promise'.

George had blown kisses and poor Winnie could not bear it, she ran inside, her apron once more mopping the tears as she sought the sanctuary of her scullery. It had been agreed that Annie would leave the keys with Mrs.Bacon and the landlord would collect them from there, he would enjoy a bonus if he let the house again quickly, the rent was paid until the end of the month but there was no consideration of a refund.

Annie's immediate concern had been to ease all three boys into the new situation so their young minds would experience no sense of insecurity, she need not have worried. The installation of Byron's old blanket beneath the scullery table and his lead hanging behind the back door, the battered old enamel bowl from which he drank positioned below the tin bath, which hung down the wall from a large brass hook, all filled the children with glee. It would seem Annie's arrival held nothing of the excitement that Byron's residency created.

Bertha's age and the after effects of her fall had limited the length of any walk she and the two boys could undertake. Now, with the long summer days and extra hours of sunshine, Annie had determined to fill their lungs with all the fresh air possible and strengthen their leg muscles in the process.

From Hood Street, Bertha was just within walking distance, as was Sarah. It was an easy distance back to Winchester Street but to The Park, even taking the pram for George and Freddy to take turns riding, it would be too far for William's legs to sustain him.

Annie had a small amount of money and one day soon she would put them all in a carriage and visit her dear friend Davina.

Charles had told Annie he would pay her fifteen shillings a month. All food of course, both for herself and George would be provided as part of the household. She would have no rent to find or coal bills to pay but personal items, such as clothes, she would provide for from her own money.

Bertha had taken delight in showing Annie the contents of a drawer in the chest upstairs on the landing.

"All these are now too small for Freddy, I thought you might use them for George, William wore them first but they are still good."

Annie hesitated, "I would be very glad to dress George in them but are you sure Charles wouldn't mind?"

"Bless you Annie, I don't think he would even notice, just so long as his sons are clean, fed and happily amused he has no further concern. The day I cut Freddy's hair for the first time the child looked quite different but Charles didn't see it, he seems to be in a world of his own much of the time. I did begin to wonder if he had met another young lady, even now something or someone seems to draw his attentions away from us. If there is a female distraction then he has said nothing and shown no sign of studying his appearance too much or bathing more often."

It was a week after Annie had moved in that one evening after the children were settled and Charles sat with his newspaper and Annie with a lap full of socks to darn, that the reason for Charles' preoccupation was made evident.

"I've rented those premises at Basford Annie, I didn't say anything before because you had such a lot to think about, one way and another."

Annie was surprised, nothing more had been said so she had presumed his interest in the place had left him.

"How large are the premises?" She asked.

"Well, allowing for storage, there's space for eight machines."

Annie went quiet for a moment, "That requires eight women to work them, already proficient unless you are willing to train the unskilled. If the machines at Basford are to produce stock items then their level of ability need not be so comprehensive but even work shirts and undergarments must be of reliable quality or your sales will fall rapidly. Have you sufficient orders to persuade the bank?"

Charles started to chuckle, "I do have some 'nous' you know, I have thought carefully enough, the bank knows its money is safe." He did not tell Annie that he had secured the loan against 14.Hood Street.

"The machines are coming by freight from Derby, they are secondhand but I've seen them and they will serve the purpose adequately. The business in Derby closed down when he was made bankrupt, silly bugger gambled everything he had, cards, fights, just couldn't resist a wager."

Annie thought of Charles' past waywardness but made no remark, he continued, "I wouldn't have got the machines anywhere else at the price, bankrupt stock is a good way forward if you can get your hands on it. I've put a notice in the window of the workshop and one in a window at Basford.

Anyone seeking work will first have to show their worth on a machine at Winchester Street."

"So you have spoken to May, Edna and Violet?" Said Annie.

"No, I put the notices up only this evening, I shall tell them about it in the morning."

Annie felt concerned for the three women. Edna had a baby to consider, it was due in December. May ever timid and nervous would feel quite insecure and Violet could be outspoken when she chose to be. Charles could find conversation at his work in the morning not to be the straightforward announcement he anticipated, telling them before putting up the notices would have been far more sensible. On this occasion, Charles had not used his newly acquired tact and diplomacy, she could only hope he might redeem himself through carefully considered words.

Over a period of several days, a number of women had applied for work and been judged either suitable, or not, on the strength of their performance at a machine in the workshop.

The vital equipment had been collected from the freight yard and taken to Basford. Under the inducement of an enhanced remuneration, Evelyn Easter had agreed to spend two days cleaning and scrubbing the premises, on the condition that a carriage convey her from Sherwood Road and back again each day.

Charles had linen, thread and all necessary fastening ready to be delivered on his instruction and eight women waiting on his word to commence.

The time spent with his sons at home became less and less. They were still in bed asleep when he left for work in the morning and already settled when he finally arrived back at night, it had been as late as ten o'clock on some days. He seemed tense and unwilling to confide in Annie so she had concentrated her efforts on the development of the three boys, remembering always aunt Bella's belief that children can learn from the earliest weeks if their senses are given something to work on. She had taken them regularly as promised to visit Bertha, always a happy time.

As they walked, Annie would prompt their thinking with various challenges, among the favourites, first to find a dandelion clock, when the last seed was propelled through the air by the eager blowing of whichever child, their continued chorus of the given time was loud enough to carry as far as the chimes of the church clock. Who can spot a catkin, first one to espy billy blue tit, count the numbers on the houses in the street? Their young legs covered the distance without thought of weariness and Byron's lead was handed to each one in turn to walk their friend, this one activity inspired good progress.

Annie was artful when it came to Sarah, she would bake a cake, some biscuits, some oranges for the girls, but never go without a bag of goodies which came some way towards returning all the treats with which Sarah would laden them on their departure.

Her great pleasure was seeing her grandson but her abiding maternal love was extended to William and Freddy also. If Samuel came home whilst they were there, his ready smile, his delight in amusing them with rides in the barrow and piggy backs around the yard would have given the onlooker, not as much as the slightest notion, that all three children were not his family.

As promised they called briefly on Winnie Bacon and Annie had introduced them to Alfred Brooks, much to his surprise they had shown no alarm at his appearance, their simple chatter, their offer of a pear drop, as naturally made as it would be to anyone else. It raised Alfred's spirits and now when he saw the boys he would hold them spellbound with his sleight of hand, taking a farthing from behind Freddy's ear, a liquorice tablet from William's hat.

'Again, do it again Uncle Alfred', they would cry and he would oblige with a look at Annie that told her, for these few moments at least, he was glad not to have died back there at the pit.

Their visits to the arboretum brought endless fun. Their circuit of the pathways in pursuit of squirrels, the tameness of the pigeons almost taking food from their fingers, peeping out from the bandstand at the people passing by, all tired them to a healthy night of sleep.

Their appetites gave Annie the need for substantial hours of baking, mostly done at night whilst they lay dreaming of their activities. The relish with which they consumed their meals gave her immense satisfaction. Reading together, doing puzzles, drawing, all had advanced the young minds. Bella Pownall would have been proud.

Charles however missed all this, even on Sundays he would take himself to the workshop to bring his paperwork up to date.

Annie and the boys had walked with him on the previous Sunday and having looked around their dad's office, discovering nothing to interest them, had not hesitated for an instant when Annie suggested they might visit Edna and Billy.

"Don't worry Edna, we won't stay long," said Annie, as she cautioned each child to be good.

Edna laughed, "Since when 'ave I been 'ouse proud Annie, I do me chores regular but there's nothin' they can 'urt and Billy needs a bit o' practice anyway, 'e don't know which way's up when it comes to babies."

Billy appeared in the doorway, he had overheard Edna's remark. "You'd be surprised what I know Edna Dodds, you're a lucky woman married to 'ansome bloke like me wi' brains an'all."

"Oh yes, an' who was it thought lactation wer' when a woman's bearin's start headin' south an' that antenatal meant a dislike o' the Scots?"

"How are things at the workshop Edna?" Asked Annie in an attempt to rescue Billy's dignity.

The boys sat quietly with Byron sharing a tin of broken biscuits.

"Things are alright," said Edna, "we've got work enough but I think the Basford place is provin' more difficult than 'e thought. May is well and Violet is Violet. I don't know what to make of 'er sometimes, she sews well but 'er tongue can be as sharp as a razor. I reckon May walks wi' 'er just 'cause she feels safer when Violet's about, 'tis a shame they don't both live on Peverell Street, that's where May could really do wi' company. I wouldn't like walkin' there on me own dark winter evenin's, gives yer the creeps."

Charles still had paperwork to finish when they returned to his office.

"You go on, I'll be home later," he said, hardly looking up from his desk.

Annie felt sad for William and Freddy, they lacked their father's company and although she filled their lives with all the good things she could, that one thing she was unable to give them, however often she reminded Charles of his unfortunate absence.

They had been to see Davina twice over the summer months. Annie had discovered, on their second carriage ride, that Edward Meade had been paid in advance to drive them to and from The Park and not just on this one occasion, he held funds in hand for Annie to bring the children regularly. She had only to send word to him and provided he was not engaged elsewhere, he would oblige.

Annie had protested. "I do not expect you to pay for our transport Davina, it is not fair, I cannot imagine that anyone else visits you without covering the cost of the carriage themselves."

"You are quite right Annie in supposing that no one else comes to call on me, carriage paid or carriage unpaid. Oh yes, one or two stuffy old women visit in the guise of friendship but once they have munched their way through all my macaroons and pralines and drunk enough sherry to mask the ache beneath their girdles, they are gone. The only exception is dear Sarah who comes seldom because of her devotion to that wonderful family. The romance between Frank and Ivy blossoms Annie, I have every hope they will announce their engagement, perhaps at Christmas." That had been at the end of August.

It was now early October, Annie and the boys were again travelling in Meade's carriage to The Park. Annie's protests had been countered by Davina's determined stance. In the end, Annie had to accept the arrangement, Davina had become tearful.

"You told me not to spoil George and I have been very careful, giving him only very few sweets but to see you and the children is my greatest joy, I have to look forward to something."

In fact it was fortunate that Annie did not have to pay Meade herself, she had received fifteen shillings at the end of July but since then, Charles had made no mention of her wages, she would have to say something soon but his mood had been strange, remote. He was anxious about the business Annie felt sure, she could not put off speaking to him for very much longer.

Ivy greeted them at the door and George presented her with a posy of Michaelmas Daisies, she looked happy.

"How is Frank?" Asked Annie, Ivy still blushed at the mention of his name, it was an endearing feature.

"He's well Annie, Mr.Lovatt has given him a small increase in pay and a new bicycle."

Annie was pleased to hear such news but nevertheless hoped the new transport would continue to delight Maggie and not be confined to merely delivering bread.

Davina watched the three little heads on the rug below, a brass trivet held their fascination. In turn, they had unscrewed all three legs from the trivet and now proceeded to put it back together again. This had been done at least twice and Annie was anxious, she had apologised at the first sight of William as he discovered it possible to dismantle the object and offered to polish his sticky finger marks from its surface.

Davina had laughed at Annie's concern. "My dear, it is a piece of old metal, it has sat in the hearth since God knows when. Unlike many trivets which I am quite sure serve a useful purpose in supporting a hot kettle or pan, that ornament has done absolutely nothing to warrant the cost of the Brasso. I have derived more actual satisfaction from that trivet in the past half hour, than I have through the thirty odd years it has sat there wasting the space."

Whilst Davina could not tell Annie of her thoughts, it had occurred to her on their very first visit, that here she now sat, looking on Nathan's grandchildren. It mattered not that Charles had no knowledge of Nathan, it was not important that Annie held no awareness of Saul's abandonment of Bella. The many ironies, which over the course of years had threaded through their lives, now entwined so profoundly, it was beyond the wit of man to unravel them.

When Annie reached Hood Street she was surprised to find Charles already at home, he had himself just returned but his early arrival home was unusual. He sat in his chair by the hearth, William and Freddy climbed over him with such enthusiasm Annie had to rescue Charles from their frenzied hugs, given by adoring arms and William's boots which jumped up and down on his dad's most sensitive regions like pistons.

For the first time in weeks they all sat together for their meal that evening. When they were washed and ready for bed, Charles was there to tuck them up and kiss them goodnight. He even looked in on George and gave the boy a loving rub of the hand across his hair. Annie sensed Charles wanted to say something, she cleared away the dishes and spread the clothes on the airer, then putting a cup of tea by Charles and one by her chair where she began to stitch a patch over the back of Freddy's trousers, she awaited Charles' revelations.

Annie had taken from his expression a need to get something of significance off his chest. She had threaded her needle and put only the second stitch in the cloth when his outpourings commenced.

"We aren't selling enough Annie, the women are producing good work but I cannot find orders to take up the stock. The workshop is doing well, although it won't be many weeks to Edna's confinement, the baby is due mid December I believe, it is the Basford operation that worries me."

"Which outlets are taking the stock?" Asked Annie.

"Drew's and Trueman's," replied Charles.

"They are both on the same side of the city, you need to persuade an outlet on the other side as well and what about Derby?" Annie had abandoned her patch and now tried to establish at what level Charles' business was actually functioning. Previously he had volunteered no information and reminding herself that her role was housekeeper, Annie had not felt it her place to ask.

"I did try Rowe's at Clifton but they already had a supplier who meets their demand, I haven't been to Derby with samples," said Charles.

Annie sighed, "But Derby is the very place you should be pushing. If the manufacturer in Derby went bankrupt through his own shortcoming then the chances are that an opportunity now exists to fill the gap his closure would have created. Tomorrow is Saturday, no shopkeeper will be interested in talking with you at a weekend. On Sunday we will devise a plan, a business plan Charles, keep Sunday free of all other activities, this must be the priority."

Byron laying on the rug at Annie's feet, raised his eyes at her stern tone, she noticed his concern and stroked his head, satisfied any wrong doing could not be his, he closed his eyes and rolled onto his side. Charles fidgeted in his chair, if Enid were here we would be having a blazing row by now he thought. He missed their arguments, those heated exchanges which led them to glorious submission.

Annie had skilfully covered the weakness in Freddy's trousers, Charles wished his own weakness could be so easily concealed.

Annie had done her chores and the boys had played without squabbling whilst she worked, so as promised, they set off for the arboretum, if they were lucky the band might play there today.

The children shuffled through the fallen leaves and took delight in throwing to the air the seed pods from the ash trees, watching them twirl in the breeze, flying back to earth under their 'wing' power. Unlike the heavier seed cases from the beech trees which fell back to earth with no attempt at a graceful landing. The activity busied them for several minutes whilst Annie sat on the bench looking on.

A voice said, "Hello Mrs.Boucher."

Mrs.Appleyard lowered herself to the seat alongside Annie and with her usual confident dialogue, began to chatter about all nature of things.

"My dear are all these children in your care?"

Annie chuckled, "I'm sure it must appear a greater number but in fact, only three little boys create this excitement."

Annie called them to her and introduced each one to Mrs.Appleyard. Their manners were faultless, Bertha's guidance and Annie's continued instruction had taught William, Freddy and George to behave as little gentlemen and Mrs.Appleyard's pleasure at meeting them was genuine. Annie had to explain the situation sufficiently for her to understand but withheld much of the circumstance, it seemed so personal and private in many ways.

"Do you know Annie, I have been complemented so many times when wearing the gowns, the nurses too look so much smarter in their new uniforms. I tell as many people as I can, that Eddowes' quality is quite superior. You should feel proud. Oh look here comes the band, or at least some of them, they played at our fund raising event in the gardens last month. I am shameless Annie, I determine myself to relieve one or two of the wealthiest in this city of just a small measure of their fortunes. To put food where tables hold none, shoes where feet go bare and coal where hearths sit empty. I haven't always known comfort Annie, I was an orphan at fifteen years of age but fate smiled on me. I am forever grateful, it is not so for a very many people." She offered no further explanation.

The band struck up to play, to the delight of the boys, hands clapping, feet tapping to the music. Byron lodged himself firmly beneath the bench, the pitch of the instruments too sharp for his sensitive ears.

Mrs.Appleyard took Annie's hand, "I am so glad we bumped into each other again my dear, I admire your stamina in keeping up with these agile young men and I envy, oh how I do envy your youth. Alas dear doggy is not too enamoured with the E flat bass and cornet, I think you might be homeward bound when he begins to howl."

Annie laughed, "He will abide it for about ten minutes, then we will have to leave before our presence upsets the fine tuning."

The two women said goodbye and Annie watched Mrs.Appleyard's stately figure disappearing behind the laurels.

Something she had said prompted Annie's thinking. The more she turned it over in her mind, the more confident she became. Tomorrow, she would tell Charles, it may well prove to be the answer to his problems.

Annie looked down from Charles' bedroom window to the back garden below, where the boys had persuaded him to push them on the swing. Her hands worked quickly, changing the bed linen and cleaning the room. She had baked last night and a piece of brisket simmered on the range. After she had fed them all she must settle the children with a puzzle and speak with Charles. Annie's skills in the kitchen achieved to stretch a joint of meat to impressive lengths, they ate only tasty nourishing meals but her grasp of simple economics she applied to the household as she did her ideas for the workshops.

Byron supervised the young ones' endeavour which today was a jigsaw of duck and ducklings, while Annie told Charles of her plan for the business.

"I shall need to go to Winchester Street tomorrow morning, the boys will have to go with me and amuse themselves as best they can while I set up a machine for the embroidered labels and do a sample run of the adapted pattern, I know you must go to Basford and open up there. Set the women to work on underclothes tomorrow, no shirts. This is what I believe you must do Charles if you are to succeed. At least seventy percent of people in Nottingham, I feel quite sure, would think many times before spending their money. Their income is low and barely covers the basic needs in life. Some items they cannot do without, food, warmth, rent, other things have to last a long time, clothing being one of them. The work shirts we must make 'special', produce them differently to any other manufacturer. Yes, they will copy but provided you are the first to do it then yours is the label everyone will seek. We shall reinforce the underarms of the work shirt. Men occupied in physical labour sweat profusely, always the underarm rots before any other part of the garment wears through. A square of linen, laid diagonally across, one triangle sewn into the sleeve, the other into the body. To do this, the shirt will be cut just slightly fuller under the arm, the increased use of material you must stand the cost of, overall it will be negligible but a shirt which will last longer than any other and cost no more, will be the one every retailer sells in number. Each shirt will have sewn into the back of the neck an embroidered label in red thread, it will identify, 'The Eddowes' Work Shirt'.

You will post notices in the workshop windows, place an advertisement in the Gazette, both here and in Derby. Go back to Rowe's at Clifton, show them the new product, stress the benefits, it will cost them no more than the old design. Take samples to Drew's and Trueman's. Go to Derby, take the new design to at least two retailers, one either side of the town, sales will rise I am convinced. The demand for these shirts will grow quickly, as will your requirement for linen, you will be able to negotiate a better price per bolt of cloth from your supplier, then you will recoup the initial expense of the extra material for reinforcing and the cost of the promotion through the Gazette."

Charles had listened to Annie's confident plan with a feeling of immense relief, he had glimpsed salvation, her words were so positive and assuring.

"I'll do all these things Annie and I must pay you what I owe you, I hadn't forgotten."

Charles spoke as though he had just been freed from a regime of cruelty and could not utter thanks enough to his liberator.

"Finished," came the chorus of voices from the living room floor, where the picture of mother duck and four ducklings beside a bullrush on the pond, had inspired three keen minds to feed the ducks and swans at the embankment.

"Can we?" Pleaded William.

For the first time in ages their father laughed at their eagerness and agreed to the request.

"Come on Annie, we'll dress up warm, bring some stale bread."

He rattled Byron's lead and the ever ready dog was first to the door.

The following morning, Edna had been amused at the antics of the young lads in the sewing room. A variety of empty cotton reels, some old thread, a handful of studs and buttons, achieved to entertain them while Annie explained to May, Edna and Violet, the new design. It was only proper to inform them that sales were not as brisk as should be but Annie stressed the reputation for quality work which they all produced. She chose her words carefully, encouraging them to realise how much a vital part of the business they were.

"You should feel proud that the name of Eddowes in a garment bears such a high regard, soon everyone will seek the Eddowes' label."

The pattern worked perfectly and required very little extra time in production. The labels would be sewn in advance on the best machine for the task at Winchester Street and sent over to Basford.

As Annie was leaving with the boys, waving to May and Violet, Edna walked with them to the gate and handed to Annie the bag of amazing creations, handcrafted by William, Freddy and George from their array of oddments.

In a low voice she said, "So 'e's buggered it up then, you bale 'im out every time."

Annie sighed, "Just pray it works Edna, say nothing to the others, May doesn't need the worry and Violet is better not being aware. If Charles is to turn things around it is crucial that this design be exclusively Eddowes', at least initially. We must keep it to ourselves for the time."

"Yer don't need to fret, me lips are sealed tighter than a duck's arse, more than could be said for me other parts, if I sneeze, I piddle meself. Mam says 'tis 'cause the baby's gettin' bigger an' puttin' pressure on me bladder, it isn't due for two months yet, 'ow big is it goin' to be for 'eaven's sake."

Annie chuckled, she had enjoyed spending some time with May and Edna and working on the machines again, if only briefly.

By Christmas an entirely changed situation prevailed, the machines stitched industriously to fulfil orders. Charles had secured sales through two shops in Derby and in Nottingham, both sides of the city were covered since Rowe's had agreed to take shirts along with Drew's and Trueman's.

From a financial position which could have been described as dire, the business now stood solid with excellent forward orders. In recent days enquiries had come in from Leicester. Annie had received her wages, four months in one payment at the end of November.

None of these happenings however, brought Annie the happiness which on December the twenty first, the arrival of Edna's baby filled her with completely. Several days overdue and weighing in at 10lbs 1 oz the baby girl brought to No.24 the greatest joy. On the third day, Christmas Eve, Annie took the boys to see the new arrival. Billy was so proud he couldn't wait to tell Annie. "We've named 'er after you, Annie Dodds, if it 'ad been a boy it were goin' to be called Harold."

The moment had pleased Annie so much. The boys each carried a small gift for the new baby, William and Freddy no longer held any disturbing memories and were able to feel excitement and wonder at the infant in the crib, without that degree of fear which previously darkened their young thoughts. It brought a magic to Christmas for them all.

At Annie's suggestion, Gertie had started at the workshop. Since Harold's accident Sarah had cocooned the young ones, keeping them close, as safe as she could. It was now time both Gertie and Jean had some paid work. Samuel never complained but he had aged very much over the last twelve months, he needed help.

"May is a wonderful teacher in all needlecraft Sarah, it will give Gertie a useful skill and stand her in good stead, she has always enjoyed her sewing and knitting."

Sarah had thought for a moment then bravely declared, "You are right Annie, it'll perhaps get Jean off her backside too, all she wants to do is paint pictures and that won't get her very far will it?"

Annie had jumped to the defence of Jean and pointed out to Sarah that in fact, Jean showed talent. "I have seen some very promising artwork on Jean's paper, it is a gift that should be encouraged, few people are able to create in that way. It would be a good thing if she attended the School of Art, I'm sure there are classes in the evenings, then by day Jean could find some practical employment.

At the middle of January, Jean Boucher was enrolled into an art class to attend three evenings a week and by day, began some hours of work for Cyril Lovatt, decorating the 'fancies'.

Davina had near' burst at the seams with delight when Ivy and Frank announced their engagement on New Years Eve. Months before she had prepared her plan for the young couple and when Davina voiced her hopes to Sarah and found support from her dear friend, she felt optimistic that Ivy and Frank would welcome it also. The bedroom in Davina's house which had relinquished its bed to Annie and Harold, with slight re-arrangement, could become a very cosy sitting room for the newly weds. Ivy's small bedroom would be vacated and she and Frank could have a double room. The kitchen of course, would be theirs to use as much as they liked. It was a desperate attempt on Davina's part to keep the company of Ivy, she feared the future with a stranger. To have Mr. and Mrs.Frank Boucher under her roof would be even more than she could have dared to dream. The offer was accepted happily and with real gratitude, the wedding was to take place on the first Saturday in April.

The weather had begun to lighten and Annie had taken the boys to the arboretum. At Easter William would begin his lessons at the school but for another month all the boys could enjoy their walks and activities with Annie and Byron. There appeared to be an influx of pigeons from other areas, the pathways were filled with birds of all colours and the oats and breadcrumbs, liberally scattered by eager hands, brought pigeons to the feet of the boys in such numbers the path had become completely covered.

A voice called out, "My goodness, what a wonderful sight." Mrs.Appleyard edged her way elegantly through the throng. "How are you Annie? It must be almost six months since we last met, I can see these young men have grown."

"We are all well thank you, and yourself and Mr.Appleyard?" Asked Annie.

"Busy my dear, always busy. Alas I am growing too old to achieve all my goals. It will be your generation Annie which will push outdated and stuffy rules and regulations aside and allow society to know more equality and fairness. Every once in a while however, I find satisfaction, today has been a good day. A family living in appalling conditions, a good, honest family, I have at last achieved to accommodate in a house which will give them a decent home, a sense of dignity. I chafe and I chase Annie, sometimes I do succeed." She gave a sigh and brought the palm of her gloved hand down firmly onto the arm of the bench.

"I know what you mean," said Annie, "I worry for May and her family. There was a shocking brawl in Peverell Street last week, only yards from May's house. Little Mabel is so vulnerable and of course May, as she walks to and from the workshop."

Annie explained the situation of Alfred's poor health, although his determination to help May by cooking and doing some simple housework was touching. Young Alfred had begun work at Clark and Brown's, Billy Dodds' aunt Jessie had found him a place there, working with her on the upholstery. The distance he must cover to reach his work meant leaving home more than an hour before time in the morning and not reaching home until seven in the evening, his only alternative was work at the tannery.

"Now this May you speak of, is that the very quiet one who came with Mr.Eddowes to fit my gown?" Asked Mrs.Appleyard.

"Yes, that's right, May Watkinson. She is timid and shy but extremely skilled at her work and as honest as the day with a total devotion to her family."

"Um, leave it with me Annie, I shall see what I can do. Where will I find you, I cannot simply hope to bump into you here, it could be another six months."

"14.Hood Street, that is where these young 'captains' of the future occupy my hours." Annie laughed, "May is very proud she would not want charity as such. A house in a safer place with an affordable rent would make her so very happy and I would love to see all her years of effort and selfless struggle rewarded."

Annie's gaze weighted the appeal and Mrs.Appleyard left the arboretum with another goal in mind.

March passed smoothly, Gertie learned quickly and already she produced good quality stitching. Edna had work to do at home, smocking and scalloping two christening gowns. Jean had impressed her tutor at Art School with her ability. Before she progressed to painting, with plain paper and charcoal she must first draw accurately the human form, part by part, the hand, ear, eye, foot, muscles and skin texture until eventually she would draw from a life model the complete body. She loved every minute of her study and proudly told Sarah and Samuel that she would work so hard, one day she would become accomplished and sell her work to buy them nice things.

Young Alfred had shown an aptitude for the work at Clark and Brown's and walked his daily marathon with a good heart. Each day Annie hoped Mrs.Appleyard might call with news but as yet, she had heard nothing.

The coming Saturday was the date of Frank and Ivy's wedding. Annie had adapted some of the boys' clothes and with careful hand sewing, had created three smart outfits for them to wear on the day.

Sarah as always, extended her kindness as far as she could, "Tell their dad he is welcome to come Annie."

Charles declined, "I really need to be at Basford," had been his response when Annie relayed Sarah's message.

Ivy's mother arrived from Grantham, Davina was anxious to show Mrs.Pilkington where her daughter would set up home with Frank. Ivy, relieved of all duties was at Sarah's being titivated for the occasion. Frank had his morning deliveries to do for Cyril Lovatt.

The wedding was to take place at the Registry Office at 2 o'clock. Sarah would not consider for a moment having food at The Park afterwards. 'No Davina, I must be occupied in baking and preparation on the day or God help me, I shall be weeping for Harold when I need to smile for my Frank'.

Annie held on to George as the words of the Registrar pulled at her emotions. William had charge of a small black cat on a loop of white ribbon, Freddy a tiny boot and George, tucked safely inside his pocket, had a horseshoe made from card and bound in silk with 'good luck' written on the side.

Ivy looked lovely, her pretty jacket and skirt in a light chocolate brown seemed to illuminate through its contrast, the double headed, deep pink camellias she carried in her bouquet.

Frank borne along by the excitement of his sisters, moved through the ceremony with an easy smile on his face but his eyes, every now and then, would catch sight of his dad and like Annie, who also observed Samuel's struggle to remain bright, the strain of fighting back tears which if once released might swamp them all, knotted his heart strings in pain.

The gathering around Sarah's table and about the living room in that small house in Mitchell Street, wrapped them all in love, just as on every other occasion which brought them together. Mrs.Pilkington seated alongside Samuel, appeared delighted at Ivy's new found family and following her third glass of sherry, turned to give him a kiss.

It was immediately declared by Maggie to be, "Ugh, a wet one." Sarah's description for Eli's tokens of affection. It caused great laughter and when William asked if he might be shown her glass eye, which Frank in his mischief had told the boy was, 'Mrs.Pilkington's left one', the tension and strain melted away to be replaced by humour and merriment.

When Annie and the boys got back to Hood Street Charles was at home. From their animated chatter and happy distribution of tit-bits, sent back for Byron, he assumed it had been a good day.

"Yes," said Annie, "It has been a really lovely time, the boys have been very good and Ivy looked radiant. I'll take off my hat and jacket and make your tea."

"No need," said Charles, "I called at The Standard for a plate of pie and mash."

Annie wished he had not, with money now in his pocket she feared the nature of his visits to The Standard. Today she would trust it had been only to seek food and not to meet any other need of distraction.

William had started school, Annie watched his anxious little face disappear through the doorway. The headmaster, Percival Dunn, Esq., took the older children for their lessons, a very severe man, not given to smile encouragement at the fainthearted. Miss Merryweather had led William by the hand and whispered to Annie.

"Don't worry Mum, he will be quite alright." Annie had not corrected her, if ever a child needed a mum, it was William on this day. In spite of her many tasks about the house and the attention she gave to George and Freddy, Annie nevertheless found concentration difficult. She watched the clock, waiting for the time to collect William from school. A special treat for after tea awaited, meringues dipped at one end in chocolate.

A knock came to the front door, Byron, beginning to feel his age was disinclined to rush to the sound and instead, watched from the comfort of his old blanket to see the caller, it was Mrs.Appleyard.

"It has taken rather longer than I'd hoped but I do have good news Annie, No.4 Melton Road is available. It is a sensible distance from both May's work at Winchester Street and her son's job at Clark and Brown's. I remember you told me that Mr.Watkinson had been a carpenter at one time. Now I realise his health would debar him from any strenuous activity but I feel quite confident he would manage the every day maintenance of a house, which at present stands in very good order indeed. Providing he could undertake this mild commitment and agree to keep tidy the rear garden, which is only small but provides a safe area of play for a young child, then at a peppercorn rent, merely to legalise their tenancy, May and her family can move from Peverell Street to Melton Road just as soon as they wish."

Annie could have kissed the dear lady but managed to retain her composure saying, "I am so grateful to you Mrs.Appleyard, May will be overcome with relief and of course gratitude, which she will want to express to you personally."

"Not necessary my dear, it is best if you give May all the details, I would probably frighten her half to death. I have the name and address to which the rent must be sent, Mr.Watkinson needs simply to make sure that it is paid as stated once a year by September thirtieth."

Annie glanced at the document. Ten shillings a year, she looked at Mrs.Appleyard in disbelief.

"It will be a reciprocal arrangement, the house will be kept safe and secure by May and Alfred dwelling there. It gives them a home and the owner, peace of mind."

Annie's face still displayed astonishment.

"Dear Mr.Appleyard, through his endeavours at his 'Lodge', has achieved to secure many such wonders Annie my dear. You need have no reservations, it is entirely genuine, honest and worthy. I do hope your friend May and all her family will know happiness in great measure from now on."

With that she was gone.

Annie's knowledge of the Freemasons was limited but if their deliberations at the 'Lodge' had produced an escape from Peverell Street for May, then she would not question further.

Now she must gather George and Freddy from their play and walk to the school, Annie could not spend time on May's house move until tomorrow when in the morning, she would go to the workshop and give her the good news.

Charles had sat at his desk in the workshop at Basford, watching the machines turn, his thoughts very much on his own circumstances, Frank and Ivy's marriage had preyed on his mind. The books at both places of business showed a healthy profit, just a few months earlier he had been close to ruin, had it not been for Annie. The thought of facing life's challenges and demands without Annie alarmed him, he felt no passion for her as he had felt for Enid but he needed her, she was the strength which compensated his weakness. He was quite sure that Annie felt no love for him, a kindliness, a caring even, but not love. He could not risk losing her, one day someone might come along and win her affections, take her away, thinking of it actually unnerved him, they should marry. The only way he might possibly persuade Annie, would be to use the boys, them she did love, deeply, devotedly, she would do nothing that would hurt his sons and her own dear George. That evening as Charles sat with his newspaper and Annie knitted for Edna's little girl, he took his chance, his lever, the vulnerability of three little boys. Annie listened but not once raised her eyes from her needlework.

"William is at school now, people can be very cruel, they will lash a child with their tongues in that pursuit of gossip and scandal. We are two unattached, comparatively young people Annie, dwelling under the same roof. Folk begin to talk, to whisper on street corners, especially as they are aware of your great knowledge of the business. Please think about it and be considerate of the harm it might bring to our innocent young sons if we allow our reputations, albeit misplaced, to become tainted."

"May and Alfred are to move house, it will be an upheaval and I shall help them as much as I can, I may well ask you to look after the boys one Sunday soon. I cannot think of the other matter until after then. You must understand my mind is engaged by the events surrounding the Watkinsons at present."

Annie reeled from Charles' request, she had not once thought of such things. That night as she lay wakeful in her bed, his words tormented her. Annie had no idea people were gossiping, they must smile at the school gate and speak their malicious 'tittle tattle' behind her back. It did not occur to Annie, herself entirely honest, that Charles could be putting doubts in her mind for his own purpose. By morning she had decided to speak with Sarah and Davina, she would not do anything which might hurt or disappoint them. Harold lived with his mother every day still and Davina had loved Harold dearly, she must ask their advice, seek their thoughts on the matter. With George and Freddy her constant companions and Byron her faithful listener, the one to whom she poured out all her concerns, Annie tussled with the dilemma through the days which followed.

Sarah stirred her rice in the pan of milk, she had shown no shock or dismay, "Annie love, you must do whatever you need to do, all I ask is that you stay close. I look at those two young lads and God knows, I've wept for them, losing their mam and her so young. Someone needs to love 'em Annie, you won't find me an' Samuel thinkin' anythin' different to that. You are our family and whoever is with you will be family as well. I can promise you that."

Annie hugged Sarah, she had lifted weight from her shoulders and made no more pain for her heart than she already bore.

Davina had looked at Annie with a strange expression.

"You are shocked I can tell, it is awful I know." Annie wrung her hands in despair.

"Hush, you will spoil the concentration being applied to that trivet." Davina smiled, "You are my dearest friend Annie, you will ever be so. Whatever you decide, I shall be nothing but happy on the condition that your visits to this silly old woman shall not cease, that I shall continue to enjoy the company of my fine young men just as often."

She cast her eyes to George and Freddy on the rug, deeply engrossed in their engineering, screwing the legs into position on the ever popular brass trivet.

So neither woman had given Annie anything other than love and friendship. If she kept that precious thing and had with her always her own son, Harold's child, then fulfilling the promise she had made to Enid and protecting the children from the hurtful tongues of people with no compassion or understanding, she would do and have no fear of the future. Aunt Bella would not allow her to fail.

May and her family had settled into No.4 Melton Road. Annie's last walk with May along Peverell Street, carrying Mabel and Alfred's few belongings had resolved her spirit. Shawcross, now looking old and grey about his jowls, sat behind the gate in his last months of life. He pleaded with his eyes for Annie to triumph over the evil that held him captive. She stroked his old head lovingly and said.

"I know Shawcross and I understand, you will ever be my friend and I yours." Just as Davina's words had comforted Annie, so she hoped that

Shawcross would end his days, trusting in their friendship, for Annie would not see him again.

CHAPTER TWENTY FIVE

Annie and Charles were married very quietly on May twentieth, so close to the date aunt Bella had died that Annie wished for the day to pass quickly and her mind to be eased. Bertha and Violet were witnesses, Bertha simply to be a familiar face and Violet to bear witness verily, to Charles' marital status.

Edna had care of the boys for an hour, whispering to Annie as she turned into No.24 with George and Freddy, "Don't you ever let 'im show you anythin' but the respect you deserve." Then with a rush of love, turned back, giving Annie a big hug, "Good luck," her voice trembled.

Now it was done, Bertha had gone home. Annie had fetched the boys, William from school and the other two from Edna's. They had eaten their tea and the children, noticing nothing different about the day had gone to bed happily.

Annie had busied herself in the scullery, scrubbing a green stain from William's school trousers where he had clambered onto an old fallen tree trunk by the side of the school yard. If she scrubbed for any longer, they would give way under the harshness of the brush. She made a pot of tea and carried a cup to Charles.

"Bring your tea and sit down." His look gave her no clue to his expectation, Annie was quiet. "We shall go up soon, I have an early start in the morning," said Charles. "You can move your things into my room tomorrow if you wish, tonight, you have only to bring yourself."

He drank the tea saying nothing more. Annie must recognise her duty, she shivered, 'remember what you are my girl, no snivelling'.

Charles pulled himself over her, with intensity he thrust up and down, up and down, like a programmed mechanism. Up and down, Annie's ears rang with the sound of the sewing machines, louder and louder as the needle pierced the cloth, time after time, penetrating the linen, securing the chosen design. Finally he rolled away, his face to the wall.

Annie felt a tear travel down each of her cheeks, falling away to the sides of her face, brushing her ears before finally dropping to the bed. She waited until she heard Charles' breathing change in sleep, Annie needed to see George.

She took a towel from the washstand to wipe herself and slipped quietly from the room. George, her George lay fast asleep, he was beautiful. She peeped over at William and Freddy in the other bed, it was no hardship to honour her promise to Enid. Annie had her own wonderful son and now two fine stepsons, it was enough.

She returned to Charles, he did not stir. Annie lay with her thoughts, the urgency with which Charles had consummated their marriage had not come of desire or the slightest shred of passion. Annie knew it had been the need to 'get it over with', that drove Charles. She would not dwell on it, instead she remembered love as it once had been, even now, with only the thread of a dream, it satisfied her longing.

Annie slept with Harold.

William had taken well to school and Miss Merryweather spoke of his brightness and advanced grasp of reading and arithmetic. It pleased Annie, she spent much time with all the children, feeding their minds as well as their bellies.

It was a fine July day and Annie was confident that George's legs would be strong enough to carry him to The Park. She had sent word to Edward Meade to collect them from Davina's at 2.30. Byron was no longer able to walk at the speed his younger days had allowed so a gentle pace would suit them all.

Davina was overjoyed to see them, as always. Ivy appeared well and happy and Frank had already made himself useful.

"Just look at that Annie dear," said Davina pointing to a chair in the corner. "Do you know, it has always been wonky, I used to put cousin Isobel to sit on it quite purposefully. Unless one concentrated very carefully and moved not a whisker, it was possible to become afflicted with the 'Mal-de-Mer' right here in this drawing room. Frank has made it as steady as a rock and he intends to fit new gauze to the meat safe this week."

Annie and Davina drank tea, George and Freddy each had the treat of an orange, carefully segmented by Ivy.

"Are you happy Annie?" Asked Davina.

Annie looked at the two boys, their total contentment, their love for each other and of their older brother William, their friend Byron, watching the disappearing orange with his deep dark eyes.

"I am not unhappy, it is enough, truly Davina, it is enough."

As they said goodbye to join Meade at the carriage, Davina handed George a small bag of candy. "To share," she said, looking quickly at Annie lest she should be scolded for spoiling him.

"Thank you," he said, his face beamed.

"It is no longer necessary for you to arrange payment with Mr. Meade, I am quite alright," said Annie.

"My dear, an old woman's pleasures are few, your visits make me very happy."

Annie kissed Davina's cheek and squeezed her hand. She lifted Freddy into the carriage first, then Byron, he sat proudly between the two boys, Annie climbed in beside George. Meade, seeing them all safely inside commanded the horse to move along, Davina waved them out of sight.

Annie leaned back in the seat and closed her eyes, that smell of the leather, the rhythm of the hooves, just as it had been that very first time she had travelled to the house with Saul.

She felt George's hand on her arm and heard his young voice say, "Would you like a sweety Mam?"

Annie turned to look at her son and saw not the childlike curls, the rosy cheeks in the cherub face, but instead, those deep brown eyes, thick dark wavy hair, the weathered complexion, that smile, and she heard Harold say, 'go on, it'll do yer good'.

She lowered her face to kiss George's head, sinking her brow into his curls so as not to let him see her tears.

Annie gathered her spirit and said, "I'm alright thank you, but I'm sure Freddy would like one and you will be able to save some for William, we shall meet him from school very soon."

George was happy, his little legs swung to and fro like synchronised pendulums, the tips of Byron's ears nodded in time to the horse's trot and Freddy sucked his piece of candy, safe in his world of simple trust. Such was the harmony within the carriage, the bond between the occupants so strong, no power on earth could breach it.

"Straight home is it Annie?" Asked Edward Meade.

"To the school first please Mr.Meade, then we shall all go home."

Somewhere afar off, Harold and Bella turned a page of their book to a new chapter, it would bring more children for Annie, more trial and more achievement but through it all, she would find strength from deep within herself. That strength of Annie's which prevailed all worlds, making each and every one, a far better place.